"Yates' ne...
romantic...
whose ch...
—R...

"The banter between the Dodge siblings is loads of fun, and adding Dallas (Bennett's surprise son) to the mix raises that humor up a notch or two."
—*RT Book Reviews* on *Untamed Cowboy* (Top Pick)

"Fans of Robyn Carr and RaeAnne Thayne will enjoy [Yates's] small-town romance."
—*Booklist* on *Part Time Cowboy*

"Passionate, energetic and jam-packed with personality."
—*USATODAY.com's Happy Ever After* blog on *Part Time Cowboy*

"[A] story with emotional depth, intense heartache and love that is hard fought for and eventually won.... This is a book readers will be telling their friends about."
—*RT Book Reviews* on *Brokedown Cowboy*

"Yates's thrilling seventh Copper Ridge contemporary proves that friendship can evolve into scintillating romance.... This is a surefire winner not to be missed."
—*Publishers Weekly* on *Slow Burn Cowboy* (starred review)

"This fast-paced, sensual novel will leave readers believing in the healing power of love."
—*Publishers Weekly* on *Down Home Cowboy*

**Welcome to Gold Valley, Oregon,
where the cowboys are tough to tame, until they
meet the women who can lasso their hearts.**

**In Copper Ridge, Oregon, lasting love
with a cowboy is only a happily-ever-after away.
Don't miss any of Maisey Yates's
Copper Ridge tales, available now!**

From HQN Books

Look for more Gold Valley books coming soon!

For more books by Maisey Yates,
visit www.maiseyyates.com.

MAISEY YATES

A Tall, Dark Cowboy Christmas

HQN™

ISBN-13: 978-1-335-47462-9

A Tall, Dark Cowboy Christmas

Copyright © 2018 by Maisey Yates

The publisher acknowledges the copyright holder of the additional work:

Snowed in with the Cowboy
Copyright © 2018 Maisey Yates

Recycling programs for this product may not exist in your area.

CONTENTS

A Tall, Dark
Cowboy Christmas

For anyone with a wounded heart this season,
and any season. May love give you hope.

CHAPTER ONE

GRANT DODGE WAS ALONE. And that was how he liked it.

He had spent the entire day out in the cold mountain air conducting roping demonstrations and leading trail rides. Not that he minded any of those things in isolation. It was the addition of *people* that made them somewhat challenging.

Worse than having to deal with people in a general sense was dealing with people who recognized him.

Not the typical small-town recognition; he was used to that. Though he could live without getting sad widower face from people he barely knew in the grocery store, but even then, at least it was people who knew him because he'd lived in Gold Valley all his life.

What *really* got to him was the people who recognized him from the news stories.

Eight years hadn't done anything to make those moments less weird. People often couldn't place where they knew him from, but they knew they did. And they would press, and press, until he told them.

The woman who had recognized him today had been a grandmother. A great-grandmother, even. Sweet and gray-haired and looking at him with sympathetic eyes that made him want to jump off the nearest bridge.

It always seemed worse around the holidays. Perhaps

because of the sentimentality people seemed to feel that time of year. And tried to inflict on him.

He didn't really know.

Whatever the reason, he seemed to have an uptick in well-meaning-but-irritating interactions.

Maybe that was why he always wanted to drink more this time of year, too.

He shook his head and settled down into his chair, looking around the small, cozy cabin that he called home. And then he looked into the full, inviting whiskey glass he called salvation.

He didn't have a problem or anything. He was functional. He considered that the benchmark. Low though it might be.

He was functional enough that his family mostly *joked* about his drinking, which meant it was probably fine.

But the one thing he didn't want to do was get in bed at night stone-cold sober. Sometimes he could. When the long, hard day of work came inside with him, resting on aching shoulders and the lower back that was getting touchier with each passing year—because *age*. Not that thirty-four was exceptionally aged, not at all. But physical labor had a way of speeding all that up.

But then, the alternative had been to spend the rest of his life working at the damned power company, living in a little house on a quiet street in a neighborhood tucked back behind the main street of Gold Valley living the life of a man lost in suburban bliss, without any of the trappings that generally made it blissful.

No children.

No wife.

Not anymore.

He never had the children, but there had been a time when he and Lindsay had hoped for them. Even though...

That had always been a pipe dream, he supposed.

But for a while, he and Lindsay had lived in a world of dreams. Reality had been too harsh. And sometimes sitting around and making plans for a future you knew wouldn't be there was all you could do.

He took a long swallow of whiskey and leaned back in his chair. This was why he didn't go to bed sober.

Because it was these quiet moments, the still ones—particularly this time of year—that had a way of crushing in on him, growing louder and louder in the silence of the room.

Solitude was often as welcome as it was terrifying. Sometimes it had teeth. And he did his best not to get savaged by them.

He took another swallow of whiskey and leaned back farther in the chair before setting the glass on the table with a decisive click. Then he let his head fall back.

He must've dozed off, because when he opened his eyes again the hands on the clock hanging on the wall had made a more pronounced journey than it would have if it had only been the few minutes it felt like.

He stretched, groaning as his joints popped. He stood, making his way over to the window and looking out into the darkness.

At least, he *should* have been looking out into the darkness.

Instead, he saw a dim light cutting through the trees.

They did have guests staying on the property, but none out in the woods behind Grant's cabin.

Grant lived well out of the way, on the opposite end

of Dodge land from the guest cabins. And if there was anyone out there right now, they were not where they were supposed to be.

He opened up the drawer in the kitchen and took a small flashlight out, and then shoved on his boots before heading outside. He supposed, if he were thinking clearly, he would have called his brother Wyatt. But then, he was half-asleep and a little bit drunk, so he wasn't thinking all that clearly. Instead, he made his own way out through the trees and toward the single light that was glowing in the woods.

When he was halfway between his house and the light it occurred to him what he was probably about to walk in on.

The back of his neck went hot, tension rising inside of him.

Odds were, anyone out in the middle of nowhere at this hour was up to one thing. And he didn't especially want to walk in and find two people having sex in the middle of the woods, interrupting his drinking and sleeping time. The teeth on that would be just a little bit too sharp to bear.

But then, if he wasn't getting any, nobody else should, either.

Especially not right next to his house.

That only increased his irritation as he continued on toward the light, the wind whipping through the trees, the bitter cold biting through the flannel shirt he was wearing. He should've put a jacket on, but he hadn't thought of it.

He swore, and then he swore again as he approached the light.

He frowned. Right. There was a cabin back here, but

it was dilapidated. One of the original buildings on the property, from back in the late 1800s. One that hadn't been inhabited in a long time. At least, not by humans. He had a feeling there had been several raccoons, and about ten thousand spiders. But not humans.

And raccoons did not light lanterns. So he could safely assume this was not a raccoon.

He was on the verge of storming in—because why the hell not?—but something stopped him. Instead, he softened his footsteps and walked up to the window.

It was not what he'd been expecting.

It *was* a person, but not *people*. And nobody was having sex.

Instead, there was a small woman, curled up beneath the threadbare blanket. She looked like she was asleep. The camping lantern next to her head was turned on, a thin, yellow band of light stretching across what he could see of her face.

She was not one of the guests; at least, he was reasonably certain. He didn't make a practice of memorizing what they all looked like.

Mostly because he didn't care.

It was also difficult to identify her positively because she was curled up in a ball, the blanket halfway up over her head. He shifted his position and saw there was a backpack in the corner of the room. But nothing else.

He frowned, looking at her again, and he saw that there were shoes on her feet, which were sticking out just past the edge of the blanket.

He dragged his hand over his face.

She could be a criminal. A fugitive from the law. But then, most likely she was a woman running from a difficult situation. Possibly from a man.

Which could mean there was a safety issue. And he had guests on his ranch, not to mention his younger sister, Jamie.

Jamie knew how to handle herself, of course. She was a tough-as-rawhide cowgirl who was often packing heat. But that didn't mean Grant would knowingly expose her to danger.

It was a lot of drama that he didn't want coming to roost.

He stood there, debating for a moment, and then he turned away from the cabin, jogging back to his house and grabbing his cell phone off the bedside table. He dialed his brother Wyatt's number, knowing that he was going to wake up spitting mad. Because it was four-thirty in the morning, and nobody wanted to be woken up at that hour. Though the Dodges were frequently up before the sun. They had responsibilities to take care of on the ranch that dictated early mornings. Though not *this* early.

"What the hell?" Wyatt asked by way of greeting.

His voice was gruff, evidence that he had been asleep.

"We have a visitor," Grant said, keeping his own voice low.

"Are you drunk?"

"No," Grant said.

At least, he didn't think he was. But even if he were he wouldn't hallucinate a *woman* sleeping in a cabin on their land.

"Really?" Wyatt pressed.

"Not anymore," Grant said.

"What's our visitor?" Wyatt asked, clearly confused.

"I woke up early," Grant said, by way of explanation. There was no need to tell Wyatt that he had fallen asleep in a chair in his living room after drinking a glass of whiskey. And that the pain in his back from sitting sleeping up had been the thing that had woken him. "I went and looked out the window and saw a light coming from the woods. I investigated. There's a woman sleeping in one of the cabins."

"What?"

"I wanted to call you and find out what the hell you want to do about it."

"You could call the police," Wyatt suggested.

"No," Grant said. He wasn't sure why that was his conclusion, only that it was. Just that… He had no idea what the circumstances might be. She could be young. A runaway teenage girl, and if they called the police… who knew who might come for her. It might be the very people she was running from. And he would rather make sure he wasn't throwing her back into harm's way.

Grant didn't consider himself a particularly compassionate person, not these days. He'd drained all that out of him over eight years of being a caregiver to the woman he was married to. He didn't resent it. Didn't resent *Lindsay* at all. But that didn't mean he had anything left to give anyone else. Particularly a random stranger.

That artery had been bled dry.

Still, he couldn't ignore the fact that there was something incredibly vulnerable in the way she was sleeping. With the light on. Like she was afraid of monsters even out there in the middle of nowhere.

"Okay," Wyatt said slowly. "Then what do you suggest?"

"She's a tiny little woman," Grant said. "I imagine

we can handle her. Go in and talk to her. Maybe Lindy should talk to her."

"Hell, no," Wyatt said. "We are not sending my wife in to talk to a random stranger squatting on our property."

Wyatt had gotten married only a couple months earlier—extremely quickly—after finally getting together with the woman he'd been obsessing over for years. Although Wyatt would never say he'd been obsessing over Lindy for that long, but Grant knew it was true.

When you were a man with no social or sex life you had a lot of time to observe things. The entire world was Grant's own personal Where's Waldo game. He had nothing to do but sit around and identify hidden feelings and truths in the lives of other people.

And drink. There was the drinking.

"We're going to end up giving her a damn heart attack," Grant said.

"She's sleeping on our land," Wyatt said. "As much as I don't relish the idea of terrifying a woman, it's not like she checked into the Embassy Suites and bought herself some privacy."

Grant shrugged. Mostly, he didn't want to hassle with her personally. He wanted to go back to sleep and wake up in a world where he didn't have to contend with another person or care about their feelings or whether or not he scared them.

"You're right there," Wyatt pointed out. "Why don't you wake her up?"

"And then what?"

"I don't know. Bring her over to the house. Give her some breakfast. Unless she shoots you."

"Which is a good point," Grant said. "I don't want to get shot."

"Bring your gun."

"I don't want to be in a shootout."

"Bring *something*."

Grant hung up the phone. His brother was just getting on his nerves now. He grumbled and grabbed hold of his hunting knife, which was in a leather case that snapped onto his belt. He put it on his hip, grabbed his cowboy hat and went back to the front door.

He was not using a hunting knife on a woman, even if she came at him. But he supposed if there was a gun involved he might have to use something.

He just felt resigned, really. If she wanted to shoot him he might let her.

Then at least he could get some rest.

He grunted and walked out of the house again, shoving his phone in his pocket, because he should probably bring that, too. In all honesty, he would need the phone before he needed the knife.

He walked quietly across the heavily wooded ground, careful not to land any heavy footfalls. Of course, if he did, he might wake her up, startle her and send her off running. And if she did that, then she wasn't his responsibility. Not anymore. If she wasn't on the property, what did he care where she was?

He didn't.

He gritted his teeth and stopped right in front of the cabin door. And then he pushed it open.

McKENNA TATE WAS used to sleeping lightly. And tonight was no exception. She had been keeping one ear tuned into the sounds around her, just in case, even while she dozed.

Not that deep sleeping in this place was likely. It was cold, and the floor of the little cabin was hard. Two days spent in it didn't make it feel any more like home.

Except it wasn't fine right now, because she heard something. And that was why she'd stirred.

Suddenly, reality slammed into her. The door to the cabin was *opening.*

She scrambled into a sitting position, attempting to push herself onto her feet, but then the door flung open completely, and she found herself stumbling back, hitting the wall and curling up there like a startled animal ready to strike.

It was a man. Which, out here in this big bad world, was the scariest thing she could think of. She would rather tangle with a bear any day. This was definitely a man.

Silhouetted in the doorway, tall and broad and terrifying. He had a cowboy hat pulled down low over his face, and she couldn't see any of his features. She could just see that he was big.

"Calm down," he said, as if a command issued from a stranger would make her feel calm.

"What?" So, now she knew he was insane, which was great. Telling a woman whose sleep he'd just interrupted to be *calm.*

"I said," he responded, "calm down. I'm not going to hurt you."

"Like you would announce you were going to hurt me if that was your plan," she said, curling up tighter.

"I have no idea what I would do if I was going to hurt

you. Because I'm not going to. I do, however, want to know what you're doing here."

"Sleeping."

"I can see that. Or rather, I could. Though you aren't sleeping now."

"Very observant. I'd give you a trophy, but I'm fresh out."

He shifted, crossing his arms. "You're awfully mouthy for somebody sleeping on someone else's property."

"And you're awfully chatty for a guy who just found someone sleeping on his property. Don't you have follow-up questions?"

"Several. But I don't want you crouched there in the corner like you think I'm about to stab you."

She snorted out a laugh. "Oh, I'm not really that worried you're gonna randomly stab me. It's other things I worry about with men."

"You don't have to worry about that, either," he said.

His voice didn't soften it all. He didn't look like he felt bad for her, or like he pitied her in any way. That would not be the angle to take with him. Crying or anything like that. She could see that right away. She could paint a glorious picture of her tragic plight, and he would probably just stand there like a man carved from rock. Unmoved. Whoever he was, he was not a soft touch.

She was pretty good at identifying a soft touch. They were the kind of people who came in handy in desperate situations. People who wanted to wrap you in a blanket, give you a piece of pie and say some encouraging words so that they could go on with their day feeling like they were decent human beings.

She had a feeling this man did not care whether or not he was a decent human being.

She recognized that in him, because it was the same thing in her.

You couldn't care much about whether or not you were decent when you mostly just wanted to be alive.

"I just want to sleep here," she said, holding her hand out. "That's all."

"You don't have anywhere else to sleep?"

"Yeah, actually, I have a mansion up on the hill. But I like a little impromptu camping. Bonus points if it's on someone else's land, because it adds to the spirit of adventure. I love being woken up in the middle of the night by large, angry ranchers."

"It's not really the middle of the night. It's almost five in the morning."

She groaned. "Close enough to the middle of the night in my world."

"This is usually about the time I get up every day."

"Don't brag to the less fortunate," she said. "I'm liable to get jealous of such decadent living."

"Are you a runaway?"

She laughed. "Right. Because somebody would care if I left." He kept on staring at her. "I'm twenty-six."

He nodded slowly, as if now he understood. "Running from *someone*?"

"Nope," she said.

Not that she'd *never* run from someone, but she'd given up counting on men to take care of her. That only ended one way. It all bumped along nicely for a while, and then inevitably it exploded and she was left with less than she had before. Always.

It was why she'd been resolutely without a man for about three years.

"Then why are you sleeping out here?"

"I'm new to town," she said, keeping her tone casual, as if they'd met on a bustling street in the bright light of day and not like this.

And she was new in town. That much was true.

"My truck broke down and it cost a crap load to fix." And ultimately she'd had to let the thing go and give it up for dead, after giving up all the money she had to get this far. "While I was waiting for the prognosis, I was stranded for a few days longer than I anticipated. Had to stay in a hotel for some extra time." And then she'd ended up hitchhiking into Gold Valley after her truck's inglorious death on a stretch of lonely highway. "Anyway. I ran out of money. I'm hoping to get a job in town, but I haven't managed it yet. Even when I do get a job I'm not going to get paid for a few weeks."

"You couldn't camp?"

"As much as I would love to sleep out under the stars beneath this threadbare blanket, that's a hard pass. I mean, obviously I would have if I *had* to."

"Homeless shelters?"

She snorted. "I'm not homeless."

With a hard bump of her heart against her breastbone, it hit her that…she was lying. This cabin was the only place she had to sleep. She had nowhere to go back to. Nowhere she was heading to.

That was the definition of homeless, and she was it.

She never figured rock bottom would look like a damp wooden floor. But hell, it seemed to be.

She had managed to stay a few steps ahead of that since she had been turfed from the last foster home she'd been in eight years ago. But now... Of course, it was the move back home that had done it.

Home.

Gold Valley was home.

A home that she couldn't remember, but it was the place her father was from, the place her mother had been born. The place she had been born. She had decided that it was time to come back. Time to try and... Find where she came from. She had to do something. Otherwise, she was going to be stuck in this endless loop. Dead-end jobs, crappy apartments. Nothing but barely making ends meet forever.

She supposed that was life for some people. For a lot of people.

But she'd hit the end of it. She'd had her birth certificate in a folder with all her legal documents—all gifted to her by the great state of Oregon on her eighteenth birthday when she'd been turfed out into the real world—and it had simply been sitting there.

Her every connection printed on a black-and-white document, as flat and dead as the paper itself.

Annie Tate was listed as her mother. And under father, a name McKenna had never even heard before. Henry Dalon.

Searches for him had turned up nothing promising.

While working as a waitress, McKenna had ended up having a conversation with a customer about a website that allowed free searches for public records. And McKenna had gone searching. She'd started with her father's name, and then switched tactics.

She'd searched her own, and discovered not the printed, digitized version of her birth certificate but a scanned version of the original. Where handwritten down in the bottom corner, and smudged, was a name that looked a lot more like Henry Dalton.

Apparently, she'd learned after calling the records office, misspellings on records were common enough. Especially when no one had requested the documents, or done any checking on them. Seeing as Annie Tate had surrendered her parenting rights when McKenna was two, it didn't shock her that her mother had never done her due diligence making sure everything on McKenna's birth certificate looked right.

From there, McKenna had printed off the certificate and folded it up in her backpack, a piece to the puzzle of her life she was actively trying to put together.

She'd started searching for him after that.

Annie Tate, with her common first and last name, was impossible to track down, and anyway, McKenna already knew she didn't want to know her.

There were a few Henry Daltons, but one in particular that was in the right geographical location to be a likely candidate. Henry "Hank" Dalton.

He'd had been all over her searches. A famous rodeo rider with three sons. Three sons who were McKenna's half brothers, most likely.

Caleb, Jacob and Gabe.

Brothers. Family.

In Gold Valley.

But she had to figure it all out. She had to get the scope of things. The lay of the land.

She watched as the man took his phone out of his pocket, and the screen lit up.

"Come with me," he said.

Panic fluttered around in her breast like a caged bird. "Are you calling the police?"

"No," he said, his thumb swiping over the screen a few times. "I'm taking you to my brother's house."

"Why?"

"Because there's food there," he said simply.

She scrambled to her feet, her stomach growling. She realized that she had only eaten a couple of times in the past three days. And trail mix and granola bars could only get you so far. They weren't...*food* food.

"Why do you want to feed me?" she asked, narrowing her eyes.

"Correct me if I'm wrong," he said. "But you're harmless."

She huffed. "I'm *not* harmless."

"Really?"

"I have a pocket knife. I can cut you up."

"Right. Anyway. Harmless. And probably hungry."

"And you care?" This offer of food and his lack of... calling the cops on her had all her defenses up. People weren't just...nice.

It made her feel compelled to push. To push him away. To push him to get down to what his deal actually was.

She didn't trust people. She didn't trust anyone.

But there was always some part of her...some small part that glowed bright sometimes and made her ache.

Hope.

Yeah. Well, for all the good hope had done her. She was filthy and cold and had no money. She'd do better to expect him to turn out to be a creep than a nice person who was actually offering to feed her for nothing.

He stared back at her, his features completely shadowed still. "No. Not really."

It was the lack of niceness that made her hackles lower, just a bit.

There was something about that honesty that struck her. People were never honest. At least, they weren't *kind* and honest. There were people who were cruel, who spent no small amount of time lecturing her about how her circumstances were her own fault.

And maybe they were.

Sure, she'd been sent out to live on her own at eighteen with a garbage bag full of her belongings, but there were plenty of people who didn't have advantages in life who probably did better than she did.

But people like this… Who could openly admit they didn't actually care, but offered help, anyway…

There were no people like this. She had no idea what kind of anomaly she was staring down right now.

"Do you *want* food?" he asked, sounding irritated and impatient now.

"Yes," she said, scrambling to a standing position. She looked at her blanket, and her backpack.

"Grab those," he said.

Right. Because of course he was willing to bait her out of the cabin with food, but it wasn't like he was going to let her stay here. She felt pressure behind her eyes, but she knew she wouldn't cry. She had quit doing that a long time ago. There was no point.

"Okay," she said, taking hold of the blanket and her bag and holding them both close.

The man took a step forward, holding out his hand, and that was when her lantern caught his face.

He was…

He was *beautiful*.

His dark hair was a little bit shaggy, and he had a

light beard that might be intentional, or might just be because he hadn't shaved for a few days. His nose was straight, his lips firm looking, set into a flat line. His shoulders were broad, and so was his chest, his waist lean, the tight T-shirt suggesting that he was also...well, fully and completely built.

She hadn't made any assumptions about his looks when he had first come in, mostly because he had shocked her, waking her from a dead sleep. And then... He had sounded a bit like a curmudgeon, so she had assumed that he was an older man. But now she thought he couldn't be much older than thirty.

"Let me take those," he said, taking the bag and blanket from her.

She started to protest, but he had taken them before she could get the words out. It made her feel naked. He had her things. Everything she owned in the entire world. Except the lantern. She bent down and picked it up, clutching it to her chest. She would hold that.

He didn't offer to take it from her. He turned, without a word, and walked out of the cabin, clearly just expecting her to follow.

There was an offer of food, so of course she was.

She scrambled after him. It was still dark outside, and it was cold. She had a jacket, but it was in her bag, and currently Mr. Tall, Dark and Cranky was holding it. So she figured the best thing to do would be to follow along.

The place he led her to was a small cabin, but he didn't go to the front door; instead, he went to an old truck. "We're going to drive to my brother's house. It's on the property. But I don't really want to walk."

She didn't, either. In fact, she had a feeling that he

didn't mind one way or another, but had sensed that maybe she didn't. Knew that she was cold.

Right. He doesn't care. Don't go applying warm and fuzzy motives to him.

She climbed cautiously into his truck, closing the door behind her. "A gentle reminder," she said when he started the engine. "I *do* have a knife."

"Yeah," he responded, starting the engine and putting the truck in Reverse. "Me, too."

"*Why* do you have a knife?"

"For all I knew you had a gun."

She sputtered. "If I had a gun and you had a knife it wouldn't help you."

"It's just a good thing it didn't get to that."

"Well. See that it doesn't."

"I know," he said, his tone dry. "You'll cut me."

They didn't speak for the short drive down the bumpy, pothole-filled dirt road. McKenna folded her hands in her lap and stared down at her fingers. There was dirt under her nails.

You're homeless. It's been days since you've had a shower.

It was amazing how you could push all of those things to the side, but the minute you had to interact with another person—a beautiful person—it all came rushing back.

"Where are we going?" Suddenly, she was full of panic.

"To my brother's house," he repeated. He had said that already.

"And he's going to be there?"

"Yes," he responded.

"Oh," she said, looking back out the window.

So, someone else was going to see her like this. She didn't really care. Her entire life had been a series of inglorious situations. It was just that this was the worst.

She'd done a pretty good job of letting shame roll off for most of her life. She'd been the poor kid. Had never had cool clothes. Had never been able to have friends over. Had been shuffled around homes, some good, some bad. She'd built up some tough armor over the years.

But this was a new low, and apparently…apparently shame still existed inside of her.

They pulled up to the house and her heart sank into her stomach. She hadn't fully realized where she was. She had hitchhiked to the edge of town, and she had fully intended on camping out in the woods. She had happened upon a collection of cabins on the edge of the woods, and then had circled around, and found a dilapidated, abandoned one deeper in. She had realized she was camping out in a place people stayed in for money, but she hadn't realized people also lived there.

Or that it was quite so fancy.

Her companion got out of the truck and headed toward the broad front steps that led to the porch. She just sat there. She took a breath, and opened the door. There was no point being timid. No point feeling like crap. She knew what she was.

And that was: more than her current situation.

It didn't matter what these people thought of her.

It mattered if they turned out to be psychotic killers, though. But she really did have a pocket knife.

And okay, she knew that wasn't the deadliest of weapons. But she had sat outside a self-defense class one time and had heard the woman talking about how the element of surprise was generally on your side when you were a woman. It was about the only thing on your side, so you had to use it. They didn't expect you to fight back.

McKenna Tate had been fighting back for her entire life. She wouldn't stop now.

And she supposed that right there was the point of that hope inside her chest she often resented. It had brought her this far. Made her feel determined. It was what kept shame and hopelessness from taking over.

As long as she never let it get out of hand, it was what kept her going.

She walked slowly up the front steps and stood next to the man. She came up to the top of his shoulder. Just barely. He was so tall. And yeah, now that she was a little bit more awake, and it was a little bit lighter out, she could see... Definitely as beautiful as she had first thought. If not more so.

She turned her face back to the door in front of her. Her new friend knocked, and they waited.

The man that answered the door was nearly as tall as the man at her side, and just as good-looking. Though in a different way. He had that easy manner about him, a charm that the other man did not have.

She didn't trust charm.

"Hi," she said. "I was told there would be breakfast."

The new man looked at the other man, and then back at her. "Wyatt Dodge," he said, sticking out his hand.

"McKenna Tate," she responded, grasping it with her own.

Of all the ways she had envisioned being caught by the owners of the property, she hadn't imagined this.

And then she realized that she still didn't know the

name of the man who had found her in the cabin. The beautiful one. The one who looked like he might not remember what a joke was, much less have a whole store of them like Wyatt Dodge probably did.

She looked at him, and he looked at her out of the corner of his eye, but didn't offer a name.

"Come on in," Wyatt said, still eyeing his brother speculatively.

She took him up on his invitation.

The inside of the house was even more beautiful than the outside. Rustic, but incredibly comfortable. Cozy. She suddenly became aware of how cold her nose and cheeks had been when they began to warm up.

She looked to the left of the entryway and saw that there was a fire in a rock fireplace. She wanted to go sit in front of it. She wanted to press her face against it.

But then, she also smelled food. Bacon.

She'd had many a disagreement with the man upstairs over quite a few of the circumstances in her life, but right about now she was feeling much friendlier to him. She sent up a prayer of thanks.

If anything could surprise the divine, McKenna Tate being thankful might do it.

"My wife, Lindy, is in the kitchen," Wyatt said.

"*Not* cooking," a voice rang out from the next room. "Just waiting for the bacon to be done."

He gestured that direction and McKenna followed the directive, walking into the beautiful kitchen, to see an equally beautiful blonde woman sitting at a small breakfast table. Her blond hair pulled back in a ponytail, her manner elegant even though she was wearing sweats.

"I'm cooking, technically," Wyatt said. "It's part of the agreement."

"Agreement?" McKenna asked.

"Yes, I agreed to marry him and move from my winery to his ranch. But only if he cooked me breakfast at least four days a week. The other three days I get a pastry from the coffee place in town."

McKenna's stomach tightened. Jealousy. She was as familiar with that as she was with hunger, and right now she felt nearly overtaken by both.

Not because she wanted the man cooking the bacon, specifically. Just that it would be nice to have an arrangement like that in general. Someone who cared. Someone who would vow to cook bacon four days a week just so you would marry him.

She couldn't imagine someone caring like that.

"What are you doing on my property, McKenna Tate?" Wyatt asked, turning toward the stove and getting bacon and some scrambled eggs out of a pan, putting them on a plate and setting them down on the table. She eyed them hungrily.

"Have a seat," he said.

She hesitantly did as he said, sitting next to his lovely wife, and feeling every inch the bedraggled urchin that she was. "Eat."

Her man said that.

Not that he was *her* man, just that he was the one that had woken her up, and she still didn't know his name. And on principle, she wasn't going to ask.

Still, she obeyed.

"Coffee?" Lindy asked.

"Yes, please," she said, trying her best to eat slow, and feeling like she was going to end up failing the moment the salty, savory bacon touched her tongue. She was ravenous. She hadn't let herself realize just how much.

"What were you doing?" Lindy asked, her voice soft.

"I just needed a place to sleep. I'm new to Gold Valley… I decided to move here," she said. She wasn't going to get into the whole thing about looking for her family. Not that she believed they were going to have some tearful reunion. She wasn't that stupid. Life didn't work that way.

Her mother, who had given birth to her, had walked away without a backward glance. A father who'd probably never even met her, maybe didn't even know about her? Why would he want anything to do with her?

The very thought of it, of putting herself in front of him and risking a rejection, made her feel…

It didn't matter. From what she had found out about the Daltons, they were well-off. Famous rodeo riders and owners of a massive plot of land just on the outskirts of town.

Surely they would be able to spare a little seed money to keep her off the streets. And they'd probably be happy to fling some money at her to get rid of her, anyway.

She didn't need a family. She'd been just fine without one all this time.

What she needed was something a lot more practical than that. A shovel to dig herself out of the hole she was in.

Money would make for a decent shovel.

She cleared her throat. "I decided to move here, but I had kind of a series of less than fortunate happenings and I ran out of money before I could get a job. So, I didn't have anywhere to stay." She wouldn't have jumped into the Gold Valley situation had she not lost the apartment she'd been in before in Portland. But the landlord had decided she wanted it for her adult son, and McKenna had been unceremoniously booted. Also, she hadn't gotten her security deposit back. Which wasn't her fault. It wasn't like she had created a mildew stain in the bathroom. That was because the roof leaked.

"It was a desperate-times-desperate-measures kind of thing," she said. "And… Thank you. For not calling the police. And for feeding me bacon. Which seems a little bit above and beyond, all things considered."

"You don't have a job yet?" Lindy asked.

"Not yet," she said.

"What kind of jobs do you normally do?" Lindy asked.

"Aerospace engineering," McKenna replied, taking another bite of crisp bacon. "But when I can't find work in that field, waitressing is my fallback."

"Sadly, we're fresh out of aerospace engineering jobs," Lindy said.

"Good," McKenna said. "Because I was lying about that."

"I had a feeling," Lindy responded. "Not because I don't think you could be an aerospace engineer, just because we're nowhere near NASA."

"I've done all kinds of things. I've been a waitress, hotel maid. You name the manual labor job that doesn't require much lifting over fifty pounds and I've probably done it."

"Basic cooking?" Lindy asked.

She shrugged. "Diner stuff."

"Cleaning."

"Like I said. Housekeeping."

"I think we could find a job for you right here," Lindy said.

McKenna frowned. "No offense. But… I'm a stranger who was caught sleeping illegally on your property. Why exactly would you want to give me a job?"

"Because sometimes life is hard and it isn't fair," Lindy said, her determined blue eyes meeting McKenna's. "I'm well aware of that. And sometimes circumstances spin out of your control. It has nothing to do with whether or not you're a good person. So, you tell me, McKenna. Are you going to steal from us?"

McKenna lifted a shoulder. "Probably not."

"Probably not," Wyatt repeated.

"I don't know. Am I gravely injured? Did a family member of mine come down with a terrible illness and the only way I can get back to them is to steal money from you?" It was moot. She didn't have any family that knew her. Or that she knew. Just family she was looking for.

"I appreciate the honesty," Lindy said dryly. "But barring extraordinary circumstances, are you going to steal from me?"

McKenna shook her head. She was a lot of things, and definitely a little bit opportunistic. But she wasn't an out-and-out thief. "No."

"Well, then, I don't see why we can't give you a job. We can always fire you if you're terrible at it." She looked over at her husband when she said that part.

"Fine with me," Wyatt said. "We were going to have to hire someone else, anyway."

She blinked. "I…"

"We also have a place for you to stay. One that isn't

that horrible cabin in the middle of the woods that doesn't have anything but spiderwebs in it for warmth."

"Oh… You can't do that."

"Sure we can," Lindy said. "We have a bunch of extra room."

Throughout the entire exchange, her man stood there mute. A solid, silent presence that fairly radiated with disapproval.

"It's fine with me," Wyatt said. "But I don't have time to train anyone right now."

He shot a meaningful look over at her man. The look that he got back was not friendly at all.

"I'm going to go get dressed," Wyatt said.

Lindy pushed up from her seat. "Ditto. Enjoy your breakfast."

The two of them left the room, and they left her standing there with… With him. And he did not look happy.

"I guess I work here now," she said, trying to sound nonchalant.

"I guess so."

"Sorry," she responded.

He shrugged. "Nothing to be sorry about."

"You don't look happy."

The corner of his mouth lifted upward. "I never look happy."

"Oh. Well. That's good to know."

And then he stuck out his hand, his dark, serious eyes meeting hers. "I'm Grant Dodge. And I guess I'm your new boss."

CHAPTER TWO

GRANT FELT LIKE the biggest asshole curmudgeon on the planet. Not that that was a new feeling for him necessarily. But he resented the fact that he had to show this girl around the ranch, and he shouldn't. Really, he should be proud of the fact that Wyatt and Lindy were using what they had to give her a shot at digging out of the bad pit she seemed to find herself in.

But Grant didn't have a hell of a lot of altruism left inside of him.

If they had done it without putting her in his jurisdiction, he might have been able to muster a little bit up. As it was, not so much.

"Come on, McKenna Tate," he said, turning and walking out of the dining area, trusting that she was going to follow him. The sound of her footsteps behind him indicated that she had.

"Where are we going?"

"I expect that you're going to want to get a look around the place. And that you'd probably like to see where you're going to be sleeping."

He would have to pull up the ledger to see which cabins were available, but that would be easy enough. It wasn't that any of this was difficult. It was all getting rolled into his daily responsibilities, after all. Wasn't extra. Not really.

But a mother hen he was not. Not even on a good day. And after the awful sleep he'd gotten, today was not a very good day.

"It doesn't really matter if I like it or not," she fired back. "I don't have any other options."

"I'm not here for this tough-girl thing you're doing," he said, stopping and turning to face her. "My brother is doing a damn nice thing for you. If you have to pretend that you don't care, you can stay quiet. Otherwise, feel free to add commentary."

Her expression went from defiant to subdued, softening slightly. Well. Apparently, she did have feelings. And wasn't made entirely of prickles and spite.

He pushed open the front door and the two of them walked out of the house. She stayed silent, her boots loud on the steps as they made their way down to the driveway. Grant paused and looked around, always surprised at how the place looked. New, and somehow the same all at once. The cabins around the main house had been restored, each one with its own flower bed and carefully manicured walk that led up to the front door.

The entire property was refreshed. The barns painted, the hiking trails into the woods cleared.

The bones remained. The foundation. The earth. Same as it had always been.

He didn't know if he took comfort in that or not.

He didn't know if he took comfort in anything, really.

He just kept on living.

To do anything else would be a damn insult to Lindsay.

"Let's walk up this way," he said. "I'm going to show you the barn, and then we'll walk out to the cabin you'll be staying in. Hitting all the highlights on the way."

His companion was much quieter than she'd been, but he imagined snapping at her had done its job. He wasn't sorry about the silence. Having to make stupid small talk was the only thing that was worse than dealing with comforting strangers over his grief.

He led her down a gravel drive that took them to the big red barn, the one that the guests liked to see, not the one that housed the equipment. But this one had hay bales, and was a fun place to hang out and drink coffee. And really, that was its primary function. They had dinners in it, and sometimes small events.

And by *they*, he meant the *ranch*. Because he didn't get anywhere near social engagements of that kind.

For his part, Grant preferred to do demonstrations with the animals. And any sort of behind-the-scenes work that needed doing. Things that didn't require talking. Just another reason this little babysitting job wasn't to his liking.

"This is like… Like ranches you see on TV," she said, looking around the barn.

Grant turned around and he couldn't stop the kick he felt in his chest when he got a look at the expression on McKenna's face. It was like something had released inside her, all the tightness in her face gone slack. Her mouth had dropped open slightly, her brown eyes wide as she took in the sight of the large red structure, and the backdrop of dark green mountains dusted with pure white snow behind.

Suddenly, the place didn't look so familiar. For one small moment he saw it for the first time, right along with her.

He was a tired man. Down to his bones. He hadn't

felt a moment of wonder in longer than he could recall. There was nothing new here. Nothing new in him.

But right then it felt like the world stopped turning, just for a second, and in that space, between his last breath and his next heartbeat, he forgot everything but the beauty around him.

And it seemed new.

But then the world moved again, and that feeling was gone.

"It's nice," he said, clearing his throat and charging on through to the inside of the barn.

He turned to make sure that McKenna was with him, and she was, almost hunched forward, looking around them with a strange mix of trepidation and wonder.

"Have you not been in a barn before?"

"No," she said.

"I thought you'd done all the manual labor there was to do. There's a lot of it to be done in barns, McKenna, let me tell you."

"Clearly I've done all the city-type varieties of manual labor."

"Have you spent most of your time living in the city?" He shouldn't ask. He shouldn't care.

"Not exclusively," she said. "I've lived in my fair share of medium-size towns. It's just that nobody was inviting me to go hang out on the ranch. I didn't get asked to a lot of hoedowns." She shrugged. "Or much of anything."

He knew that a lot of people would feel sorry for her. He didn't. She was standing in front of him healthy and on two legs. Life was tough, but it was a hell of a lot tougher when you were dead.

"You'll probably end up at a few. Depending on how

long you stay. My sister-in-law has grand plans for some big-ass Christmas party over at her winery. So."

Her expression went soft, and then shuttered again. "I doubt I'll be here through Christmas."

"Don't make me waste time training you. I don't mind if you skip out before Christmas, but you better do the work you say you're going to do. Understand?"

"You're grumpy," she said.

"Yeah," he agreed. "I am."

"Most people don't like being called grumpy," she said.

"Well, I told you I wasn't going to deal with your tough-girl act, so I suppose as long as we're being honest, I have to take that one on the chin."

"So this is what you do," she said, following him out of the barn as he led them both down the path that would take them a long way to the mess hall, and would give her a good sense of the size of the property. "I mean, you're a professional... Cowboy."

"That's about the size of it."

"Did you always know you wanted to be a cowboy?"

"No," he said.

There had been a time when all he had wanted was to get the hell away from the ranch. From his dad. From everything familiar. When he had wanted to escape and start over. Get out of Gold Valley. He hadn't cared what he did or where he went. The only thing driving him had been anger.

And then he met Lindsay. And all he'd wanted was to make her happy.

All he'd wanted was to be a good husband.

A good man.

Because she knew he could be, and if Lindsay believed it, he wanted to make it real.

"When did you decide you wanted to be a cowboy?"

"When did you decide to become an interrogator for the police?"

"I'm curious," she said. "First of all, I don't get to talk to very many people. Or I haven't talked to anyone in a while. I've been by myself for a couple of weeks. Second of all, I really don't meet very many people like you."

"Grumpy assholes?"

"Cowboys," she said. "Assholes are par for the course, at least in my experience. Though not very many that are so aware of what they are."

"I didn't really decide to do it," he said. "My brother decided to revitalize the ranch. I hated my job."

"What did you do?"

"I worked in the office for the power company."

"Well… That does sound boring."

"It is. Pays well. Retirement. Benefits. All that."

"I bet this doesn't."

"Yep," he agreed.

She stopped talking for a while as they walked on the trail that wound down toward the river. The smell of the frigid water filtered through the heavy, damp scent of pine around them, the sound of the rushing rapids a comforting whisper beneath the wind in the trees. She had that look on her face again. That one that made his own eyes feel new.

He wasn't sure that he liked that.

Wasn't sure he liked at all that this stranger had the power to affect anything in him.

The path they were on led to the back of the mess hall, to the outdoor seating area that had a good view of the river. Even though it was just the beginning of November, his sister-in-law had put up white Christmas lights around the perimeter. Because, she said, winter was dark and any cheer was welcome. And she had also argued that white lights were not necessarily holiday specific.

She had argued these things with Wyatt, Bennett, Bennett's wife, Kaylee, and the youngest Dodge, Jamie.

She had not argued it with Grant.

Because Grant didn't care.

He wasn't going to waste a moment of damned breath arguing about the appropriate date to string lights.

In the end, he'd been the one to put them up.

Somehow, he'd been the deciding vote, since he was seen as neutral ground in some ways.

Funny, he wasn't sure he considered himself neutral. Just apathetic about pretty much anything that didn't involve alcohol.

Well, that wasn't entirely true. He liked to ride horses. In some ways, he thought that this endeavor at the Get Out of Dodge ranch had saved him. Sitting behind that desk had been a slow path to hell. When he'd been working at the power company still, his only solace really had been drinking.

He had spent so many years ignoring the way that other men his age lived their lives. Had spent so many years pushing down the kinds of appetites men his age had. Had honed his entire focus onto his wife. Not on the things they didn't have, but on what they did have.

Their small, perfect house down in town, within walking distance of all the cute little shops that she loved so much. Cozy dinners in on the nights when she felt like eating. And sometimes, Ensure shakes on the couch with a movie on when she didn't.

On those kinds of nights he waited until she went to bed, then heated up a TV dinner after she fell asleep. Not because he was hiding the fact that he was eating. She wouldn't want him to do that. He just didn't like to remind her of anything she might be missing.

He'd stripped his life down to the essentials because he didn't want to be out living a life that Lindsay couldn't. There was no one on earth he could talk to about it. And anyway, he spent as much time as possible talking to Lindsay when she had been alive.

The problem was, after she'd died, after he'd clawed his way out of the initial fog of grief, what he'd found on the other side was that he didn't exactly know how to live anymore. Not like a normal person. He didn't have a confidant, didn't know how to talk to anyone about it.

And there had been so many things he had mentally put a blockade around. Things he couldn't do. Things he couldn't have.

Hell, staying at his job was a prime example.

He didn't love it. Not even a little. But when Lindsay had been alive it had been a necessity. He'd needed that exact amount of money to keep up payments on their house. Had needed that specific kind of job so he had the kind of health insurance required to pay for her extensive treatments.

When she was gone, he hadn't needed the job. Not anymore.

But he'd stayed in it. For years longer than he needed to. Had stayed in the house, too.

Routine, as much as anything else.

Sometimes he'd even had those chocolate meal-replacement shakes with a shot of whiskey for dinner because he'd missed them.

Realizing he was stuck, realizing that he didn't have to live that way anymore, had been the first realization on the other side of that initial punch of grief.

That was when he'd started boxing things up. Returning some items to Lindsay's parents, keeping just two things for himself.

Her wedding ring set and the country Christmas snowman, carved from wood that she had insisted on setting out every holiday season. He'd hated it. Had given her a hard time about how god-awful it was. Made from knotty wood, with wire arms, and strange, knitted mitten hands. He thought the thing was everything that was wrong with a holiday craft bazaar.

In the end, of course, it had been one of the things he hadn't been able to part with.

It lived in a box up in his closet, but he had it.

The rings he kept on a chain around his neck, along with his. Hidden under his shirt, but there all the same.

It had been three years before he'd taken his own ring off his finger. He hadn't done it for a specific reason. Not really. It was just that at some point he realized he was putting on a wedding ring every morning, and he wasn't married.

That was when he'd added it to the chain that had her rings.

The chain seemed right.

He wasn't married. But it was impossible not to carry that marriage with him.

It had shaped him. Changed him.

Even if there was no reason for him to live like she was still here.

Sometime after deciding to put the house up for sale, while he was still working at the power company, his drinking had gotten worse. Mostly, because he didn't know what else to do with himself. He'd gone from one box to another.

And it was only Wyatt deciding to make some changes on the ranch that had really pulled him out of that dark, well-worn routine he'd found himself in.

His older brother had saved his life.

Damned if he'd ever tell him that, but it was the truth.

"Is this where you…eat?"

It took him a moment to realize he'd been standing there in complete silence while McKenna poked around the deck.

"Sometimes," he said. "Sometimes we eat in the mess hall. Because it's a little bit more centrally located than the main house. Though, when we have guests, not as much."

"Do you have guests right now?"

He nodded. "Some. So, if we eat inside, we just make sure to avoid mealtimes. Though the appearance of ranch hands adds to the experience, I guess."

"I would think a lot of the women would pay extra for you guys to come wandering through." She smirked, her expression taking on an impish quality he hadn't seen before.

He didn't know quite what to make of that. He supposed she was saying he was good-looking.

He didn't know why.

And he didn't know how to feel about it, either.

"I'll suggest Wyatt and Bennett pencil being living props into their schedule."

"Not you?" she asked.

He shifted, feeling uncomfortable. "I think I might scare them away."

She shrugged. "Some women dig the asshole thing."

He cleared his throat. "I'll make a note of that."

He pushed open the back door, led her into the dining hall. No one was in the large room. There were rows of vacant tables and benches, all clean and ready for the next meal.

Two large dispensers of coffee from Sugar Cup were set up on a long, bright blue table that was pushed up against the back wall, along with fixings for cider, hot chocolate and tea. In exchange for sending people on to the coffeehouse, they provided the ranch with coffee. And as far as Grant was concerned, it was a pretty good deal. An employee brought out fresh urns in the morning, and picked them up in the afternoon.

Caffeine that he didn't have to make was about the best thing he could imagine.

Except for possibly a self-refilling whiskey bottle.

"You can get coffee here in the morning," he said. "That's what most of us do. Wyatt and Lindy have coffee at their place, but most of the ranch hands come here."

"Am I a…ranch hand?" she asked.

"I guess so," he said.

The corner of her mouth tilted up, a dimple denting her cheek. "How funny."

"Mostly, you'll be doing chores in here, or housekeeping type stuff. Not a whole lot of heavy lifting."

She lifted her arms, which were slim like the rest of her. "For the best."

"Come with me, I'll show you to your cabin."

They walked down a long dirt road that led away

from the guest cabins. Not all of the Get Out of Dodge staff lived on the property, but depending on weather or projects that were happening, it was convenient to have the lodging.

This particular little house was set far away from most of the main buildings, nestled into the trees.

It was small, with a tidy porch and a red door. It was near one of the ponds, providing a nice view from all angles. The mountains at the back, the water out the front.

He found himself looking back at her, to see if she had that look on her face again. She did. A little bit of wonder. A whole lot of awe.

"Is this it?"

"Yes," he said.

He imagined that was an opening for witty banter of some kind. But he honestly couldn't be bothered. He didn't have enough experience with that kind of thing.

He walked her up to the door and punched in a code. "Four three six," he said. "That will get you in. I'll write it down for you."

He pushed open the door, and held it for her. Her expression went blank as they walked inside. Like the rest of the cabins, this one had been furnished with all new stuff.

Hell, it was nicer than his place.

Small, but nice.

"Think this will work for you?"

She blinked several times in rapid succession. "Yes," she said, her voice sounding a little bit tight. "Yes, this is fine."

"Are you okay?"

"Are you really letting me stay here?"

"Yes," he said. "Though, to be real technical about

it, Wyatt is letting you stay here. He's in charge. I'm just a shareholder, so to speak."

"But I mean… You're letting me stay here for… Nothing?"

"For work."

She sucked in one side of her cheek, looking away from him. "I don't have to sleep with you or anything, that's what I'm asking."

Heat shot down his spine, pooling in his gut. The shock of her bringing up sex, and the fact that he might be looking to trade lodging for it, caught him off guard.

"Hell, no," he said, the denial vehement and easy.

She lifted her hands. "Sorry. I didn't mean to be offensive. But you know, women on their own have to look out for these things. Most situations that seem too good to be true are. And most of the situations I've been in that were too good to be true fell apart because… Some guy expected a form of payment I wasn't that interested in."

"That's not going to happen here," he said.

She took a deep breath, clasping her hands together and looking around. "Okay. So, when do I need to start work?"

"You said you've worked in housekeeping at a hotel?"

"Yeah. I've done that a ton of times. Hotels, motels. You name it. I've cleaned it."

"Okay, make the rounds on the cabins today. The supplies are in the mess hall, where we just came from. You can start in a few hours. Get some rest."

She nodded. "I don't… I don't really have much in the way of—"

"Toiletries should be in the bathroom. You can use the washer and dryer in Wyatt and Lindy's place."

He hadn't verified that with his brother and sister-in-law, but he figured if they were going to start giving homes to strays he could give their washer and dryer.

"So." She looked at him. "Is he your younger brother?"

"Who?"

"Wyatt."

"No. I'm his younger brother."

She made a musing sound. "You seem older than him."

He had to laugh at that. He probably did. "No."

"You have other brothers?"

"One," he said. "And kind of a surrogate brother. And a younger sister. She's around. If you need anything, and you see the girl with dark hair, that's Jamie. She'll be happy to help out."

"Thanks," she said.

"You're welcome. I guess I'll leave you to it, then." She nodded. "Okay."

He lifted his hand, brushing his fingertips against the brim of his hat, and their eyes caught and held. She was pretty. He wasn't sure if he'd realized that yet. Well, he noticed she was pretty in that way he tended to find women pretty. They were female—he liked that, and he generally liked looking at them.

But McKenna Tate was something more. With her large brown eyes and delicate, pointed chin. Her dark hair was tangled, but still glossy, hanging around her face in a wild mane. And her mouth...

Pale pink with a deep curve at the center of the top lip, the lower one round and full.

He felt...*hungry*.

Dammit all. *That* wasn't new. Not really. But he

wasn't used to that hunger hitting hard and specific, with a woman standing right in front of him.

General craving he was used to. It was part of him. Part of his life. Wanting sex and not having it was printed on his DNA.

This was specific. Sharp and focused.

He didn't want *a* mouth.

He wanted that mouth.

Those lips.

Hell. No.

He forced himself to turn away. It was that or do something stupid he couldn't take back. Dammit, he wasn't one for guilt or pity but the woman had asked him outright if she was going to end up owing him anything and now he was staring at her lips like a sex-starved beast.

Because he was.

He walked out the front door without saying anything, taking in a deep breath of the cold early-morning air. Hoping it would do something to jolt him. To get rid of the deep, dark need that was coursing through his veins, ten times more potent than any alcohol.

He had work to do, and he was going to focus on that.

And he wasn't going to give one more thought to McKenna Tate's mouth.

CHAPTER THREE

MᴄKᴇɴɴᴀ ᴇᴍᴇʀɢᴇᴅ ꜰʀᴏᴍ the cabin a few hours later feeling strangely numb. Like she might be wandering through an alternate dimension and wasn't quite connected to her body. The cabin was so cute and neat, and she had felt weird putting her old, threadbare clothes away in the solid wood chest of drawers. Like they might dissolve the pretty cedar.

She wished that she had something warmer than what she was wearing, but her spare few items were what they were. And only what she could fit into a backpack.

A free promo phone she got on a pay as-you go plan, pajamas, two pairs of pants, two shirts, one pair of boots, some scattered and nearly used-up toiletries.

There were no warmer clothes in her possession at all. So she went ahead and braved the chilly afternoon, which didn't seem like it was going to thaw at all, judging by the textured gray of the sky.

She followed Grant's instructions and found the cleaning materials, then went to the first cabin and knocked. No one answered so she used the code he had provided for her to get inside. It was laid out similarly to her cabin, and she found cleaning it was a lot more fun than cleaning usually was. Mostly because she was used to cleaning whatever terrible apartment she lived in, or gross hotel rooms that were never going to lose the general film of seedy filth no matter how much elbow grease McKenna applied.

She moved through the row of cabins quickly and easily, feeling strangely accomplished by the end.

She was also hungry again. It had been hours since breakfast, and she had been running on empty, anyway. Of course, breakfast had been better than anything she'd had in a couple of months, so she would have thought it might sustain her. But no. It had just reminded her what it was like to have a full stomach. And now she wanted one again.

She wandered outside, wondering if it would be all right for her to go to the mess hall. Grant had mentioned that the ranch hands ate there during off-hours, and she wondered if two o'clock constituted off-hours.

She decided she was going to chance it, because she was really hungry.

She opened the door cautiously, peeking around before stepping inside.

The coffee station was still set up, and she decided that whatever there was to eat she was going to have caffeine with it.

There didn't seem to be anyone around, so she went to the kitchen and helped herself to a bowl of soup, taking it out to the tables and sitting next to the window, bathing herself in the anemic light that was trying to get through the cloud cover. She felt warm. Warm and…safe.

She hadn't really been aware of feeling like she was in danger, but that was partly because there had been nothing for her to do but soldier through. But now, now that she had a little bit of respite from the truly horrendous situation she'd found herself in, she could fully acknowledge how awful it had been.

She blinked, her eyes stinging slightly. She wasn't going to cry. She didn't do that. At least, not without a reason. Tears could be useful. They could soften your look, make people feel sorry for you.

Tears, on a personal level, were pointless.

Her thoughts drifted back to her tour guide. Grant Dodge.

Just thinking his name made her stomach tighten a little bit. And that was stupid. He was handsome. But she'd quit caring about how handsome a man was quite a while ago. Handsome didn't mean anything.

The door to the mess hall opened and McKenna jumped, every reflex inside of her getting ready to run if she had to. Like she was in here stealing soup, instead of eating like Grant had said she could. But she felt like an outlier. An interloper.

It was her default setting, and it was difficult to just turn it off at a moment's notice.

The woman who walked through the front door had wild, carrot-colored curls, and pink, wind-chapped cheeks. Her smile was cheery and friendly, and McKenna was taken off guard when it was immediately aimed at her. "Hi," she said. "Are you one of the guests?"

"No," McKenna said, reflexively wrapping her hands around her soup bowl and pulling it closer to her. "I work here."

"Oh," she said. "I work with Bennett Dodge. At his veterinary clinic."

"Oh," McKenna said. She had no idea that Bennett Dodge worked at a veterinary clinic. She could only assume that he was one of the brothers Grant had talked about. She didn't like being caught off guard, and she didn't like looking ignorant, so she chose not to ask any follow-up questions.

"I'm Beatrix," she said. "Beatrix Leighton. I'm also Lindy's sister-in-law. Well. I'm her ex-sister-in-law. She used to be married to my brother. But now she's married to Wyatt."

"That seems complicated," McKenna said, somewhat interested against her will.

"Not really," Beatrix said. "My brother was a terrible husband. And I love Lindy, and all I want is for her to be happy. Damien didn't make her happy. Wyatt does. That's about as simple as it gets."

"I guess so."

"How long have you been here?"

"About twenty minutes," McKenna said, lifting another spoonful of soup to her lips.

Beatrix laughed and walked over to the coffee station. "No. I meant at the ranch."

McKenna laughed. "Not much longer than that. I got here this morning."

"Wow," Beatrix said, filling up a coffee mug and, much to McKenna's chagrin, taking a seat at the table across from her. "Where you from?"

"Out of town," McKenna said.

"Okay. How did you find out about the ranch?"

"Oh, I kind of… Stumbled upon it."

"I think you'll like it here. They're all great."

"Well, that's good to know." From a total stranger. But McKenna wasn't going to say that, because she was going to do her best not to alienate anyone in this place. It was warm, it was dry, there was food and coffee. While she planned her next move, there was no better place she could be. She had gone and stumbled into some kind of Hallmark Christmas movie, and she wasn't going to question it. She was just going to accept the hospitality while she figured out how she was going to approach the Daltons.

She needed an idea that was a little bit better than wandering onto the property and announcing that she was a secret half sister.

If all else failed, she would definitely do that. But she was going to try to come up with something a little more sophisticated first.

"Have you met Jamie yet?" her chatty new friend pressed.

"No," McKenna said.

"She's the sister. The only sister. She's one of my best friends. I'm here because we're going to go riding. You can come along."

McKenna shifted uncomfortably. "Thank you. But I have to keep working." She also had no idea how to ride horses. She wasn't sure she had ever been within thirty feet of one.

"Some other time," Beatrix said. "Jamie is a great guide. That's what she does here."

For a moment, McKenna let herself wonder about the kind of alternate reality that might have existed where she could have… Lived on a ranch and ridden horses for a living. This whole place seemed like a sanctuary of some kind. And the whole family was just… Here. Not moving around. Not wondering where they might stay next. Not waiting for the other shoe to drop, or worrying about what might happen if a sour relationship went so sour that they had to leave it, and lose the roof over their head.

"Sure," McKenna said, but there was basically no way in hell.

Still, she didn't want to say that. She wasn't sure why.

But this was such a strange, easy connection made with someone who wasn't afraid to smile at her, and didn't seem to want anything from her. Those kinds of connections were few and far between. McKenna wasn't entirely sure she'd ever had an experience quite like it. So the last thing she was going to do was ruin it by being unfriendly.

"I'm sure I'll see you around. I come by quite a bit."

"Okay," she said, "see you around."

Beatrix stood, taking her coffee with her, offering a cheerful wave as she walked out the door, leaving McKenna alone with her soup.

"What the hell is this place?" she asked the empty room, obviously not expecting an answer.

She finished her soup and stood up, walking back to the kitchen. Right then, the back door opened, and Grant came in. She froze, her empty soup bowl in hand, as she stared at him for a moment, then blinked and looked away. "Hi," she said.

"Hi," he returned, his voice gruff.

"I was just having lunch."

"Good," he said.

"Do I just…wash the bowl… Or…?"

His face remained immovable, taciturn, but he reached out and took the bowl from her hand, walking over to the sink. It was one of those large, commercial sinks with a detachable nozzle right on the spout. She wasn't sure what they were called. Because she had certainly never lived in a place nice enough to have a kitchen that would have one. He set the bowl and spoon down in the sink, and then he did something truly unexpected. He pushed his sleeves up to his elbows, and turned the water on.

She just stood and watched while he filled the sink partway up with water, adding a little bit of soap. He looked at her out of the corner of his eye, one dark brow lifting slightly as he did. He didn't say anything.

So she just watched him.

His movements were direct. He didn't waste any, she noticed. He was a no-nonsense kind of guy. His profile was strong, his jaw square. The dark whiskers that covered it only enhancing that sense of masculinity.

Her eyes dropped down to his forearms. They were strong, the muscles there shifting and flexing as he moved. She imagined *he* lifted objects over fifty pounds often. At least, his physique seemed to suggest that he did.

"Thank you," she said, because she realized it was weird that she was standing there staring at him, and neither of them were saying anything.

"Not a problem," he said.

"I could wash the bowl," she said.

"Yeah, but I would've had to show you how it all worked. So I might as well do it. Anyway, you can learn for next time."

"I'll owe you. Next time you eat soup, I've got the bowls."

"Much obliged," he said, nodding his head.

Normally, she would have said that cowboy hats were cheesy, and in no way hot. But the way that he nodded just then, that black hat on his head… He was like some weird country-boy fantasy she'd never realized she had.

You're not going to make a fantasy out of the nice guy cleaning your dishes. You don't need guy trouble and you know that. Men are terrible dead ends with muscles, and that's all. Just make the most of this living situation and don't screw it up.

That didn't mean she couldn't look at him. Looking didn't mean doing anything. So there.

She wasn't sure when she had gone from thinking of him as a grumpy asshole to thinking of him as a nice guy. But she supposed the two weren't actually mutually exclusive. He was grumpy; there was no denying that. Even now that he was doing something nice for her, he hadn't spared her a smile. Maybe *nice* was the wrong word.

Good.

He seemed like one of those mythical *good men* that she hadn't ever really been convinced existed.

Even the long-lost father that she wanted to meet couldn't actually be that good of a man. He had knocked her mother up and left her alone. He had a whole family, which she certainly wasn't part of. And sure, maybe he didn't know about her. But still, a guy running around indiscriminately spreading his seed was hardly going to go into the *good man* category.

There was something about Grant that just seemed *good.*

Of course, she was a terrible judge of character. Or maybe she couldn't be much of a judge at all, because she tended to need to ally herself with whoever was willing. That meant sometimes putting blinders on out of necessity.

McKenna was very good with necessity.

"Don't worry about it," she said. "I might even wash two soup bowls for you."

"I couldn't begin to accept such generosity."

"I'm very generous," she said, a smile touching her lips.

Grant didn't smile at all. She studied his eyes, kind of a dark green that reminded her of the trees that surrounded the property, trying to find a hint of humor. A glimmer of something. The man was unreadable.

"I have some work to do," he said. "Need to get lunch and then get out."

He was dismissing her. Which was fine. She didn't care. "I don't know what I'm supposed to do next. I cleaned all of the cabins."

"Why don't you get some rest? Come back in here at dinnertime and get something to eat. You can worry about doing a full day tomorrow."

"Okay."

The door to the kitchen opened, and Wyatt came in. "Hey," he said, greeting her first, then nodding at his brother. "How's the day going?"

"Fine," McKenna returned.

"Good. Hey, we're all going out to the bar in town tonight. Do you want to come?"

She was blindsided by that question. She blinked, not quite able to process the fact that her new boss had just invited her out for drinks. And suddenly, she wanted to crawl out of her skin. "Thank you," she said, edging toward the door. "But I think I'm going to… Just rest. It's been… It's been a hell of a few weeks."

"Is there anything we can help with?" Wyatt looked

genuinely concerned. Grant's expression was like a wall of granite.

"You're helping enough. Giving me a place to stay is more than I…" Her throat tightened, and she did her best to speak around it. "Anyway. Thanks for inviting me. I'll—"

"Grant will meet you in here tomorrow," Wyatt said. "Breakfast time. We're a bunch of early risers."

"Six a.m.," Grant said, those unfathomable green eyes settling on her. "Don't be late."

McKenna nodded, and backed out the door, tripping down the path and heading toward her cabin. Her cabin.

A wave of emotion swelled up in her chest. Less than twenty-four hours ago she had been curled up on the cold, damp floor of an abandoned structure out in the middle of the woods and now she had… People talking to her. People offering to help her.

A group of people inviting her out for drinks.

When she'd been younger she had something of a social group, but the last couple of years…

Everything had been so grim and stripped back, and she wasn't sure she had even fully realized it until… Well, until she had been in Grant's truck this morning accepting the fact that she was homeless, and without very many options.

She entered the code to her cabin, pushed open the door and shut it, leaning against it for a moment. She let her head fall back, closing her eyes. It was completely quiet. Nothing but the sound of furniture settling over the hardwood floors.

She pushed off from the door and walked down the hall toward the bathroom, stripping her clothes off as she went. She turned on the water and waited for it to heat up. Then she got inside and stood beneath the spray. She let the hot water roll over her face. Something inside of her chest cracked. Everything felt too big to be contained. She kept her face tilted up, steadfastly refusing to find out if there were tears running down her cheeks, or if it was just the shower.

It made her feel better to blame the shower. So she would leave it at that.

And tomorrow she would report for work at 6:00 a.m. By then, hopefully, she would be done with all this emotional crap.

When she got out of the shower she changed into her pajamas—something she hadn't done since going on the road, because pajamas didn't feel like the kind of clothes you could make a quick getaway in—and crawled into bed.

She felt that same wave of emotion begin to build inside her again. She closed her eyes. It was early, way too early to be getting into bed. But she was exhausted. Drained.

And for the first time in a very long time, McKenna Tate closed her eyes and let herself fall all the way asleep.

GRANT LEANED BACK in his chair and surveyed the surroundings. People were filtering into the Gold Valley saloon in large numbers, the end-of-workday crowd eager to get that first drink into their systems. Anything to begin that relaxation process after a day spent at the desk. He could remember that well.

His work didn't stress him out now. He drank for other reasons.

It surprised him how relieved he was that McKenna

had not taken his brother's invitation to join them tonight. She made him feel tense. On a good day he might try to make excuses as to why that might be. Lie to himself a little bit. But today wasn't an especially good day. He couldn't pretend it was a mystery why.

She was beautiful. She was a woman. He wasn't accustomed to being in proximity to a woman he found not just pretty but attractive.

Beatrix Leighton was around all the time, particularly now that she had started work at Bennett's veterinary clinic, and had made fast friends with Jamie. She was cute, and he recognized that. But he wasn't attracted to her. When Lindy had started coming around to the property when she and Wyatt were working on their joint venture between the winery and ranch, before the two of them had gotten together, he had known she was pretty. Closer to his age than Bea, and closer to his type—assuming he had a type—and still, she hadn't made his skin feel too tight.

His younger brother Bennett, and Bennett's wife, Kaylee, walked over to the table and took a seat next to and across from Grant. Kaylee was holding a bottle of beer, and Bennett had a glass of whiskey in one hand, and a bottle of beer in the other. He slid the whiskey over to Grant.

"Thanks," Grant said.

"You're welcome," Bennett said, lifting his beer bottle.

Wyatt and Lindy were on their way, and apparently, Bea and Jamie would be joining them, too. It was a little bit more social than Grant was in the mood for. But he was already here. And he had whiskey, so it was fine.

He found that most social situations could be easily

navigated with an alcoholic drink that he pretended required a lot of concentration. Everyone else would pick up any and all slack in the conversation and he could just sit there and drink.

"Anything new at the ranch?" Bennett asked.

"No," he said, because he didn't want to have a conversation about McKenna. Besides, he couldn't remember the last time he had felt pressed to keep Bennett apprised of new hires at Get Out of Dodge.

He wasn't even sure why McKenna came to mind just then.

"I'll be around to put in a workday this weekend."

"Don't worry about it," Grant said. "You're busy."

"Wyatt said there was some big fencing project. Dallas wants the payday," Bennett said, smiling at the mention of his teenage son. "I figured I would go and make him spend quality time with me while he earns his paycheck."

"I'm sure he'll enjoy that," Grant said.

Bennett had only discovered he had a son a little over a year ago. It had been a big adjustment for both Bennett and for Dallas. For the whole family, really. Bennett was the first one to have a kid, and he had showed up a teenager. Only good had come from it, though. Bennett was a great dad, and Dallas was flourishing living in Gold Valley. Plus, something about the change, whether it was the pressure of the whole event or what, had finally pushed Bennett and his best friend, Kaylee, into becoming more. It had been obvious to Grant that they should have been from the beginning. But he didn't stick his face into people's love lives.

Mostly, because his own was currently nonexistent. And then also because the one he'd had wasn't anything like anyone else's. And also wasn't anything most people would aspire to.

"He's mostly okay with me," Bennett said.

"And he's not having any girls back at the house while you and Kaylee are out?" Grant asked.

Kaylee shot Bennett a look out of the corner of her eye. "Hopefully not."

"Dallas had a pretty rough upbringing," Bennett said. "And I'm well aware he's had a lot more... Experience at his age than I would like. But then, he's also my walking, talking cautionary tale about what happens when you mess around at sixteen. So, hopefully he'll just remember that."

Kaylee laughed. "Yeah. Because the threat of consequences keeps teenagers from having sex."

Grant didn't know how to respond to that at all, so he just lifted his glass of whiskey to his lips while his brother groaned. The idea that his sixteen-year-old nephew was having sex while Grant...

Life was not fair.

Of course, he'd made his choices.

He wanted to make some different ones. But that was the problem. He didn't know how. And at thirty-four, the conversation that he would have to have with his partner was...

It was just layers of complicated and hard and he honestly couldn't figure out how to navigate it right now.

But then he thought of McKenna. Her brown eyes, and that soft-looking skin. Her lips.

She was managing to take over his bar time without actually being here.

"I did tell him that I was not helping him out if any

angry dads came onto our properties with shotguns. He's on his own."

"That's just mean," Kaylee said. "I bet your dad defended you from a few shotgun-wielding parents."

"I didn't get caught," Bennett said.

Grant took another drink. Their upbringing had been… Not so great. Bennett had been six when their mother had died. Grant had been ten. Their father was a good enough dad, but he had been fully emotionally unavailable after that had happened. Jamie had been a newborn, and their dad had been consumed with trying to parent her. Grant couldn't blame him for that. They'd all reacted to it in different ways. Wyatt had taken his anger and channeled all of it toward their father. They had a big dustup involving their dad's fiancée when Wyatt had been seventeen, and Wyatt had left home for years after that. Bennett had been the good one, but had been blowing off steam with sex obviously. He'd just been doing all his misbehaving under the radar.

Grant?

Grant had turned into a monster. He'd been so angry, and he hadn't known what the hell to do with it. He hadn't brought it home. Hadn't brought it to his father. No. He bled it all over everyone else. By the time he'd gotten into high school he'd been the biggest asshole bully. Nothing made him angrier than happy kids with happy lives, and he'd gone out of his way to add a little misery to their existence.

The only thing he'd hated more than them was what he'd turned into. But he hadn't known how to be any different. He didn't talk to his brothers. He didn't have friends. When he walked by people in the halls they cowered. And for good reason. He'd been known to shove kids straight into the wall. A quick, satisfying outlet for the rage that burned just beneath his skin.

He'd been failing every class. More than that, he'd been failing at being a person.

He'd spent a lot of time in detention, but he didn't much care. Home. School. It didn't matter. He didn't feel any different wherever he went.

He could still remember, so clearly, being seventeen years old and walking into the school library and seeing her.

Blonde and beautiful with blue eyes. She'd smiled at him, and he... He'd felt it. He hadn't been able to remember a time when he'd felt anything other than anger.

She talked to him. Like he wasn't scary. And she'd offered to tutor him.

And he didn't know why in the hell, to this day, he'd taken her up on it.

Except that his life had been so damned bleak he'd thought, *Why the hell not?*

She'd been so nice to him. Unfailingly. And that hungry, desperate part of him had fallen for her hard and fast.

You don't have to be this way, you know. I know you're a good guy, Grant. You're just angry. I can understand that. I feel angry, too, sometimes.

He swallowed hard, the memory washing over him, blotting out the scene around him.

It was one of his favorite places in Gold Valley. A little out-of-the-way place just off a dirt road that wound up the mountains, right by a small creek. It was where he went when everything at school and home felt like too much.

The sunlight filtered through the trees, making Lind-

say's hair look like it was spun from gold. Like there was a halo over her head.

He'd never felt the way he did for her about anyone. Like he wanted to protect her. Keep her safe forever.

Before Lindsay, he'd only ever wanted to destroy things.

He hadn't touched her. She was sweet. Too sweet for a guy like him.

"You get angry?" He looked at beautiful Lindsay, with her bright eyes and hopeful expression. He couldn't imagine her being angry.

She nodded slowly. "Yes. Don't you know I wasn't in school last year?"

He shook his head. "No. Weren't you guys out of town or—"

"I had cancer, Grant. I could get it again." Her blue eyes locked with his. "That's always a possibility. I need you to know that. I know it. It scares me. It makes me angry."

He didn't know what possessed him, all he knew was that he wasn't able to make another choice. He gripped her chin and closed the distance between them, kissing her on the lips.

He blinked, finding himself back in the present. He'd been so careful with her. Because she was sweet and delicate. Because she thought he was good. Sometimes he regretted just how careful he'd been. When the cancer came back, her prognosis wasn't good. They'd gotten married as quickly as possible. Always thinking it would go away. Always hoping. Even though, deep down, he'd known.

They'd both known. Her life wasn't going to be long; there was no way it could be, barring a miracle. But he'd imagined that they could have something. Maybe not the kind of marriage everyone else had, but something like it.

They'd never had normal. But they'd had something pretty damned precious. In the end, being with Lindsay had changed him profoundly.

Without her… The path he had been on only ended a couple of ways. Dead young or in jail. She had saved him. And whatever he had or didn't have now, whatever he hadn't done…

He couldn't regret the choices he'd made.

So, if his sixteen-year-old nephew was getting play, he had to ask himself at what point he was going to start figuring out how to live some kind of normal life.

He'd tried. Once.

He'd driven to a neighboring town and gone to a bar. He hadn't even gotten past saying hi. The damned woman had recognized him. He was that famous guy who'd married his terminally ill high school sweetheart even knowing their life together would be short. She'd given him the saddest eyes he'd ever seen, and he'd been sure he could have gotten pity sex.

That was when he realized he didn't want pity sex.

That had been two years ago. Two years since he'd last tried to go out and get some and had stopped himself on some kind of principle. Right about now, he was starting to think that maybe he would take pity sex.

A hot kick to his gut told him that wasn't true. Not by a long shot.

He didn't just want *any* sex. That was the thing. If he did, there were a bunch of ways to get it.

He was a man who didn't want an emotional connection, at all, yet was unable to stomach the idea of an anonymous hookup.

He'd had enough emotional connections to last him from here to forever. He'd had an emotional connection with a woman for eight years. He didn't want to do it again. Not ever. He valued it, over any other experience, over any other relationship, he'd ever had. He didn't have the energy to do it again.

Lindsay had made him a better man, and he was never going to go back on that. He wouldn't do that to her memory. Yeah, he'd given her those eight years, but she'd given them to him, too. He wasn't perfect. Far from it. But she saw him as somebody worthwhile, and he had needed that, more than air.

Maybe that was part of why the shallow hookup thing didn't work for him.

He almost laughed. Actually, he could see Lindsay telling him to go for it.

You're too serious, Grant. Go have some fun.

He gritted his teeth and took another drink of whiskey. Thankfully, after that, the rest of the crew arrived, and pushed his thoughts out of that maudlin territory.

Lindy and Bea were talking about Lindy's brother, Dane, and his recovery from a recent accident he'd suffered on the rodeo circuit. "When he's up and around, hopefully we can get him a job on the ranch," Lindy said.

Bea's forehead creased. "How long do you think that will be? He was… Not so great when I saw him the other day."

"Yeah," Lindy said. "He's not so great."

Well, Grant could relate to that. Though maybe that wasn't fair. He hadn't been trampled by a bull. He was just… Constantly trying to figure out what the hell his life was supposed to look like.

That, he related to. The fact that your life could change completely, look nothing like you wanted it to, and you could do nothing but go on living.

Grant figured that the chances of Dane getting back to riding were slim to none. Also, knowing his brother Wyatt like he did, he knew that bull riders didn't take kindly to the idea that they might be human, or fallible in any way.

"So what's the deal with the new girl?" Jamie asked. "The new hire?"

"You said there was nothing different happening at the ranch," Bennett said, looking at Grant pointedly.

"We don't talk about every new ranch hand we bring on board."

"This sounds like something other than a random ranch hand," Bennett commented.

"It's a woman," Jamie said. "She's young."

"She's twenty-six," Grant said. All heads swiveled toward him. "She told me," he added, knowing he sounded a little defensive. "Anyway, Jamie, she's older than you."

"You seem to be an expert on the subject," Kaylee said.

"I'm not an expert," Grant said. "But I found her this morning sleeping in one of the abandoned cabins on the property. She was homeless."

"What?" Jamie asked.

Bea was looking at him with wide eyes. "She was homeless? She didn't say anything about that when I talked to her today."

Leave it to Bea to have struck up a conversation with

McKenna. Bea was a collector of strays, though mostly they were of the furry variety. It didn't surprise him that she had a soft heart when it came to people, too.

"Yeah, well, I doubt it comes up in polite conversation," Grant said.

"She didn't... Well, she didn't look homeless," Bea said. "Not that there's... I mean... That sounded mean."

"Don't worry about it, Bea," Lindy said, putting her hand over Bea's. "I know what you meant."

"I found her this morning," Grant said. "And today she was put in my charge. So, I spent time showing her around the ranch, and helping her figure out the job."

"I invited her to come out tonight," Wyatt said. "She didn't want to."

"Possibly because she didn't have money to pay for drinks," Lindy said gently.

Wyatt frowned. "I would've bought her drink."

"She probably didn't want to assume," Lindy said.

"Well, next time I'll make it clear."

"I wonder what happened," Jamie said. "I mean, it has to be pretty rough to end up sleeping in one of those god-awful cabins on the ranch property. Those things are full of spiders."

Yeah, Grant imagined McKenna had had it pretty tough. Not just because he'd found her curled up on the floor this morning, but because her whole demeanor was like a shield. Fully designed to keep people away from her.

"Why didn't Luke and Olivia come tonight?" Bea asked.

"From what I heard," Jamie said, "they couldn't get a babysitter."

That was when Jamie held up her cell phone and

showed off pictures of Luke and Olivia's baby. Not that she was much of a baby these days.

Grant didn't look at the pictures. He made a show of it, but he let his eyes skim over the screen. Not that he wasn't happy for Luke. He was. Luke was like a brother to him, and the guy had had it rough growing up. He deserved every bit of happiness with Olivia that he could get. But that didn't mean Grant wanted to look at it.

"Does anybody want another round?" Grant stood up and gestured toward the bar. "I'm going to get another drink."

All hands around the table went up, and Grant took that as a great excuse to take a small break away from the revelry.

He was good at that. Good at using alcohol as a distraction.

Another image of McKenna filtered through his mind. McKenna would be a damned good distraction.

He gritted his teeth, pushed that out of his mind and walked over to the bar.

CHAPTER FOUR

McKENNA COULDN'T BELIEVE she had slept all the way through the night. Not considering she'd lain down at two o'clock. But at least she was feeling revived. Renewed in some way after sleeping for so many hours. Even though it was still dark outside. She was a couple of minutes late heading over to the mess hall, but not late enough that it should matter. At least, not in her opinion. Whatever the opinion of her gruff, grumpy guide was, she didn't know.

The conclusion she'd come to that morning that was most important was that she needed new clothes. When she got her first check from this job, that would be the thing she took care of right away.

She would also have to figure out transportation. But she didn't want to waste money on a car. And she didn't want to save up that long for anything. Not right now.

But today, in a pair of worn jeans, another threadbare sweater, with the heavier sweater she'd been wearing over the top of it, she was feeling slightly day-old. And then some.

At least her hair was clean. Clean and brushed and silky feeling for the first time in weeks.

As victories went, it was a small one, but she would take it.

When she walked into the mess hall, Grant was

standing against the back wall, leaning against the display with the coffee on it. He lifted his cup. "You're late."

"I know," she returned.

"If you know what time it is, then why didn't you come at the right time?"

"Because it's early? And it took a little longer for me to get ready and get over here than I realized it would."

"Get it figured out for tomorrow," he said, his tone hard. Uncompromising.

"Do you let anyone make mistakes?"

"Nope."

"What about yourself?" she asked. "Are you allowed to make mistakes?"

He stared at her, the moment stretching out into two. "No," he responded.

And the funny thing was she absolutely believed him. The gravity in his green eyes was far too severe for her to even consider that he might not be deadly serious.

"Come on," she said, reaching past him and grabbing a coffee cup, her elbow brushing against his solid midsection. She clenched her teeth, trying not to think about just how solid that midsection was. "Mistakes are like walnuts in the cookies of life."

"What does that mean?" he asked.

"It would be better without them, but somehow they end up in there half the time, anyway."

The corner of his mouth twitched, lifted upward slightly, and McKenna's heart leaped up half a foot in response. She didn't know why she was reacting to him. He was hot. Big deal. Men were often hot. Sure, not commonly as hot as this one, but whatever.

Of course, there was no reason to be too...too

guarded with him. He'd been nice to her, and anyway, it was better for her if he liked her. Or whatever his version of liking someone might be.

"Careful," she said. "You almost smiled at me."

"Won't happen again."

She arched a brow. "Does that make your smile a mistake, Grant?"

"No," he said. "Just an unplanned facial tic."

"Damn. You're a hard case."

"Not the first time I've heard that one."

He took a sip of his coffee and her eyes were drawn to his mouth. She had never really been into the cowboy thing or the beard thing. But she liked his. His mouth was… Well, it could almost be called pretty. Except for all the ruggedness that surrounded it. She shouldn't be staring at it.

She popped the lid on her coffee cup and lifted it. "I'm ready."

"Just fifteen minutes late now," he said.

She chose to ignore that. She had hot coffee. She wasn't going to spoil it with a fight. "I can't tell you how long it's been since I've woken up to some decent coffee." She took a long sip. "It's blessed."

"Blessed?"

"If there was a patron saint of caffeinated beverages I'd be saying a prayer of thanks to him right about now. Or her."

"So tell me," he said, pushing away from the coffee stand, the only indication that he was ready to get moving. McKenna started to follow him out the door. "How exactly did you find yourself in a position where you're waking up without coffee in the morning?"

Her stomach twisted, her guard going right back up.

She squinted at him, trying to read his face. "Why do you want to know that?"

"I'm curious," he said. "Also, maybe wanting to make sure you didn't murder someone and are now on the run."

"I told you I wasn't on the run from the law," she said.

"It's entirely possible you're running from becoming identified by the law. Which makes you not on the run from the law on a technicality."

"No," she said. "I'm pretty sure that makes me on the run from the law on a technicality actually."

"Whatever."

"It's a whole series of bad choices, Grant," she said, trying to sound light and not ashamed or depressed. "The main one being that I got screwed out of my apartment and my deposit and decided to come here."

"Why here?"

"I found out that I have... A family connection. But I'm not sure how to approach it. You know, since random family members showing up at the front door aren't always welcome." She wasn't going to tell him about what the family relationship was. Certainly wasn't going into the fact that she was Hank Dalton's secret baby.

"Is this your only family?"

She nodded. "At least, the only family I want to find. I could maybe track my mom down, but she gave me up. I'm not looking for a tearful reunion. Anyway, I'm not even sure why she gave me up. For all I know she had good reason."

"Right," he said. "So you found out you had some extended family here."

"Yes," she responded. It was kind of a lie. But not totally. Not that it really mattered. She lied all the time. What was one more?

"But your truck broke down."

"Dead as a doornail." She waved her hand in a broad gesture. "At least, barring me finding a thousand dollars. Let me tell you, that is not likely."

"Right."

"I don't really have any connections. The last couple years... There hasn't really been anyone. I figured why not start over. Totally. Somewhere new. I had a plan. Not the best plan, but I had one. I should know better than to make those by now."

"You're preaching to the choir," he responded.

She thought about pressing for more information, because she was curious. Curious what force on heaven or earth had ever dared oppose Grant Dodge. He seemed far too formidable for anyone or anything to dare. But she also had a feeling—a pretty rock-solid one—that he wasn't interested in having heart-to-heart talks. Least of all with her. The man was a fortress, and she had a feeling that was by design. That he was keeping things locked up for a reason.

Hell, she could understand that.

"Don't you want to know what we're doing this morning?" he asked.

"Yes," she said, taking a sip of hot, fortifying coffee. "My brain is feeling just awake enough to handle that information."

"We're painting the barn."

She thought of the pretty, bright-red structure he had showed her yesterday morning. "Isn't it painted?"

"One of them."

"There are more barns? Multiple barns?"

"Several. This is the one we keep supplies and machinery in. But Wyatt thinks that we should freshen it up for the tourists."

"And you don't?"

"I don't have a thought about barns, or the color of them, at all."

"Oh, just the way you said it. Made it seem like it was something he was into, but maybe not you."

"I'm here to support Wyatt. I would rather be here than working at the power company. That means I do whatever the man wants."

"It must be tough," she said. "Working with your brother. Taking orders."

"Why do you think that?"

She shrugged. "I don't know. I'm an only child." She frowned. Because maybe she wasn't an only child. If it turned out she was a Dalton, then she had half siblings. But still, she had been raised one, so that counted for something. She had foster siblings sometimes, but ultimately, she was alone in life. There was no group that moved with her. No one she could reach out to when she needed something.

"I always admired the hell out of Wyatt," Grant said. "He used to be a pro bull rider in the rodeo."

"Really?" she asked. "That's kind of badass."

"Pretty *damn* badass," Grant agreed.

He pushed open the door on a barn that had been worn down to the original wood, and held it for her. She went in first. There were dropcloths and ladders, paint rollers and buckets of paint, all ready to go inside.

His demeanor changed when he talked about his brother. He was a little bit less serious. A little bit less of a wall. It intrigued her. Made her want to dig a little deeper. See what other reactions she could possibly get from him.

And why not? Allies were an important thing in this world. It wouldn't be a terrible thing to make one out of Grant Dodge if she could.

"Where are we starting?"

"Outside," he said. "I'll do up high, if you want to do down low."

She huffed out a laugh. "Is that what the kids are calling it these days?"

He shot her a look she couldn't quite read. It almost had humor in it—almost. "I have no idea what the kids are calling much of anything these days."

"I guess I don't, either," she said. "What a sobering thought."

"You're closer than me."

"Not by much."

"Twenty-six? I'd say."

"How old are you?"

"Thirty-four."

"Wow," she said, rolling her eyes. "So advanced. So aged. Can you even remember what you were doing when you were my age?"

His expression turned to stone. It was an immediate shift. That little glint of humor she had seen in his green eyes, just a hint, gone flat. And just like that, her stomach fell.

"Yeah," he said. "I do."

She'd said something wrong, and she wasn't sure what. It would be nice if she could find a segue, but she needed at least one more coffee to be that nimble on her feet. "Well, I guess we can cart some paint outside." Her verbal soft shoe was nothing to write home about.

"Right," he said.

They hauled out one of the big five-gallon paint buckets, and he started messing around with some piece of equipment she wasn't familiar with.

"Compressor," he said. "I'm going to use that on the upper level.

"Wait a minute, you get the power tools? Is that because you're a man?" She eyeballed her classic, totally uncool paint roller.

"No, I get the power tools because I know how to use them. If running a compressor was something that you did for one of your manual labor jobs, please feel free to inform me, and I will happily turn that work over to you."

"All right, that's a good reason. Because no, I haven't ever used a compressor."

He pried open the lid on the paint can and started to stir, and she found herself captivated by his movements, even while he was all covered up. This morning he had on a dark jacket and gloves, the same hat he'd been wearing yesterday on top of his head.

"Is this what you would be doing if you weren't babysitting me?"

"I'm not babysitting. I'm training."

She shrugged. "Well, is this what you would be doing if I wasn't here?"

"Yes," he answered. "Probably by myself."

"How much of a charity case am I, Grant?"

"I'll get the job done faster with you here." His sidestep didn't go unnoticed.

"That doesn't answer my question."

"Do you *want* the answer, McKenna?"

"I don't actually care if I'm a charity case. People in my position can't afford to put pride over a warm meal."

"Fair enough. It's probably about fifty-fifty. Because let's face it, the cleaning work that we need you for doesn't exactly cover pay and a place to stay. And it sure as hell isn't full-time."

"Fair enough," she said.

"How did you end up—"

"Working a string of menial jobs and having no connections in my life?"

"Yeah," he said, hefting the five-gallon bucket of paint and pouring a measure into a tray.

"Foster care," she said. "Which kind of gets you used to the transient lifestyle. Also, not the best for forming long-term attachments."

"All your life?"

"From the time I was two."

Most people looked at her with pity after she told them that. Most people said they were sorry. Grant Dodge just seemed to absorb it. Like she had spoken the words to a mountain, and not a man.

"I did not get good grades in school. Didn't know how to even begin applying for financial aid for college. Didn't want to, anyway. I struck out on my own with a guy that I met in my last home. That didn't turn out. Had a little run of *didn't turn out*. Decided that at least if I was on my own I was never going to get screwed for anyone else's mistakes. Which ended up not being true, since my last landlord sold the place out from under me. Thought that was more a deliberate action than a mistake on her part."

She looked up at Grant. His expression contained

neither judgment nor pity, and she didn't know quite what to do with that. Typically, it was one or the other.

"Aren't there tenants' rights to protect you?" he asked.

"Sure," she answered. "But how am I going to take anyone to court? How am I going to make sure that those rights are enforced? Mostly, it isn't going to happen."

He frowned. "That doesn't seem—"

"Life is not fair, Grant. Not even close."

"Yeah, I'm actually familiar with that principle."

Again, she didn't ask. It was strange, because he was asking her quite a few questions. More than she had expected a guy like him to ask, certainly. But she could tell the reverse would not be welcome.

"Well, then we understand each other to a degree. I don't expect life to be fair. And that's why when I'm given unexpected charity, I don't kick up a fuss. I've had enough of the alternative to know that if something good is going to cross my path, I'm going to take it for however long it lasts."

"Pretty solid principle to live by," he said.

"I haven't got a whole hell ton of principles, but the ones I do have have served me pretty well." She dipped the long-handled roller into the tray of paint and moved it back and forth a few times, sliding it through the ridge part of the tray to get rid of the excess.

"Anywhere?" she asked.

"Anywhere," he responded.

While he set up the air compressor, she set about making her mark on the side of the barn. She had thought yesterday's work was satisfying, but this was somewhere beyond that. It was therapeutic in a way.

Bright red strokes over weathered, worn wood. Making something new out of something old. It was more than just cleaning, it was transforming. She and Grant worked in relative silence, nothing but the sound of the air compressor, which blended into white noise and became somewhat meditative as she worked through the lower sections of the barn. They worked until her arms ached, and she was hungry.

"Why don't we take a lunch break?" Grant asked.

"Sounds good to me."

He covered her paint roller in plastic, and then the two of them walked back down the trail toward the mess hall. This time, when they walked by one of the covered arena areas, there were horses, and a girl with dark hair was riding one around a set of barrels.

"That's my sister," he said. "Jamie."

McKenna found herself glued to the scene in front of her. She walked over to the fence, draping her arms over the top, and just watched. Grant went to stand next to her, a silent, tall figure at her side. "She's pretty good, isn't she?"

"Amazing," McKenna answered.

"You want to ride sometime?"

She turned her head toward him, her expression contorting into one of shock. "I don't know how."

"I can teach you," he said.

"You could teach me?"

He hesitated. "Or Jamie could."

She wanted Grant to teach her. And if he had been a different man she might have said that. Hell, they were talking about him teaching her to ride. If it had been a different man she probably would've made an innuendo out of it.

But then, if it had been a different man she wouldn't have felt like it. There was a reason she hadn't been with anyone in a couple of years. She was sick of all the ridiculous nonsense that came with men. The way that a nice relationship turned into a series of transactions, and then faded out into boredom before the guy abandoned her. There was always hope in the beginning. That was one of the things she hated about herself. She could never quite squash that out. She knew women who could. At the last diner she'd worked at, there had been a whole crew of women on swing shift who had been shiny and sharp like obsidian.

Pretty, but hard.

Every client that wanted something extra with his meal was met with laughter and a cutting jab, and McKenna could hold her own there. But then, they also were all in relationships, and McKenna had recently sworn off them.

She remembered talking to the shift manager, Ruby, about that.

"Why don't you have a man, McKenna?"

"Too much trouble," McKenna said.

"Sure," Ruby had replied. *"But they don't have to be. If you know what you're getting into."*

"That's the problem," McKenna responded. *"Part of me always hopes that I'm getting into something else."*

Ruby had laughed and blown a smoke ring into the cold, early-morning air. "Oh, I quit hoping a long time ago, honey."

"Something in me always does."

"Give it ten years. Give it ten years and you won't hope anymore. You'll just be glad for a place to sleep."

Part of McKenna had envied that. That grim resignation.

Another part of her had been afraid of it.

She wasn't sure she wanted a life without hope. And she supposed that coming to Gold Valley, and holding out hope there was a right way to tell Hank Dalton that she was probably his daughter, was a testament to that fact. That she wanted hope. That she carried it somewhere inside of her.

But then, if there wasn't hope at all, she didn't see the point in walking on.

If what she had so far was representative of what she would have in the future...

Well, she might as well go lie down on that arena dirt next to Jamie Dodge's next barrel and let her horse trample her to death.

But McKenna didn't want to be trampled.

She wanted to live for better.

"That would be nice," she said.

"Yeah, she's the best, too. She's starting a job at the Dalton ranch soon, training horses that used to be in the rodeo. The Daltons are, like, rodeo royalty."

McKenna's breath felt like it had been sucked from her body.

All that air had been replaced by hunger. A hunger to know more. These details about her family were something she'd had no idea she'd been desperate for.

But she was.

"Oh, yeah?" she asked, trying to sound casual. "Rodeo royalty, huh? What does, um...what does that look like?"

"I'm not totally sure. I don't know them that well. Wyatt knows them better. He used to ride with the brothers in the rodeo. Hank, though, the father, he's as famous as a cowboy gets."

"Really?" she asked.

"Yeah," Grant said. "Back in the eighties he did some big campaign for cigarettes or something. Famous advertising."

"Wow."

"Yeah. But I hear he settled down in recent years. I guess you have to eventually."

"Why is that?"

"He has a reputation. Of course, so do his sons. They're cowboys and smoke jumpers. So, you can imagine."

"They get a lot of play? Is that what you're saying?"

"By all accounts, yes."

"I mean, firefighting cowboys are pretty compelling, even I have to admit."

"What does that mean?"

"What does *what* mean?"

"That *even you* have to admit they're compelling."

"I'm not easily compelled by men," she said.

He gave her a strange look. Like he didn't know quite what to do with her. Or like she was an alien life form that had dropped down from another planet.

"Shall we go get lunch?" she asked.

"That would be good," he responded.

The two of them turned away from the arena and walked the rest of the way toward the mess hall. "For what it's worth," she said, "I think you're a good babysitter."

"Thanks," he said, giving her a slight grin. Friendly expressions from that man were worth their weight in gold, and as she was a woman short on gold, she would take those smiles. She wasn't sure why it mattered. Maybe because she couldn't remember the last time she had made another person smile. She'd been in a particular kind of poverty for most of her life. But it was the poverty of connections that was starting to get to her. Living without things she could endure. But this little bit of time she'd spent with Grant—with the entire Dodge family—made her realize how starved she was for the rest.

"So," she said. "Riding lessons, huh?"

"If you're up for it."

"I think I might be."

She had no idea if she was or not. But what she knew was that she desperately wanted to spend more time with him. Whatever that might mean.

"Tomorrow after work, then," he said.

"Tomorrow after work."

CHAPTER FIVE

McKENNA COULD BARELY concentrate on the tasks at hand the entire day. Thankfully, the act of cleaning toilets was a relatively mindless one, and it gave her the opportunity to worry and look forward to the horse-riding endeavors she'd agreed to with Grant. She didn't know anything about horses, except that of course she had gone through a phase when she was younger and had read books almost exclusively about kids who had them. *Black Beauty. The White Stallion. My Friend Flicka.* If there had been a horse and a scrappy kid, she had read it and fantasized about putting herself in that position.

But much like anything else, she learned early on that fantasy wasn't reality, and it never would be.

She'd read *Anne of Green Gables* in one of her foster homes. Well, half of it. It had made her so angry she'd shoved it in a small space between the couch and the wall. When the foster mother had asked about it, McKenna had denied any knowledge of it, and had gotten a lecture on being more responsible with personal property.

McKenna was happy to take that one on the chin.

No one in that house needed to read that book.

It was filled with things that would never, ever happen. She couldn't believe it. Not for one moment. No nice couple was going to show up at a train station and see a skinny, redheaded orphan girl they didn't actually want, then take her back home and love her like a daughter. It wasn't fair. Reading it had made her chest feel swollen, had made her cheeks feel prickly.

She had hated her. Anne with an E, who had unusual red hair and adoptive parents who loved her, and *still* complained about her life and her looks.

The horse books, she had decided, were a safer read. Because she didn't harbor fantasies about living on a ranch or finding a beautiful, wild steed to ride. It had nothing to do with her life. It hadn't even been anything she wanted. It had just been an escape. Something so different from the life she lived, being shifted between suburban neighborhoods.

A life riding horses over rolling hills with golden sun filtering through the trees. There was a lot of dappling sun in those books. And in McKenna's mind, dappling sun was one of the most romantic images, to this day.

But it was a fantasy that didn't get its claws into her soul, because it seemed impossible. Not like having a family someday, which seemed both impossible and like it should be as possible for her as anyone else.

It seemed surreal she was coming closer to actually having the horse fantasy than ever having the loving family fantasy. But who knew. Maybe the Daltons would fold her into their loving embrace.

The thought sent a sharp pang through her chest. Like she'd been run through with a shard of glass.

She stopped walking for a moment and stood, looking out at the mountains that surrounded the ranch. Maybe she had internalized that Anne stuff a lot more than she had realized. Because obviously part of her believed in it, even as she railed against it. Oh, that bright light of optimism that seemed to burn inside of her no matter what.

"Maybe I'll fall off the horse and break my neck," she said cheerfully, taking a step forward and kicking a pinecone out of the way. "Maybe the horse will hate me, and Grant will take it as a sign of my bad character and tell Wyatt to send me packing. Maybe this is all just a dream and I'm still sleeping in a hollowed-out cabin in the freezing cold."

"Or maybe, you're just about to have an uneventful riding lesson." She looked up sharply, and saw Grant move onto the path.

"Good Lord, Grant," she said. "Are you part puma? You scared the hell out of me."

"Are you nervous?"

She flattened her mouth into a line. "I'm not the most Zen."

"The horse I got for you could safely ride in circles at a kid's birthday party."

"Well. Now I feel condescended to."

"Would you rather be condescended to, or did you want to get bucked off a horse today?"

"Condescension, please," she said.

"Your horse is completely safe, and nothing is going to happen."

"You're just trying to make me feel better."

"Have I *ever* tried to make you feel better?"

"No," she said, puzzling. "That's the weird thing about you. You're not too nice, but you're not mean, either."

"Is that weird?"

"Yes," she said. "It's really weird. My experience

is that when you have the kind of life I had, people either look at you like you're a very sad little puppy that they pity deeply, or they want to lecture you about how something you've done has put you in this position. You haven't done either thing."

"Well, it sounds like you've had some things go down."

"Understatement."

"People end up in weird situations, McKenna. Situations they didn't plan on. All the damned time. And anyone who doesn't think that? They're just scared. They can't stand the idea that they might find themselves homeless, trying to find a cabin to sleep in on someone else's property. If they don't blame some kind of moral failing in you, then what's to keep them from suffering something that puts them in the exact same place? It's the same with a lot of life's crap. Sickness. People always want to know what *you* did. If you prayed hard enough. If your body was alkaline, or you ate enough kale. They want to believe that in the end they would have been able to do something. And most of all, they want to believe that somehow you deserve something they don't. Fact of the matter is I'm not sure any of us deserves to have good or bad things that happen to us. They just happen. So I don't judge you. In the grand scheme of things, I don't have a whole lot of reasons to pity you, either."

McKenna blinked. "My mother abandoned me."

"I'm sorry about that." His face stayed that same shade of beautiful neutral it almost always was.

"But you don't feel sorry for me."

"If I did, would it change anything?"

She frowned. "It might... Affirm my feelings."

His brown eyes were unreadable. "You don't need your feelings affirmed. You just have to decide what you're going to do."

"Well, I'm here, so obviously I've made some decisions."

She didn't like the fact that he had now graduated to lecturing her. In fact, she preferred a little mindless pity over this.

"I speak from experience when I say that people feeling sorry for you doesn't help you do a damn thing. Especially if they are sorry without offering help."

"I guess you're offering help."

"That's Wyatt and Lindy. I'm offering to teach you how to ride a horse."

They approached the barn—one she hadn't been in before—and walked inside slowly.

It smelled sweet. Dense and dusty, but not entirely unpleasant. She looked around and saw stacks of hay, and could just barely see the tops of a few horses' heads in the stall.

"What's the smell?"

"Everything," he said.

"What does *everything* mean?"

"Shavings. Hay. Dirt." He paused and looked back at her, his expression partly shaded by the brim of his cowboy hat. "Horse urine."

"Well." She wrinkled her nose. "That's a bit… Earthy."

"Horses are. It's not a bad smell, though."

She inhaled, letting it kind of roll over her. "No. I guess it isn't."

"You've really never been around horses?"

"No. I mostly lived in the suburbs. In around different places in Oregon. Predominantly the Portland area. I guess we went to…pumpkin patches and things? And did hayrides? But it seemed like everything was… cleaner."

"Probably because it wasn't a working ranch."

"Well, okay, probably not. But I always thought it was fun."

"This will be fun for you, too," he said.

"Unless I *do* fall off and break my neck," she pointed out.

"I won't let that happen," he said, his tone firm.

"Are you going to rush to lay a pillow out on the ground if my steed starts to act up?"

His green eyes were unbearably serious when they clashed with hers. "I said I won't let that happen. I'm not going to let anything happen to you, McKenna."

"Are you the horse whisperer?" she asked.

"I already told you I don't make mistakes."

She couldn't give him a hard time about that. His tone was so very grave, and mostly, it had nothing to do with his sensibilities and everything to do with the fact that… She just wanted to believe him. Everything in her wanted to believe that Grant Dodge was a unicorn. A good man who did what he said, and who just might keep her from harm. Which made her wince internally, if only a little bit, because if life had taught her anything it was that she had to be her own savior. Not hope that someone else might be. But then, if winding up sleeping in a frost-ridden cabin with nowhere else to go had taught her anything, it was that sometimes someone had to lift you up and help you stand on your feet, or you were going to end up a tragic, modern-day rendition of the Little Match Girl.

Grant walked down to the third stall from the door, and lifted his hand to the bars on the door. A horse came forward, pressing his nose against Grant's hand. "This is Sunflower," he said. "She's going to be your...what did you say? Your steed for the day."

He unlatched the stall door, grabbing hold of a horse leash, or whatever it was, and lashing it to the thing on her face, leading the large beast out into the main area. His movements were unhurried. Easy.

She was completely glued to his every motion as he prepared the horse for the ride. The horse was beautiful, a light caramel color, all the way down to her hooves, with a white mane and tail. And as for Grant...his hands were large and firm, his muscles working with an ease that she couldn't help but marvel at.

He did the task with the skill of a person who had done something a thousand times. She realized then that she hadn't done anything a thousand times ever. Nothing beyond the basics.

She'd never stayed anywhere long enough or had the time or inclination to learn anything like that.

She had a skill for picking things up quickly, because in her life, adaptability had been king. She prized that. But this was...

Grant made putting a saddle on a horse look like art.

Or maybe it was just because he was so gloriously... hot.

He went to another stall, and got another horse out, this one a black, glossy animal with slim legs and a longer nose than Sunflower. And she watched him repeat the process over again, watched as a line pleated the space between his brows, watched his mouth firm as he worked.

He lifted his hat up for a moment and wiped his forearm over his brow, then set the hat on a hook on the wall, leaning forward while he tightened the horse's saddle. His hair fell into his eyes and she felt overcome with the desire to push it back into place, even more overcome by the desire to run her fingertips over his jaw, over the bristly-looking hair there.

She had known the guy for three days, and she was obsessing over him. She wondered if she was really just *that* sad. That all it took was a decently good-looking man being nice to her and she was halfway to buying him a rabbit just so she could boil it later.

In fairness to her, he wasn't just *decently* good-looking. He was *stunning*. Like he belonged in a movie and not on a ranch. Except he wasn't as refined or polished as any of the men in movies.

She wondered if Grant even had any idea of just how good-looking he was.

He didn't have that cockiness that gorgeous men typically possessed. Hell, she'd known men with much less going for them than Grant Dodge. Men who had swanned around like they were glorious lights of masculinity put on earth to make women swoon.

McKenna was not given to swooning.

Grant didn't posture. He didn't swan.

He just *was*. In all of his glory. And it was a whole hell of a lot of glory.

"What's his name?" She directed her focus to Grant's horse.

"He's a *she*," Grant responded.

"Oh, really?" She crouched down slightly, taking a peek beneath the horse's belly. "I suppose she is."

Grant shook his head. "Just verifying that I was correct?"

"Well, now that you mention it, I imagine if he were a *he* it would be pretty apparent. The phrase *hung like a horse* doesn't come from nowhere."

His face did several things right then. His brows pinched together slightly, the corners of his mouth pulling down, before returning to their neutral, flat position all before she comment on any of it.

She smiled, hoping to diffuse whatever tension had just walked its way up his spine and left him standing there stiff.

"I expect it does," he grunted.

"I would think you *know*," she said. "Having been around horses for such a long time."

"True," he said. She gave him her best impish grin. Men often found that charming. *Many* people found it charming. She *could* be charming when she wanted to be.

He didn't seem charmed. Instead, he continued to ready his horse in a rather taciturn manner.

"Her name?" she pressed.

"Guinevere," he said.

"As in… King Arthur?"

"King Arthur. Lancelot. The whole bit."

"Did you name her?"

"Hell, no," he said.

She didn't know why she found that vaguely disappointing. Maybe because it seemed, for a moment, that Grant might have something of a romantic soul. He did not. Apparently.

"Well, what would you have named her?" she pressed. "If given the choice."

"I don't know. Something less ridiculous than Guinevere."

"What's a nonsilly name for a horse?"

"Jessica?"

She let out a guffaw of laughter. "*Jessica*. A horse named... Jessica?"

"It's a sensible name, McKenna," he pointed out, his tone deadpan.

"Why did you say it like that?" she asked through a gasp of laughter.

"Why did I say *what* like *what*?"

"*McKenna*. You said it as if Jessica is sensible, while McKenna is firmly in the same column as Guinevere, which you do not find sensible."

He lifted a shoulder. "It's a weird name."

"Okay. *Grant*."

He took his hat off the hook. Then he ran his hand over his head, sweeping his hair back before putting it in place. She was sad she wasn't the one to do it. "Grant is a normal name."

"Sure. I guess if you're a film star from the 1920s."

"I take it that's a reference to Cary Grant. And he was not a star in the twenties."

She lifted her hands, simulating surrender. "Fine. Grant is a sensible name. McKenna is King Arthur levels of silliness. I would lecture my mother about it but I don't know where she is."

"Mine's dead. So I can't exactly scold her for mine, either."

Her stomach hollowed out. "I'm sorry."

"Don't be. I mean, I didn't say that because I was trying to one-up you. Actually, I think your situation might be worse. My mom didn't choose to leave."

"No," McKenna said. "I guess not. We can just agree it sucks. No one has to out-suck the other."

One side of his mouth lifted. "Is that so? That's not my experience with hard knocks. Typically, people want theirs to out-hard yours."

"People with terrible lives so rarely have chances to go on and compete in the actual Olympics. Training is expensive, and all that. The Life Sucks Olympics is basically the best we've got. So, it's understandable in some ways."

He snorted. "I'll share the gold-medal podium with you."

"No," she responded. "The gold medal is mine, Grant Dodge. You were not sleeping curled up on the hard-wood floor a few days ago."

"Fair play," he relented. "I'll take silver."

"Silver would also be a nonsilly name for a horse, I imagine."

"Not a black horse."

She shrugged.

Grant took both horses by the reins and began to lead them out of the barn. She followed closely, watching as he walked between the two large beasts. He led them with no effort, without a single concern. It captivated her. The animals were huge, and they made her feel uncomfortable. Grant was guiding them around like they weighed nothing, like they were an extension of his own body.

The horses had to know that they were stronger than him. They had to. But they seemed happy to follow where he led.

When they got outside he put the reins into position, and gestured to Sunflower. "Okay," he said. "I'm going to help you get on, all right. You come up beside her and put your hand on her."

McKenna froze. She wasn't scared of much. Honestly, when you lived with the threat of hunger, possible rape and inevitable homelessness hanging over your head, it was tough to be too scared of the average, everyday nonsense in the world. But for some reason the big-ass horse scared her.

Grant reached out, wrapping his fingers around her wrist, and lightning scorched her. All the way down to her toes. If there were blackened footmarks beneath her shoes, she wouldn't be surprised.

His green eyes were steady, giving no indication that he felt the same heat that she did.

He drew her closer to the horse. "I'm right here with you," he said, his voice steady. "Remember I said nothing was going to happen to you."

Calm washed through her, interspersed with crackles of lightning. A storm of epic proportions raging inside her.

He guided her as she pressed her palm flat against the horse. One of the horse's muscles jumped beneath her touch, and McKenna nearly jerked her hand back, but Grant held her steady. Her heart was racing hard, and she wasn't sure if it was because of the feel of his hand, wrapped so tightly around her wrist, the touch of his calloused, bare skin against hers or because she was standing in front of a giant animal.

"Don't be nervous," he said.

She realized that he would be able to feel her pulse, pounding in her wrist, the way that he was holding on to her.

She swallowed hard and took a deep breath.

"Okay," he said slowly. "Now what I want you to do is put your left foot in the stirrup."

"My left foot?"

"Yes."

"It seems backward."

"No. Backward is what you'll be if you don't follow my instructions. Now. Lift your left foot and put it firmly into the stirrup."

She followed that direction. And he was still holding on to her wrist.

"Now reach up," he said. "Grab hold of the horn."

"I assume that's the knob on the saddle?"

"You assume correct. Now grab hold of that and hang on to it."

"Okay," she said, extricating herself from his hold, and grabbing the horn of the saddle with both hands. "Now what?"

"Heft yourself up there."

"*Heft* myself."

"Yes," he said. "Heft yourself."

"I, sir, have never hefted myself in my life."

"Better get started if you want to go for a ride."

She lifted, using the muscles in her leg, and her arms, finding it surprisingly easy, and a little bit faster than she anticipated.

"Swing your leg up over her," he guided. "That's a girl."

And then she found herself seated on the back of the horse, perilously high off the ground.

"This is terrifying," she said.

"You'll be fine."

"What if I'm not?" she asked.

"You'll be fine."

She huffed, hanging on to the saddle horn.

"You can't hold on to that the whole time," he said.

"Why not?"

"Because," he responded. "You've got to hold on to the reins."

Grant handed them to her, his hands covering hers again as he guided her, showing how she was supposed to hold them. "This is a good beginner's hold," he said. "Eventually you'll be able to do it one-handed."

"That's definitely what she said," McKenna said.

"I'm going to ignore that," he said.

"Great. Ignore that. But telling me you're going to ignore it isn't exactly ignoring it."

He did ignore that. "Pull this way to go left, this way to go right. When you want to stop, you pull back. When you want to go, give her a kick."

"A kick? That seems mean."

"This horse could flatten you without giving it much thought. A little kick from your rounded heel to the flank doesn't hurt. It's a nudge. And that's all you're doing, because you're just walking. A gentle nudge, and she's going to go."

"And pulling back is the brakes?"

"Pulling back is the brakes. But believe me. She's an old girl. She's not going to get frisky on you."

"Okay," she said, feeling nervous. "I guess I'm… Ready?"

"You're ready," he confirmed.

He went back over to his horse, mounted with complete ease. The grip he had on his reins looked different than hers, and he guided Guinevere into position as effortlessly as he had led the horses out of the barn.

"I'm going to lead us down the trail," he said. "Give

her a tap, and she's going to start walking. Don't freak out."

"Hey," she said. "Do I seem like the type of girl who freaks out?"

"In general? No. On a horse? Maybe."

She breathed in deeply, giving Sunflower an experimental tap. And indeed, just like he said, the horse walked forward. She seemed to keep an effortless following distance between her nose and the ass on Grant's beast. In fact, the horse might be a better driver than McKenna.

"There," she called up to him. "I'm not freaking out."

"Good job," he said.

"Why do I get the feeling that wasn't entirely sincere?"

"It was sincere."

She rolled her eyes, but didn't say anything. Instead, she focused on the scenery around them. Many of the trees that were spread across the flat land were bare, their branches like bony fingers reaching toward the sky, just a few lone brown and yellow leaves clinging on for dear life.

But up ahead, and growing up the mountainside, was the thick blanket of evergreens that never withered or changed. The wind blew down the hillside, across the trail, kicking up the scent of pine, damp earth and moss.

She wondered if after today she would find comfort of some kind in smells like this. In the strange, heavy scent in the barn, and in the fresh woodsy scent of the pine.

The horse's gait was strange at first, difficult to get used to, but after a while, she settled into it. Learned to move in her saddle along with Sunflower. They rode the horses into the thick line of pine, the trail continuing on up through the evergreens and to the mountain.

It was so quiet. There was no sound beyond the intermittent breeze, the swish and flick of the horses' tails.

It was *vast*. Even now where they were, closed in on the trail, surrounded on all sides by trees, she sensed that vastness. She felt like nothing more than a tiny dot, in the center of the world.

It was a strange, heavy feeling.

McKenna was often the biggest thing in her own world. Her wants. Her needs. Her hunger. Her cold. And right now, she felt like nothing. Like gold dust. A glimmer of something, but not so substantial all on her own.

It wasn't an awful feeling. It was clarifying.

Like a relief.

If she wasn't the center of everything, then she didn't need to strive quite so much. Then maybe she didn't need to worry the way she often did. Maybe she could set down concerns for the future for just a moment and be here. With the strong silent cowboy riding in front of her as she lived a moment out of time that she could never have imagined she might find herself in.

She didn't have to pretend to be anyone else. Didn't have to fantasize about an alternate reality. She was the one existing here, free of concern, out in the middle of nowhere, on the back of a horse.

And she felt… The strangest thing, starting at the center of her chest and spreading outward like warmth. A still, calm feeling that was like nothing else she'd ever felt.

Was it contentment? Peace?

Had she truly come out to the country and found something she hadn't been able to find anywhere else?

She would worry about being a cliché, but she didn't want to worry. Not now. Not now. The trail wound around, narrowing slightly, boulders rising up on either side. She was worried for a moment that her horse might not want to go through, but Sunflower kept on going. Clearly, everything that Grant had said she was. The sound of rushing water grew louder and louder, and when they made their way through the rocks, there it was. Water rushing in a torrent, flowing over the side of a cliff.

"What's this?" she asked.

"Wishing Well Falls," he said.

She stared at it, in absolute awe. The water was a wicked beast, churning and frothing as it spilled over the side of the rocks.

If she'd felt small before, this diminished her further. She was on the back of an animal that could dispatch her with one quick move, near water that could sweep her away before she could call out for help.

All those stories of people going into the wilderness and finding themselves made sense. You could find your own insignificance out here. Your place as a thread in the patchwork of the world, rather than imagining you were the whole damn quilt.

"Let's ride the horses down to the swimming hole," he said, tugging his reins and starting down the trail.

"What?" The trail up ahead was steep, and the very idea filled her with dread.

"They'll be fine," he said.

He urged his horse forward, and she watched as Guinevere made an easy trek down the path, surefooted even on the rocky ground.

Sunflower at this point didn't have to be urged much

by her, but kept on following her leader. McKenna held on tightly, leaning back and gritting her teeth as the horse made her way down the trail.

When they reached the bottom, Grant looked back at her.

"What do you think?"

Now that her heart wasn't racing so quickly from the stress of making it down there, she was able to appreciate the beauty. "It's like a secret garden."

"Like a what?" he asked.

"It's a book I read. When I was a kid. *The Secret Garden*. It's about this girl. Her parents died. And she ends up living with her aunt and uncle. But her cousin is sick, so he's not allowed to go outside. And while she's wandering around trying to entertain herself she finds a secret garden."

She hadn't minded that book much. As books about orphans went. It was realistic enough in that no one had much cared about the girl, but had taken her in out of a sense of obligation. Granted, she had held out some hope for a while that she might discover she had a distant aunt and uncle in England, so that she might have a rambling manor home to wander around.

But alas. That was not to be.

Still, she had enjoyed that book. Because it was the orphan girl who'd had something to give to the boy who still had his family. Because she had been smart, and she had been valuable.

Sometimes she wondered if the reason she had hope in her heart was because of all the books she'd read. Because they had often depicted bleak things, and sometimes had shown her things she didn't like. But they had also taught her things about herself, and things about the world. The terrible things people believed and did, and the wonderful things, too. And the ways in which people could triumph as long as they always believed in *something*.

Like magical waterfalls named after wishing wells, and cowboys who seemed good, straight down to their bones.

"Do you want to explore for a minute?" he asked.

"Will the horses be okay?"

"They'll be fine."

Grant dismounted, and then walked over to her, reaching his hand up. She was grateful, because she wasn't sure she could manage the dismount on her own.

She reached down, taking hold of his hand, something that still sent a shock through her, even though their hands had touched several times that day.

She leaned forward, not quite sure how to proceed, and slipped just a little bit. But even she, in all her nervous state, wasn't as terrified as Grant looked in that moment. His eyes went wide, and then he reached up, large hands grabbing hold of her waist, and lifted her down from the horse as though she were as light as a child. He was strong. Stronger even than she had realized. And when he set her down, her toes nearly touching his, their eyes met, and she realized that he was even more handsome than she had thought.

His green eyes were blazing into hers with absolute ferocity, his chest rising and falling with a hard, heavy pitch.

He felt it, too.

She couldn't do anything but stare. She didn't want to move away. She felt drawn to him. To his heat. His intensity.

His hands were still wrapped around her waist, the heat from them bleeding into her skin. He flexed his fingers. Almost imperceptibly. But the slide of the fabric from her shirt against her skin, and the rasp of heat from his fingers beyond, sent a shock of attraction straight to her center like a lightning rod. She looked up, her eyes landing on his lips. She was fascinated. By the whiskers there. She wanted to touch them. She lifted her hand, her fingertips brushing him, a shudder racing through her when her hand made contact.

And then, abruptly, she found herself being set away from him, his expression ferocious.

"That's enough," he said.

"I..."

"We should go back." The words were hard, brisk.

"But why?"

"Because we've been out long enough." The clipped explanation wasn't an explanation at all.

"You said we were going to explore," she said.

"That was before I realized how late it had gotten," he said.

He was lying. She knew he was lying. And she felt... Like someone had taken a drawer full of expectations inside of her and turned it upside down. She didn't know whether to laugh or cry, whether to be offended or relieved.

Apparently, even sun-dappled horse rides could turn into total messes when she was involved.

He didn't want her to touch him. That much was clear. He didn't want to chase the attraction that seemed to be building between them—and not just on her side.

That made him... That only made him better, she was sure of it.

Because he was in a position of power and he could demand anything from her, and in order to keep her job, in order to keep the roof over her head, she might feel compelled to say yes.

Except the problem was, she felt compelled to say yes because she wanted to. And he was being...noble.

There was a certain sense of triumph over being right about his goodness, but a hell of a lot of frustration over the way his goodness was making him behave.

"Okay," she said.

She got back up onto the horse all on her own. She wasn't going to touch him. Not again.

She spent the entire trail ride back stewing, not able to enjoy the scenery.

Somewhere in there, she felt like this was just her life. There might be horses, and a beautiful scene, there might be a moment of serenity, of feeling content with her place in the world.

But then the good man was going to push her away, and she was still going to be alone.

"You've been fine by yourself all this time," she muttered as she entered her cabin. "At least now you're not alone and homeless."

She looked around the tiny room, and she tried to convince herself that—for now at least—this was enough.

CHAPTER SIX

Grant got an unnecessarily early start on painting the next morning.

He needed to expend all the pent-up...

He couldn't even pretend he didn't know what it was. Sexual frustration.

McKenna was... She was a hell of a lot of things he wished she weren't. A hell of a lot of things he wished didn't appeal to him. Because he had to deal with this, he knew that. He had to deal with himself, and where he was at, but he just...

He wanted to skip ahead.

He had spent eight years of marriage wanting to slow the years down. To hang on to what he and Lindsay had. He had spent the eight years since bogged down and walking his way out of a fog. And now he wanted to fast-forward through the part where he figured out what to do next, and just *be* there.

But no one—human, divine or other—had ever seemed to care what Grant wanted out of life and time.

Seeing as there was no way to solve that, for now, he would just paint the barn.

The sun was starting to rise, and his joints ached. He hadn't slept. Not at all. Instead, he had been replaying that moment down by the waterfall.

He'd given thanks throughout the whole ride that she

was behind him, and not in front. That even though he could sense her presence, he couldn't see her. She'd been scared of the horse at first, but then gradually a look of awe had settled over her face and he'd had to look away.

He couldn't see her for the whole ride, and she'd been silent for most of it. Uncharacteristic for McKenna, as far as he could tell.

He'd wanted…he didn't know. To show her more. To show her something good. Because it was clear her life had been tough, and damn if he didn't relate to that. So he'd decided to take her to the falls, and then he'd been even dumber and decided they should stop.

And when she'd started to dismount…

She'd slipped and there hadn't been any thought in his mind other than taking hold of her and making sure she didn't fall.

And all he could think was that he had promised she wouldn't get hurt. So immediately he had grabbed on to her.

And that had been a mistake. A damned fool mistake.

She had been soft. So alive. He hadn't touched a woman in so damned long… He hadn't touched a woman where there was a possibility of something happening in a hell of a lot longer.

He had been a caregiver for years. But care was not what he wanted to give McKenna.

He couldn't compare touching her with touching Lindsay, not remotely. He didn't want to, anyway. Comparison was the last thing he was after here.

His marriage was sacred.

And maybe that was part of the problem. He had made certain promises to his wife, and he knew that death had done them part, and that was it. But the problem was...

They'd had all the sickness, none of the health. They had never gotten to half the things in those vows. He'd known there was a chance—a good chance—it might be that way. He had known they wouldn't be together till they were old and gray. But he'd hoped...he'd hoped they'd have some healthy times in there. A few years.

They never had. It had been hit after hit. Illness, barely a recovery, infection, reoccurrence, repeat. It hadn't been fair. Not to her. Not to them.

But he'd forsaken all others. Even though he hadn't been able to have her.

Part of him didn't know what to do with the fact all that could be *over*.

That really, truly, he could have followed that desire he'd felt for McKenna down there by the water.

She was complicated, though. Prickly and wounded and living on the same property. Entwined in his life, in his family. He had no desire to be entwined ever again.

It couldn't be her. It could be *someone*. Hell, it needed to be. Soon.

He needed to get out of town. That was the only answer.

He went back into the barn to find the other bucket of paint, and then he heard footsteps behind him.

He turned around, and saw a disgruntled-looking McKenna standing in the doorway.

"You started without me."

"I didn't even say that was your responsibility for the day. In fact, you should go find Wyatt and see what he wants you to do."

"I thought you were my...my Yoda. My guide."

"Well, maybe you should find another guide."

"What's your problem?" she asked. "You were weird yesterday at the end of the ride, and you're being weird now."

"I'm not being weird."

"Yes, you are. And I was going to let it go. I wasn't going to say anything. But you're being grumpy with me this morning."

He dropped his paint roller onto the ground, not caring if it got dirty. "McKenna," he said. "I don't know exactly what you think this is, but let me clarify a few things for you. You work here. You work for me, you work for my brother. We are not friends. When we do work we're not hanging out. Me taking you on that trail ride yesterday? I wasn't being *friendly*."

"No," she said. "You weren't being friendly at all. You just offered to take me on a completely extracurricular activity that you totally didn't have to take me on."

"What I did was not extraordinary. Don't start thinking there's anything more to this than just basic human decency."

McKenna rolled her eyes, tossing her glossy brown hair back, angling her chin up toward him. That pouty mouth was schooled into a rounded shape that told him she was about to launch into a whole thing. As little time as he'd known her, he knew that much.

"Why are you so married to this idea that you're grumpy?" The word *married* hit him like a bullet, but she carried on. "That you're an asshole? Let me tell you something, Grant. I have known a lot of assholes. Like, *a lot*. You're not one of them. You're difficult, I'll give you that. But you're good. Just… Straight up good." She waved her hand. "Hell, from my point of view you're practically a saint."

He didn't hear the rest of what she said, because it was those last two things that hit hard and stuck. That rattled around inside of him, collecting speed, turning into a molten ball of flame that settled into his gut. Good. *A saint.*

For the first time he wondered if she knew who he was. If she knew more about him than she was letting on. It had been stupid of him to not consider that before now.

She was young, which was one reason he'd assumed that she hadn't been glued to his human interest piece he didn't sign on for that had played out on *Good Morning America* sixteen years ago, or the repeat of it eight years ago after Lindsay passed.

But it was possible she'd talked to Jamie or Bea, or hell, anyone. It wasn't like it was a state secret he was a widower.

He didn't want her to know. But she must.

That he was somehow better than other people was what everybody thought of him when they knew. That he was this great, sainted man who had married his high school sweetheart in spite of the fact that she was dying. That was what every news outlet had always said. Like Lindsay was a burden. And he was something special. When the fact of the matter was the only reason he mattered at all was because she had believed in him. Because she had come into his life and taught him to be something more than a raging, angry bully that was headed on a one-way ticket straight to prison or hell, possibly both.

And now he was... He didn't even know what he was.

Just an idiot stuck in limbo who had no idea how to get out. He'd moved enough, just enough, over the past few years to convince himself he was making progress but it was a damned lie he'd told himself. As much of a lie as this idea that he was *good*.

And somehow this woman, this woman who made his thoughts into something entirely separate from saintly, had bought into the same lie about him.

Good. A saint.

Before he could think it through, he found himself walking toward her. The distance between them closing with each step he took.

He wasn't good. He wasn't good at all, he had just spent a hell of a long time on a leash. And yeah, he had chosen it. He had put it on gladly. But it wasn't there now.

No one was here to be disappointed in him. To see him acting like an ass.

McKenna's eyes caught his and she took a step back, then another, until she was pressed against the barn wall. And he should feel guilty. Because she looked uncertain. Because her dark eyes were wide, and her mouth was now slack, held open slightly, and she was looking at him like he might take a bite out of her throat.

The idea sent a kick of lust through his body. Yes, he did want to take a bite out of her.

He was consumed with the idea. It was all he could think about. He pressed his hand against the barn wall up by the side of her head, and leaned in. And then McKenna did something completely unexpected. She pressed her palm flat against his chest, right over where his heartbeat was raging, and met his eyes.

There was a challenge there, one that he wasn't sure

he could ignore. Because he was past the point of reason. He was past the point of himself. Of everything.

He felt more like the boy he'd been back in high school than he had for sixteen years. Feral. Angry. About absolutely everything.

And along with that came intensity. An intense desire to do something. Destroy something. To make someone pay.

But it was McKenna who was right there in front of him. Looking at him with cool assurance now.

He didn't feel cool. Not at all. And he didn't feel assured of a damn thing. Why she could stand there looking like that, while they were so close, while she had her fingertips pressed to his chest, right where his heart wanted to try and escape his body, didn't seem fair. Along with everything else.

She wanted the gold medal in the Shit Olympics, but there was just no way in hell.

The gold medal was *his*.

And right about now he could only think of one thing that would make adequate compensation for that.

He slammed his hand hard against the wood, and she jumped, but her eyes never left his.

He reached his other hand up beneath her chin and held her there, staring down at her. But she never wavered.

Her tongue darted out, touching her upper lip. And it was like a lit match had been pressed against a pool of gasoline.

He ignited.

And beyond that point, there was no more waiting. No more thinking.

He angled his head, bringing his lips down to hers.

She was frozen for a moment, and then the hand that was pressed to his chest curled into a fist, wrapping the T-shirt around her hand, as she parted her lips for him.

She was trying to take control, and he wasn't going to allow that. This was his moment. His moment where he didn't have to be in control. Where he could feel angry. Where he could take what he wanted. Prove he wasn't good. Wasn't a saint. Maybe then she would get it. Maybe then she would understand.

Hell, maybe he would.

He released his hold on her chin, wrapping his arm around her waist, and bringing his other hand around to cup the back of her head as he took the kiss deep and hard, sliding his tongue into her mouth because he wanted to. He didn't know the rhythm of kissing. Not hers, not anyone's, not really.

It had been such a long damn time since he'd kissed at all. And he had never, ever been unrestrained. He'd always had to be gentle. And it hadn't been hard. Because it was what she needed, so he gave it. Gave whatever he needed to.

This wasn't about anyone but him.

It was about not holding back, not anymore. For just one moment.

The silky strands of her hair slid through his fingers and he shifted, holding her more tightly, her firm breasts pressed against his chest. He was so unbearably aware of every inch of her. Every sweet, subtle curve. He moved his hands down, cradling her ass, and he groaned into her mouth. And McKenna surprised him by groaning right back. She lifted her hands, forking her fingers through his hair and holding him to her, her tongue sliding against his as she pushed her pelvis up against his hard length.

That blazing red tide that had lowered itself over his vision—anger, rage—blended seamlessly now with his need. And now he didn't know which was which. He wasn't even sure it mattered.

She slid her hands down, bracketing his face, delicate fingernails scraping his skin as she drew them down his neck, down to his chest.

He was so hard it hurt. But he was used to that. *That* was nothing new. What was new was having a woman in his arms when he felt like this. What was new was having a woman touch him like this. Kiss him like this. Having a woman with her tongue sliding against his in a slick friction that was driving him closer to the edge of sanity all while her soft lips moved in time with his.

He wanted to consume her. Whatever this was, he wanted more. Deeper. Harder. He didn't want there to be anything between them. He wanted to be...

He pushed her away, just as he had done yesterday, but this time, he did it about three minutes too late.

"I'm going to finish painting the barn by myself," he said.

"Grant." She said his name like a question. And he didn't have any answers.

"No," he said. "This isn't happening. It's inappropriate. I shouldn't have to explain to you why it's inappropriate. You might be used to transactions, McKenna, but that's not what this is. And it's not who I am."

"Right," she responded. "But you're not a good boy. No saint. Isn't that what you were just trying to prove to me?"

Her words dug deep. Hell, yeah, that had been half of that. He was no saint. But that wasn't why he was stopping now. The real reasons... He wasn't getting into that. Not now. Not with her. Not with anyone, ever.

"Go clean. Find Wyatt. Find Jamie. Figure out what you're supposed to do for the day. Leave me the hell alone."

Her entire face turned red, anger and humiliation radiating off her in waves. He didn't need a ton of experience with women to know exactly what all that was. "Don't pretend you're trying to protect me. You're trying to protect yourself. You don't want to sully yourself with me, that's the real issue. Am I too much of a slut for you? Is that the problem?"

"I didn't say that," he responded.

"No. But you keep coming back to 'transactions.' So that means you made a lot of assumptions about me."

"Did I make assumptions, or did I make some guesses based on things you told me? When you first got here?"

"All right, fine. I know I said that. But that was before I knew you. I didn't kiss you hoping to find a paycheck in your tonsils, Grant. I kissed you because I think you're hot."

"You don't feel sorry for me?" he asked, the question acrid on his tongue.

"Why would I feel sorry for you?"

He stared at her, at those dark brown eyes. She was angry. But he didn't think she knew anything more than she was showing. Unless McKenna was a better liar than he'd given her credit for. The fact of the matter was, she had no reason to lie. Not about this.

"Nothing."

"Are you with someone?" she asked.

"What?"

"Engaged. Dating. Married. In a convenient bed-buddies arrangement with a milkmaid down the lane?"

"No."

"Then what's the problem?" She stood there, breathing hard, her eyes shining with…*hurt*. It was the hurt that did him in. The hurt that acted like a needle in the swollen balloon of his rage, popping it effectively and firmly.

"It's not a good time," he said, the words coming out rough and weary.

He suddenly felt tired. Just bone-deep tired. Of this barn. Of this life. Of himself.

Most of all of himself.

"It's not me it's you?" she asked, sounding bitter and acidic.

"Basically."

"Whatever, Grant. I'll go. I'll stop bugging you. You don't have to be my Yoda anymore. I'll find another one."

Perversely, when she turned to walk away, the thing he wanted to do most in the world was grab her arm and haul her back. Hold on to her and stop her from going. He wanted to pull her back into his arms, and he was the dumbass who had let go of her in the first place.

He didn't deserve a moment of this regret, a moment of this sense of absolute frustration. Because he had caused every damned issue he was contending with right now.

But he let her walk away.

And then he went back to painting the barn. Because God knew what else he was supposed to do.

CHAPTER SEVEN

THE NEXT MORNING McKenna didn't see Grant at all, but after she had finished with breakfast and returned to her cabin, there was something in the little mail slot by the door waiting for her.

A paycheck.

She tore open the envelope with shaking fingers and read the amount, breathing a sigh of relief. It would be small if she were paying for a number of real living expenses, but given the current situation, it was more than adequate. She needed to get something more than the same three outfits she'd had on for the past week. She needed to get off the ranch.

But that presented the next problem. She would just have to hitch a ride into town. It wouldn't be that hard. Either with one of the Dodges or with a passing motorist.

Nothing she hadn't done before.

She tucked the check into her pocket and walked back on the trail toward the mess hall, hoping that she could track someone down there. She felt a kick of excitement when she saw Jamie and Beatrix sitting inside talking.

"Hi," McKenna said, working at giving off her friendliest smile. "Beatrix, are you headed back into town at some point today?"

"We were both about to head into town," Jamie said. "I have to get a couple of things."

"I do, too," McKenna said quickly. "Would you mind if I... If I hitched a ride?"

"Of course," Beatrix said. "We can shop together."

McKenna drew back sharply. "Together?"

"Unless that bothers you," Jamie said.

"I just... I need to get some clothes," McKenna said.

"I like shopping for clothes," Beatrix said.

Jamie looked pained. "I like...new riding boots."

"It's fine," McKenna said. "You don't need to come with me. I just need to hit up a place that will cash a check and then I need to go by my stuff."

"Well, the feed store will cash a check. And they do have clothes," Jamie said.

"You're the only person under the age of sixty-five who buys clothes at the feed store," Beatrix said.

"If you're trying to say that my tastes are mature, I'll take it," Jamie said.

"That wasn't what I was trying to say." Beatrix looked up at McKenna, her expression apologetic. "We can go down the main street and look for clothes there. Christmas decorations are going up—it's going to be really pretty."

"Thanks," McKenna said, privately thinking that there wasn't a single outfit that she would be able to buy on the main street of a place like Gold Valley. Likely, it was filled with spendy boutiques. Not designer stuff like you would find in a city, but still stuff that was more boutique and high-end than, say... Your average feed store. Which McKenna had a feeling was more in her budget. Some sturdy jeans, a couple sweaters and a pair of gloves would do nicely. She didn't need to look fancy. She just wanted to be warm.

The weather was starting to cool, and McKenna wanted to be ahead of it.

"I'm looking forward to the feed store," McKenna said.

Jamie smiled. "I knew I liked you."

McKenna shook her head, feeling a strange spot of warmth in her chest.

"We can take my truck," Jamie said, standing and leading the way out of the mess hall and back toward the gravel drive. She had a big, old beast, with a bench seat in the front, and one in the back. Beatrix climbed over the seat and took the back spot, fitting since she was such a little thing. McKenna breathed a sigh of relief over it, too, because she didn't want to squeeze in and get cozy or anything.

McKenna wasn't the get-cozy sort.

Well, she'd like to get cozy with Grant.

Why? What's the point?

A good question, really. She liked him. She was attracted to him. It was nice to feel close to someone. She would prefer that kind of closeness came from someone she liked, and thought was good-looking.

She ignored the slight ache in her chest that made her wonder if it was more than that.

It was pointless was what it was. She needed to get on her feet, and needed to figure out how to approach the Daltons about their possible family connection.

She didn't need to be...having a crush or whatever the hell this was.

She got into the passenger seat and buckled up,

thanking Jamie again as she started up the engine and drove the truck toward the main road.

"It's really no trouble," Jamie said. "It's the damnedest thing," she continued. "Suddenly, it's not just me and a bunch of men hanging around on the ranch all the time."

"Was it?" McKenna asked.

She didn't know why, but she wanted to be able to picture the place as it had been. Suddenly felt hungry to know some history. She was never really part of anyone's history. Not in a meaningful way. She was always passing through. Towns and people.

It made her want to take some history of this place with her, if she wouldn't leave any of herself behind.

"Yes," Jamie said. "My mom died when I was a baby. I don't even remember her."

Oh. Of course. "Grant mentioned something about that," McKenna said softly. "I'm sorry."

Jamie looked over at her quickly, taking her eyes off the road for a moment, her expression speculative. "Grant told you?"

"He's been helping show me around. I might have forced him to engage in conversation a time or two."

"Well, that's a neat trick."

"I don't know. It's not that hard to get him to talk. Anyway, you were telling me about being inundated by men."

"Well, when my mom died it was just me and my brothers. And my dad. Then, for a while, it was me and my dad. Then Wyatt came back, my dad got remarried, but when he married my stepmother, they moved away. Now Wyatt is married to Lindy, and they live here. And I've gotten to know Bea a little bit through that."

"I don't live at the ranch, though," Beatrix pointed out.

"I figured," McKenna said.

"And now you're here."

She wondered if growing up had been lonely for Jamie. She might have been surrounded by men, but it sounded like she had been surrounded by a whole lot of people. And even though she didn't have a mother, she had some kind of…consistency. That just wasn't in McKenna's experience.

When Jamie pulled her truck past the cheerful, carved wooden sign that said Welcome to Gold Valley, Jamie's jaw dropped. It was like a Christmas card. Not just because of the white lights that were being put up over the windows, but because of the sheer quaintness of the place. Redbrick buildings lined either side of the main street, with wooden overhangs and uneven, cobbled sidewalks. It was like something out of a Western, a classic gold rush town, brought right into the modern era.

"This is… It's adorable," she said. And she rarely said things like that.

"It kind of is," Jamie said cheerfully. "I hardly notice it. At least, unless someone from out of town comes in. The first time my stepmother saw it she was completely overcome. But it's way too cold here for her. She went back to New Mexico, and my dad went with her. They usually come home for Christmas, but this year they're going on a Caribbean cruise with their new friends. And if you knew my dad…" Jamie laughed. "Let's just say that's a miracle."

"You must miss him," McKenna said.

"Sometimes. But I'm glad he's happy. He was alone for so long. He was engaged one other time before

Freda, but that didn't work out. I just…want him to be with someone."

"Isn't that what we all want?" McKenna mumbled. "For ourselves."

"I don't know," Jamie said. "It would take… Hell, I don't even know. I need a man who's not going to tell me what to do. Who will let me do exactly what I want when I want to do it. And if I can't find him… Then I'd be happy enough being alone."

"Not me," Beatrix said. "I don't want to be alone."

She sounded wistful. Sad. It made McKenna wonder if she had a particular man in mind.

"Well, being with the wrong person is not better than being alone," McKenna said.

"Really?" Beatrix asked.

"Of course," McKenna said. "Believe me. I have an epic comet trail of douchebags blazing out into my past. It all seems good for a while. Then it goes bad."

She needed to remember *that*. The going-bad part.

Jamie shook her head. "I wouldn't take any crap."

"Unfortunately," McKenna said, "I've taken a lot of crap in the name of not being by myself."

Beatrix made a sound that McKenna thought might be a sad sort of agreement.

Jamie spoke with all the confidence of a younger woman. One who hadn't been hurt yet. McKenna supposed she couldn't be that much older than Jamie, but it seemed as though she had kind of a sheltered life on the ranch. McKenna wondered how old she would feel if she had a life like that. As it was, she felt like she might be about a hundred.

They turned left at the end of Main Street, past the little diner and down through a different part of town, where newer buildings mixed with the old. A grocery store, a large old house that looked like something out of a Jane Austen movie, with Christmas decorations being hung there, as well. And down just a little farther was what Jamie had undoubtedly referred to as the feed store. There was a large sign that said Big R, and McKenna was curious if it was one of those local things, where they never actually called it by the name. One of those local things that she'd never really been a part of, because she'd never been local to anywhere. Not really.

They parked in the nearest available space, and when they got out of the truck, McKenna planted her boot over the top of a rainbow slick on the wet blacktop, the remains of oil, most likely. It was funny how something like that could be so pretty.

It was also funny how feeling so far out of her element, feeling like an outsider, made her so philosophical.

She shrugged her shoulders, stuffing her hands into the pockets of her jacket and walking toward the entryway of the store with Jamie and Beatrix. The doors slid open, and they were greeted by the sound of country music being played over the speakers, and the smell of sawdust layered over the top of a heavy, spiced potpourri.

There was a large, raised box at the center of the store, with bright red heat lamps up above. She took a step over and looked down inside, raising her brows when she saw a collection of rabbits, curled up in shavings. They looked like little piles of fluff, all bound up in each other. Their ears were twitching, and every so often a back foot would give a kick.

A smile touched her lips, and she moved closer.

Beatrix stopped at the box with her. "They're so cute," she said. "I want one."

"Do you have any more room for any more animals in your place?" Jamie asked.

"No," Beatrix said wistfully. "Anyway. I had to make a commitment to only take in rescue animals."

"That's very principled of you," McKenna said.

"Not really," Beatrix said. "My place was getting overrun. I had to set a limit somehow. I'm not good at setting limits with animals."

Jamie shook her head. "Not a problem I have."

"Right," Beatrix said. "How many horses do you have?"

"That's different. Anyway, most of them aren't really mine personally. They belong to the ranch. Horses are useful. Name one good use for rabbits, Beatrix."

"They're adorable."

"That's not *useful*."

McKenna laughed. "Okay. I'm gonna go cash my check. I'll catch up with you."

She wandered over to the customer service counter and pulled the check out of her pocket, taking it out of the envelope and signing it, making a show of taking out her wallet and getting out her ID. The older woman behind the counter kept a close eye on her, and McKenna kept her movements deliberate and smooth. She couldn't afford for anyone to decide that she might be a problem. And since she was a stranger in a small town, it was entirely possible that she might come across as suspicious. And she needed the money today.

Fortunately, the older woman didn't question her, and a few moments later McKenna was armed with a couple hundred dollars. She wandered through an aisle that had fencing, and found a Western-wear section, where there were jeans folded and stacked on a table, plaid shirts hanging on a round rack and straw hats and beanies on the wall.

It was basic. Very basic. But exactly what she was after. She got two pairs of jeans, some warm work gloves and a couple of shirts.

She was headed back toward the front of the store when she intercepted Beatrix and Jamie. "Are you sure you want to get your clothes here?" Beatrix asked.

"Yes," McKenna said. "I just need work clothes. I'm not doing anything but hanging out on the ranch right now. And I'm kind of on a budget."

Beatrix looked abashed by that. "Sorry. I didn't mean to…"

"It's fine," McKenna said. If she let every moment that reminded her she had less than others get under her skin, she would never be able to get anything done. It was a fact of life. In her experience, other people were more uncomfortable with it than she was. Case in point—Beatrix, who looked completely and utterly embarrassed. "Really," she added.

"Hang on," Jamie said. "Grant just texted me. I have to get him a pair of work gloves. He said he wore through his pair." She paused, presumably responding to the text, while McKenna grappled with the unexpected mention of the man who had kissed her yesterday. It made her feel things. Topsy-turvy and off balance. She really wasn't a fan of this whole high school crush thing she had going on with him.

She followed Jamie back to where the work gloves were, and then the three of them went to the register, where McKenna paid, and fortunately had money left over.

"Why don't we park somewhere and walk down the main street," Jamie suggested when they were finished at the store. Beatrix agreed enthusiastically, and that was how McKenna found herself being shepherded down the uneven sidewalk on Gold Valley's main street, bright white twinkle lights all around them, evergreen boughs wrapped around each and every support beam, red bows adding cheery pops of color every few feet.

The window displays in the shops were as festive as the rest of the town; little displays, half done up for Christmas, and half not quite yet, were all carefully arranged. Some of the windows had holiday-oriented stencil. White and gold trimmings, red candles, ornaments and stars, and a blue-and-white menorah. The window of the toy shop at the end of the street was overflowing with teddy bears and plush lions, all wrapped in tinsel, and appropriately made festive.

"Let's stop in here," Jamie said, pausing at a store that had a wrought-iron buffalo and hanging metal bats in the window. "The Gunslinger. I used to work here."

"Okay," McKenna said, following after her leaders.

The store was like something out of a holiday TV movie. Decked out in Western decor from floor to ceiling, glass cases with handmade jewelry around the room and everything from the somewhat kitsch to more high-end items on display.

McKenna's personal favorite was the wooden clock behind the counter that had John Wayne on it, with the small sign that said Not for Sale.

And why indeed would you sell such a thing if you were fortunate enough to own it?

"I love their things," Beatrix said, making her way to one of the racks that had jackets that looked heavy and made of money.

She reached out, touching one of the leather coats. It was butter soft and her fingertips could sense how many dollar signs had to be on the tag. She released her hold on it quickly, afraid that she might have gotten residue on it, or something. Like she wasn't fancy enough to even put her hands on it.

"These are nice," Beatrix said, grabbing hold of a dark-colored jacket that looked like it was made out of a heavy canvas, lined with white fleece.

"Very nice," McKenna said.

Beatrix was staring at her now, her eyes filled with a strange kind of determination. "What size do you wear?"

"Why?"

"I'd like to get you a coat," Beatrix said.

McKenna felt like she'd been punctured, a small balloon deflated, floating sadly down to earth. For a little while she had felt like she was out with friends. Which was kind of silly, because it wasn't like she knew Jamie or Beatrix, much less had anything in common with them. But Beatrix was treating her like one of those bunnies they had just looked at in the feed store.

As something adorable and vaguely sad.

Beatrix dealt in rescues, after all.

"No," McKenna said. "I'm not…" She looked around. "Beatrix, I'm working. I'm not a charity case."

She remembered telling Grant only the other day that she couldn't afford to turn charity down. But that was true when it came to lodging, and if it were a case of taking the jacket or dying of frostbite, she would take the jacket. It was just that…

"I know," Beatrix said quickly. "I just… I want you to have it."

"You can't possibly have the money to just randomly buy me a jacket."

Beatrix looked her square in the eye, straightening and tossing her hair back. "I do," she said. "I just came into my trust fund actually. And believe me when I tell you I don't really need it. So it seems silly to let it sit there when I'm not using it."

Jamie looked over at her friend. "I didn't know that you had a trust fund."

Beatrix frowned. "Because it doesn't matter. Sabrina didn't get one," she said. "My sister. Damien got almost everything, because he's the boy and he matters more, and you know, Sabrina and my dad had that falling-out. Just because my dad was happy to let me have some of the family fortune doesn't mean I… I'm not like him. I'm not like them. I never have been. I have my cabin in the woods and my job at the veterinary clinic and I like it. I'm still figuring out everything I want to do with the money. Well, right now I want to buy my friend a jacket."

It was still charity. But somehow, the ferocity of the way Beatrix talked about it changed something inside McKenna. Maybe it was the fact that Beatrix didn't feel obligated to do it. Or sorry. Or sad. It was that she wanted her to have it. Wanted something good for McKenna, and McKenna couldn't remember the last time that had been the case.

"I won't be able to pay you back," McKenna said softly.

She suddenly felt completely unequal to Jamie and Beatrix, and all the things they had given her today. What had they gotten out of the deal? A chance to spend a couple of hours in McKenna's slightly sharp and spiky presence?

"Friends don't have to pay each other back. You can buy me a coffee sometime."

McKenna could have laughed at that. Because of course she could buy Beatrix coffee now. But the idea that she would be around in a few months to have those kinds of ongoing dates was…

Well, not realistic.

Unless she stayed. Unless things worked out with the Daltons.

It was so hard to imagine that it would. She had to try, because that was that little seed of hope, that thing that lived in her, fighting against all the things that life threw at her, to continue on shining like a beacon in the darkness. It was why she tried.

But it was tough not to be somewhat fatalistic about the whole thing.

Beatrix took a jacket off the hanger and held it out toward McKenna. McKenna slipped it on, enveloped by the warmth and the intense softness. She didn't think she had ever worn anything quite so… Nice. She knew she hadn't.

"I'll take this," Beatrix said, pointing at the jacket.

McKenna started to take it off, and the woman behind the counter waved her hand. "I can scan it while you wear it."

McKenna's throat felt clogged with emotion and no small amount of embarrassment when Beatrix swiped her card and completed the transaction for the coat.

Then she thanked the woman working behind the counter, and the three of them left.

Beatrix, for her part, looked triumphant, and that helped with McKenna's feelings. Because it wasn't like the other woman was smug, or anything like that. She just sensed that she was elated to have gotten her way. And to have been able to help.

"Why don't I buy you a coffee now?" McKenna suggested.

God knew there was no guarantee she would be around to do it tomorrow.

Well. Probably tomorrow. But still.

"I won't say no to that," Beatrix said.

"Neither would I," Jamie added.

"You're going to have to show me the way to the best coffee," McKenna said.

"Happy to do that," Beatrix replied, directing them across the street and around the corner. "Sugar Cup," Beatrix said as they pushed open the black door that led to the inside of the rustic coffeehouse.

There was a large chandelier hanging in the center of the room, spray-painted black, a strange contrast against the roughhewn wood walls and floor. It was surprisingly full in the coffee shop for being the middle of the afternoon on a weekday, people occupying nearly every table. Some with friends, some alone with their laptops.

It was warm and cozy, and the scent of coffee and cinnamon filled the air. The pastry case in the front was packed full with everything. Muffins, bagels, cinnamon rolls. There were scones and cookies and something called the Sugar Bar.

McKenna's stomach twisted.

"We might need to get pastries, too," Jamie said seriously.

"Definitely," McKenna said.

They each got coffees and a treat, and McKenna paid, and they took a seat in the back at the only unoccupied table. McKenna dug into her cinnamon roll enthusiastically, while Beatrix ate a scone and Jamie picked up her Sugar Bar—a concoction with coconut and chocolate chips, and what looked like caramel drizzle.

"Hopefully it's okay that I took the whole day away from the ranch," McKenna said, taking a fortifying sip of coffee.

"Wyatt won't mind," Jamie said. "And if he does, I'll punch him in the face."

The door to the coffee shop opened, and with it came a gust of cold wind. McKenna looked over, just in time to see an incredibly tall man with dark hair and a black cowboy hat walk inside. There was something about him that felt… She didn't even know. Familiar maybe. Except she couldn't figure out why he would.

Jamie followed McKenna's gaze, her lips tightening at the corners when she saw who McKenna was looking at. "Oh," she said, her tone vaguely disdainful. "Him."

"Who's that?" McKenna asked.

"Gabe Dalton," Jamie said, taking a bite of her Sugar Bar. "Women *love* him. Like they loved my brother before he got married, and like they drooled on Lindy's brother before he got hurt. That cowboy…thing."

"Gabe Dalton," she repeated. *"Gabe Dalton."*

"Do you watch the rodeo, or something?" Jamie asked.

"No," McKenna said, forgetting why that was a relevant question.

"Oh. You sounded like you knew who he was, so I assumed you knew from there. He and Wyatt rode together for years. Not bulls like Wyatt does. Broncos. And he's an asshole. Like they all are."

"Are they?" she asked, desperate to know if she meant like all rodeo riders were or all Daltons, or what.

Was he…was he her half brother? Really and truly? Hank's name was on her birth certificate, but she supposed it could be wrong. Suddenly, it all felt huge and desperate and…she needed to know.

"Yes," Jamie said. "All of those guys think they're God's gift." She snorted. "Wyatt wasn't exactly immune to that, either. But Lindy has taken him in hand nicely."

So, she meant rodeo riders. Which was something of a relief.

She didn't want her only potential family to be a pack of assholes. Though, honestly, even if they were she'd be several steps ahead of where she was now. She'd rather have terrible family than no family at all.

"I don't get it," Jamie continued. "A guy does a stupid job liable to get him trampled—like poor Dane Parker—and women lose it over them. If I see a guy riding a horse… I'm usually a lot more interested in the horse."

Just then, he looked over at their table, and McKenna froze. She could see the moment recognition flashed across his face, but it wasn't directed at her, but at Jamie.

Jamie's posture went a little stiff, a bit of color creeping into her cheeks. And McKenna thought that perhaps Jamie was not as immune to rodeo dudes as she liked to pretend.

"Hey, Jamie," he said, closing the distance between them, his long legs easily eating up the space.

"Gabe," she returned, smiling.

"Have you given any thought to seeing what you can do with my horses?"

She straightened. "I didn't know... Wyatt said it wasn't anything you'd finalized or made decisions about."

"I've made decisions," Gabe said. "I've got six retired rodeo horses set to come to my place in a couple of months. If you're not too busy, I'd really love to have you come out to work with them. You're the best around for that kind of thing."

"Not you?"

"I'm not staying. I will for a while, but I've got a couple of years left on the road. My dad wants me to start taking over management of the place." There was a strange, hard note in his voice when he said that. "So I need someone who can manage the horses while I'm gone. And hell, a gentler touch might be in order."

Jamie scoffed. "I'm not a gentler touch necessarily. But I am good. I'm an intuitive touch. But by then... I'm going to be doing a lot of trail rides for the ranch."

"I'm willing to work with your schedule. But I'd love to hire you on. Talk to Wyatt about it."

McKenna could only sit there and stare, and eventually Gabe noticed. "Who are your friends?"

"Beatrix Leighton," she said. "And McKenna." She blinked, as if suddenly realizing she didn't know McKenna's last name.

"McKenna Tate," McKenna said, extending her hand, wondering if the use of her last name would jog anything. It didn't seem to.

His eyes met hers. And in spite of the fact that his

were blue, and hers were whiskey brown, there was a sharp kick of familiarity. "Nice to meet you," he said.

"Nice to meet you."

He shook Beatrix's hand, too, and said the same thing, then excused himself, but McKenna was having a difficult time staying engaged in the moment. She felt like she was having an out-of-body experience.

"Come back to earth, McKenna," Beatrix said. "Is he really that hot?"

McKenna cleared her throat. "Isn't it obvious?" She was not going to get into the actual reason she was fully spaced out.

"He's good-looking," Beatrix said. She looked down. "I guess I just… There's someone. Someone I… It doesn't matter."

"Oh, really?" McKenna asked.

"It's not happening," she said. "It doesn't matter."

Jamie huffed "He's just so… He has no morals."

"Who?" Beatrix asked, clearly afraid that Jamie was talking about her man.

"Gabe Dalton."

"He's not my type," McKenna said, shrugging.

"Tall, dark and handsome isn't your type?" Bea asked.

That made her think of Grant. She supposed that Gabe was equally tall, dark and handsome, but it just didn't hit her the same way. Probably because they were related. Half siblings. Family. She might have just shaken hands with the first person she could ever remember meeting who shared her DNA.

Yeah, that was something else. But not the something that Jamie was thinking.

Grant, on the other hand…

"No one is my type right now," McKenna said, finishing up the rest of her coffee. "I'm getting my life back on track. Men don't help with that. In my experience."

"Right," Jamie said in a tone of firm agreement.

"I'm not going to fight you for him, Jamie," McKenna said, doing her best to offer a conciliatory smile. A tough thing to do since she felt so rattled, and as a result didn't feel like she had any control over her face.

Jamie huffed. "He's, like, a thousand years old. He's my brother's age."

McKenna laughed. "By that you mean in his thirties? I think that just makes them better. A little maturity. A little skill."

"Absolutely not," Jamie said. "Remember what I told you? I'm not going to be with a man who thinks he can tell me what to do. And believe me when I tell you, cowboys are stubborn pricks. They think they run the ranch, and they think they can run the cowgirls, too. Absolutely not. I don't want anything to do with that crap."

"If you say so."

"Oh, shoot," Jamie said, looking down at her phone. "I have a ride scheduled for the day. And it's a lot later than I thought. We need to get back."

They packed up the remains of their sweets and got in the truck, making a quick trip out of town and back to the ranch. "Can you give Grant his work gloves?" Jamie asked, handing the entire bag from Big R to McKenna.

She hadn't seen Grant since the kiss, but it wasn't like it would kill her to see him. "Sure," she said.

"I have to head back to the winery. I'm still doing double duty between there and the clinic." Beatrix smiled. "See you later, McKenna."

"Wait," McKenna said, clutching her bag and the one

that Jamie had just handed her. "Thank you, Beatrix. For the jacket. It means a lot to me."

Beatrix flung her arms around McKenna and gave her a squeeze. "Of course," she said. "And my friends call me Bea. You can call me Bea."

"Okay," McKenna said. "I... Thank you, Bea."

McKenna couldn't imagine what man was holding out on a person like Bea. All she wanted to do was give to people. She was easy and cheery and a hell of a lot nicer than anyone McKenna had ever encountered before. Whoever it was, he was an idiot.

"See you later," Bea said.

McKENNA TOOK BOTH bags into the mess hall, but didn't see anyone there other than one of the ranch hands whose name she didn't know. "Do you know where Grant is?"

"Not sure," he said. "Last I saw he had gone back to his house. There was something with the cow pasture earlier. Fence fixing, and I'm pretty sure someone fell in the mud."

McKenna smiled. "You look clean."

"Wasn't part of my shift today."

"Lucky," she responded.

She turned and walked out of the mess hall, remembering vaguely which direction Grant's cabin was. Though it had been dark when he had driven her over to the main house that first morning she had arrived at Get Out of Dodge.

Still, she could set the work gloves on a chair by the door, or something. Maybe hang them on the handle.

The walk was cold, and brisk, but she didn't mind. Especially not now that she had her jacket. She looped the plastic bag handles around her wrist and stuffed her hands happily into the pockets, almost whistling as she walked, the icy gravel crunching beneath her boots. It was beginning to get dark, even though it was only four o'clock, a hazard of the season.

But given the way things were going, she almost didn't mind. She had a place to stay, a warm coat... Yeah, it wasn't that bad.

The edge of the small pond came into view, and then she rounded a curve, and the trees seemed to shift, giving her a view of the small cabin that Grant lived in. She quickened her pace, and a few minutes later was tramping up the front porch, knocking on the door.

There was no answer, and she was about to leave when the door jerked open.

It was... Grant.

In nothing but a pair of blue jeans. His chest was bare and it was...

She had never seen a man like that. Ever.

She had known Grant was muscular, but this went beyond that. Well-defined, with just the right amount of hair. And his abs... They didn't even look real.

She was so distracted by all of the muscle, and the genuine male glory before her, that it took her a moment to realize he was wearing a silver chain around his neck. He moved, and the necklace moved with him, the three tokens at the center of it shifting.

Then she realized it was a set of rings.

A thick band, a slimmer one, and another that had a diamond on it. The rings sat in the center of his chest, which was glistening slightly, and she didn't know if that was just a fevered imagination thing, or if *he* actually glistened a little, too.

A set of wedding rings.

"Can I help you?"

"I… Yes," she said, shoving the bag toward him. "Jamie sent me to give you your work gloves."

"Thanks," he said, taking hold of the handles. "I just got out of the shower. We had a catastrophe with the fence, and some cows. I slipped and fell in the mud."

"Oh, right. I didn't realize that was you. Jedediah mentioned that when I ran into him in the mess hall. When I was trying to track you down."

"I wore through my work gloves. Trying to fix the fence. That's why I needed another pair."

"Right," she said.

Her eyes traveled back down to the rings. One was definitely a man's wedding ring. The other a woman's, and possibly an engagement ring. He cleared his throat, and took a step back. "Want to come in?"

"Sure," she said, wrapping her arms around herself and stepping inside.

"Just a second," he said, walking back down the hall, and appearing a moment later with a dark T-shirt in his hand, pulling it over his head and covering up his body. And the rings.

She edged close to the door, not quite sure what was going to happen with the situation, or even what she wanted to happen.

"I owe you an apology," he said.

"No, you don't," she said, fighting to hold back a snarl, because this was not the discussion she wanted to have.

"I do. I was an ass to you yesterday."

She shrugged. "Yes. You were. But you don't need to apologize. It's fine."

"I do."

"You don't," she said. "And I'm not going to fight with you about whether or not you need to apologize. Because you don't. My feelings are not hurt, honestly."

"That doesn't mean my behavior was acceptable."

"Are you apologizing for kissing me or for being a jackass about kissing me? Because I need to be sure that we're talking about the same thing."

"Both."

"Don't apologize for kissing me, Grant," she said. The way he was looking at her made her feel hot and jittery and something about those rings felt like a slap. She had no idea why.

She didn't need to know anything about Grant, his past or his life now. But she felt like she should, anyway. And she didn't want to feel it. Not at all.

But after everything today—Bea and the coat and meeting Gabe Dalton—she just felt…wrong and weird. Shaken. This wasn't helping.

Grant was just… She hadn't wanted to be with anyone in forever, and she wasn't sure she'd ever wanted someone the way she wanted him. And she hated it. Hated it but loved it, because it felt like something. And she'd had a whole lot of nothing for too long.

And while her brain worked to try and right itself, while her heart tried to find a rhythm, her mouth kept going. "If you wanted to blow off a little bit of steam with me? That would be great." She tried to sound casual. Even though she didn't feel casual at all. She felt jittery, and like the words that were coming out of her mouth were all wrong. She had just been thinking earlier about how it would be stupid to do anything with Grant. And yet, here she was, practically propositioning him. Again. "If not, it's not a big deal. I don't take this kind of thing that seriously."

Except it felt like the thing that was leading her from one breath to the next.

She hadn't been with a man in almost three years. And it wasn't like she was into casual sex. Serial monogamy, maybe. But she was always in a relationship with the guys she slept with.

"I don't know how to do that," he said, his voice rough.

She frowned. "You don't…"

"Casual stuff. It's not my thing."

Her face went hot, icy pinpricks breaking out over her cheeks. "It's not really… I mean…"

"That's not a judgment, McKenna. I'm just saying. And that's a problem because, look, I hurt your feelings. And I didn't mean to. But you're here, and I'm here… Not a good idea."

Why?

She stopped the word from coming out of her mouth. Because it was sad. There was no reason to be… Needy for the guy.

He was just a guy. That was the thing. And apparently, there were hot men all over the place around here. Of course, the one she had just met was probably her half brother. But that aside, he couldn't be the only other one in town.

"Okay," she said, backing up another step, her heel hitting the door. "It's fine. No… Hard feelings or anything. It doesn't need to be weird."

"Of course not. It's not weird."

"Okay. So stop acting weird."

A slight smile curved his lips. "Okay."

"Enjoy your work gloves. I'll see you."

She opened the door and went outside, the cold air stinging her cheeks, making her eyes water. She told herself it was the cold that made tears stream down her face the whole walk back to her cabin.

It wasn't emotion. It couldn't be. Private tears were useless, and she knew it. Tears were useless if you couldn't use them.

As useless as caring about a man she could never, ever hope to keep.

CHAPTER EIGHT

GRANT HAD FORGOTTEN that Wyatt had prepared some kind of guys' night poker game that they were all supposed to get involved in. It was being held at Bennett's house, and was designed to make sure that even with the responsibilities of marriage and children, they didn't forget how to hang out and have a good time.

Grant found the whole thing slightly ironic, considering he was now the one without a wife, and while they had been having their carefree single years, he'd been about as unhappy as it was possible to be.

Not that Luke, Bennett and Wyatt weren't perfectly happy to be tied down, as Wyatt had jokingly put it when first organizing the night. No, they were positively smug about it. Which made the whole thing grate even more.

Grant grudgingly walked up the front steps of Bennett's farmhouse and rung the bell. He was holding a bottle of whiskey and a bag of chips, because even when it was his younger brother, he didn't believe in showing up to a gathering empty-handed.

Because you're such a good guy?

That angry little question manifested itself in McKenna's voice. Which he deserved, he supposed.

A gorgeous, spectral woman glaring angrily in his mind.

The whole day he had been asking himself why. *Why* he'd pushed her away. *Why* he'd said no.

There were reasons, and they partly made sense. Except... She was there. She was right there within arm's reach, and he could have her if he wanted to. So, he wasn't sure why the hell he wasn't having her.

Because he didn't want to have a talk? Why did they even need to have a talk?

Well, the talk was necessary because she needed to understand that he was not in the market for a relationship.

"You came," Bennett said, smiling in the doorway and looking far too chipper for how Grant currently felt.

"Yeah," Grant said, stepping over the threshold and into the entryway, passing off the chips and whiskey to his brother. "I did say that I would."

And he'd needed to get out. He was driving himself crazy in the cabin, which was unexpected. Since he usually enjoyed being by himself. Well, maybe *enjoy* was too strong a word. It was his preference, anyway.

But after seeing McKenna today...

He'd been hard and on edge ever since.

She'd been looking at his chest. Then at the rings.

Which seemed like a metaphor for all the stuff he didn't want to deal with.

What he'd wanted to do was pull her into his arms and kiss her again. What he'd wanted to do was say to hell with the consequences and just...

"True," Bennett said. "If you say you're going to do something, you usually do."

"Damn straight," Grant replied, clearing his throat. "It's why I often don't commit to anything."

"Probably also true." Bennett gestured toward the

kitchen. "We can save the whiskey for later. Feel free to grab yourself a beer. Then meet us in the living room."

"You'd think you'd bring the drinks into the living room," Grant grumbled as he made his way into the kitchen, jerking open the fridge and hunting for the type of beer he liked. "And I could use whiskey now."

Dammit, could he ever.

"Glad you could make it," came a voice from behind him.

He grabbed a bottle and straightened and turned to see Luke Hollister standing in the doorway.

"I said I would," he repeated.

"Yeah," Luke said.

"How's the baby?" Grant asked.

"Good," Luke replied. "I mean, keeping us up at night and giving me gray hair. But isn't that what they're supposed to do?"

"It's my understanding," Grant said.

"Olivia's a great mom," Luke said, his smile broadening.

That was an unexpected ice pick to the heart. Lindsay would have been a great mom. Sometimes he regretted not pushing harder toward adoption, but she hadn't had the energy. Still, he could have taken care of the kid. She could have just loved them. Been a mom, like she should have been. If the world were fair.

"I bet she is," he said, forcing a smile.

It wasn't Luke's fault that his brain was stuck on the past right now.

"I hear you have a new girl working out at the ranch."

He'd almost rather think about the past than McKenna at the moment. "We do."

"Is she pretty?"

Grant narrowed his eyes. "I'm not sure whether to be more offended that you might be asking for yourself or for me."

"For you," Luke said. "Obviously, I would never look at another woman. I have Olivia. Let me tell you, I don't want anyone else. Ever. You, on the other hand…"

"My brothers get on me about this enough. I don't need you on me about it, too."

"I'm practically a brother," Luke said. "And anyway, they might get on you about it, but I doubt either of them would suggest that you hook up with a woman working at the ranch. Wyatt has too much invested in the place. Bennett is way too much of a rule follower."

"There are rules for a reason," Grant pointed out.

"Sure," Luke replied. "Because they're fun to break. At least, that's what I've always assumed."

"You're no help, Hollister," Grant said.

"Seriously, though," Luke said. "Think about it."

"Why?" Grant asked. "Why her?" He wasn't sure if the question was more for Luke, or more for his own damn self.

"I saw the two of you together the other day. I drove up to the ranch, saw you standing outside the barn talking. Painting. She likes you."

Grant gritted his teeth. "You can tell that how?"

"I'm not blind," Luke said. "She likes you. And I think you like her."

"I'm not in high school."

"No. When you were in high school you fell in love with a great girl. But then you lost her. And in all that time you didn't do the things that normal people did. So, if you like her and she likes you, you should go make out behind the bleachers. God knows you deserve that, Grant."

"I don't need you in my business, Luke."

Luke held up his hands. "Fine. I'm just throwing it out there that I endorse it. Officially."

Grant lifted his hand and held up his middle finger. "And I'm just throwing this out there."

Luke laughed. "You know I appreciate that. If you want to get out of town... Look, I would take you, I would go be your wingman, but with the baby, I can't really get away. This is about as far as I can go."

"I don't need a wingman. More to the point, I don't want one."

"Okay," Luke said, sighing heavily. "I know this is personal stuff, and I know we don't do this. But... look, Olivia changed my life. She...she gave me things I didn't know I could have and healed things I didn't even think could be healed and... I don't want you stuck where you're at forever. It doesn't need to be love, but maybe it needs to be something."

Grant firmed up his jaw. "There's a reason we don't talk feelings."

"Has there been anyone since Lindsay, Grant?"

He knew what Luke meant. Luke meant sex. And there was absolutely no way he was going to follow up that question with the truth.

That there had *never* been anyone.

Not even Lindsay.

"No," he said.

"The first one's going to be the hardest."

If he were in a laughing mood, the irony of that damned statement would have made Grant guffaw. "Is that so?" he asked. "You say that from experience?"

"The only thing that I'm experienced at is loss. Another kind than you had. I'm not going to pretend that I get it. You lost your mom and your wife. I lost my mom, and I didn't have anyone. Not a dad, nothing. I know what it's like to lose the life you had. And to mourn the hell out of it even if that life was hard. I took care of my mom, Grant. She was fragile. She needed someone. And when she was gone…"

"It's different," Grant said, his voice rough.

"I know."

"No," he said. "You don't. You were born your mother's son. You never made a choice about it. You took care of her because you were a good son. You did what you could. But you didn't choose it. You got dropped right in it. I loved Lindsay. I chose it. I chose her. I knew she was sick before we got married. I wasn't going into it blind. I chose it."

Luke nodded. "I know. I respect the hell out of that."

"Don't," Grant said. "That makes it sound like it was charity."

"I don't mean it that way."

"If Olivia were sick, if you knew that she was going to die, you would have married her. It's not about being the right man to do it. It's about loving the right woman. It has nothing in hell to do with me."

Luke nodded slowly, his expression grave. "I suppose that's right."

Grant huffed out a laugh. "I'm not a great guy. And you know what? I really want to get laid."

"Then do it."

"I…"

"If you're not a *good guy*, nothing else matters, right? There's plenty of women who want a night of fun. It doesn't have to be a big deal. Doesn't have to be complicated."

He sighed heavily. The problem was, now he just wanted the one woman. And he had gone and walked himself into an unwinnable situation. He had thought that all he needed was a woman to attach his lust to. That generalized lust was too difficult. Then he had imagined that his notoriety stood in his way. And now, he was blaming the fact that he wanted one woman in particular. It really was never going to end until he ended it.

"Well," Grant said. "This was a little bit too much talking about our feelings for my taste. Let's not do it again."

"We don't have to talk about our feelings, but I am going to give you some advice. Just try not to take everything so damn seriously for a little bit. It doesn't have to be forever. Just for a while. Just be... Happy for a while. Have some fun. Blow off some steam. You don't have to marry anyone."

"I would rather have the pointy end of a pitchfork shoved under my toenails than ever get married again."

"There you go. You know what you want. And I imagine if the pretty stranger living on the ranch knows what she wants, too, it could be convenient and fun."

"No more meddling, Hollister," he said.

"Fine. I'm done."

Luke turned away and began to walk out of the kitchen.

"Did Wyatt send you to do that?" Grant asked.

"No," Luke said, turning partly. "But Bennett is too careful of your feelings. And Wyatt is such a bastard. He always sounds like he's joking, and sometimes I think that's him, and sometimes I think it's because he doesn't want to push you. But you sure as hell need to be pushed, Grant. That's just a fact. Otherwise, you might not move forward. So, consider this a shove from me. Hopefully it was in the right direction."

Grant popped the top off the beer and followed Luke into the living area. Bennett and Wyatt were seated at the table, cards in hand.

"We'll have to make this a monthly tradition," Bennett said.

"We should see if we can invite Dane," Wyatt said.

"How's he doing?" Grant asked of Wyatt's brother-in-law.

"Still not fit for human company. The wheelchair is getting to him big-time. It's not a permanent situation, it's just both legs are too messed up to get on crutches yet, and I think it's really getting in his head."

"Is this how you guys talk about me when I'm not here?" Grant asked.

"Don't be an idiot," Wyatt said. "We say that about you when you're here. I mean, the thing is, you're here. So, you're a step ahead of him."

"Yeah, well," Grant said, "his accident didn't happen eight years ago. Give the guy a little time to recover."

"Do you think that's what he needs?" Wyatt asked, his expression sincere. "Time?"

"I don't know what it's like to get physically injured like that," Grant said. "I can do anything I ever did. So, I get that I'm your touch point for loss and grief, but it isn't the same. Anyway… Time doesn't hurt. But there is such a thing as too much time…and you settle in."

"You think you've settled in?" Bennett asked.

He didn't want to have this discussion now. He

wanted to have it never. But the fact of the matter was, there was no other group of men he could ever have it with. This was all bare bones, no real personal info, and it still felt a little too deep for him.

But they all…loved him, he supposed. And they were here.

In the moment he was grateful for that.

"I think I settled in for too damn long," Grant said. "But that needs to change."

He took his jacket off and pulled his wallet out, surfing through it for twenty. "Get me some change. I'm in."

He looked across the table, and his eyes met Luke's. The other man gave him an imperceptible nod, and Grant returned it.

As much as he hated to admit it, Luke was right. He had his push forward. Now he needed to take a step. Otherwise, he was going to stay where he was forever, and die there.

He thought of McKenna. The way she'd looked at him earlier, back at the house. The way she'd tasted when he'd given in and kissed her in the barn.

He wanted her. And the simple truth was, it had been a long time since he'd wanted. That in and of itself was a small miracle.

Now he just had to figure out what his next move was going to be.

CHAPTER NINE

IT WAS LATE. He shouldn't go over to McKenna's cabin. He should sit on this new decision. He certainly shouldn't go barreling over there as soon as he left his brother's house. Shouldn't go over without talking to her first. Without thinking on all of this for a whole night.

But the problem was, he'd done too much damn thinking in the past eight years and not enough doing.

McKenna lit him on fire and he had been beginning to think that he was made of ice. That there was no one and nothing that could begin to thaw out the block he was frozen in.

And that was the other truth that had hit him on the drive back to the ranch, a drive that turned McKenna's cabin into his final destination.

If he had truly wanted to do this at any point over the past eight years he would have.

But he hadn't found the right woman.

Now he'd found McKenna.

McKenna was the one he *wanted*.

He wanted her. And she had said that she wanted him, too. She had propositioned him earlier, for God's sake. He was done with self-denial. Fully done with it.

He was decided. For his part, he knew exactly what he wanted. And he was going to go in, tell her what that was and wait.

He parked, his jaw set in grim determination as he turned the truck engine off and got out. It was so damned cold out. But he would be shocked if the frost crunching beneath his boots didn't melt with each step he took up to her house.

He wasn't frozen anymore.

He knocked. He didn't really care if he woke her up. He didn't care about anything. Not a damn thing, except having her mouth underneath his again.

He had denied himself. Denied and denied. In his defense, the first time they'd kissed had been all tangled up. Something about it being wrong to take advantage of her, it being too complicated.

His life was an endless complication. An endless web of being recognized in the strangest places, for a tragedy that would define him forever. Whether or not he let go of it, the town never would.

He and Lindsay were Romeo and Juliet, as far as the town was concerned. The problem was, he hadn't drunk any damned poison. He was still alive.

He needed this.

The door jerked open, and there was McKenna, standing in a thin, long-sleeved top made of some soft material that immediately announced she wasn't wearing a bra.

She blinked in surprised. "Grant."

He stepped in without waiting to be invited in, grabbed the back of her head and hauled her toward him, kissing her mouth with all of the pent-up savagery inside of him. She was frozen beneath his kiss, and he kept on, sliding his tongue into her mouth, coaxing a response from her. She lifted her hand, her fingers brushing against his cheek, a soft whimper on her lips as he continued kissing her.

When they parted, they were both breathing hard, and she was looking up at him with confusion in her dark eyes.

"Do you want me?" he asked.

"I... Yes," she responded.

"You don't sound certain." For the first time in a long time, he was sure. And he needed her to be sure, too.

"I'm sure." She kept her eyes trained on his. "I'm just confused."

"Here's the deal," he said. "If we do this, there are rules, do you understand?"

"Sure," she said, nodding slowly.

He could tell that she was a little bit nervous, but that she was going to let him finish.

"First rule, this is between you and me, do you understand? Nobody else."

She nodded. "I understand."

"Second, this is just sex."

"Right."

"Third, no talking."

"We're talking right now," she pointed out.

"No talking after this. Except I want you to tell me if something doesn't feel good. Tell me what you like. Otherwise, we're not talking."

His heart was thundering in his head, and he was honestly surprised it was beating at all, considering all of his blood was down below his belt.

She was still staring at him, her eyes wide, her expression frozen.

"Is there a problem with any of that?"

"No," she said.

He looked around the room. It was small, but cozy. And she had a fire going in the fireplace.

"Should we go to the bedroom?" he asked.

Her shoulders lifted slightly, and she clutched her own arm, just above her elbow, like she was bracing herself. "It's really cold in there."

Right. Well, he didn't want that. Because he didn't want her hiding under any damned blankets.

The fact of the matter was, he had waited a long time to get his hands on a naked woman, and he didn't want to miss anything. Not a thing.

"Wait here," he said.

He went down the hall. All the cabins had more or less the same layout, so it didn't take long to find her bedroom. He grabbed every blanket off the bed and a pillow, and hauled them out to the living room, laying one blanket on the floor, then another, tossing the pillow down at the end. She just stood there watching him, not saying anything. Clearly trying to keep to the agreement.

He crossed the room, taking her into his arms and kissing her again. Then he lifted her up off the ground, holding her up against his chest as he kissed her deeper and deeper.

He felt reckless. The blood rushing through his veins hotter and faster than the flames licking in that fireplace. She pressed her hand to his chest, and he knew that she could feel the way his heart was pounding. Knew that she could tell just how affected by this he was. But they weren't going to talk about it. So, it didn't matter.

He carried her over to the blankets and laid her down on them gently.

He touched her face again, kissing her. He could kiss her forever. Except for the impatience pounding in his blood. Pounding in his groin. She was so warm. So vital and alive. Strong. A woman who had been out on her own for all this time, who had fought and fought to keep on going.

She could handle him. Could handle this.

He wouldn't have to hold himself back.

Tonight, he didn't have to have a caregiver's hands. Tonight, he could have a lover's hands.

He felt like a damned traitor being relieved by that. Felt like the worst kind of ass for holding some of those regrets deep inside of him. But they weren't aimed at Lindsay, of course. Just at the world. At the unfairness of it. That he'd had to be a nurse when he touched his wife and not a husband.

But he wouldn't think of her. Not now. Because this wasn't about anything in his past. This was about now.

The darkness beyond the reach of the orange glow of the fire seemed to close over them, cocooning them in warmth, in intimacy. Making it feel like they had disappeared into some part of the world created just for them. That existed out of time and space and sanity.

He pulled back, pressing a soft kiss to her lips as he sat back on his knees, looking at her lying down on her back on the blanket, propped up slightly by her elbows, her knees bent.

The way the fire caught her skin made it look like she was glowing. Her dark eyes glittered, her full lips held partway open, swollen from kissing him.

He could look at that forever. Her, staring at him like that. Wanting him. Wanting him the way that he wanted her.

There was no pity in those eyes. Just desire.

He looked down, studying the curve of her breasts, visible through that thin shirt. The stiff, pointed outline of her nipples. The corners of his mouth kicked up into a smile. He couldn't help it.

This...this was worth smiling about.

He didn't feel like a saint right now, far from it. He didn't feel like a *good man*.

He was just a *man*.

A man who wanted a woman with every part of himself.

He leaned in, keeping his eyes locked with hers as he pushed his fingertips beneath the hem of her shirt. She was soft. So damn soft. He groaned as he moved his hands over her stomach, around her back, up the elegant line of her spine, between her shoulder blades and back down. He pushed both hands beneath the fabric, bunching it up, pushing it over her head in a swift movement.

The breath gusted out of him in a rush as he looked at her. Topless, with the flames dancing over her skin. Her breasts were full, her pink-tipped nipples pointed upward, begging for him to touch them, kiss them. And he would. Soon. Very soon. But for now, he wanted to stare. To take it slow. Because this was a moment a hell of a long time in the making, and he was in no hurry for it to pass him by.

It was like that moment McKenna had first seen the ranch all over again. When he looked at her bare body... he felt new.

All that tired, all that weary, seemed to fade away. In its place was an overwhelming sense of wonder, a sense of awe.

He reached out, pressing his fingertips lightly against

her collarbone, tracing a line down between her breasts, down her stomach, to the waistband of her sweatpants. He hooked his fingers in the elastic and dragged them down her thighs, along with her panties. Surprised that the totally foreign action seemed so natural. Maybe it was because he'd thought about it so many times. How it would go. Except this was nothing like he'd imagined.

He was sober. For one thing.

For another... He never would have been able to dream up McKenna.

He gritted his teeth, staring down at her naked body. At the dark shadow of curls between her legs.

He had never seen anything so beautiful in all his life.

Not a sunrise or a sunset, not a mountain capped with snow, not the main street of town decked out for Christmas. Not a single damned thing could come close to the beauty of McKenna Tate naked in the firelight. He was almost afraid to move.

Afraid to breathe.

She was staring at him, and she looked like she wanted to say something, but he had warned her not to, so she didn't. He put his hand on her thigh, then moved it down to her calf, her ankle. She was just so soft. So damn soft.

"My hands are rough," he said, the words gruff.

He hadn't meant to say them, but it had struck him then that it had been so long since he'd touched another person in any way that he hadn't been conscious of what it might feel like for them if he ever did. He'd been a lot more conscious of what it would feel like to him to touch someone, but now...

He wanted her to feel good, too.

He had calluses; he knew he did. The hazards of working the land. He was scarred up, nicked up, jacked up, from life. From the kind of work he did.

And her body was perfect, unmarked. Smooth.

She bit her lip, like she wasn't sure if she was allowed to talk. "I like them," she said finally.

Relief coursed through him. He leaned in, kissing her, not touching anything but her lips with his own. Then he moved away, lifting his hands and cupping her breasts. His thumbs skimmed the delicate skin just beneath her nipples, teasing her, teasing himself. Withholding it from himself. Just a little longer. Letting the anticipation build, and build, until he was sure vital parts of his body were going to explode.

Then he shifted, just a little bit, his thumbs moving over those tightened buds. She moaned, low and sweet, her head falling back, and the only thing that could entice him to tear his gaze away from her breasts was the desire to see the look on her face. Her eyes were closed, her lips rounded into a perfect circle. He dragged his thumbs back and forth, satisfied as she squirmed, pressing her knees tightly together, shifting her hips.

"You like that?"

She said nothing, just bit her lip and nodded.

He slid his hand up, back behind her head, pushing his fingers through her hair, leaning in and kissing her on the neck, down to her collarbone, down to the plump, soft curve of her breast. Then he moved down farther, drawing her nipple into his mouth, sucking it in deep. He couldn't stop the groan of satisfaction that rumbled inside of his chest as he tasted her.

He moved to the other breast, teasing and sucking, glorying in the way she wiggled beneath him, the little sounds of pleasure she made spurring him on. He moved down, kissing a line across her stomach and down farther.

She froze, going stiff when he reached that place beneath her belly button.

"You don't like this?" he asked.

"I don't know," she responded.

"What do you mean you don't know?"

"No one's ever... Done that." Color bled into her cheeks, that pale skin going scarlet. "You know. Gone down on me."

He couldn't stop the growl that rumbled in his chest. A feeling of total satisfaction and anger overtaking him, and he didn't know what to do with the feeling that was such a perfect combination of the two. It was damned perfect, really, that no one had ever tasted her like that. Because he'd never tasted a woman like that before.

But McKenna wasn't a virgin.

She'd had lovers, and they damn well should have done this for her. He was angry. Not just because it was selfish, but because there were men out there wasting opportunities like that.

Stupid assholes.

He pressed her legs open, staring down at her, open and beautiful for him. His cock jerked inside of his jeans, just looking at her taking him so close to the edge he could hardly hold back. He pressed his face against her inner thigh, kissing her deliberately, waiting for her to react. He looked up. She was breathing hard, her breasts rising and falling with the motion, her eyes fixed on him.

He moved his hands down beneath her ass, cupping her, holding her up. Then he brought his mouth down to her center. Salty and sweet and female. He wanted to devour her. Utterly. And so he did. He didn't hold back.

It was years—*years*—of desire, unleashed on her beautiful body. Because she was everything. And every other damned idiot man that had touched her before him hadn't known it. Hadn't realized everything he had. So wet and gorgeous and every fantasy that had kept him awake at night for the past eight years.

He didn't think. Didn't worry about whether or not he was doing good, or making the right moves. He pressed his hand between her legs, working his fingers inside of her slick passage as he continued to lap at her with his tongue.

He kept going as she pressed her hands against his shoulders, dug her fingernails into his skin. So hard he was sure he might be bleeding.

Good. He hoped he was.

He wanted to be scarred by *her*. Not just work. Not just death.

Damn, he'd count himself lucky if he could come away from making love to McKenna Tate with ten half-moon scars on his shoulders.

He felt her internal muscles start to tighten around him, and he kept on licking, working his fingers in time with his mouth, increasing his rhythm, following the rise and fall of her hips against his face. And then he felt it happen. Felt her explode around him, her orgasm the sweetest, most satisfying sensation he'd ever felt.

He withdrew from her body, pressing both of his fingers into his mouth and licking them clean, taking every last taste of her that he could.

She was staring up at him like he'd set the earth off its axis, and of all the things he'd expected, it hadn't been that. Whenever he'd imagined this, it had been his own desire, his own pleasure, that had been at the forefront of his mind. He hadn't realized how much it would mean to be able to give it to his partner.

To make her body feel good.

She reached up toward him, clawing at his shirt, dragging it up over his head, her movements clumsy. His necklace fell forward, the rings bumping together. She looked down at them, her eyes fixed. But she didn't say anything. He took them off and set them with his T-shirt.

There was no guilt about it. Guilt was never why he'd held himself back from this.

She undid his belt, pulled it through the loops, then undid his button on his jeans, slid the zipper down. She reached inside his underwear, wrapping her soft hand around him. He gritted his teeth, her touch almost undoing him completely. He reached down, grabbed hold of her wrist and pulled her back. He managed to get his jeans off, moving back to her, kissing her deeply.

She wiggled away from him, looking down at him with intent. "Let me," she said, moving toward him, licking her lips.

"No," he said, the denial coming out much harsher than he had intended it to.

But the touch of her hand had almost finished things, and if she put her mouth on him he was going to lose it completely.

He had to get through this. This part. Without embarrassing himself. Without turning what had been an incredible experience so far into one that required explanation.

He grabbed hold of his jeans, took his wallet out of

the back pocket and took hold of the condom in there. He'd kept one in there for a while. Rotating it out, to make sure it didn't expire. He'd been doing that for years now.

So, clearly part of him was hopeful. The part that was currently so hard he was afraid he was going to sustain an injury.

It hit him that he'd never put one on before. They hadn't even done that dumbass banana thing in health class. Or, if they had, he'd missed that day.

But McKenna took the packet out of his hand, a sly smile curving her lips upward. She tore it open and applied it quickly and efficiently, squeezing him, her touch nearly undoing him.

She kissed him, and when they parted, he just stared at her for a moment. At the soft, well-satisfied look on her face. At least he'd made her come once. He pressed her down into the soft blankets, settling between her thighs. When the head of his erection pressed against the slick entrance to her body, he froze. She put her hands on his back, sliding them down toward his ass, and he reached back, grabbing one of them, pinning it up over her head. She could not touch him like that. She needed to let him get a grip on himself.

He grabbed hold of her other hand, pinning it down with the first, holding both of her wrists easily with one hand, as he guided himself inside of her with the other.

He closed his eyes as he entered her. Inch by agonizing inch.

It was the first time he'd ever been inside of a woman.

He opened his eyes and studied her face, watched her as he filled her. His heart was pounding so hard he thought it might burst out of his chest, his lungs aching, because he was holding his breath and he hadn't even realized it.

He waited for the overwhelming sensation of being surrounded by her, gripped tightly in her wet heat, to subside slightly. But it didn't. If anything, the need to move, the need to take her, increased. There was no getting used to this.

His hips bucked, of their own volition, and he drew back, thrusting deep inside of her, shuddering as he did. He wasn't going to last. There was no way. And he was just going to have to apologize later. Or maybe he wouldn't. They weren't talking. Maybe they could keep to the no talking. And it would just be better next time.

He withdrew again, slamming back into her, his movements harsh, rough. Unpracticed.

Pleasure blurred his vision, stole his control. He bucked against her, and the world went blank, then bright white as his release shook him, tore him apart.

He was shaking with the force of his orgasm, couldn't *stop* shaking. She hadn't come yet. He reached between them, rubbing his thumb over her clit, stroking her until he felt her internal muscles tighten, until she stiffened, pulsed around him, a harsh cry on her lips. He released his hold on her wrists then and she grabbed hold of his face, kissing him deep.

He withdrew from her body, pulling her up against him, her bare breasts crushed to his chest, both of their breathing ragged. And all he could think in that moment was...

Sex was not overrated at all.

MCKENNA WANTED TO HIDE. But perversely, she wanted to hide while curled up against Grant. Wanted to bury her face in his shoulder to avoid having to look at him. To avoid having to separate from him, or have any kind of awkward conversation.

Most of all, she wanted to hide so that she wouldn't cry.

She didn't know what was happening to her. Didn't know why she felt like something inside of her had shifted. Why everything that had happened between them felt so... Big. So singular.

Typically, she was in a relationship with a guy before she slept with him. And she hadn't been with all *that* many. Even so, she wasn't totally inexperienced.

But he had been different. This had been different.

The way he had looked at her... The way he touched her... No one had ever done that before. And not just the oral sex stuff, but the touching in general. The way he moved his hands over her skin like she was something fragile and precious. The way he looked at her like he'd never seen anything like her. Like she might be rare and special rather than another set of tits for him to get his hands on.

Frankly, most guys looked at her like a collection of body parts. Body parts they appreciated, sure. Body parts they wanted to touch. But not body parts that were special.

Grant seemed to look at her. And yes, at her body, but there was something reverent in it. In his gaze, in his touch.

And then there was that necklace. With the rings.

Suddenly, he shifted, and her moment of hiding up against him was over. He extricated himself from her hold and pushed himself to standing.

She watched him, the way the firelight looked over

his skin, the way it highlighted the hard-cut lines of his body. That broad chest, the well-defined abs and that angled line that served as an arrow, drawing her gaze down to that most masculine part of him.

He was incredible. So much more than any man she'd ever seen naked before.

She didn't realize they made men like him outside of books and movies.

It would be easy to write off the fact that it had been the best sex of her life because he was hands-down the hottest guy she'd ever been with. The most well-defined.

The biggest.

But it was more than that. Deeper. Chemistry and something else that made her heart feel swollen.

She didn't like it. She scrambled up so that she was sitting, because she didn't like lying there flat on her back where she likely appeared as physically devastated as she felt.

He turned and walked down the hall, disappeared into the bathroom. She let out a long breath and flopped back down, staring at the ceiling for a second before pushing herself up again and getting to her feet.

She decided that she had better get dressed before he came back. Mostly because she didn't want to be standing there bare-ass naked like a fool.

She hunted around for her pants and found them, wiggling them up her hips. She was still standing there topless, fussing with getting her shirt turned right side out, when Grant returned.

Her eyes connected with his, and the expression on his face made her skin feel hot all over. He was looking at her like he might eat her up all over again. Not that she was opposed to that. At all.

He made his way over to the couch and grabbed hold of the necklace, putting it on, before grabbing his jeans and putting them on, too. Clearly, he was not staying. But then, she had started getting dressed first, so she supposed she might have set the tone of that.

But she had just felt so…so incredibly naked. In a way that went beyond skin. Being actually naked in combination with that was not going to work for her.

She jerked the shirt down over her head, right as Grant finished with his. Covering up his body. Covering up the rings.

She was so unbearably curious about him. And she didn't know what to do with that. Because obviously if he wanted to have a conversation about his life, about himself, they would have it. The obvious thing would be to explain the jewelry that he wore. But then, that would be if he wanted to talk about it. And he clearly didn't.

And if they were in a relationship, maybe she would push that. But they weren't.

They'd just had sex on the floor of the cabin his family was letting her live in for charity.

That wasn't even close to a relationship.

She wasn't used to feeling cautious. Wasn't used to feeling tentative. But then, she wasn't used to caring whether or not she pushed someone away. But yeah, the guy who had looked at her like she mattered… She was afraid of pushing *him* away.

She was also afraid she might launch herself across the room and throw herself on his body and beg him to stay with her all night. Beg him to hold her.

That was what she wanted. More than anything. For Grant to stay and get in bed with her and hold her all night long. For him to treat her like she was precious even when she had all of her clothes on.

That was so pathetic, just thinking it made her want to curl up into a ball of shame.

She certainly wasn't going to say it. She wasn't going to do anything to let him know that she felt that way, that she was curious about him, about his life, or why he wore that jewelry.

Obviously, she had suspicions. And obviously, she had spent a little bit of time pondering it. He must have been married at some point. Or engaged. But kept the rings. That seemed reasonable enough.

He'd also mentioned that his mother had died when he was a little boy. It was possible that he wore his parents' wedding rings, she supposed.

But she had a strong feeling it was much more personal than that.

There was something so dark in his eyes now. Something pained, and she had no idea what to do with it. With his...

Need.

It wasn't physical need, but he needed something. And she had no earthly idea what.

She'd never been in a relationship with a man who needed something from her other than her body and a part of her paycheck to help with rent. She'd always wanted someone to be in the house with her. Someone to help pay the bills.

But there was something in his gaze now, something demanding. And it scared the hell out of her.

Made her want.

She needed to clear her damn head.

"I guess..." She cleared her throat, trying to find

her bearings. She would graciously hold the door open for him. Metaphorically. "I guess you should probably go get some sleep. I know you wake up really early."

He nodded slowly, his green eyes unreadable. "Yeah," he agreed.

"We should…" She scrambled forward, pressing her hand to his chest, feeling the ridge of the chain he wore beneath his shirt. "We should do this again," she whispered, kissing him on the mouth.

It was as close as she would get to letting him know how she felt. To giving him an inside look at how much she wanted to hang on to him. The kiss wasn't enough. She wanted more. She wanted to strip his clothes off again and get skin to skin.

She just didn't want to be alone.

He had made it feel like she might not be.

Pathetic.

She was so very close to potentially forging a connection with her family. She didn't need to latch on to Grant Dodge. And obviously, he didn't want her to. Because he was stepping away from her. Moving toward the door.

"See you tomorrow, McKenna," he said, his tone grave.

"See you tomorrow."

Then he opened the door, and walked through it, shutting it decisively behind him and leaving her alone, wearing her pajamas just like she had been when he'd arrived. And if it weren't for the way her body still burned, if it weren't for the tangle of blankets on the floor, and most especially the tenderness in her heart, she might have thought that she'd hallucinated the entire thing.

CHAPTER TEN

IT WAS AFTER his second cup of coffee, in the total emptiness of the mess hall, that Grant finally allowed himself to remember the events of the night before.

That he had gone over to McKenna's cabin. Kissed her. Laid her down by the fire. Made love with her.

Left her.

It had been a strange, charged moment. The time after things had finished between them. She had been half-dressed by the time he had gotten out of the bathroom after disposing of the condom. She'd wanted him to stay. He could see it in her eyes. Along with a slight uneasiness. And he had known that while part of her wanted him to stay, another part wanted him gone. He knew it, because it was exactly how he felt.

Part of him wondered what kind of idiot he was walking away from a woman who wanted him. Who would have him again that same night. But another part of him needed the distance. He had gone back to his cabin and had too much whiskey to drink, and passed out in his chair, rather than getting into bed.

All he could think was that he should feel some sense of triumph. He had. For a brief, blinding few seconds after his orgasm.

But then he'd remembered who he was. Where he was.

And everything had seemed a hell of a lot sharper. More complicated.

A kind of complicated he needed to go and work out on his own.

Which he hadn't done. He had gotten drunk instead and had a blessedly dreamless sleep.

But he figured maybe it wasn't reasonable to expect for him to change everything about his life in one night.

He lifted his coffee to his lips and closed his eyes. Remembering what it had been like to have her underneath his hands. Underneath his body.

She was…

She was everything he had known she would be. Which was a damn strange thing, all up. Considering he didn't have any sexual experience, the fact that he had known, instinctively, that he and McKenna Tate would fit like a glove seemed to reach somewhere beyond reason. But then, maybe men felt that kind of certainty about any potential partner.

Though he hadn't. And there had been potential partners before.

He still hadn't…

They hadn't been her.

In a weird way, it made him think of how drinking had been when he'd been a younger man. Anything would do. As long as it could get him a buzz. Didn't matter if it tasted good. And now that he was a little bit older—though he drank too much—he did have standards.

It wasn't just about getting hammered. It had to be good stuff.

It had to be something he liked. Something he wanted.

Maybe sex was a little bit like that.

He hadn't been single in his younger years, but he could see how that worked. How you could train yourself to care more about quantity than about the specific chemistry you might have with another person. About getting any, rather than getting exactly what you wanted.

He'd had an entire relationship that hadn't included sex. Had been entirely in love with the person he couldn't be with. A lot of people advocated sex without love. He'd had love without sex. And he knew that was possible. That you could love a person with all of yourself without being able to get naked.

The emotional intimacy that it required was…

Something.

And it made him wonder if it was part of why he couldn't quite wrap his head around sex with a stranger. Or sex with someone who didn't appeal specifically.

Whatever it was, McKenna was exactly the right shot of whiskey for him.

The door opened and in walked Wyatt and Jamie. Wyatt was looking harassed, while Jamie looked enormously crabby. "I can get everything done."

"I'm completely fine with us taking on some of the Daltons' rescues," Wyatt was saying. "I'm just not sure I can spare you for as many hours a week as Gabe is wanting you to come over and do training. We can house some of the horses here and train them."

"So you can supervise me."

"I didn't say that," Wyatt said.

"But that's what you mean. You don't want me over there with the Daltons because they have hideous reputations with women. And you don't think that I can handle myself."

"I didn't say any of that," Wyatt returned.

"What's going on?" Grant was happy for the interruption of his thoughts.

"Jamie wants to take a part-time job at the Dalton ranch. Gabe has asked her to come and train some of his rodeo horses to be good beginner horses for trail rides and kids and things. I think it's a great idea. In general. But I need Jamie here. He's going to need her during busy season and I can't see how that will work."

His eyes clashed with Wyatt's, and he saw the concern in his older brother's gaze. He was about to defend Jamie's stance, because she was a grown-up woman who could more than handle herself, when scenes from last night flashed through his mind again. It was like a key had turned in the lock and opened a door to a room he'd never been in, and in that room was an onslaught of understanding.

Both the way and the *why* men were driven to get laid, and exactly what all that entailed. The way that McKenna had looked at him. Vulnerable and scared. The way it had felt to leave her.

Grant had seen porn. He was a single man with no sexual outlet. And frankly, he had thought it best to be forearmed before getting out there. But *seeing* sex was a hell of a lot different than *having* it. And he hadn't appreciated that fully until just now.

"You should have the horses here," he said.

"Really?" Jamie asked. "*Et tu*, Grant? You're usually the reasonable one."

"Am I? I thought I was usually the drunk one."

"Sure. But reasonable. Wyatt is a hypocrite of the

highest order. He's just as bad as any of the Dalton brothers. And he doesn't trust me around them because I'm his sister. Even though he treats women just like they treat women."

"Treated," Wyatt said. "Past tense. I am completely and totally monogamous now. I'm a married man."

"Good for you," Jamie said. "I don't see what that has to do with me taking on work with Gabe Dalton."

"I don't trust him."

"You're his friend," she pointed out.

"Yes. Away from all women I'm related to or care for at all. I don't trust him around you."

"He is *a thousand years old.*" Jamie's vehemence about the agedness of a man in his midthirties was almost funny.

"He's younger than me," Wyatt said.

"Yeah. So? Anyway, I don't need you to trust him. I need you to trust me. And remember the fact that you taught me how to fire a rifle with total accuracy when I was twelve years old."

Wyatt shook his head. "That isn't why I don't want you over there. I actually need you here heading up the trail rides."

"Then we can hire someone else. And Dallas is ready to take some of it on, he's fantastic with horses. I love doing the trail rides, Wyatt, don't get me wrong, but this gives me a chance to do something really great. I feel… This is bigger than what I'm doing now, and I want to do it."

The door opened again and McKenna slipped in. Their eyes collided and she froze.

"Good morning," Wyatt said, clearly oblivious to the tension between them.

"Good morning," she said, looking between Wyatt and Jamie, and then back to him.

She slipped past all three of them, making her way over to the coffee station. "Are you hungry?" Wyatt asked.

"No," she responded, sneaking a glance at Grant again.

"Are you sure? Because there's some leftover bacon and eggs in the kitchen."

"I'm sure," she said quickly.

"McKenna," Jamie said. "Remember when we talked to Gabe Dalton at Sugar Cup?"

McKenna's eyes darted between Jamie and Grant. "Yes?"

"Gabe called and he offered me that job officially. But Wyatt doesn't think he can spare me for enough hours."

"Well," she said slowly, "I'd help, but I definitely can't help out with the riding and stuff. The fact that I've been on one trail ride does not make me guide material. But any of your other responsibilities... I need more hours. More work, anyway."

Jamie's expression turned triumphant. "There you go, Wyatt. Surely we can rebalance some things. We have McKenna here helping out."

"Sparing you a few days a week right now while you go get familiar with the place is nothing. But the real job will be during the summer," Wyatt said. "You know that's much tougher."

McKenna looked like she'd been lanced when Wyatt said that. "Well..."

"Whatever," Jamie said. "That gives us time to find new people. And we already have McKenna."

McKenna tucked her dark hair behind her ear, and Grant couldn't help but think about how soft it was to touch. She looked up, meeting his eyes again, and she bit her full lower lip. He found himself totally distracted by the way her teeth sunk into the soft pink flesh.

He wanted to push her into the kitchen and do some biting of his own.

A kick of lust hit him straight in the gut, all his blood rushing south. Holy hell. He was literally about to get a hard-on in front of his brother and sister. He had just been congratulating himself on his maturity. On the fact that sex when you were in your thirties was clearly different than when you were in your twenties or teens, and because he had waited so long he had skipped all the immature nonsense.

Apparently, he was no better than any other man. And his dick was just a dick.

He took a step backward, getting some distance between himself and McKenna. Because, good Lord, he had to get a grip.

"Grant—" Jamie looked at him with pleading eyes "—you know I'm being reasonable. And I really want this."

"You can do it," Grant said. "And you don't need permission from either of us."

It hit him suddenly that Jamie's life hadn't been any less stagnant than his own for the past few years. They had both gone all in with Wyatt, getting the dude ranch off the ground. And Jamie...

Jamie, for her part, had thrown herself into the ranch. Whether their father was running it, or they were running it. And Grant had never stopped to ask himself, or Jamie, whether or not it was what she wanted.

But she wanted this.

And whatever was going on with him didn't matter. Not right now. It was so easy for him to get caught up in everything he'd been through that sometimes he took his strong, resilient sister's presence for granted. Her happiness. But she had gone from being a kid to being a woman during the years he'd been grieving, and sometimes he wondered if Jamie was here because she wanted to be, or if she felt like she had to be out of some sense of obligation.

"I might not need your permission," Jamie said. "But I care about the ranch, and about making sure it runs smoothly. Plus, I don't hate you guys, so it's nice to have your approval."

"If you think you can handle both, Jamie," Wyatt said, his tone a bit more challenging than Grant's had been, "then go for it."

"I will," Jamie said, her tone defiant, clearly in no mood to be conciliatory with Wyatt.

Wyatt shook his head and went over to fix his own coffee, leaving Jamie, Grant and McKenna standing in a circle.

"I don't really have that many responsibilities," Jamie said, loud enough for Wyatt to hear. "He's being a drama queen. But a couple times a week I might need your help feeding horses. If I'm still going to be over at the Dalton ranch."

"I would be able to handle that," McKenna said, her tone cautious.

The *if I'm still here* was unspoken. But Grant heard it all the same.

"Hey," Wyatt said to Grant, coming back over to the group, "do you want to come check the fence with me again? Those cows did such a number on it the other day."

"Sure," Grant said.

He looked at McKenna one more time—she was getting pink in the cheeks and staring at him—and he had no idea what she wanted him to do. He wasn't going to... Do anything special with her right now. While his family was standing there.

"See you around," Wyatt said to both Jamie and McKenna, and Grant waved on his way out the door. But the entire time he couldn't shake the feeling that he had done something wrong.

Which he resented. They had rules.

He had assumed that things could continue on with them as they had during the day. At night...

But then, he supposed that was the problem. He had assumed some things, and she had assumed some things.

That was something he hadn't thought of. The fact that being with someone would mean needing to talk about stuff like this. Except he wasn't with her.

Images of his hands on her skin flashed through his mind again. Of what it had been like to be inside of her.

"What's up?" his brother asked.

"Nothing," Grant responded. "Let's go fix the fence."

And later, he might have to fix a metaphorical fence. But that was a problem for later.

McKenna didn't know why she was behaving like such an absolute baby.

But it had... It had hurt. Having Grant look *through* her this morning like he barely knew her, much less like he had ever been inside of her. Like they hadn't had amazing, transformative sex that had made her question everything she knew about herself and men and her body.

Grant, as a lover, had been a revelation.

A man who had touched her like she was something precious. Something special. A man who had been so strong and so gentle all at once. A man who had cared as much for her pleasure as his own.

In bed—or on the living room floor, as it were—he was completely and utterly unlike any man she'd ever known.

But now...now in the aftermath, he was being so damned *expected*.

A man who could clearly keep sex and interaction separate. When she had thought that...

She wanted to pound her head against the wall of the cabin she was currently scrubbing, because she didn't actually know what she wanted.

For him to acknowledge her and the sex they'd had? To what end?

She *should* be thinking about Gabe Dalton and the fact that Jamie was going to be working with him, which meant that she could probably finagle a way to get to know him a little bit better before she dropped the bomb on him about being his secret sister.

Before she went to his dad and dropped a bomb about being a secret daughter.

And she *would* be a bomb. There was no getting past that.

She had concerns. Concerns about disrupting the Daltons' life. Obviously, Gabe was older than she was, and she didn't know the state of his parents' relationship. From the brief bit of digging she'd done she'd found a couple of divorce records, but it also looked like Hank Dalton had remarried the mother of his children at some point.

Where she fit into all that, she didn't know.

It was a mess. That's what it was.

But she needed to get in there and wade in the mess because she didn't have a whole lot of other choices. Plus, she had felt… It was like she could feel the shared blood in their veins when she looked at Gabe. She felt a connection to him. She hadn't been able to stop staring when he had come in, and it wasn't because he was an attractive man. Though he was.

But it was different. Like the blood that made her heart thump had recognized the blood in his veins. And it had responded.

She hadn't been in the same room as someone she was related to since she was two years old. Since before her mother had decided that she wasn't worth the time.

She sighed heavily and reached the end of the kitchen counter that she had been wiping down.

She was done with her very last cabin of the day and she would be meeting up with Jamie in a little bit to go over the logistics of feeding horses.

She looked around the cabin, felt a sense of satisfaction swell in her chest in spite of her earlier sense of discomfort.

She had done a good job cleaning. She did a good job at the ranch in general. And she enjoyed the work. And tonight she would go back to her own little cabin and do some scrubbing there.

Maybe she would go and see Grant, even though she was mad at him.

She felt… She didn't know. She had come to Gold

Valley to deal with the Daltons. This stop at Get Out of Dodge had been unexpected and unintentional. The stopover in Grant's bed even more so, and utterly ill-advised.

Becoming friends with Jamie, getting to know Bea...

She hadn't counted on any of those things, and yet she felt...

She didn't know how to describe it. She wasn't sure if she was happy. Because there was too much left undone. The whole thing with Grant was making her feel strange and she knew that she had the task of contending with what might happen if the Daltons rejected her.

Knew that she had to approach that with caution so that hopefully it could... Work out.

But for the first time in her life she felt like there might actually be a space for her here. Like in this place she fit.

Her little cabin nestled back in the trees belonged. And she felt like she belonged in it.

It wasn't comfortable necessarily. There were edges. Sharp ones. And when you fit snugly into a space, what she was noticing was that the edges dug in a bit deeper. The thing with Grant was sharp at the moment. And the worst part was she wasn't sure she was upset with him or upset with herself.

For what she was feeling. For giving in, in the first place.

For not knowing what the hell she even wanted.

"You want to find your family, not stay in this one. You need to figure out where you're going next. Not whose bed you're going to sleep in tonight."

She scolded herself as she gathered her cleaning supplies and walked out of the cabin. Then she wandered back to the mess hall to put them all away.

She walked from the back and into the dining area, which was empty, except for Grant, who was standing by the coffeepot pouring himself a cup and looking so hot it should be illegal.

And now she knew.

Knew that his hands were as strong and capable as they looked. Knew that the dark whiskers on his jaw scraped against her skin when they kissed—and that it felt damn good. Knew that he was better than any fantasy she'd ever had, and a hell of a lot better than anything she'd actually had.

"Fancy meeting you here," she said.

"Yeah," he responded.

Yeah. He was *such* a dude.

"So, what was this morning about?" she asked.

She didn't have to make this easy for him. She was feeling wounded and a bit spiky, and she didn't know why he shouldn't have to feel some of it, too.

"This morning?"

"Yes," she said. "Don't play stupid."

"Oh, you mean this morning when we were standing in a group together with my brother and sister? What exactly did you expect?"

"For you to not treat me like I was a stranger."

"McKenna," he said, his voice maddeningly gentle. She was hoping that he would get angry. That he would prove to be exactly the basic bro she had begun to think he was over the course of the day. A guy who engaged in a little *wham bam thank you ma'am*, then couldn't remember the woman's name. Because she didn't like the alternatives. Yes, there was an edge of disappointment in thinking maybe Grant wasn't the saint that she had initially believed he was, but there was also a bit of relief.

It was easier, in some ways, to believe those old-fashioned, handsome, chivalrous, decent men didn't exist. Because then she wouldn't want one.

It was a whole lot like *Anne of Green Gables*, really.

If she didn't believe those kinds of people existed—people who would happily take in a skinny orphan girl when she wasn't even what they really wanted—then she couldn't long for it.

Otherwise…

Otherwise, there was this great, beautiful thing somewhere in the universe and she didn't have it. Couldn't have it for whatever reason.

Because of who she was, most likely.

It was why she wanted a fight right now. Why she wanted him to give it to her. But he wasn't.

"I thought we agreed that we were going to keep what was happening between us separate," he said. "I couldn't exactly grab hold of you and kiss you in front of Wyatt and Jamie."

"You could have been friendlier."

"I don't know if I could have," he said. "I'm not sure how to do the middle ground thing."

"Well," she sniffed. "That doesn't work for me."

"I'm sorry," he said. It was an apology, and it seemed sincere, but it certainly didn't indicate that he was willing to change what he was doing. More like: *sorry you feel that way, but nothing is going to change.*

"You don't get to have everything your way," she pointed out.

"Bear with me here, McKenna," he said. "I've never done this before."

"What?"

"The just-sex thing," he said, his jaw firming up, his eyes getting closed off. And she knew, more than anything, that she was treading right around a sensitive area for him. Around those rings that he wore on that chain, she had a feeling.

She could push. She could push, and she could shut him down, and she could probably earn herself a big old fight.

"I haven't really, either," she found herself saying instead. "I mean, I've been with guys. But always in relationships."

"Okay," he said. "So clearly we're both a little bit raw and we don't know how to do this. Even though I think it's what we both want."

"I guess," she said.

Because what was the alternative? Having everybody know they were sleeping together? It didn't really matter, she supposed. Not to her. But then, she was passing through and Grant had to deal with everybody after she was gone. So, logically, however he felt about the situation was the right and true feeling on the subject.

She really didn't want to be reasonable. She wanted to be hurt and upset because she was. Because she was, and she didn't know why, and that made her feel unsettled.

Because everything that had happened between them last night made her feel unsettled.

"I guess…" She fought against the words that were trying to come out of her mouth. Fought against her desire to protect herself with her desire to connect with him. Because this morning, when they had been so close but not connected, she felt terrible. Because she wanted to embrace what she'd felt last night and run away from it at the same time.

Because she didn't know her own heart. Her own mind. Anything.

"I guess I don't know how to do this, either," she finished finally. "I thought just… Wanting it to be just physical would be enough. But…"

"You let a man inside of your body, McKenna, and that's always going to feel intimate."

She had never, not once in her life, had a man say something like *that* to her. She'd had boyfriends; they'd had sex with her. But they'd never seemed to treat it as intimate. And on her part… She'd wanted so much to feel close to someone. But so often, it was just physical closeness, and nothing more.

She told herself it was for the best. Each and every time when one of her boyfriends would lie there sleeping afterward, and she felt completely alone and disconnected, that it was for the best. That there was someone there in case she needed them.

That the physical presence of the other person was all that mattered. That it was okay if nothing else was connecting up. If it didn't feel amazing for her body or her heart. It was closeness. And it was the closest she could be to someone.

But she'd often ended up feeling hollowed out and more alone than she had before, and she'd never understood why.

For some reason Grant's words, that acknowledgment of the fact that letting someone in mattered, brought all these things flooding into her. Through her. Was that why last night had felt different? Because Grant understood? Because maybe he even felt it, too?

In her experience, men really didn't. In her experience, they seemed to be able to take their pleasure and feel nothing.

She always felt something. Usually kind of sad. Sad that she couldn't find the connection she knew she shouldn't want, anyway.

Because loving people was a dead end.

She'd loved her mother. So much. And even though she couldn't remember her, she remembered the ache her leaving had left behind. Love hadn't brought her back. She'd loved her first boyfriend, too, or at least had wanted to. She'd wanted it to be something because she'd wanted…a connection.

Love hadn't made it last. It hadn't made him care for her.

Anyway, love didn't matter. It wasn't like air. Or water. Or even a soft bed. She needed a place to stay. Maybe even a place in general to call home.

She didn't expect the Daltons to love her. She didn't even expect them to like her. But maybe…who knew. Maybe guilt or whatever would entice them to help her.

She needed help, and God knew she'd been through enough in her life. Had struggled enough. Hank Dalton was her father, and he should owe her something.

All her relationships had been built on that same kind of need.

Maybe that was the difference. That Grant had made it very clear he wasn't trading sex for anything. That she was safely cared for, with lodging and a job, no matter what happened between them.

That the sex between them was just about pleasure. Just about attraction. And not about trading.

Maybe it was removing that layer that had allowed for the emotional stuff to creep in.

"I'm dysfunctional," she said. "I know that. It's just... I don't know what I want sometimes. I'm here to find my family, I told you that. I don't know what I expect out of it. And I think maybe this whole thing got tangled up in it. But I liked what we did last night. And you're right. We don't need anyone here to know."

Actually, the idea of Jamie finding out that she was sleeping with her brother made her stomach feel sour. Jamie was becoming a friend and she didn't want Jamie to think that McKenna had been using her to get to Grant or anything like that. Mostly, she didn't want to tangle this up. She didn't want to complicate it.

As places went, this was the happiest she'd been in for quite some time.

Even with the sharp edges.

"Maybe we can be friends," McKenna said. "I mean... Separate from the sex stuff. Maybe there *can* be a middle ground."

The corner of his mouth tipped upward. "Maybe you didn't notice, but I don't exactly have a lot of friends."

"You have your family. They seem to love you."

"They're stuck with me."

"Have you always been this grumpy?"

He got a strange look on his face, as if he was really thinking about how to answer that question. "Yes and no."

"What does that mean?"

He let out a slow breath, raised one of those gorgeous, masculine hands and rubbed the back of his neck. "I was an asshole when I was in high school. Let's put it that way."

"And after that?"

"Better," he said.

"Very descriptive, Grant," she said.

"I'm not trying to be descriptive, McKenna," he said.

McKenna fought the urge to get closer to him. To touch him. Instead, she rocked back on her heels, shoving her hands into her pockets. The pockets of her new coat. The one that Bea had bought her. She had no idea how life had gotten so strange in a matter of a few weeks.

"I was *extremely* popular in high school," she said. "Probably a combination of my warm, winning personality and my superfashionable clothing choices."

She didn't know why she was doing this. Why she was badgering him. Pushing him to give more. She didn't know why she was giving more. Except that she wanted to know him. Whether that was silly or not.

"Is that a fact?" he asked.

"No. It's a lie." She grinned widely for effect.

"Were you nice to other people?"

It was such a strange question. She wasn't sure anyone had ever asked her that before. In fact, she was sure no one had. "Not particularly. But then, I guess you kind of get that way eventually. When other people are jerks to you."

He nodded slowly. "I guess so."

"Were you nice to other people?"

He shook his head. "I was a bully."

She blinked. She couldn't imagine that. Couldn't imagine the man that she knew being a bully. Yes, he was grumpy. He wasn't always effusive or anything.

But… She kept coming back to that *good man* thing. No matter what, that seemed to be the truest thing about him. That at every turn he defied what she knew about men and people in general, because his motivation was never based in selfishness. It was always a hell of a lot more complicated than that. *He* was a hell of a lot more complicated than that.

"You probably weren't."

He shook his head. "No. I was. Nobody liked me. Everybody avoided Grant Dodge. And my dad… He was so lost in his grief that he couldn't really do anything about it. The school called him, I assume. But he never talked to me about it. He barely made eye contact with me half the time. I love my dad, McKenna, don't get me wrong. But it was not a great time for us. I mentioned that Jamie was a baby when my mom died, but I mean… She died because of complications. Just a few weeks later. She had a blood clot, and it took her suddenly. My dad was completely overwhelmed. And that lasted for… Years after."

He closed his eyes, and she could see him battling with something. Memories. Old anger. She didn't know.

All she knew was she felt it. Deep inside. This pain that lived in him. And she wanted to do something about it, which was as foreign a feeling as she'd ever had.

She could only ever worry about herself. That was survival.

But here she was, aching for this beautiful man in front of her who had a family and a whole damn ranch.

"I was angry," he continued. "And the only alternative to letting it out at home was to unleash it at school. And I did. On anyone weaker than I was. I wasn't a bully in the way that jocks are. I didn't do it for a crowd.

for a show. It wasn't for my friends. I didn't have any friends. I was that lowlife that hung out by himself, shoved the skinny kids in the halls. Failed half of his classes. You wouldn't have wanted to know me. And I wouldn't have been nice to you. I would have recognized all your weaknesses and I would have used that against you. Made you feel worse, because I felt ugly inside and didn't know what to do beyond making other people feel ugly, too."

McKenna forced a laugh, trying to shift the weight that had settled in her chest. "Honey, I would have cut you with the knife in my boot. I was nobody's victim."

"I bet you didn't make victims of people, either."

"I didn't have the time or the emotional energy. I didn't have the anger, Grant. That takes energy. I was just trying to survive half the time." That much was true.

She wanted to touch him now even more. Wanted to do something to reach that lost, lonely boy that she was convinced still lived inside of him. That anger that she had a feeling was still there. Most of all, she wanted to unlock all of his mysteries. Wanted to pry him open and figure out how he had become the man he was now, and why she still sensed that darkness underneath.

The goodness was real; she knew it was. But so was the anger.

But just wanting that terrified her.

Made her want to pull away.

"How about now?" he asked. "Are you just still surviving?"

An image flashed through her mind, one she hadn't ever let in before. Of her sitting with the Daltons. Together in a room.

Just together.

No. No, it would never be that.

Food. Shelter. Money. That was what she needed. Once she had that…once she had that, she could have a whole different life. A whole new set of wants.

But it started with those essentials.

"I'm on a quest to find something other than survival," she said honestly, truthfully. "I'll let you know if I find it."

Their eyes caught and held, and something hot and tense stretched between them. She thought about that time spent in his arms. That had been something other than survival. Maybe that was the difference. She'd wondered that earlier.

From the time she had left the foster care system, she'd been with men for survival purposes. Like everything else in her life. She hadn't seen it that way, not strictly. She'd had feelings for her boyfriends. She had been attracted to them. But it hadn't been like this.

Grant being in her life but not being a necessity to her survival added something different to it. It made the sex feel luxurious and decadent. Like eating past the point of being full. Having dessert. Grant Dodge was dessert.

She was so very desperate to have him again.

And when she put it like that, it wasn't quite so scary. It made sense.

It wasn't different because of him, so much. It was different because of where she was at. And hell, like she'd just said, she was on a quest to find something other than survival, so she might as well enjoy this unexpected little piece of it.

"I think I'd like to find that, too," he said, his voice rough.

She wanted to touch him, and she wanted to pry deeper into his secrets. But this time, she just went with touching. She closed the distance between them, reached out and placed her hand on his cheek. "I don't see why we can't have that."

"As long as you're here," he said.

"As long as I'm here."

She knew it was risky, but she didn't care. She leaned forward and pressed her lips to his. It was brief, but it was so very needed. It made her heart feel like it was going to burst, made the blood in her veins feel like fire.

She wanted more. Needed it. Craved it. But they had to keep going. Had to have a normal day, so that they could get to the part that was just the two of them.

"See you tonight," she said.

He nodded slowly. "See you tonight."

CHAPTER ELEVEN

GRANT WAS WONDERING exactly what *tonight* meant in McKenna's terms. What time she would come over. Or if he was supposed to go over there. He had eaten dinner at his brother's house quickly, and made excuses about not feeling up to going out when Wyatt had invited him to the Gold Valley saloon for a drink.

He was now back at his house pacing the floor, looking at the time. It was only five-thirty, and he imagined that was a little bit early for a hookup. But then, he didn't know what the usual time frame for hookups was. He wasn't sure he cared what the usual time frame was. He was about to go storm the door of McKenna's place.

Talking to her today had been…

He had never told anyone that. Had never actually talked about why he was such an asshole bully.

His brother Wyatt hadn't been at the same school as he was, and hadn't known about it, because he had left home at seventeen. Bennett hadn't been in high school yet when Grant had straightened out, thanks to Lindsay's intervention. And Lindsay… She had known him. They had never talked about the whys. First of all because Grant had been a teenager then, and it had never occurred to him to really search himself and figure out why he had been such a raving jackass to everyone who had crossed his path.

And then… Then their life had been consumed by Lindsay's health, and Grant had been happy to leave behind the memories of who he had been.

He hadn't liked that man, anyway, so there was no real reason to talk about him.

Telling McKenna… It had been strange, and yet at the same time he realized he had missed it. Missed connecting with another person. In a way, it had felt good. To stand there and talk like that. To hear about her.

He hadn't thought he would like that. Not at all. He resisted things like that on a daily basis. If Wyatt had his way they would talk about his feelings a hell of a lot more. Wyatt was always wanting to know how he was. So was Bennett. Jamie a little bit less.

His phone buzzed and he looked down, his stomach going cold when he saw who it was.

His former mother-in-law. Dammit.

It had been enough years that he didn't talk to Connie often anymore. He had his own family, after all. And they had each other. He and his ex-brother-in-law, Cooper, had never been overly close, since the other man had a job that took him out of town often, and since Lindsay's death he had been gone constantly.

But there was no bad blood between himself and his in-laws, and he did love them.

It was just that sometimes he didn't quite feel up to maintaining the connection.

He felt like a jerk for thinking that. Then he answered the phone. "Hello?"

"Grant," Connie said, and Grant could tell immediately by her tone that she was having one of her rough patches.

Connie had always suffered from anxiety, and hell,

Grant couldn't blame her for it. She had been nervous the entire time he and Lindsay had been married. But her daughter had been sick, and frequently uncomfortable. Always one terrible infection away from dying.

"Is everything all right?"

"It's just almost Christmas," Connie said. "You know that's a hard time of year for me."

Grant nodded, swallowing hard. And he remembered last night. Being with McKenna. Apparently, that was how he was coping with Christmas this year.

Again, he waited for some kind of guilt. But he didn't feel it. Lindsay was gone. He hated it. But she'd been gone for a lot of years.

There wasn't guilt but a feeling of being tangled up in the past and connected to it in a way he didn't know how to escape. In a way he didn't feel like he could or should escape. But it wasn't the letting go that got him. It was the moving on.

How did you do it when you lived in the same place? With the same people. With in-laws that you cared for but couldn't have around all the time, because they couldn't change their life in the same way that you could.

He didn't the hell know. He just didn't.

"I know," he said, keeping his voice gentle.

"I was just wondering if you had gone up to her spot yet. If you had brought any poinsettias."

Lindsay had loved poinsettias. And usually they took turns bringing some up to the place where they'd sprinkled her ashes.

The place where he and Lindsay had had their first kiss.

That place he had showed her the day he had realized that he was in love with her and she had told him that her cancer was back.

It was the place where he knew his life had changed forever. Where he knew *he* had changed forever.

A place that meant something to the both of them, and that added to all that tangled-up emotion that clung to him, wound itself around his life and made it so he couldn't take a step without feeling a tug backward.

"I haven't been up yet," he said honestly. "I will go, though. I promise."

"Cooper is coming back into town," she said, trying to keep her voice cheery.

"That's good," Grant said. He hadn't seen his brother-in-law in years.

"He doesn't like to come back," she said. "Especially not around Christmas."

"Yeah, I know," Grant said.

"It's hard for him," Connie continued.

Of course it was. It was hard for all of them. And Grant tried not to judge another man's grief, but it was difficult to do sometimes with Cooper. He wished that he was able to be here more for his parents. But then, part of that was out of Grant's own desire to not have to be the one that was there for them.

And so, he was back to not being able to judge another man's grief.

In some ways, he felt guilty whenever he was around her family. She was their daughter. Cooper's sister. They'd had expectations for her life starting from when she was a child. And then she had gotten sick.

Grant had known. And that was the thing that was difficult to untangle even inside himself sometimes.

He had chosen to get deeper involved even after

knowing she was sick. He had married her knowing that till death did them part would come much sooner than it would for most people.

In fact, with as sick as she had ended up being, it had seemed like it would come sooner than it had. The fact they were married for eight years had surprised everyone.

And within that, so many things had been different than Grant had thought they would be. The fact that they had never been able to consummate being the big one.

The fact that he had been much more caregiver than husband.

Sometimes he felt like a fraud. Everyone imagined he was grieving a very specific relationship. A very specific loss.

It made his stomach turn to admit that even to himself.

He had loved her. He *did* love her.

They also hadn't lived as husband and wife in a traditional sense. He hadn't been able to give that to her.

He closed his eyes, memory washing through him.

"It's not...fair to you, Grant."

"Marrying you was never about fair. It's not fair that you're sick, Lindsay. It's not fair that we won't get old together. Sex is nothing."

"It's not," she said.

"It's nothing to me." He put his hand on her forehead. *"We've never pretended we were the same as everyone else. You told me...you told me when you got diagnosed you were going to die."*

"And you said everyone dies," she pointed out.

"And I'm right about that." His throat was impossibly tight, and she felt so light and small in his arms. It

was one thing to say that, and it was another to watch it happen. "No one has a guarantee, Lindsay. No one. I wish you felt better. But not for me, for you."

"I wish I felt good and that...everything wasn't painful. The plan was never to die a virgin."

"Well, I'm one, too."

She put her hand on his face. "You won't die a virgin, though."

Right then, he doubted that. Because the alternative was to go find someone else, and holding Lindsay's fragile body in his arms, he couldn't imagine doing that. "We're in this together, babe," he said. "I promised. I meant it."

"I know you did," she said, her voice sounding thinner, weaker, than it had a moment ago.

He swallowed hard, an ache in his chest spreading to his throat. It hurt. It all hurt.

"I love you," he said.

"I don't know why."

He felt like she'd punched him. "You made me someone better, Lindsay. Better than I was, or ever would have been without you. Other people might have a normal marriage, but ours is the only one that could have saved me."

"Just think." She smiled, her pale lips curving upward. "You could be out at a bar, picking up chicks."

He looked around their little living room, perfectly organized. Just like Lindsay liked it. He did his best to keep it that way so she wouldn't expend too much energy trying to make it perfect. Same with their yard. Immaculate, on the corner of their little street.

"That would be a shame," he said, "because this is where I want to be."

That felt like a lifetime ago.

He had a feeling that last night was a big part of why he could feel that distance like a yawning void, more now than ever.

"I'm glad he's going to be back. Hopefully I can catch up with you between now and Christmas."

Though, right now, the idea of seeing them…

He didn't want to. He didn't want to deal with that part of his life. Not now. He'd been dealing with it for so long. He wanted to bury himself in McKenna. In being naked by the fireplace. In being with somebody who didn't know about that part of his life.

Did that make him selfish? He didn't know. More to the point, he didn't know if he cared.

He had been a husband.

But never a lover.

Right now, he just wanted to be a lover.

Not a husband, or a grieving widower. Not a son-in-law or even the steady, even-keeled brother everyone saw as responsible and good, because he'd been through some hard things and that somehow elevated him in the eyes of his siblings.

It hit him then that what he really wanted was to keep McKenna completely separate from his actual life.

That would be impossible. She talked to everyone at the ranch, and if she didn't already know that he'd been married before, she would find out soon enough. He sure as hell didn't want to talk about it.

He wondered if that was why he had told her about the high school stuff so easily. It was a separate part of his life in many ways. A different time. A time before Lindsay.

But he couldn't do that. Because he was going to

have to go and leave poinsettias. Because whatever he wanted didn't necessarily mean what he could have.

And when it came right down to it, *want* was an awfully complicated concept.

"It would be nice if you could stop by the house," Connie said.

"Sure," Grant said, the response exiting his mouth by rote, no thought at all behind it. "Let me know when it's a good time. And if you need anything."

"I will."

There was a long, deathly silence on the other end of the phone, stretched with tension and filled with what he knew were quiet tears. "You've been better to us than you needed to be, Grant. You were so very good to her."

Suddenly, Grant's chest felt heavy. Swollen. "No," he said. "She was good to me. If you can understand that, I hope you will. I never did her any favors. I just loved her."

"Thank you," Connie said.

He got off the phone then, feeling numb. Strange.

And different than he had before the call. He wished that he could have just focused on his arousal. On his desire to repeat what had happened between himself and McKenna last night. But now it all felt weighted. His whole body did.

He sighed and looked toward the liquor cabinet. He was tempted to drink.

But he knew how that ended, and he was tired of the predictability of his life as much as anything else.

No, what he really wanted was to escape this cabin. Escape his skin.

Then he remembered McKenna touching his skin last night.

Last night his body hadn't been the prison it had been for all this time. No, his body could make him feel things. *Good* things. Not just grief. Not just pain. Not just this tangle of emotions and connections and past hurts he wasn't sure how to release hold of.

He was through fucking waiting.

He turned away from the whiskey bottle and he grabbed his jacket off the peg, along with his cowboy hat, flinging the door open and walking out into the cold. He slammed the door shut behind him and shoved his hands in his pockets. He walked away from the house, leaving his phone. His link to anyone and anything other than what he was out to find.

He was going to find McKenna.

He walked, his head bent low, his breath a cloud in the crisp night air. If anyone saw him walking around this late they would probably want to know what he was doing, but thankfully Wyatt and Lindy were out having a drink, and the odds were Jamie had tagged along with them. So that meant he was probably safe from the deepest of interrogations.

Plus, he just didn't care enough to be cautious, not when the promise of McKenna and the oblivion that she could give him was only a few paces away.

When he reached her front porch, he pounded on the door heavily, not taking any care with being polite.

When she opened the door, she looked grumpy. She was wearing a soft-looking sweater and a pair of jeans, no shoes. Her dark hair was falling around her shoulders in a curling, damp tumble. She looked like she had just gotten out of the shower, her cheeks rosy and freshly scrubbed.

"You didn't tell me you were coming over yet." Her

tone would have been comically grouchy if he had it in him to find anything funny.

"We didn't actually come up with the time," he said.

"No," she responded. "But I was getting ready."

"You look plenty ready to me."

She frowned, wrinkling her nose. "In what way?"

"You look sexy as hell," he responded, crossing over the threshold and slamming the door shut behind him.

His patience was severely compromised. And he just felt… Like he was trying to run away from everything building inside of him. From phone calls and memories and damned reality. And McKenna, her cabin, represented a vacation from that reality. He desperately needed it.

He stomped back to her bedroom, flinging open the door. It was cold in there. He needed to get her a space heater. He wrenched the blankets off the bed and brought them into the living room, set them in front of the fire that was burning cheerily in the hearth.

"The rest of my day went well, Grant, and how was yours? Good. Very nice to hear. Did anything fun and unexpected happened to you today, McKenna? No, not especially." McKenna was going back and forth, imitating both of their voices.

He paused his movements, turning to look at her. "What?"

"It's just…" She waved a hand toward the blankets. "Often, men pretend to be interested in their partner before getting down to the sex."

"I'm sorry, did you want me to lie about why I'm here? Pretend we don't know what's going to happen?" He took a step toward her, need and anger coursing through his veins. The need was for her. The anger wasn't. But it was a heady cocktail that was going to his head faster than a shot of whiskey. "We could talk about the weather, but we're in the same damn place, so we can both step outside and see that it's cold as hell. We can talk about how our days went, except we both work at the same place so we know nothing catastrophic happened or we would have already heard about it. We got together earlier today and talked about some real stuff. About the fact that I was a bully in high school and you were poor and didn't have friends. But we can do small talk if you really want."

He closed the distance between them, wrapping his arm around her waist and pulling her up against him. "I've been inside you, McKenna. I've tasted you. We can try to be polite, but I think we're past polite, don't you?"

She shivered in his arms, deep, pink color spilling into her cheeks. "When you put it like that…"

"How was your day?" he asked.

"Fine," she said. "Uneventful, as we've established."

"It's about to get more eventful."

"How was *your* day," she said, squeaking as he lifted her up off the ground and carried her over to the pile of blankets, depositing her on top of them. He stripped her shirt up over her head, growling when he saw the black, lacy bra she was wearing. "It *fucking sucked*, thanks for asking."

"Why did it suck?" she asked.

"Not in the mood to get into it."

"But you're in the mood to get into me."

"Hell, yeah."

He claimed her mouth with his own, and he consumed her. There really was no other word for it. He wanted her. All of her. And Lord, he would not ever take for granted the absolute privilege of being able to touch a woman like this.

Being able to touch McKenna.

He had closed-off places inside himself out of necessity. Told himself he didn't need it. Told himself his life was enough without it.

What did a physical connection matter? What did physical satisfaction matter?

Now... Now he couldn't remember how the hell he had found that acceptable for the last eight years.

Love had filled the cracks in his life when he'd been married. Had been what held him together. Whatever else he was missing, he'd had love. And for the past eight years, he'd had nothing at all. And he told himself if he'd survived that long he would be fine for longer, but now he couldn't imagine how in hell that was true.

She was life underneath his fingertips. Warmth and vibrancy that he hadn't experienced in so damned long. Maybe never.

She filled him with heat, with desire. And it wasn't desire that wasn't going to go unmet. He had never experienced desire and *enjoyed* it.

No, for him, desire had always been an enemy. Something that chipped away at him, that made him want, made him need, and never brought about satisfaction. But not now. Not with her.

Desire was a razor blade, and a knife's edge that cut into him deep, but knowing satisfaction was on the other side made it sweet. Made the pain a delicious indulgence that he could finally afford.

They were both down on the floor on their knees now, kissing like they might die. McKenna shoved lightly at his chest, separating from him. The look in her whiskey-sharp eyes was mischievous. "Get on the couch, cowboy," she said.

"Why?"

"Because I want to do something."

She grabbed hold of his hand and tugged, like she was leading him toward the couch. He pushed up, then sat, just as she commanded. She stood, pressing her knee onto the couch, between his spread thighs, and pushed her hands beneath the hem of his shirt, pushing it up over his head.

His stomach turned to ice when the rings jingled together. He might have left the phone back at his cabin. Might have left that much behind, but he had brought these with him.

They were part of him, in many ways. It would be strange for him to forget to wear them, rather than it actually being a conscious choice for him to put them on.

She looked up at him, her eyes searching. And then she reached out, slipping her hand beneath the rings and pulling them out toward her, examining them in her palm.

"Grant..."

He reached out, cupping the back of her head. "Not here," he said. "Not now."

"I just..."

"This is you and me, McKenna. Nothing else. I need this. I need you." She looked like she was going to argue again. "Please."

He wasn't above begging. Not for this. Not right now.

She nodded slowly and lowered her hand, the rings going back to rest on his chest. McKenna gripped his shoulders, pressing a kiss to his mouth, then to his neck, down to his chest. She kissed down in a line, skipping over the rings that fell just above his abs. Then she moved down to his stomach, and down lower still, her lips skimming the waistband of his jeans.

She flicked the button open, unzipped his fly. And then she reached inside of his underwear, wrapping her hand around his throbbing body. His breath hissed through his teeth, his whole body going tense.

She pushed his underwear down, pushed his jeans down partway and drew him out, stroking him slowly as she kept her eyes on his.

"I want you," she said, her voice thick. "I can't say I've ever really wanted to do this before. But with you…" She leaned in, her tongue a stroke of fire over his erection. "I want it. I want you. I want to taste you. I've never seen a man like you, Grant. I've never had a lover like you before."

He tightened his hold in her hair, clinging to her, trying to keep himself together.

There had never been anyone like her, because there had never been anyone. But it was more than that, and he knew it. Because there had been opportunity, and he never felt moved to take it. Now, with McKenna, he couldn't fathom not being with her like this. She had become like water, like air, so quickly.

But the fact that he was somehow singular to her? That was a damned *miracle*. And it did things to him. Pushed at the edges of his already frayed control. She leaned in again, pulling against his hold, a heavy, thick sound of pleasure building in her throat as she parted her lips and wrapped them around him, slowly taking him in, an agonizing glide of pleasure that he thought might well kill him.

He bucked his hips upward, not able to keep control of himself and immediately relaxed, afraid that he might have done something he shouldn't. But McKenna didn't seem perturbed at all. She looked up at him with those knowing eyes, her hands wrapped around the base of him, her lips and tongue working magic over the rest.

And he lost himself. In this pleasure that was unlike anything he'd ever felt before. The kind of thing he never even let himself want.

The kind of thing that he never imagined could be for him.

Beautiful and hot and wet and just for him.

He didn't know how long he was going to be able to hold back. How long he was going to be able to control himself. And he was bound and determined to make this time last longer than the last time had.

Yes, she'd come twice last time, but he still felt like he owed her more than a couple of quick thrusts once he was inside, and he aimed to give her that this time. But with all the attention she was giving to his body, he wasn't sure he was going to manage it.

"Not like this," he said, his voice rough. "I need you."

She looked up, her lips swollen and red, her eyes bright. "I don't mind if we finish like this."

"I do," he said.

He reached down and picked her up, drawing her up onto his lap so that she was straddling him, the seam of her jeans pressing against his arousal.

She arched forward, kissing him as she rubbed herself against his length, making sweet little sounds in the back of her throat as she did.

He reached behind her and unhooked her bra, unable to stop the growl that rose in his throat when he saw her, bare and gorgeous, in front of him.

He kissed her between the valley of her breasts, then undid her jeans, reaching down inside to find her slick and hot, as he moved his mouth to one tightened bud and drew it in deep.

He pleasured her in both places, sliding his thumb over her clit and pushing his fingers into her while he continued to suck.

She wiggled, squirmed, wrenching her mouth away from him and panting, while she ground her hips against his hand.

"That's right," he said. It was like training a new horse in some ways. There was a lot of coaxing involved, but half of it was for his own benefit. So they could both learn each other. "Come for me," he said, the words a dream to say, the final realization of so many years of fantasy.

There was finally a woman beneath his touch, finally a woman in his arms.

Not just *a* woman.

McKenna.

He had known her for only a little while, but he felt like he had waited for her all his life.

He pretty much had.

Thirty-four years.

He pressed his fingers in deeper, increasing the rhythm, going until she let out a hoarse cry, until her internal muscles pulsed around him.

She collapsed against him, shaking and boneless. "That's not fair," she said. "You wouldn't let me do that for you."

"Yeah," he said, not sure at all how his voice remained steady. "But you can come as many times in a row as I can make you. Men's bodies have limits."

Though he had a feeling his might not, right about now.

He couldn't imagine not being hard for her. Couldn't imagine anything that might take the edge off this. But he wasn't willing to risk it.

He had put three condoms in his wallet for tonight. He had some grand plans, that was for sure. He just had to be certain he was going to get this first time. Just like he wanted.

Buried deep inside her.

He shifted his hips, lifting them up off the couch so that he could get hold of his wallet, and took a packet out.

Then he tore it open and rolled it over his length.

McKenna stood, pushing her jeans down all the way, and then she straddled his lap, the tight, wet heart of her pressing against his sensitized head.

He didn't know about this. Because it put him out of control. If she was in charge of the movements, it might be over a hell of a lot quicker than he wanted it to be. He was about to tell her no, but she began to lower herself down on him and he couldn't say a damn thing. Mostly because his brain didn't work. Not anymore. There was nothing but feeling. Sinking into her body was like a baptism. Something physical that reached down into the spiritual and changed him.

Hell, right about now it felt like it was saving him.

And when she had seated herself on him fully, her head thrown back, her eyes closed, a sound of ecstasy on her lips, it was easy to believe that this was all there was.

He could see her like this, and it was glorious. Her

whole gorgeous body, those round full breasts and the shadow of hair between her legs as she rode him like the confident cowgirl he knew she wasn't.

He bucked up against her, unable to help himself wanting more. Harder. Faster. And McKenna kept up.

She dug her fingernails into his shoulders, the sounds she made getting deeper. Less controlled.

And he matched it. There was nothing civilized about this. Nothing gauzy. It was so bright and real. It was sweat and labored breath, intense heartbeats and slick friction. It was need, so pointed it stabbed right through him. Desire so heavy he thought he might be crushed beneath the weight of it. And yet he wanted more. Even as he thought it might kill him.

This was why men destroyed their lives for sex. It was why they risked scandal, loss, war, to have the woman they desired.

It was like a whole world of knowledge was suddenly revealed to him. Mysteries that had confounded him before suddenly became clear as day.

He cupped her face, his other hand gripping her hip, holding her steady as he drove up into her, reveling in the satisfying sound of flesh meeting flesh. He moved his hand back through her hair, combing his fingers through the silken strands before gathering it in his fist and holding tight, drawing her head back so that he could kiss her neck, so that he could take one of her nipples into his mouth again. Her movements increased, the harsh sound she made more animal than human, and he gloried in it.

Lost himself in it. In her.

He moved his attention to her other breast, circled

her nipple with his tongue before sucking her, and he felt her orgasm break over her again.

And that was all the permission he needed. He gripped both hips now, holding her steady as he drove up inside of her, as he chased his release.

He came on a growl, his entire body pulsing, pleasure consuming him. It was like a cleansing fire, wiping away everything that had come before it, leaving everything burned out, devastated and somehow new even in the destruction.

She curled up against his chest, resting her head over his heart. He swept her hair back from her face, a tangled mess now. They were both a mess. Both deeply and utterly affected by the burn that had just claimed them both.

"I just... I'll be back," he said, shifting and lifting her from his body so that he could go deal with the condom.

He took care of it quickly, then turned on the faucet, filling his palms with water and splashing his face with it.

He braced his hands on either side of the sink, his breathing still heavy. The rings hit the porcelain, and that was when he realized he hadn't taken them off this time.

He straightened and looked up at his reflection. He wasn't sure he knew himself right now. He wasn't sure if he cared. There was something symbolic, he supposed, about forgetting to take the necklace off this time.

It spoke to the baggage he carried with him even if he wanted to leave it behind. To the fact that he couldn't separate what he'd been through in the past with who he was now.

But that didn't mean he wanted to have a conversation about it with McKenna.

Because there was something about her seeing him as a man divorced from all that… Yeah, there was something about that.

She didn't feel sorry for him. She just wanted him. She didn't expect him to be nice. She seemed to like him to be a little bit bad.

He didn't want to lose that.

He walked back out into the living room, gratified when McKenna's eyes roamed hungrily over his body.

There was something deeply satisfying about being lusted after. Not that it had never happened before. Women thought he was good-looking. When he went out, they checked him out. But if they knew who he was, it was always tinged with that sorrowful pity. If they didn't, it was just a passing thing. McKenna was his lover, and she desired him still.

And that was something he had never experienced before.

"Gabe Dalton is my half brother," she blurted.

CHAPTER TWELVE

McKenna didn't know what the hell she was doing.

She felt torn apart and stitched back together loosely, vulnerable and very easily damaged. There was something about the way they'd come together this time. Something deep and emotional. Grant had needed her. Really and truly. He had been radiating with some kind of dark emotion when he had come to the house, and it had only grown more intense.

She shouldn't have asked about the rings again, but she knew—somehow—that whatever he was feeling was related to that.

If he was hung up on an ex it would kill her. Well, not literally but it might feel like something close to death.

The idea that there might be a woman out there that Grant Dodge loved, when all the while he touched her and kissed her like she was a miracle, then… Then maybe she wasn't the miracle.

Maybe he was thinking of the other woman the whole time.

The thought made her want to die inside and it shouldn't matter. Because the sex felt great either way. And shouldn't she just enjoy the passion?

But the very idea still made her feel like she'd been stabbed through the heart.

And she just wanted… She wanted to give him something. Share something. So that maybe he would share with her. So that maybe she could know him.

"Gabe Dalton is your half brother?" he repeated.

"Yes," she said. "But please don't tell anyone. I have to figure out how I'm going to deal with all of this. And I didn't expect… I met him. I didn't expect to just run into him at a coffee shop. But apparently, he knows Jamie, and wants her to work with him. So… They're my family, Grant. They're the only family that hasn't rejected me maybe. I mean, maybe Hank Dalton did. I don't really know. I don't know the story. But Gabe and his brothers… Maybe they don't know. Maybe they don't know they have a sister."

"They're why you came to Gold Valley."

She nodded. "At the very least, I think they can bail me out of my current situation. But that's not… That's not primarily what I want."

"You're looking for family."

"Yes. Though I want… I mean, look, it's not like I think they're going to fold me into a loving embrace. I'm not stupid. If they'd like to have me over for Thanksgiving or whatever sometime, I don't exactly have…better offers. I wouldn't say no. But mostly I think I'll get some…child support or whatever."

"But that isn't what you *want*."

She bit the inside of her cheek, feeling totally naked still even though she was clothed. "I don't know. It's weird being here. Watching the way all of you work together. I want… I just want to be part of something, Grant. I never have been. I've always been the add-on. I've never belonged. But I have family here. I could have… Something. It's hard not to want that. I know better. But this place is weird and it's making…watching your family… It makes me want things I didn't even believe were real before I came out here."

"You know what *this* is, right?" he asked, his tone suddenly biting.

His words gave her whiplash, because she had been trying to build a bridge, and she felt like his retort had knocked down her new construction efforts.

"This?" She pointed to the ceiling. "It's a cabin, I think."

"You and me," he said. "Because when we started this it was based on the idea that I thought I knew exactly what you were here for."

"Wait a second, are you telling me that you don't like the idea I might not just be a stone-cold bitch set out on using people? The fact that I have feelings bothers you, Grant?"

"I can't have a relationship right now."

"That's a real shame, because my life is just a yawning, relationship-shaped void." She said it lightly, but with how lonely she'd been feeling lately, and how badly she wanted to fix it, she was afraid that there was a little bit too much truth in that. But she was not going to show him that. He didn't get to kiss her like she mattered and then dismiss her ten minutes later. She would not be cautioned by him.

It wasn't that she didn't know he had some tragedy in his life. He'd lost his mother, and she felt sympathy for that. Her mother was alive, but she wasn't in Mc-Kenna's life and she knew all about the empty space that left behind.

But he had this place. He had his family. He had more stability, more support, than she could ever imagine having. To her mind he was sheltered. She was not going to have him lecturing her on how the world worked. On how these sorts of relationships worked.

"I didn't want to pick a fight. I just want to make sure we're on the same page."

"You're the casual-sex novice," she said, her tone getting icy. "You're the one that seems to have a problem figuring this out."

"You said you weren't particularly experienced with casual sex, either."

She lifted a shoulder. "I'm not a bar-hookup kind of girl, but I've certainly been in my share of relationships that weren't all about love and lasting commitment. I don't have any problem keeping my emotions out of the bedroom. In fact, I'm not entirely certain they've ever crossed the threshold. And hell, Grant, we've never even been in my bedroom."

"I just…"

"You're just full of this ridiculous savior complex. I didn't ask you to try to make me feel better about what we were doing. I feel pretty damned good about it. Or at least I did until you started acting like you had to put me in my place. You're here. I figured maybe we could talk for a minute. I'm sorry if you're not sure where the line is between conversation and a woman begging for marriage."

"I don't want to hurt you," he said.

"It's adorable that you think you could."

He could and she knew it. And she fought the urge to rub her chest right where her heart was starting to burn. Where all of this felt like a deep, terrible ache. "Worry about yourself," she said. "I want to see what I can make work with the Daltons, but trust me, if they don't want me, I'll take their money and run. Finding out I'm related to rodeo royalty? Now that's a gift for someone in my position. If they don't want to know me? It's no skin off my nose. Someone like me can't afford to be sentimental." She forced a laugh. "I'm a practical person. I've never had my heart broken, Grant. But I've broken a couple."

She'd never broken anyone's heart. No one had ever cared about her enough to have their heart broken by her.

And clearly, that wasn't going to happen here, either.

She wasn't going to let him see that his words left her dented. Anyway, she wasn't going to let them dent her. Maybe it kind of hurt. Because he was hands-down the best lover she'd ever had, and it was tempting—very tempting—to imagine that the focus he applied to her body somehow went deeper. But it didn't. That was fine.

The alternative was living here and not having amazing sex. She would rather have amazing sex.

"I'm not worried," he said.

He was *such an ass*.

"You should probably go," she said. "I don't want you getting the wrong idea."

"You should go talk to the Daltons," he said.

"I'm sorry, why are you giving me advice now? I thought we just agreed that this was physical. Only physical."

"If you want to build a connection here, if you want to find a family, then go find a family, McKenna. Don't hide."

The fury that rose up inside of her was quick and decisive. It compelled her to lash out. Right to the center of his chest. To the most vulnerable target she could think of. "Right. Says the man clinging to tokens from the past, refusing to talk about them, even though he wears them deliberately to his lover's house, where he knows she'll see them. Please, go ahead and lecture me about hiding, Grant. I'll add it to the earlier lecture you gave me on making sure I move forward in my life. You're clearly an expert on both of those things."

He straightened, his expression turning to stone. He said nothing as he gathered his coat, and his hat, clearly getting ready to leave. He sat to put his boots on, the silence getting thick and irritating.

She wasn't losing anything. If he didn't come back after that, what did she care? Plus, he would. The sex was too good. And he was just a guy.

But she didn't have to say yes if he did come back.

She gritted her teeth, ignoring the fact that she wasn't entirely sure she was strong enough to turn him away. She wished she were strong enough. She would really like to be.

"For God's sake, if you're going to storm out you might want to be a little less methodical about it," she said, tapping her foot impatiently as he laced up his work boots.

He looked up at her, those green eyes taking on a winter frost, much like the trees outside. And he didn't move any faster. If anything, he became more deliberate. He was such a jackass.

She stood there, her arms crossed, her foot tapping restlessly. And then Grant finally stood.

He walked out, slamming the door shut behind him, and McKenna let out a primal scream, then bent over and picked up one of the cushions from the couch and flung it across the room.

How dare he? How dare he try to tell her what to do

when he didn't have a damned idea what he was doing. How dare he try to… Let her down easy. How dare he…

She sat down hard on the arm of the couch, then slowly slid backward, falling onto the cushions.

How dare he read her so accurately. How dare he see that she was starting to have feelings for him.

That was the real problem. He wasn't wrong. She did need a reminder that nothing was happening between them. Because while she could say that she didn't want a relationship, and while she knew—if she laid it all out logically in front of her—that she and Grant could never work, could never be together, part of her was starting to want it.

She pressed her hands over her face and scrubbed hard.

Regrettably. Grant was right. About quite a few things.

She didn't regret punching him in the chest—metaphorically—as she'd done. But he was right.

She needed to get down to the business of meeting the Dalton family. Figuring out where she fit there.

If she wanted a family, she would find it there.

She wasn't finding anything with him.

She was just going to have to accept that.

CHAPTER THIRTEEN

APPARENTLY, WYATT'S SPONSORSHIP of the Christmas parade meant a few things for the crew at Get Out of Dodge. First of all, there was the assembly of wreaths and garlands. Second, that Jamie was going to be doing an old drill team routine out ahead of the Girl Scouts during the parade. A fact that had her playing cranky, but Grant thought that she was probably secretly pleased, considering that she was doing it.

Jamie Dodge didn't do a single thing she didn't want to do. She was hardly going to get strong-armed into a parade she didn't want to be in.

But the day before the festivities they found themselves occupying the freshly painted barn, a long table with benches running the length of either side set up as an assembly line for evergreens, bows and fake berries.

Everything had been supplied by the Gold Valley Garden Club, along with a short tutorial on how to do it all. Apparently, several businesses were tasked with assembling various decorations. It seemed to Grant that the whole town was going to be completely buried beneath an overkill of cheer.

Right now, the cheer grated a little bit.

He was still angry about the other night. Angry at McKenna. Angry at himself. There was something about her vulnerability when she had confessed to him that Gabe was her half brother that had…

His first inclination had been to wrap her up in his arms. To ask what he could do. And along with that came a deep, cold fear.

He didn't want to take that responsibility on.

He wanted to be a lover. Nothing else. He'd been everything else. Husband. Caregiver. He'd been in love. Had given his whole heart to someone, and he'd never gotten it back. Would never get it back.

Didn't want to.

Right now, he just wanted to share his body. He wanted something new. Something different. And he didn't mind if they talked. He didn't mind if they got along. In fact, he preferred it. If he had wanted to go out and have a one-night stand he would have done it by now. There was something in it that just didn't appeal.

He liked that McKenna made him laugh. That she was interesting and funny. But he liked all that as a kind of peripheral to the main event.

And when she had started confessing her deep need for a connection…

It wasn't like he hadn't realized that was there. He had. But she was the one who had said she didn't have any grand designs on settling in Gold Valley forever. And hearing her talk about her desire for connections, for a family like that…

He didn't want to be invested in that. He didn't want to get tangled up. He just wanted to make it clear that they were on the same page. But he'd known the moment he opened his mouth he had seriously put his foot in it.

He didn't have any experience fighting with women.

That was the thing. Eight years of marriage and they'd never had a fight. He'd gotten frustrated sometimes, sure. But he'd always felt bad about it later. He'd always pushed it down and dealt with it on his own.

Lindsay didn't need his stress and concern on top of everything else. She certainly didn't need him getting frustrated with her about anything.

Concerns about bills and household repairs, about health insurance…he'd shouldered it. And she'd been a haven from it.

Mostly, the time with her had been peaceful. All that anger he'd walked around with before Lindsay had been put on the back burner during that time.

But McKenna wasn't his wife. And he didn't love her.

That stuff about the rings had been a step too far. She made him rage. And she made him burn.

He wasn't used to either.

He'd avoided her ever since.

Thankfully, she hadn't showed up to the barn yet. He was currently cutting wire to prescribed lengths before passing them down the table to Lindy and Bea, who were busily attaching greenery to said wire, before giving it to Bennett, his son, Dallas, and his wife, Kaylee, to add berries, before it went to Wyatt and Jamie for ribbon.

"Wyatt has a hidden talent," Jamie commented from down the table.

"What's that?" Bennett asked.

"He's wonderful at tying dainty little bows."

Lindy smirked. "That he's good with his hands and good with fine detail is not news to me."

"Agh!" Jamie flung her arm over her eyes. "No. *Please.*"

Wyatt laughed, damn near falling out of his chair. "You have to be careful," he said. "My wife plays dirty. And she's Team Me."

"I am," Lindy agreed.

Wyatt grinned. "Because of my magic hands."

Before McKenna, Grant would have felt... Irritated by the exchange. Not in the way that Jamie was. Not horrified by the fact that his brother had a sex life. But irritated because of his own lack.

That wasn't the case at the moment. Though he might be on the verge of another dry spell if he didn't figure things out with McKenna. Of course, he wasn't sure he wanted to figure things out with McKenna. Or if he should. That was the issue. Right at the moment, he wasn't entirely certain that things should go any further.

"Think of the children," Bennett said, grinning.

"I know you don't mean me, Bennett," Jamie said.

"Obviously, he was referring to me, Aunt Jamie," said Dallas, who at sixteen was hardly a child.

"Obviously," Bennett commented.

Grant huffed out a laugh. He realized that everyone had stopped what they were doing to look at him. "What?"

"You laughed."

"It was funny," Grant said. Everyone kept on staring. *"What?"* he asked.

The barn door opened and McKenna breezed in, barely sparing him a glance. "All right," she said. "I'm ready to help with parade nonsense."

"There's a whole stack of nonsense over there," Wyatt said, indicating the pile of greenery in the corner.

"Thank you," she said, moving confidently through the space and heading over to the greens, taking a seat next to Lindy, and very much not making eye contact with him.

He found that part of her fascinating. She wasn't overly warm, yet she seemed completely at ease in any group of people. He wondered if it had to do with the amount of time she'd spent moving around over the years. The way she'd gone from house to house, school to school.

As someone whose life had been conducted entirely in a ten-mile radius, it fascinated him.

He felt like he couldn't escape all of the connections in his life. Ones that wrapped around him like creeping vines. Holding him together sometimes, supporting him, and threatening to choke the life out of him at other times.

He deliberately avoided looking at McKenna. Instead, he looked down at the end of the table and caught Jamie's eye, offering her a smile. She smiled back and went back to ribbon tying. He wondered how it had ended up that the two of them were the last remaining single ones. Bennett had discovered he had a son a few months ago, and had married his childhood friend, Kaylee. Wyatt and Lindy were the newest happy couple. And even though their surrogate brother, Luke, wasn't here, he was with someone, too.

It made sense that Jamie was the last holdout. She was the baby.

And Grant… Well, back in the beginning he'd been the first to get married. And that was it. Now he was destined to remain single forever.

But he wondered what Jamie thought about all of this. Sometime he might have to ask her.

It hit him again how long it had been since he'd had

a conversation like that with Jamie. Since they'd had a conversation at all. He'd been so wrapped up in his life. In getting every last moment with Lindsay that he could. And then…he'd kind of disappeared into his grief. Back into some of that anger that he'd been mired in when he was in high school. Even if it hadn't taken hold of him in quite the same way as an adult.

Well, he supposed his first clue to all of this could have maybe been when everybody looked at him in absolute shock because he laughed.

It hit him that McKenna might have an easier time sitting down and having a conversation with his family at this point than he did. It wasn't like he didn't talk with his family. When his brothers had been going through things with the women they eventually married, he'd been around to listen. But he didn't share about himself. Ever.

And they'd tried to get him to. They tried to get him to talk about the future, the past. He resisted all of it. He had so many off-limits areas that no one was allowed in.

"We need more cider," Bea commented from over by the refreshment table.

"I'll get it," McKenna said, standing quickly.

"You don't have to get it, McKenna," Bea said.

"It's fine," she responded. "I need to grab myself a snack, anyway. Does anyone else want anything?"

"I'm starving," Dallas said.

"I'll bring cookies and pastries," McKenna said. By now she was intimately acquainted with the contents of the pantry, and the things that they kept on hand at all times.

And Grant knew he had an opportunity here. To either spend some time alone with her, or to avoid her.

He should avoid her. Probably. He should just let the whole thing die a natural death instead of pushing all this.

"I'll help you," he said, setting down the wire cutters and the piece of wire he was working on.

"Thank you," she responded, her smile turning wide and somewhat brittle. It resembled a snarl, really, and he had a concern that he might end up getting savaged once they were out of sight.

But he could take it.

The fact of the matter was, if she was still angry, he had hurt her.

He felt a kick of conscience that he'd been spared up until this moment. He'd been angry at her because of what she'd done, and that had given him a little bit of a pass on his own behavior.

But just like earlier, he could find some middle ground here. He was sure of it. Middle ground between being more cautious with what was happening between them and letting the bridge simply burn away.

And he should make sure that she was okay.

He led the way out of the barn, holding the door for her, then letting it shut behind them.

"I wanted to make sure you were okay," he said.

She halted in her steps, then whirled around. "Excuse me?"

"I wanted to make sure you were okay. After the other night."

Her eyes widened, then she took on a shocked look while she poked her own arm. "I feel normal. Probably fine."

Then she turned away from him and kept on walking toward the mess hall.

"McKenna," he said, his tone warning. "I'm trying to do the right thing here."

"You're welcome to apologize to me," she sniffed, her tone arch.

He was still pissed at her, but honestly, he probably should give her an *I'm sorry*, if only to make her feel better. "I'm sorry."

"Thank you."

"Are you okay?" he asked.

"I'm mad at you."

"I apologized."

She skipped. She actually skipped for two steps. "Doesn't mean you weren't a jerk."

He frowned. "I thought you wanted an apology."

"I will take one. I'm *owed* one. Because you *were* a jerk."

That was just obnoxious. She was so beautiful and annoying. Enraging. She touched him physically in ways no one else had. Made him feel things—intense things. Dark, dirty and sexual. And she made him want to punch a damn wall.

"What about you?" he asked. "And everything you said to me."

"I stand by it," she returned, the words crisp and sharp.

He huffed out a breath that hung in the air like a cloud. "You don't know anything about me."

"Because you choose not to share it," she bit out.

He stopped walking, his heart hammering. "Did you ever think for one second that maybe it's because it's important to me to have a space where someone doesn't know all of my business? Everyone here knows me. Everything about me. My family. Everyone in town. Did you ever think that maybe—"

"No," she said, her voice cold. "I didn't think that. Because we're just having sex, Grant. So, I don't need to think about you. Or your personal life. And you don't need to think about mine."

"I care about what happens with you and the Daltons."

"Don't." The word was flippant and casual. The lightness in her tone, and the anger beneath it, was maddening.

He reached out and grabbed hold of her, stopping her in her tracks. "What can I do to fix this?"

"You can't. I'm angry at you. I have every right to be."

"Maybe I can talk to the Daltons…"

"No. Stop it. I don't need you to fix this. I don't need you to fix me."

The words hit hard, just about knocked him on his ass. He didn't want to fix her, anyway. This was what he was trying to avoid. He didn't want to get in deeper with her. Be a fixer, a caretaker… And she…

She didn't need him to.

"I'm not trying to fix you," he said.

She shook her head. "You don't know what you're trying to do."

That was truer than he would like it to be. He knew what he wanted. At least, what he thought he wanted. And what he felt like he should do. They were two different things.

That, he supposed, was the thing about living a somewhat stagnant existence. You didn't have to make big decisions very often. And because you didn't make a lot of big decisions, or a lot of big changes, there wasn't a lot of questioning involved.

When he had decided to sell his house, had decided to quit his job and work on the ranch, that hadn't been hard at all. He'd known exactly what he wanted. He wasn't used to this.

He didn't know what the hell to do.

"I guess… I guess we're done, then," she said.

She squared her shoulders and pushed open the door to the mess hall, looking around to see if anyone was there. It was empty.

"Why?" he asked.

"We're mad at each other."

"We're just having sex. Why does anger have to stop it?"

"Because 'just sex' should be a lot less… of this."

"You really want to be done?" he asked.

"Yes."

His face felt like it had been struck with a hot iron. He had been ready for this. For her to tell him it was over. At least, he had thought so. But it turned out he really wasn't quite ready for it. Right then, he felt like he would give just about anything for another night in her arms. But it was getting to be too much. Too tangled. And the fact that he was confused about what he wanted in his head and what his emotions seemed to want from him was as good an indicator as any that it needed to be done.

"Just like that?"

"I mean, just like a huge fight the other night after a tentative beginning and a whole lot of missteps. You're a great lover, Grant. The best I've ever had. I don't see the point in lying to you about that. But this… It's not worth it. You're right. I need to focus on what I'm doing with the Daltons. Not with you."

He gritted his teeth and fought against the desire running through his veins, hot and reckless. The desire to push her up against a wall and show her none of this was okay. To show her that the physical connection was enough. To convince himself of it, too.

Instead, he nodded. "Okay."

He didn't want this to be the end. He wanted to push. Wanted to take back what he'd said, to tell her it didn't matter if they didn't see eye to eye right now, they could still talk using their bodies, and that was good enough.

But the fact that he wanted to do that so badly told him he had to let it go.

The fact that it made him feel like he was being torn apart was all the evidence he needed that it had to be finished.

"Great." He stalked back to the kitchen and grabbed pastries and cookies, and when he came out, McKenna was fussing with a Crock-Pot that had cider inside. "Trade," he said, handing her the cookies and picking up the heavy Crock-Pot.

They headed back toward the barn, neither of them saying anything. When they reached the door, McKenna stopped. "I had a good time," she said. "Most of the time."

"Me, too," he said.

This really was for the best. She never had to know about him. Or when she did inevitably find out about the life he'd had before she'd arrived in town, there would be distance between them, and he would never have to talk to her about it.

Anyway, he'd done it. He'd had sex. He'd torn the

Band-Aid off. There was no need to have an awkward conversation with anyone about his stubborn virginity, because it was gone.

And if nothing else, he would always be grateful for that.

Even if he could never tell her.

"I wish you the best, McKenna Tate," he said.

She forced a smile. "And I kind of wish you'd go fuck yourself, Grant Dodge."

And on that, she pushed open the barn door and slammed it shut behind her, leaving him alone outside.

CHAPTER FOURTEEN

MCKENNA WAS TIRED, grumpy and gritty by the time she and Jamie headed over to the parade.

She thought deeply about backing out of helping. After all, it was actually her day off. But Jamie had seemed like she wanted her to come and McKenna really didn't want to do anything to reject the younger woman's friendship.

The simple excuse for that was because she was going to try to finagle an invitation to the Dalton ranch. If Jamie was going to be working there, then McKenna figured she could use that to her advantage.

But the reality of the situation was...

She was lonely. The Dodge family made her feel less lonely.

Not so much Grant. Who was the reason for her terrible night's sleep, and the fact that she felt grumpy and her eyes felt like they'd been rubbed with sand.

You're the one who put an end to things.

Maybe she was. But Grant had had one foot out the door about the time he lectured her on what all this really was. She had known what was coming. She'd been broken up with enough times in the past to know how it was all going to go down.

Why draw it out?

It had been fun. It had felt good. She'd been celibate for three years and she had broken that spectacularly with him. She should just focus on that. That he'd shown her something new in terms of passion. Something new about herself.

It was a growth opportunity.

Or something.

McKenna was jittery and keeping herself from pacing while she waited by the barn, next to Jamie's truck and horse trailer.

Jamie emerged finally, leading her horse into the trailer, her dark hair in her signature braid, a white hat on her head. She had on a fitted navy blue top with white fringe.

"I know," she said when she popped out of the trailer and shut the gate. "It's a little over the top. It's what I used to wear when I was on drill team."

It wasn't remotely over the top, but McKenna realized that she'd never seen Jamie in anything that didn't skim loosely over her figure, so she wondered if the shirt made her uncomfortable.

"I think it's great," McKenna said. "You look like a rodeo cowgirl."

"I'm not a real one. Maybe someday," Jamie responded, smiling. Then she rolled her eyes. "A little bit awkward to be leading the Girl Scouts in the parade. But fun."

Wyatt and Lindy had gone early with the greenery they'd spent yesterday assembling, and to man the booth that would have free cider, hot chocolate and roasted chestnuts.

McKenna wasn't sure what Grant's responsibility was in all this. Maybe he was holding down the fort. Maybe she wouldn't have to see him today.

She kept her eyes fixed on the trees that lined the side of the road while they took the winding two-lane that led downtown.

"I think it's really great," McKenna said. "The way that you all get involved with the community."

"It's home," Jamie said. "I like things like this. It makes me feel… Connected. It was hard. Growing up without my mother. And I think for a while… I dreamed about running away. About having a different life. I… It's hard. To know that your birth caused your mother's death, McKenna. It doesn't matter whether it was my fault, really. It's just… Because I exist she's gone. That was really lonely for a long time."

The way Jamie talked, McKenna had to wonder if it was still lonely. If anyone understood that. If anyone realized. Her first instinct was to tell her that of course that wasn't true. That of course it wasn't her fault at all. But Jamie was twenty-four years old and she felt that way now, had for a long time. Obviously, if trite, simple words were enough, they would have already been enough.

"I know what it's like to be alone," McKenna said. "And feel like maybe you're responsible for something not so great. I don't have any great insight into how to escape that. I just… I get it."

"In the end, it's Gold Valley that helps me not feel quite so lonely," Jamie said. "Roots. A sense that I belong here. That I can…matter."

McKenna shifted, resting her elbow on the armrest and looking out the window. "I'd like to find that."

"Well, this is a pretty good place to start."

McKenna was starting to think it might be.

When they rolled into town there was already giant

orange detour signs set up on the four-way stop. They were rerouted around the back of the cute little buildings on Main, down past the fire station, as well as an old, rickety barn that had been standing since the mid-1800s and currently served as an art studio. They went around the back of the historic, brick post office, and back up the street, where they could park behind Sugar Cup. Those side streets were lined with groups of people all getting ready.

McKenna waited while Jamie got her horse out and saddled up, mounting before they began to make their way down the streets that were serving as the staging area.

Bright orange cones were set beside each group marching in the parade, with a number placed on each.

The fire trucks were already being decorated with boughs of evergreen with two large wreaths hanging from the grilles in front of the vehicles, while the firemen were decked out in their red suspenders, black shirts and Santa hats.

There was a large section blocked off for a classic-car club, with members coming from all over the state, and also from Washington and California, to drive their cars through the parade. From two-tone cars with chrome detailing and fins, to old milk trucks and cars that would be at home in a gangster movie from the 1930s.

There was a group of men in kilts, warming up their bagpipes, their legs bare in spite of the cold.

McKenna wrapped herself more deeply into her coat, looking around at the unusual amount of bustle as she, Jamie and the horse continued on to the number they'd been assigned. They passed a crew of young marines in their camouflage fatigues, all boys except for one stern-faced-looking girl with her hair pulled back in a bun, her hand wrapped tightly around the American flag.

There was an intertribal dance group from the high school rehearsing their routine, dressed head to toe in buckskin with bright fringes and elaborate headdresses.

Down past a one-man band was a local motorcycle club predominantly made up of retirees who did charity rides, along with the high school drill team for the Cub Scouts, the Gold Valley Garden Club and a crew of Girl Scouts dressed as cookies. The girls stared up at Jamie, bright-eyed, and Jamie dismounted, talking to the girls about the horse, and about the routine she would be doing, and how they could join a drill team, too, someday. She gestured down the way at the high school girls, their horses even flashier than Jamie's, with glitter on their rumps.

McKenna felt at loose ends, and wondered if she should go find Wyatt and Lindy and take a shift in the cider booth. "I'm going to wander," she said, touching Jamie's shoulder.

She picked her way through the festivities, down onto the main street, to the area by the Christmas tree, which remained as yet unlit. There were several booths set up. A big one from Mustard Seed Café where there was chili in bread bowls on offer, and another from Sugar Cup with coffee. There were other booths, too, with crafts from local artisans, and down at the end was free cider and roasted chestnuts, a station currently being helmed by Wyatt and Lindy.

There was also a man in a wheelchair next to the booths, black cowboy hat on his head, and a tall, overly familiar figure with his back facing her. Based on the conversations she'd heard bits and pieces of over the past weeks, she assumed the man in the wheelchair was Lindy's brother, who had been injured in the rodeo a few months earlier.

He looked like her, though he was definitely an extremely masculine version.

"Hi," she said, registering the exact moment Grant realized she was the one standing behind him. His shoulders went stiff. But he didn't turn. Not quickly.

"Hi, McKenna," Lindy said. "Come back here and grab a cup of cider. You can be the nut girl for a while."

McKenna smirked. "The nut girl. That sounds dirty."

"It's not dirty at all. We just need you to handle the hot nuts," Lindy returned.

McKenna lifted a brow and shot another look at Grant's stubborn back. "Is that all? I think I can handle some hot nuts."

Grant finally did turn then, and his expression was baleful. "Is Jamie ready to go?" he asked.

"Yes," McKenna responded. "She is."

She looked down slightly at the man she assumed was Lindy's brother. He was stunningly handsome.

His face, sculpted and beautiful, was also marred by a collection of scars. His eyes were blue, the same shade as Lindy's, but there was no happiness in them. Not right now. They were flat.

"I'm McKenna," she said, sticking her hand out. "Let me guess, you're Lindy's brother?"

That did earn her a slight smile. "She might call you out for insulting her," he said, shaking her hand steadily. "I'm Dane."

"Nice to meet you, Dane," she said.

"Likewise," he said, but she wasn't sure if he meant it.

Not that she took it personally. She had a feeling it had nothing to do with her and everything to do with him.

"Where's Bea?" he asked.

His casual query about Bea made McKenna wonder…

It just made her wonder if he might be the man Bea was hung up on.

"She's walking with the Humane Society," Lindy said. "They're having her wrangle what I think she called…a passel of corgis."

"She must be in heaven," Dane said, a smile tipping his lips up just a bit.

She didn't get the sense that his inquiry about Bea had anything to do with him having sexual feelings for her. But he could see that he had a soft spot for Bea. Though it looked much more brotherly than anything else.

If he was the guy Bea had a thing for…

Well, McKenna felt a little sorry for her.

"Why don't you take her some cider," Lindy said, thrusting a cup of it at her brother.

His face went stony. "If I was going to navigate all around I would have brought some crutches."

"It's treacherous," Lindy said, "and I'm pretty sure you can get over there in the chair just fine. You're not steady enough on crutches right now."

"You're not my doctor, Lindy."

"No," Lindy said. "But you're a dumbass man who isn't trustworthy enough to look after his own recovery."

"Good to know you feel that way."

"You were dumbass enough to ride broncs, Dane,

and it's why you're here. So, maybe be a little bit less defensive."

"Hey," Wyatt said, looking at his wife. "That was kind of my thing, too."

"And you quit before you broke yourself."

"I'll be back at it as soon as I'm not broken," Dane said, taking the cider from his sister and maneuvering his chair the other direction. "I'll be back."

Lindy made a growling sound when Dane was out of sight. "I didn't mean to be hard on him. It just kills me to see him that unhappy."

"He's fine," Wyatt said. "I mean, he'll be fine with you giving him a hard time. Honestly, someone has to give him a hard time. You're right, he needs to take care of himself."

"He'll do better when he can work again. When he isn't going stir-crazy living by himself over at the winery and not going anywhere."

She was… She was completely unable to remain unaffected by the way they all cared about each other. To have a family like that, to have a safety net like that… She couldn't imagine it. This was all twining together with what Jamie had said earlier about this place. About it being home. Roots, even when she felt disconnected from the people around her.

It made McKenna long for something she didn't have a name for.

Or, at least, things she didn't want to name.

"I came to see if you wanted a break," McKenna said. "If you want to go watch the parade…"

"We can see it from here," Wyatt said.

"Sure," McKenna said, "but if you want to go look at the booths or anything…"

Lindy let out a breath, seeming to fortify herself. "I'd like a break," she said. "Thank you. You want to walk around, Wyatt?"

"That's not a question," Wyatt said, addressing both McKenna and Grant. "You okay to hold down the fort?"

Wyatt took his wife's hand, and the two of them wandered off down the row of vendor booths.

"We meet again," McKenna said, eyeing Grant from her position behind the table.

"So we do," Grant said.

"Did you sleep well last night?"

He snorted. "You know I didn't."

"Well. That's the price you pay for being an asshole."

He laughed. "I don't know what the hell to do with you."

"What do you mean?"

"Most people avoid uncomfortable conversations. You tend to just dive right in."

"Uncomfortable conversations are the only truly interesting conversations, Grant. What's the alternative?"

A couple dressed in matching knit scarves and black wool coats walked up to the booth and treated Grant to strangely intense smiles before following them up with a request for cider.

"I'm the nut girl," McKenna said.

The woman didn't look amused, so McKenna grinned back, hoping she managed to infuse as many pointy edges into her own smile, and got two cups.

"How are you?" the woman asked, her tone like that of a small child talking to a puppy, directed at Grant.

"Good," Grant said, his answer strangely definitive.

"Aw. Good to hear," the woman said.

"Take care of yourself," the man said, and the two of them left.

"Anyway," McKenna said. "The alternative would be the two of us standing here pretending that we didn't have a fight yesterday. Pretending we've never seen each other naked. That's just silly. It's one thing to lie to other people. Why lie to ourselves? We were there."

"I don't want to have this discussion in town in front of everyone."

"Is everyone looking at us?" She looked around theatrically. "It doesn't seem like they are."

The woman that she had seen at the Mustard Seed booth came over to the cider station just then, a smile on her face, concern lurking in her dark eyes. "Hi, Grant," she said. "How are you doing, honey?"

"Just fine, Lucinda," he responded.

She reached out, her dark hand covering his, and gave it a squeeze. "Good to hear."

She released her hold on him, then turned her focus to McKenna. "I don't think we've met."

"McKenna Tate," McKenna said, sticking her hand out. "I'm working at Get Out of Dodge."

"Nice to meet you," she said, looking between Grant and McKenna. "Come by and get some chili on the house later."

When Lucinda was back at her station, McKenna turned to Grant. "You're popular," she said. "Which calls into question some of your statements about your jackassery."

"They feel sorry for me," he said, his voice rough.

"They feel sorry for you?"

"It's pity. It's not friendliness. There is a difference."

She thought back to what he'd said yesterday. About

not wanting her to know about his past because he liked for her to be disconnected from it.

"Grant..."

"I'm a widower," he said. "It's over between us, so there's no reason not to tell you. It's not a secret."

She felt like she'd been punched in the stomach. A pain that grew into a twisting vine that made her entire body hurt. She had seen the rings. She knew there was someone else. She had known there was a marriage. She had come up with other scenarios, but she had never thought...

That his wife had died.

"I'm sorry," she said.

He let his head fall back and the sound he made was somewhere between a laugh and a sigh. "So is everyone else. All the time."

She looked away from him, not sure what the hell to say to that. To anything.

He'd lost his wife.

That realization echoed in her head, louder and louder, like building thunder.

They continued to give out cider, working in stilted silence, their elbows brushing sometimes as they moved around, heat igniting in her blood each and every time.

She was turning over everything he'd said to her in a totally new light. That he didn't do casual sex. Of course not. He'd been married.

He'd loved someone enough to marry them. And he hadn't chosen to be without that person.

It made her feel small and insignificant. Because she was not the kind of woman that...

She blinked hard, embarrassed at how emotional she was getting over the whole thing. Over him.

"It's nice to see you here, Grant."

She looked up to see an older woman with blond hair that had gray streaks around her temples, her blue eyes kind, but sad. There was a man standing next to her, gray all over. His hair, his complexion, his eyes.

She felt, rather than saw, the intense gathering of energy within Grant. And then he moved from behind the table, around to the other side, where he pulled the woman into a hug, and shook the man's hand. "Hi, Connie," he said. "I'm sorry I didn't call you back. I haven't made it up yet with the poinsettias."

"It's okay," she said, her voice thin. "I think Cooper will help me."

But McKenna knew that it wasn't fine. She could tell by the nervous way the woman held herself, the way her voice trembled slightly.

"Is Cooper here?"

"No," she said, "he's coming into town tonight. He's going to miss the tree lighting."

"Well, let me know if you end up needing me," Grant said.

"It should be fine," the man said, his tone firm, his hand on his wife's arm. "We don't want to trouble you, Grant. We know you have a family. And that you have obligations to them around the holidays."

McKenna felt like the man was speaking for his wife's benefit.

"You're still family," Grant said, his tone heavy.

A cold feeling hit McKenna in the chest and spread outward. She knew. Without having to be told who they were. And she suddenly realized the counterpoint to these roots. A whole weight could be tied to them, could drag you down.

Grant couldn't be out in public without being reminded. He had to tell her because of the way people treated him... Like he was a wounded puppy.

And if she guessed correctly, these were his in-laws. His former in-laws.

The woman looked at McKenna, her blue eyes suddenly taking on a sharp light. "Who is this?"

"Her name is McKenna Tate," Grant said, keeping his voice even. "She's working over at the ranch."

"Yes," McKenna said, keeping her hand wrapped firmly around the ladle. "I'm McKenna Tate. I work at the ranch." Her repetition of what Grant had just said was silly, and probably sounded self-conscious. "We are just manning the station until Wyatt and Lindy get back."

She was protesting too much, and she kind of knew it. But for some reason, the overexplanation seemed to placate the woman.

"Merry Christmas," the man said.

He guided his wife away from the booth, and McKenna stared after them.

"Were they..."

"My in-laws," he said. "Lindsay's parents."

Lindsay.

His wife's name was Lindsay.

"Grant..."

"Let's not talk about it," he said, his tone hard, decisive.

She nodded, then immediately had to paste a smile on her face when another person came up to get cider and chestnuts.

When they left, she turned toward him. He was very determinedly not looking at her.

She opened her mouth to say something else, and he cut her off. "The parade is about to start. I should go watch Jamie."

"Okay," she said.

And she watched Grant walk into the small crowd that had gathered for the spectacle. She had the strangest feeling he had taken a part of her heart with him.

CHAPTER FIFTEEN

GRANT SAT DOWN on the curb, somewhat gratified by the discomfort he felt when the concrete bit into his ass, and the cold bled through his jeans, threatening to freeze his balls right the hell off.

He rested his forearms on his knees and settled in as the mayor welcomed everybody to the parade and kicked off the festivities with "The Star-Spangled Banner" sung by the elementary school choir. For that, Grant stood and put his hat over his heart. But then he sat back down, welcoming that pain in his butt again, because it served as a reminder of the fact that his current situation was exactly that.

The parade began with the fire department, and all the little kids around him went slack-jawed over the vision of the giant red truck wrapped in tinsel. Not that he could blame them. He remembered that. When simple wonder had been only a giant backhoe or a fire truck away.

He hadn't particularly enjoyed being a child. After all, it hadn't been the happiest time at his house.

But there was something about that wonder you felt when you were a kid that he envied sometimes.

He thought back to McKenna. To the first time he'd seen her naked.

Okay. Maybe it wasn't a fire truck that made him

"FAST FIVE" READER SURVEY

Your participation entitles you to:
✴ 4 Thank-You Gifts Worth Over $20!

Complete the survey in minutes.

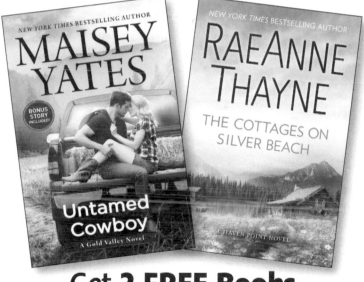

Get 2 FREE Books

See inside for details.

Dear Reader,

Since you are a lover of our books, your opinions are important to us... and so is your time.

That's why we made sure your **"FAST FIVE" READER SURVEY** can be completed in just a few minutes. Your answers to the five questions will help us remain at the forefront of women's fiction.

And, as a thank-you for participating, we'd like to send you **4 FREE THANK-YOU GIFTS!**

Enjoy your gifts with our appreciation,

Pam Powers

To get your
4 FREE THANK-YOU GIFTS:

✴ Quickly complete the "Fast Five" Reader Survey
and return the insert.

"FAST FIVE" READER SURVEY

1 Do you sometimes read a book a second or third time? ○ Yes ○ No

2 Do you often choose reading over other forms of entertainment such as television? ○ Yes ○ No

3 When you were a child, did someone regularly read aloud to you? ○ Yes ○ No

4 Do you sometimes take a book with you when you travel outside the home? ○ Yes ○ No

5 In addition to books, do you regularly read newspapers and magazines? ○ Yes ○ No

YES! I have completed the above Reader Survey. Please send me my 4 FREE GIFTS (gifts worth over $20 retail). I understand that I am under no obligation to buy anything, as explained on the back of this card.

194/394 MDL GM3Z

FIRST NAME	LAST NAME

ADDRESS

APT.#	CITY

STATE/PROV.	ZIP/POSTAL CODE

go slack-jawed anymore. A pair of nice breasts sure did it, though.

Breasts he no longer had access to, so there was no point in thinking about them. And if he hadn't been reasonably certain they were done before, he was sure now. Things had gotten real. She had seen exactly what his life was like here. And she knew. Well, not everything. But either way, she had crossed out of the realm of fantasy and straight into the real hell that was his life.

The parade had moved on, a cavalcade of classic cars driving slowly down the main road, and he knew that bagpipes weren't far behind, because even though they weren't in view he could already hear them.

Right then, a boot touched his hand. He looked down at the familiar, ratty brown shoes. And then, a moment later, McKenna sat next to him. "Wyatt and Lindy came back," she said, her fingers curling around the curb.

"Is that so?"

"Yes. So they sent me off to enjoy the parade. I figured I would find you."

"Why exactly?"

She lifted a shoulder. "Just because."

"Because you feel sorry for me?"

"Maybe," she said, edging closer, the worn toe of her boot touching up against his. "Can you honestly tell me that you've helped me without feeling sorry for me at all?"

"We've talked about this," he said. "I don't feel particularly sorry for you. I'm sorry that you've had it rough, but people have had it harder."

"You, you mean," she said.

"My wife."

He wished that he hadn't said it quite like that. Because her face went slightly ashen, and her lips were tight. "I'm sure," she said. "I'm just... Pity isn't a bad thing, Grant. Pity is the one thing that has gotten me this far in life. Even when people do things out of the goodness in their hearts, the root of it is always that they feel sorry for you. For something or someone. That kind of has to exist for people to want to help. I wouldn't have had a place to live or food to eat if people didn't pity me off and on over the years. And you know what happens when they don't? A lot of times it's all sneering, or it's..."

She swallowed hard, her pale hands clasped together tightly. "Or it's men like my last ex. Who was happy to have me living with him and sharing the burden of bills, but also happy to tell me all the time what a waste of space I was. And how I was a pretty disappointing lay for someone who costs so damned much money. It's either charity or someone is making trades. And believe me, the trade thing really sucks."

"So does pity," he said. "Trust me on that. She died eight years ago, McKenna. But when people see me they think of her. And I can't even be upset about that. Because I don't want her to be forgotten. But I can't go out without being reminded. It's the word that's attached to my name. *Widower.* That's what I am. When people run into me in the store, and they know me but their friend doesn't, when they walk away from me, I know they say, 'That's Grant Dodge, his wife is dead.' They still ask me how I am in that way they do."

She nodded slowly. "I mean, I noticed. You know, the people were very concerned for your well-being. And as someone who has never had a very large amount of people concerned for her well-being, it stuck out to me."

Jamie rounded the corner then, on the back of her horse, holding an American flag, a trail of Girl Scouts throwing candy behind her. Grant lifted his hand and waved at his sister, who couldn't acknowledge him with a wave, but did smile. Then he saw a small jolt in her face as she looked between himself and McKenna.

He realized then that they were sitting closer than acquaintances normally would. But then, they were also crammed into a crowd of people. Still, he didn't make any effort to put distance between them.

"There's more to me than that," Grant said.

Though, right then, he wasn't sure if he believed it. There hadn't been more to him for quite some time. And while some of that was easy to blame on circumstances, some of that was him.

"But it's a pretty big part of you," McKenna said softly. "Would you rather I not feel anything about it?"

He met her gaze. "We weren't supposed to feel anything about any of this."

"Sure," she said. "But admit it, even though you're kind of a hard-ass you feel a little bit sorry for me, too."

"No," he said.

"I'm an abandoned child who spent years being shuffled about from home to home. My last boyfriend stole my money and punched a hole in the wall of the apartment. Not because we were fighting, mind you. But because he lost the Xbox game he was playing. He didn't feel that passionately about me. Not even close. Hell, if we'd had a fight that rated him punching the wall, the rest of our relationship might not have been so boring."

"Well…"

"You know what I think?" she asked.

"I'm sure that you're going to tell me."

"I think that pity isn't really the bad thing. I think it's whether or not it's the only thing. You're right. You're more than that. So am I. Sometimes it feels like that's all I am, because I'm dealing with the fallout of it all the time. I had a rough start in life, and that's translated into a rough everything in life. I've never had support, so I had to figure out how to be on my own. I didn't have anyone sitting down and teaching me how to do adult things, so it's been a constant learning curve. Figuring out how to open a bank account, how to write a check. Stupid things that other people just know. But those are my circumstances. And I like to think that I'm a hell of a lot bigger than they are."

She cleared her throat. "I understand why you wanted… I mean, I can understand why you didn't tell me. I saw the way everyone talked to you. And I get why you didn't really want me to join in their number. But I'm also glad I know."

She turned toward him, her dark eyes serious, and she reached out, pressing the exact spot where the rings rested against his skin.

"You know, I was convinced that you must know," he said.

"Why would I know?"

"Well, my sister has a big mouth. But then…" He hesitated. But she already knew, so there was no point in her not hearing the whole story. "Lindsay and I got married when we were eighteen. She was ill. At the time… They really didn't know how much longer she would live. She was very, very sick at the wedding."

"And you married her… You married her knowing that she might die?"

He shook his head. "I married her knowing she was *going* to die, McKenna."

There was persistently cheery Christmas music playing in the background as a jazz dance troupe went by, and it made a very strange backdrop to the topic of the conversation.

"Everyone dies," he said.

He echoed the words he had told Lindsay, over and over again. He wasn't sacrificing anything marrying someone who was going to die. It was something everyone had to contend with. The biggest burden was knowing they couldn't be together as long as most couples.

"You know what I mean," McKenna said. "You married her knowing that she was going to die before you."

"I knew that, barring a freak accident, it was very likely the scenario, yes."

"Grant…"

"I'm not a saint," he interrupted. "But there was some national media outlet that picked it up, and I ended up on all those websites that collect feel-good stories and things like that. Not so much when we first married, but when she died. When she actually died, that was when everybody read the inspirational story. And they featured it on a morning news program and it… I never wanted that." He said those words with a hefty amount of disdain. "And that's what people know me from. And people love… They *do* feel sorry for me, McKenna. They do. But they also love a tragedy that isn't theirs. It's romantic to them. Because they're not the ones that watched someone they loved suffer and struggle for years. Fade in and out, depending on whether a treatment was working or wasn't. Or whether or not the cancer had come back in a new place. They're not the ones that waited for test results, and then more orders, and more test results."

"Damn," McKenna said. "Cancer. I'm sorry."

"Me, too," he said.

"Was she ever well?"

He shook his head. "Not really. We would get a few scattered months of remission here and there. But there was always something. She was on so much chemo for so long her immune system was completely screwed."

The grand finale was just starting to come down the parade route, a float put together by the garden club, covered entirely in flowers and evergreens, lights. There was a crescendo of music, and everybody around them began to stand.

"We never had sex," Grant said.

McKenna froze, the two of them the only people seated on the entire street.

"What?"

"I was never able to have sex with my wife. When we got married she was very nearly dead. That all hit so fast... I swear to God, if I would have known I would have quit being such a gentleman and had her before. But I didn't know. She got sick, and everything went downhill fast after that. It didn't seem like she was responding to treatment. We got married. Knowing that there was just no way we could be together. Not like that. But then she pulled through. And I was grateful. But there was never... There was always an infection risk. And when there wasn't... Her body hurt. She had nerve damage. Neuropathy. Her skin was sensitive to the point where... Touching didn't feel good. It's unusual to have it happen like that. But that was our reality. That was... Nobody knows that."

McKenna nodded slowly, but he wasn't entirely sure she understood.

He started to stand, but she grabbed his arm. "Grant… You… You hadn't been with… Grant, were you a virgin?"

Nice to know that his male ego was so strong that even while the topic centered around deeply emotional things he'd never spoken of, he managed to feel a stab of humiliation right in the center of his chest.

"Yes."

McKENNA'S EARS WERE BUZZING, but Grant had stood up to applaud the end of the parade, and right after that it seemed like Jamie had appeared, followed closely by Bea. And they were all being ushered back toward the cider booth, where Dane and Wyatt and Lindy were waiting.

She was having difficulty processing the entire conversation she just had with Grant. From the story about his wife, to the fact that he had married someone who had been ill, and had been ill for their entire marriage. To the fact that he had been a virgin.

The sexy, gorgeous man—who was hands-down the best lover she'd ever had—had been a virgin.

She was the only woman he'd ever been with. And she had no idea how to wrap her mind around that.

She'd lost her virginity in high school, in the back-seat of her homecoming date's car. It hadn't even been prom. Which would have at least had some cachet. It had been awkward and she'd found it vaguely distasteful.

But she'd enjoyed the fact that someone had wanted her.

That he'd been excited to be with her.

She hadn't even been annoyed about not having an orgasm. She hadn't even known to want one.

There hadn't been anyone for her to talk to, to tell her how things should be. The closest thing she'd gotten was a foster mother who had taken the girls down to the county office and told them how to get free birth control there. Then proceeded to tell them they'd better all start taking it.

Which McKenna had done, because God knew she didn't want to bring a kid into her sad life. She couldn't even take care of herself, let alone anyone else.

She could not reconcile her early experience with sex with… What had happened between herself and Grant.

And she also had to not be thinking about that, because she was surrounded by his entire family, and it was weird.

"Once we're finished up here why don't we all head back to the ranch for a barbecue?" Wyatt asked. "I'll invite Luke and Olivia, and Bennett, Kaylee and Dallas."

"Sounds good," Lindy said, her eyes on Dane. "Are you up for it?"

"I can eat," Dane said, his tone hard.

Bea was looking on hopefully. "Of course you're invited, too, Bea," Lindy said.

"Thank you," she responded.

She practically glowed when in Dane's presence, and it was so painfully obvious to McKenna that she almost felt sorry for her. The girl had no chill.

She looked to the left and saw that Jamie was looking at her, and she had to wonder if she was currently lacking chill herself. She didn't think that she was staring after Grant in wide-eyed wonderment. Even though she felt a bit of wide-eyed wonderment where he was concerned.

No one knows this.

Those gruffly spoken words echoed inside of her. No one in his family knew that he'd never been with a woman before. No one knew that he hadn't been able to sleep with his wife.

She was suddenly so curious about who that woman was. A woman that a man would stay with like that when he couldn't even get sex. No man had ever been willing to do such a thing for her, no man would. It had been very clear in all of her relationships that that was basically what she brought to the table. That and whatever meager earnings she got from her waitressing job.

Was that love? Something that held you together like glue when all those other things that usually stuck you to someone didn't hold?

She pondered that while they packed up the stand and tore everything down. While she got into the truck with Jamie to head back to the ranch. She had wanted to drive with Grant but she knew that it would seem strange, and obvious. They were going to have to talk later.

She was going to have to make it through a large group dinner. Which she didn't really want to do.

"So," Jamie said, once they were on the road. "You have a thing for my brother?"

McKenna blinked, whipping her head toward Jamie. "Excuse me?"

"I saw you. With Grant. During the parade. Your shoulders were touching."

"It was crowded," McKenna said, feeling like a jack-ass. She shouldn't lie to Jamie, but she didn't exactly want to blurt out that she'd had amazing sex with Grant and now it was over, but today he had told her some things and her feelings were about to boil over.

Mostly because she doubted Jamie wanted to hear it. And also because… Everything she and Grant had discussed today was off-limits. And now that she knew that Grant had never been with a woman before her, the sex felt especially personal, too.

She wanted to cover him up. To protect him.

She wanted to keep that conversation between the two of them.

"There was space. You were touching him pretty deliberately."

McKenna gritted her teeth. "He's been really nice to me," she said.

"He's had it really hard," Jamie said. "I mean, he's had his heart broken and—"

"Are you… Warning me off your brother because you think I might hurt him?"

"I love Grant. I don't want to see him hurt. Not after everything he's been through."

"I've heard of overprotective older brothers, but not so much overprotective younger sisters."

Jamie let out an exasperated sound. "I told you. They didn't have a mother because of me, and I know they like to think they protect me but… I do a damn lot of protecting them actually. I like you, McKenna, but Grant—"

"I know about his wife," McKenna said. "I would never hurt Grant, Jamie. Not in a million years. He's one of the nicest men I've ever met." When he wasn't being a tool. "And honestly, just knowing a nice man is… Kind of revolutionary for me. But I know who I am.

And I know who he is. I know that… Nothing would ever happen." Nothing real. Nothing lasting.

Not with him. Not for her.

Everything about him made a lot more sense now that she knew his wife had died, and not only died, but that he'd been taking care of her for so many years. That he'd lived with a dark specter of grief even before he lost her.

That was the one thing about living the kind of life McKenna had. She'd never loved anyone enough to be devastated by the loss of them. Life just kind of went on.

She just got moved to another family, found another roommate, found another boyfriend. An endless rotation of cookie-cutter people to fill the space that the last person had been in.

Grant wasn't like that.

And it suddenly made all the sense in the world why he'd been so strange after they'd made love the first time. She was the first woman he'd been with. And all that time he hadn't been with anyone, and he could have been. Which made… Maybe it made her matter. Maybe it made her not a cookie-cutter person.

She felt a fragile sliver of hope begin to cut through the heavy, dark feeling in her chest and she pushed it back. She didn't need that. She didn't need hope.

Not about him.

She needed to save it for everything that lay ahead in her life.

The fact of the matter was, Jamie was right to be concerned. But not because she would ever hurt Grant. But because she needed to be reminded just why she couldn't get in too deep with him.

"But you like him," Jamie said, pressing. Her stress

on the word *like* let McKenna know exactly what she meant by it.

"Yes," McKenna said, because there really was no point in hiding it. It was obvious. At least, it had been obvious enough for Jamie to go into full mother-bear mode.

"Are you going to—"

"Things wouldn't work out with me and Grant. We've… We've discussed it. It's… The way that I feel isn't a secret to him."

There was a very long pause, the only sound in the car the wheels on the asphalt. "Does he… Does he feel the same way?"

"No."

"I wish he did," Jamie said. "I wish he would be happy."

"You were just warning me off him."

"Well, because I wasn't sure what all you knew, or how you felt. And I… As much as I've lost, he's lost so much more. He remembers our mom. They all do. I don't. And then Lindsay… Of course he had to go fall in love with a woman who died. And I just feel… Helpless. Like I've escaped the worst of the grief and there's nothing I can do. But if… If he likes you, too…"

"I'm sorry. I think that someday… Someday there will be a woman for him." What kind of woman did a man like him even deserve? Certainly one that wasn't someone's throwaway baby. An accident that no one had felt blessed by.

"Just not you," Jamie said.

"No," McKenna said. "I don't think it can be me."

They didn't talk anymore in the car, and when they got to the ranch she hung back while Jamie put her horse away, and then headed over to the house with her. The living area of the house felt packed full of people.

Wyatt was grilling and there were bowls of chips being passed around, and she marveled at the surplus of food and the generosity with it that the Dodges exhibited with such ease.

Her whole existence had been so spare she'd never had the chance to share with people like this.

Except…except she felt like she'd shared something pretty serious with Grant. And her body was a slightly bigger deal than potato chips.

She started looking for Grant, but ended up getting waylaid by Lindy, who wanted to make sure she met Luke and Olivia Hollister, very close family friends of the Dodges. She stood wide-eyed as the situation was explained to her. That Luke was a friend who had lived on the ranch from the time he was sixteen years old, and had ended up falling in love with Bennett's ex-girlfriend. But that was before Bennett had discovered he had a son he'd never known about, and fell in love with his best friend, who he was married to now.

"That sounds like a movie," McKenna said, blinking.

Luke laughed. "It kind of does."

"Especially compared to us," Lindy said, elbowing her husband. "We're pretty normal."

"Yeah," Wyatt said. "Totally normal. I just used to hang out with your ex-husband before I knew what an ass he was, all the while suppressing the fact that I fell in love with you from the moment we met."

"You suppressed it pretty well," Lindy said.

"They didn't like each other very much at all," Luke said.

"Really?" That intrigued McKenna. Because she

would have never known there was any kind of strife between Lindy and her husband, who seemed obnoxiously, wildly in love to McKenna.

"That's just because Lindy was suppressing her desire for me," Wyatt said, the corner of his mouth tipping up.

"I thought it was because I wanted to kill all men with a steak knife after my divorce."

"That, too," Wyatt said. "But it was also a little about me."

"You think everything is about you."

"That's not true," Wyatt said, wrapping his arm around his wife. "I think everything is about us."

The exchange made an ache spread from the outer edges of her heart on out. It was great. So very, very great that the two of them were into each other like that. That all these people around her seemed to have found love, and belonging.

But that just made her think of Grant again. She scanned the room, and she didn't see him. "Where's Grant?" she asked, not caring if it seemed weird. Jamie already knew that she *liked him*, which was a pretty feeble way of putting it. But if Jamie knew, she imagined that it would end up trickling out to the rest of the family. Not because she didn't trust Jamie, just because she got the feeling that the Dodge family didn't keep very many secrets from each other.

Except the one.

Her stomach felt hollowed out. Yeah, Grant certainly hadn't shared the fact that he was a virgin with his family.

He's not a virgin now.

No, he wasn't. Courtesy of McKenna. A fact that

made her feel honored, smug and like she might burst into tears all at once.

"He said he wasn't hungry," Lindy said.

She cast a worried glance over at Wyatt.

"This time of year is hard for him," Wyatt explained.

McKenna nodded. Of course. Of course this time of year would be hard for him. Because it was Christmas, and all of this family stuff. And things like what happened to him in town. It wasn't just his grief; she had a pretty clear vision on that. It was the fact that he lived in a small-town *Groundhog Day*. Always exacerbated by the fact that people remembered him as one thing.

She also understood, without even needing to ask, why he hadn't left.

She lived a rootless life. A life where no one was waiting for her to come home. A life where nobody checked up on her well-being. A life that was much more transient than anything else.

She knew exactly why you wouldn't leave the familiar to head into that. She imagined there might be some comfort in it. But there was comfort here, too. It was just that life had teeth wherever you were at, and it didn't hesitate to bite you in the ass when the opportunity came up.

He could undoubtedly slip into some kind of anonymity if he left. And for sure, that bit of media notoriety would make it tricky, but she hadn't known who he was. And there were probably a lot of people who didn't. Who would never recognize him.

But then, there wouldn't be any hand reaching out to keep him from slipping completely into the darkness, either.

She nodded, and worked her way away from the

group. Then she planted her feet firmly and pressed her hands against her forehead. Yeah. She needed to go find him. It was so nice that everyone was including her in this get-together.

But she needed to be with Grant.

Not because she felt sorry for him. But because in some way she thought he might be the only person who understood. A man with too many roots and a girl with none, but somehow, it felt like it fit. She wanted to connect. She wanted to connect with him.

It was easy to slip out of the house unnoticed; there were so many people that she simply picked through the group and made a quiet retreat, wrapping her new coat around herself tightly as she planted firm footsteps on the frozen ground.

She moved quickly to Grant's cabin, chilly but not really caring.

She knocked on the door but no one came. She waited. Maybe he wasn't home. She tried the knob and the door opened.

There was a fire going in the fireplace and she could hear water running from the back of the small cabin. The shower.

They'd never been together in his place before. Not like she was intending to be with him now. She didn't know what he'd…think of that. If he'd want it.

But she had to see. She had to try.

She walked into the living room and closed the door behind her. Then she stood for a moment, trying to make her decision. There really was no decision to make. She shed her coat, whipped her sweater up over her head and began to walk down the hall. She took off her T-shirt, her bra, her shoes, her pants. Leaving them all behind as she left behind her other protective layers.

She remembered that first time they'd been together. When she'd been desperate to cover up after because he made her feel so much, and she couldn't stand being unprotected like that.

It wasn't possible to shield herself now. Now after everything he'd told her.

She didn't even want to.

The last thing to go was her panties, right when she walked into the bathroom. It was full of steam, and she had a feeling he'd been in there for a little while. She looked through the fogged-up glass, at his glorious, masculine silhouette.

He was so beautiful. It wasn't fair that a man that gorgeous should have had to go through so much pain. But somehow, all that made him more beautiful. Made his strength that much more profound. That goodness that he carried down inside of himself even though it was all covered up with a rough, gruff exterior.

"I was looking for you at the party," she said softly.

His silhouette jerked in the shower. "You found me, I guess."

"I know I probably shouldn't have come in uninvited."

"What is it you want, McKenna?"

She didn't have words. She didn't have words for the desperate, clawing feeling in her chest right now. All she had was need.

Without another word, she pushed open the shower door and joined him, wrapped her arms around him and rested her cheek against his back.

The hot water poured down over both of them and

she held him tight, closing her eyes and letting the steam curl around them, sheltering them from everything.

She wished it could shelter them forever.

When they didn't have clothes on, everything always seemed so simple.

It was when the clothes came on, when they had to talk, when other people were around and when their pasts came up that it all seemed so much harder.

He turned, sharp and fierce, backing her against the wall, the cold tile a shock against her shoulder blades. There was something desperate in his eyes. Not a saint. Not a nice guy. Just a man. A man who needed her. "Do you feel sorry for me?" he asked, his voice rough.

She didn't know what to call the feelings that were sharp like slivers of glass ground into her chest. She felt everything. Scared and sorry and needy.

But there was one thing she knew. One thing she understood.

"I *want* you," she answered.

He kissed her, fierce and hard and intense, and she wrapped her arms around his shoulders, sliding her hands across his slick skin, across all that muscle. She moved her hands around to the front, over that chest, his rough chest hair and down farther, wrapping her hand around his length and working her palm over him, squeezing him.

And he kept on kissing her. Rough and desperate and everything she'd wanted.

Not just everything she'd wanted *tonight*, or everything she would want tomorrow. It was everything she'd ever wanted from the first moment she'd realized there was a hole in her life. For someone to be desperate for *her*. Intense and needy and *everything*.

He moved his hands over her body, sliding them easily over her slick curves, pressing his fingers between her thighs and stroking her there, making her feel weak, making her feel strong because this big, broken man wanted her.

Wanted her to come apart right along with him.

It didn't matter what they'd said. What they'd reasoned. That they both agreed they couldn't do this, and that it needed to stop. This was the honest truth. What was happening between their bodies now.

She needed him. Needed him now that she knew she was the only woman he'd ever touched like this.

Now that she felt like she might be special. She needed it. Just for a little bit. And he needed her, too. So maybe it was okay. Maybe it was okay to pretend for just a while that *she* mattered.

He moved his hands down to her hips, gripped her, pulled her against him and arched forward. He growled, moving his hands down farther, gripping her thighs and lifting her up off the floor, using the back of the shower to brace her, to brace them both. He flexed his hips, dragging his length through her slick folds. She thought she might be dying. But she'd thought that before. That she might die of cold. That she might die of hunger. Thinking that she might die of pleasure was a gift.

He pressed the thick head against her entrance, and then he pushed inside of her, the sensation of being joined with him, being filled by him, so perfect it made her want to cry.

The water beat a steady rhythm over his back, and he pounded a steady rhythm into her. Hard. A sharp edge of the tile bit into her skin, and she didn't care. She loved it. Because this was the most real anything had ever been for her. He was deep inside of her, nothing between them, out of control. They both needed. Equally.

There was no exchange.

It was just a desperate desire to connect. A desperate desire for each other. For the pleasure they only found between the two of them. He'd never had a lover, and she had, but even still, there had never been anyone like him.

He stood apart. Only Grant had ever made her feel like this. Only Grant had ever made her need, and then fulfilled it.

She opened her eyes, looking into his, at the wild, animal desire there. She pressed her hand against his cheek and rolled her hips against him as he thrust inside of her, as the steam from the shower wound itself around them, seeming to press them in tighter together.

"Grant," she whispered. "I need you, Grant."

That was when his control snapped. His thrusts became wild, hard, and she welcomed it. Whether he was giving or taking, she couldn't tell, but she couldn't care. Because whatever he was doing, it worked for her.

He shattered, and she broke right along with him, until the two of them were nothing but splintered, jagged edges. She wasn't sure if they locked together in place perfectly, or if they could ever be fully healed. But at least they weren't alone in being broken. Their pieces were all mixed together, and somehow, somehow that worked.

There was no sound after that, just the broken sound of their breathing and the spray of the shower. He slowly lifted her down to the ground.

"I'm sorry," he said, the word splintered.

"For…"

"I didn't use a condom. I'm sorry. I didn't think."

"It's okay," she said, her hands still on his face. "I'm on the pill. And I know that you're safe. I am, too. I haven't been with anyone in a long time," she added. Because even though he never made her feel bad about any of her past, sometimes she did, whether she should or not. "It's been a couple of years actually. Almost three. It's just... I have a standing date to collect three months at a time with the county, and it doesn't cost me anything so it always seems like it's probably the better part of valor, or something."

He nodded slowly, and then he picked her back up again, taking them both out of the shower. He shut the water off and set her down, wrapping her in a fluffy towel and drying her, before drying himself.

Then he picked her up again and carried her back toward his bedroom.

"What are you doing?"

"Stay with me," he said, setting her down on the bed. "Stay with me tonight."

Her throat went tight, painful. "Okay," she said softly.

He drew back the covers and settled her onto the mattress, and then he joined her there, drawing her into his arms.

She curled up against him, resting her head on his cheek. And she didn't think she'd ever felt half so peaceful as she did lying against Grant Dodge, his heartbeat lulling her to sleep.

WHEN GRANT WOKE UP he was starving. He also wasn't alone. He was naked and tangled up around McKenna Tate.

It was dark outside, unlike when they had fallen

asleep, and for a moment he wondered what time it was. Then he decided he didn't care. It was just as well to have this moment exist outside of everything in his normal life. Exist outside of time, and everything real.

He would call it a fantasy, but the feel of her skin beneath his fingertips was far too real for that. Her soft breasts pressed against his chest, her breath hot on his neck.

He bent his head down and kissed her forehead, then shifted. And so did she. "Grant?"

"I'm hungry," he said.

"Me, too."

"Want to get food?"

She burrowed more deeply against him. "It's probably a little bit late to go to Wyatt's for hamburgers."

Grant laughed. "Not only that, I have no desire to see my brother's face right now."

"Really?"

"Not at all. This is for us. This moment is for us."

He thought she might hit him or say something snide about that bit of sentimentality. He almost hoped that she did, because he didn't know where it had come from, and it made him feel slightly off balance.

But she didn't. Instead, she just traced shapes he couldn't picture over his chest with her fingertips.

Then she sat up. "Food." She scrambled out of bed, completely naked. Then rooted around on the floor for clothes, and came up empty. "I think my clothes are spread all over your house."

"I don't mind that."

"Can I have a T-shirt?"

He got out of bed and opened up his dresser drawer, fishing out a thin, white T-shirt, which McKenna put on hastily, covering up her curves. He was a little bit sad to be deprived of the view, but at the same time, the novelty of seeing a beautiful woman wearing nothing but his T-shirt was something else.

He grabbed himself a pair of jeans and pulled them on, leaving the button undone, and led the way to the kitchen.

"Between the two of us we have a whole outfit," McKenna pointed out.

He chuckled. "I guess so."

"So," McKenna said, leaning against the counter in the small kitchen. "What are you going to fix me?"

"You're not going to cook for *me*?"

She tossed her hair. "I am a terrible cook. I can make, like, two things and neither of them are very good. I basically spent most of my life eating ramen noodles or bringing home leftovers from the restaurants I worked at."

"Well," he said. "I cook."

"Excellent."

He opened up the fridge and hunted around for a moment, producing eggs that had come from their chickens, and some sourdough bread.

"It's going to be basic," he said. "Eggs and toast okay?"

"Yes," she responded enthusiastically. "I'm starving."

He set about frying the eggs, and toasted the bread and butter in a pan on the stove, he and McKenna not speaking.

There was something unspeakably domestic about the moment, and none of it brought back parallels to the life he lived before.

He'd had a kind of domestic bliss with Lindsay. But

it hadn't been like this. There had been no random, late-night meals after sex. When he looked at McKenna, memories of touching her, of being inside of her, were never far behind. It was just a whole different way to know someone.

"You're not wearing your rings," McKenna said softly.

He looked up from the stove. "I don't wear them to bed."

"The last times we were together you put them back on really quickly. I thought maybe it was a… A guilt thing. I mean, since I've been thinking about it the last few hours. Trying to process all my newfound Grant information."

"I don't feel guilty," he said.

"Then why weren't you ever with another woman, Grant? I mean… You're hot. You're really hot. I imagine a host of women would have lined up to be your first. You could have auctioned your virginity off and made bank."

He laughed, for the third time in only a few minutes. He couldn't remember the last time he laughed as much as he did with her. And he had never imagined that someday he would laugh about his lingering virginity. That had been a frustrating, enraging marker of just how caught up in the past he was. There had been nothing funny about it. And it was still weighted. But somehow he could see the humor in it, too.

McKenna seemed to navigate her whole life that way. With a sense of wry humor directed at the ridiculous things life threw at her. It was a strange and marvelous thing to have her manage to bring it to him.

"Thank you," he said. "But it isn't like I didn't get offers."

"From women who wanted to deflower you?" She lifted her eyebrows suggestively.

"No," he said. "I told you, no one knows about that."

She cleared her throat, her expression sobering. "I won't tell. I am… Grant, I can't really believe that you trusted me with that. Not just with the secret, but with your body in general. That you waited all that time and then… That you wanted to be with me. It's… Thank you. For trusting me with that. With you."

"You really don't need to thank me," Grant said. "All the things I've ever needed are in the way you respond when I touch you."

She ducked her head, blushing. "I've never had anyone look at me the way that you do."

"I've never seen anything quite like you." He cleared his throat. "I went out a few times. I meant to hook up. It never seemed right. That's the problem with waiting for things sometimes. You know how when you wait to eat all day and you're starving, and sometimes you hit a point where the pressure on it to be just the right meal is so intense. It can't just be satisfying. It has to be great. It has to be right."

"As someone who has been actually starving, the metaphor might be lost on me. But I take your point."

"I didn't want to care about whether or not it was right. But I definitely wanted to want the woman without any kind of hesitation. And when I realized that with you… With you I was having to fight the desire I felt for you, not force myself to make a move, but fight against it, I just…"

"That was when you knew it was right. Or at least that it was inevitable."

"Either one," he said. "I don't feel guilty. I don't wear the rings because I still feel married. She's gone. I've accepted that. I haven't worn the ring on my finger for five years." He paused for a moment. "Remember I told you that I was a bully?"

She nodded. "Yes. I remember that."

"I was so angry. And I was bound and determined to make sure the people around me were as miserable as I was. I was failing all my classes. And I got assigned to a tutor. I remember the first time I met her. In the library after school. She was pretty. And she didn't look at me like she was scared. She was happy. And she... She said she believed in me. That I could do it. The work... And being a better person. I've never been in love before. But I fell for her hard. She made me want something else. Something other than being angry. I had gone right into my own swamp, had embraced every bad feeling inside of me. She made me want something good. Something light. She made me better. If I'm a good man, then it's because of her. I wear the rings to remind me of that. I didn't want to sink into that anger again. I wanted to be... I wanted to be better for having been together. I want to keep that next to my heart."

He had never explained that to anyone. He had never talked about why he wore the rings. He kept them under his shirt so that other people wouldn't comment on them. And he was sure that his siblings were well aware of the fact he wore them, but they certainly never discussed it.

McKenna was a first for so many things. But she had been the first woman to touch his body like that, and now he just wanted to share these things with her. These things no one else knew.

"I don't think you need a necklace to remember to be a good man," she said softly.

"I might," he said.

He put a piece of toast on each plate, then topped them with a fried egg, and hunted around for some forks, and two bottles of beer. McKenna wrinkled her nose, but lifted the beer to her lips. "Beer and eggs."

"An unexpected combination," he said.

"That's what they'll say about us," McKenna said, taking a sip of beer. "McKenna and Grant. They go together like beer and eggs."

He smiled and took a bite of the egg.

"You don't actually have to let anyone know that this is happening," she said. "I understand why it works to keep it to yourself. It won't... It won't hurt my feelings."

"Won't it?"

She shook her head. "No. Look, I understand wanting to keep your cards close to your vest. I don't exactly want to shout from the rooftops that the Daltons are my family. I have to figure out how to approach them. It's not fair to them to spread it around. And it's not... I don't know what I'm going to want to do about it yet, either. I don't really know them. Maybe I'll hate them."

"Do you think so?"

"No," she said. "It's hard to explain. But I met Gabe. I've never felt... He's my brother, Grant," she said, her voice getting sick. "My big brother."

She didn't say anything else. She lowered her head and picked her plate up, cutting off a piece of bread and egg.

"That must be something," he said. "Finding out you have family."

"Yeah. It is."

"It pains me to say this," Grant said. "But I can see how you kind of look like Gabe Dalton."

McKenna grinned. "It pains you because it pokes at your fragile masculinity to think that I might look like a dude you know?"

"Yes," he said. "Exactly."

They ate in silence for a while longer. Then suddenly, McKenna looked up. "For what it's worth, Grant, I don't think Lindsay made you a good man."

He didn't know what to say to that. So he said nothing, opting instead to shove a bite of food into his mouth.

"I think you were always a good man," McKenna continued. "But even a good man needs something to care about before he acts on it. She gave you something to care about. She gave you a reason to push past the pain. But I don't think she took a bad man and turned him into a good one. I don't think that's possible. Believe me. I've dated enough bad men to have come to that conclusion. I think… I think that people who maybe seem bad or hard… When they change like that… They always had it in them somewhere. I think you always had it in you."

He didn't know what to say to that. Mostly because it conflicted so intensely with what he thought about himself for so long. He didn't think he liked it. Wasn't sure he could accept it.

"Lindsay was amazing," he said.

"I don't doubt that. I can… I can tell that she changed

your life in a really serious way. And no one who isn't amazing could do that."

"Does it bother you to talk about her?"

That little piece right there was him spoiling for a fight, to shift the uncomfortable feeling swirling around inside of him. But McKenna paused for a moment, and then shook her head slowly.

"It doesn't bother me. She's part of who you are. I can't… I can't imagine what you went through. But as much as the struggles, and the jackasses that were there for them are part of my story, she's part of yours."

"Tell me about your first time," he said.

McKenna knew his first time story, and knew the whys of it. It seemed fair he should know hers.

"We were in foster care together." She pulled a face. "I moved enough that I never thought of any of the other kids I lived with as siblings. He was just a guy I knew, who happened to live with me. I let him take my virginity after homecoming. It was awful. But I wanted him to want me. I wanted him to keep me. I figured… That was how you did it. We moved out together, us against the world. But he had addiction problems and he went from being a decent guy to being an awful guy whenever there were issues with drugs. Honestly, more money related than the way he acted when he was high."

He hated that thought. McKenna being shoved out into the world with no safety net. At eighteen he'd been married, had secured a stable job. And yes, he'd had his trials. He and Lindsay had been dealing with illness and mortality in a way eighteen-year-olds should never have to.

But they had a network of support. Her parents and his father. His brothers and sister. A whole town that cared deeply about them and their marriage, their happiness. A town who'd done fundraisers to help with medical bills whenever it was necessary. That had organized meal trains and little gift baskets with soft socks and lotions and other things to help her with her chemo symptoms.

They were there now, to give him endless sympathy. For better or worse.

Whatever the pain, whatever the struggle, Grant hadn't been alone.

McKenna was alone.

He looked up at her. "Did you ever have..."

"Drug problems?" she asked. "No. I watched it take too many people. A lot of the kids that I was in care with... That was the kind of cycle their parents were caught in. Or that they were already because they've been exposed to it at such a young age. That was the one thing that my mother did for me. The one thing I'm grateful for. That she didn't take drugs while she was pregnant with me, so I wasn't born with those kinds of issues. That she didn't give them to me when I was a kid, and never took any around me. As far as I know, they weren't a factor for her. Which means she just left me because she didn't want to take care of me, but that's its own whole drama. I have abandonment issues, but not addiction issues."

"Do you think Hank knows about you?" Grant pressed.

She lifted a shoulder. "I don't know. To be honest with you, I wouldn't be surprised if he did. If he just didn't... Didn't want me. No one else ever has. I don't know why he would have. That's why this whole thing feels like a fool's errand. But I... I've never had a lifeline to reach for. This is the one I have. This is the first time I've ever had the chance to grab hold of someone else's hand and get pulled up. I can't say no to that." She took the last bite of her egg and toast. "Whatever the risk, I can't say no to that."

"Makes sense to me."

"Good. At least it makes sense to you. I question it about a thousand times a day."

He moved closer to her, pressed his hand over the top of hers. "As someone who loved someone I knew I'd lose, I can honestly tell you it's always worth the risk."

He felt something deep and intense move through him, and he let go of her hand, taking a step back. "You have to see," he said. "You have to try."

"Should I... Should I go back to my place?" McKenna said, pushing her empty plate aside.

It would be easier if she did. Easier to put all this behind them. Easier to maintain boundaries he wasn't sure were there anymore now, anyway. But he couldn't bear the thought of getting back in that bed and having it be empty.

"Stay the night with me," he said.

"Okay."

He took her hand and led her back to bed. And for the first time in more years than he could remember, Grant Dodge went to sleep sober.

CHAPTER SIXTEEN

McKENNA HAD SNEAKED back to her place before the sun rose, and had managed to get herself out the door and ready for morning chores. She was on breakfast duty, which meant being up early enough to receive coffee delivery and then start cooking up eggs and bacon and other things to keep the troops fed.

There were three groups staying with them this week. An older couple on an anniversary trip, a group of women on a girls' trip and a family with three small children. That at least provided McKenna with a distraction while she dealt with her general unhappiness.

By the time she finished cooking and was sitting down with a plate, Jamie and Wyatt were strolling in.

"Good morning," Jamie said, taking a seat across from McKenna. "You left awfully early last night."

"I was tired," McKenna responded, and she ignored the speculative glance that followed her explanation.

"It's for the best," Jamie said. "They ended up playing charades. Drunkenly."

Wyatt laughed. "Hey, sober or not, I'm good at charades."

"Keep telling yourself that."

"I thought you cooked bacon for your wife every morning, Wyatt?" McKenna asked.

"Lindy had to be at the winery early this morning.

It's a little bit tricky sometimes, balancing the two, because now she's so involved in both enterprises. She used to live there. Now it's just her mistress."

"I'm heading over to Gabe Dalton's today," Jamie said. "Getting a tour of the facility and having a talk with him about exactly what he expects."

Wyatt looked stony-faced at that. "Yes indeed."

"I'll go," McKenna said. "I mean, I'm happy to go with Jamie. I'm really interested. I can be back before it's time to clean."

"That would be a good idea," Wyatt said, not surprising McKenna at all. He clearly felt wary of his sister being around Gabe Dalton, and that was going to work to McKenna's advantage.

"Sure," Jamie said, trying to sound bright, even though she was bristling a little bit. McKenna couldn't blame her for that, either. And truly, if McKenna didn't have an ulterior motive, she would not have horned in on the situation. Because Jamie was an adult, and Wyatt was treating her like she was a vulnerable kid. But McKenna did have an ulterior motive, so weaseling she was.

"It'll be fun," McKenna said. "And it will give me a chance to get a look at the kind of work you're doing. I'm honestly fascinated." She was. It was true enough. "Plus, I've heard a lot about the Daltons. Aren't they, like...rodeo royalty?"

"I like to think of myself as rodeo royalty," Wyatt said.

"Maybe the court jester," Jamie said.

"That hurts, Jamie."

"Well. Anyway," Jamie continued. "From a dynastic standpoint, yes, I suppose the Daltons are rodeo royalty."

"I think that's really fascinating," McKenna continued, hoping she wasn't laying it on too thick. "Plus, I liked what he was saying about rehabilitating the horses."

They finished shoveling down breakfast, and McKenna and Jamie got a couple of cups of coffee to go. Then McKenna shot Grant a quick text, letting him know what she was doing. She hesitated, then added: Wish me luck. I'll see you later.

She felt thankful then that she didn't have a smartphone or she would have been tempted to add a heart emoji.

Feeling giddy and high on adrenaline, she hopped into Jamie's truck, curling and uncurling her fingers, trying to contain her nervous energy.

"Okay," Jamie said, "what's going on?"

"There's nothing going on." She had to hedge, because she wasn't exactly sure what Jamie was talking about. If she was wondering about Grant and McKenna, or if she was meaning something to do with Gabe.

"I want to know why you jumped on this trip so eagerly. Because I don't believe any of what you just said to my brother. And I know that he's totally clouded by the fact that he really wants me to have a chaperone, but I'm not."

"I've discovered a newfound love of horses?" She tried to sound innocent.

"Have you discovered a newfound love for Gabe Dalton?" Jamie asked. "I thought you liked my brother."

McKenna let out a tense sigh. There really was no

reason to keep it from Jamie. She was about to talk to Gabe, anyway.

"I'll tell you," McKenna said, "but you have to promise not to tell anyone. Because I'm not going to keep it a secret forever. In fact, I'm working at telling someone a secret. But I need to be able to do it in my own time. And in a way that doesn't… Hurt anyone."

"Okay."

"Gabe is my half brother."

Jamie pumped the brakes, the truck jerking. "What?"

"Gabe is my half brother. At least, I am ninety percent sure. I think that Hank Dalton is my father. I grew up in foster care, Jamie. And all I have is Hank's name on my birth certificate. I've done some digging and figured out where he was. That's why I'm here. I didn't come to Gold Valley by mistake or by accident. I'm here to get to know my family. And I thought… I felt connected with Gabe the moment I met him. I want to talk to him. I just… I want to tell him. I want to tell him first."

"Wow," Jamie said, her voice small.

"I know. It's a whole lot of wow. And it really freaks me out. I don't know if I'm doing the right thing. I mean, the right thing for them. I think it might be the best thing for me, and I've spent so long being by myself that I—"

"I understand," Jamie said. "If I could… If my mom was just out there somewhere, even though I've never met her… I would do whatever I could to find her. No matter what. Anyway, it's not your fault that he had a secret baby. You don't have to protect him. He should have protected you."

Jamie's words were like a balm for her soul.

It shocked her, how much it meant to hear something like that. To have someone think she deserved something good.

"So, I'm sorry about using you to get to him. But you can see why I couldn't just say what I was doing. And you can see why it's important. I'm trying to approach everything with caution."

"I totally understand," Jamie said. "Like I said. I would do the same thing."

"My mom is out there somewhere," McKenna said. "But I already know she doesn't want me. Maybe Hank won't, either. But... I have to try."

They drove the rest of the way in silence. All the way through town and out the other side, up a winding, two-lane road that went way into the hills. It turned to dirt, and there was a sign posted that said Private Drive.

They rounded a corner, and McKenna curled her fingers tight, her fingernails digging into the skin. There was a house, large and beautiful, made of stained wood the color of honey, three floors with windows that overlooked an incredible tapestry of dark green trees and mountains below. The lawn was well manicured, green and bright, spreading from the front of the house, to the edge of a row of tall trees.

This was her family home.

She didn't know how quite to process that.

She had never owned anything in her life. Nothing really except for that truck she'd had to abandon back at the mechanic shop. And this was her father's house. Where all her half siblings had grown up, where they lived now. "It's beautiful," she forced out of her scratchy throat.

"It really is," Jamie agreed.

Jamie drove past the house, down a narrow, gravel road that had been well oiled to keep any dust from kicking up. They drove until they reached a section that had barns, not unlike the layout at Get Out of Dodge. Except everything here was newer, more modern.

Her heart lurched when she saw Gabe exit one of the barns, lifting his hand in a wave. Jamie parked, killing the engine, and got out quickly. McKenna just sat for a while. She let out a long, slow breath, and then got out of the truck.

"Hi," Gabe said, his eyes landing on her. "McKenna, right?"

"Yes," McKenna confirmed. "McKenna Tate."

He nodded slowly. "Still working at the Dodge ranch obviously."

"Uh-huh," McKenna confirmed. "Still."

"Great." He nodded once. "Come on, Jamie, I'll show you around."

McKenna followed along, her heart pounding heavily as Gabe took them out to a pasture where there were six horses grazing. "These are ours," he said to Jamie. "But in the summer we're going to be taking horses who have retired from the rodeo, so there will be a lot more of them," he said. "You sure you're up to it?"

Jamie nodded. "I'm sure."

"So I'll have you come out here and work," he said. "And there will probably be a rotation of horses. Some of them will make good trail riders for beginners, too, I think. By the time all is said and done."

"Yes," Jamie said. "I agree."

They continued to talk logistics, and McKenna watched him, trying to see as much family resemblance as she could. The way that he talked, the way that he gestured. The way his mouth curved up a little more on one side when he smiled. She could see it. She could see that he was her brother.

She wondered if she would see it in the other brothers. And Hank. Obviously, the Daltons had strong genes. She had never really known if she looked like her mother. But she could see now she was almost purely like her father's side of the family.

"Okay," Gabe said, "that about covers it. Do you think you can have your schedule cleared up enough in the next six months?"

"I think I can handle that," Jamie said.

"All right," Gabe said, extending his hand.

Jamie looked down at it like it might be a snake, but then took hold of it. "You have yourself a job lined up, Jamie Dodge."

McKenna noticed that when Jamie released her hold on his hand, she wiped it on her jeans.

"I need a quick word with you," McKenna said, blurting it out before her nerve could desert her.

Gabe's brow shot up. "With me?"

McKenna nodded. "In private."

"Okay," he said. "Come this way."

Jamie nodded awkwardly, then began to head back in the direction she had parked, while Gabe and McKenna walked down to the side of one of the barns. "We've never met before," Gabe said.

"No." She blinked in surprise. "I mean, other than the coffeehouse."

"Thank God," he said, looking visibly relieved. "I didn't think I was that much of an asshole."

She frowned. "What?"

"You had me scared, thinking maybe we had hooked up or something."

"No." She drew back. "We have *never* hooked up."

He shook his head. "I guess the fact that I had to ask doesn't say a whole lot of good about what I've been up to for the past few years."

She could definitely see why Wyatt was not thrilled to have her sister around Gabe.

"No. But... I do have something... Something that I need to tell you. I think... No, I mean I'm really sure that I'm your half sister."

Gabe looked like she could have pushed him over with her index finger right about then. "My half sister?"

"Hank Dalton's name is on my birth certificate," she said.

He said nothing for a moment, a muscle in his jaw jumping. She could see him putting pieces together in his head, figuring out how to proceed.

"How old are you?" he asked, finally.

"I'm twenty-six."

"Younger than any of us," he said.

"I know. I mean, at least I kind of do. I did quite a lot of searching around before I decided to come. I didn't... I didn't decide to look for my birth father until recently. I... I didn't have anywhere to go. It's... I don't want to cause any trouble. But I exist. And I thought maybe you should know."

"I don't know why I'm surprised," Gabe said, looking at her, a strange expression in his dark eyes.

"I have the birth certificate. I didn't bring it with me today, but... If I can talk to your dad. Our...dad? Well, then I'll bring it with me."

"I believe you." The sincerity in his tone left her in

no doubt. "I just don't know why it surprises me that one of his kids showed up after all these years. If I think about it… The real surprise would be that you're the first one."

"Really?"

"My dad… *Our* dad… He has quite the reputation. He… He cheated on my mom forever. All their marriage while he was on the rodeo, and she divorced him. She was the manager for his career, and even then… They could never stay away from each other. Even when they weren't actually together. But my dad couldn't stay away from other women. They were together, though, about the time you were… Conceived." He pulled a face when he said the word. "That was when my mom actually kicked him out. It didn't last long. It never does. They're back together now, though she won't marry him again. But he's… You know, he's old now."

"Well. I… I have to say, of all the things, I don't think I expected you to just believe me."

"We kind of look alike, don't we?"

McKenna ground her teeth together, biting the inside of her cheek to try and keep from crying. "I didn't know if I was the only one that noticed that. When we met in the coffee shop… I wasn't expecting to see you there. But I knew… I felt like I recognized you. I know you have family here. But I don't have anyone. I just… I don't have anyone."

Gabe hesitated for a moment, and then he reached out, pulling her in for a quick, one-armed hug that lasted just long enough for both of them to feel a little uncomfortable. "I'll help you figure out a time to meet with my dad. Do you want me to tell him what it's about?"

She thought about that. Of being spared that moment

of either shock or… No shock on his face. "Yes." She hesitated before speaking her next words. "I'm not entirely sure he didn't know about me."

"Our dad is a really flawed person," Gabe said. "He's made a lot of mistakes, and I don't know the extent of them. But I don't think he's cruel. And I don't think he's…bad. I think if you have a talk with him…well, I don't see how he could turn you away."

She admired Gabe's confidence, and she supposed that she should defer to it. After all, he was the one who knew his dad, she wasn't.

But then, on the other hand, he had grown up in this beautiful house surrounded by people who loved him, and she had seen the cracks in humanity from a very early age. She knew that good people did bad things when they needed to simplify their lives and she couldn't even blame them for that sometimes. But she would like for him to have time to prepare. Maybe he would come up with a better story. And maybe… Just maybe whatever the past was, he would embrace her now. She could have some part in this place. With these people.

"I'd like to meet your… Our brothers, too."

"They're on a training thing right now. They're smoke jumpers. But they'll be back."

She laughed. "Right. I forgot about that. You know, I can't imagine that I'm part of a family with a bunch of badass cowboy firefighters."

"*I'm* just a cowboy," he said.

"Do you know… That until a couple of weeks ago I'd never ridden a horse?"

"Really?" He sounded in utter disbelief, but then

she had a feeling Daltons learned to ride before they could walk.

"It's true. I'm kind of a city slicker."

"Now that's going to be the hardest thing to get past," Gabe said, smiling slightly.

"Grant Dodge taught me to ride."

Gabe's expression turned curious. "Is that so?"

"Yes," she said, knowing she was blushing a little bit.

"McKenna... I'm glad to have met you. And... I hope..."

"I do, too."

"I'll talk to Dad."

"Okay. Then maybe after that you could talk to your brothers."

Suddenly, she felt like everything was so much more high stakes.

She'd met her brother.

She really liked her brother.

She wanted to meet the other ones. But if they didn't want her...

What would she do now if they didn't want her...

"Sure," he said. "Jacob and Caleb will be... Well, probably no more surprised than me. It's always been brothers in our house. Who knew all this time we had a sister."

McKenna felt like her chest was cracking, and all she could do was smile. But what she really wanted to say was: *Who knew all this time I had a family?*

SHE DID SAY it to Grant when she got back to his house that night, and they talked it over some more over breakfast, since they had gotten distracted over the intimate dinner at his place and had wound up in bed. She had spent the night again, cradled in his arms, and he had told her not to bother to go back to her place first before breakfast this morning. So they had walked over to the mess hall together, and no one had noticed. Or if they did, they were too polite to say.

Everyone lived in close quarters, anyway, so there was nothing overly remarkable about it.

They did it that morning, and every morning after the whole week.

Then during breakfast on Friday, she got a text from Gabe, telling her to come over in the afternoon.

"I don't think I'm ready for this," she said, setting the phone down and looking up at Grant. "My dad wants to meet with me. Today."

"That's good," Grant said.

"I guess," McKenna responded. "But it's also kind of terrifying."

"You said that Gabe was happy to see you. To meet you. You said that he wasn't surprised his dad had a secret child."

"Sure," she said. "But I also think that he maybe has a little more faith in humanity than I do."

"Okay, yeah, that's fair enough."

"I just… I couldn't stand it, Grant. I couldn't stand it if… It's been my dream for the past few weeks. And now it's like… A week until Christmas? I'm either going to have a family or have lost my dream of one forever. I'm not sure I can cope with it."

"You've coped with harder stuff than this, McKenna. I know that you can cope with anything life throws at you."

She huffed out a laugh. "Okay. Well, maybe I don't want to cope with this."

"That I relate to."

"Somehow that doesn't surprise me."

"Would you like for me to go with you?" he asked.

She would. More than anything. But the fact that she felt vulnerable enough to ask him to go with her made her feel small and sad. And afraid.

She couldn't start depending on him. She was so dependent on her fantasy of the Daltons as her family, her forever family, that all of this was starting to psych her out. What was going to happen if she got dependent on Grant, too? On the comfort and the sense of home that she had here at Get Out of Dodge. It wasn't supposed to be like that. *She* wasn't supposed to be like that. She knew better. She damn well did. But she… She really did want Grant to come with her.

"Please," she said.

He nodded slowly, his green eyes never leaving hers. "I have a stop to make today. Do you want to come with me?"

"A stop? Where?"

"I have to go put out some flowers."

CHAPTER SEVENTEEN

GRANT DIDN'T KNOW what the hell he was doing. Bringing McKenna with him to Lindsay's spot. But it felt... She was the only person who understood the deeper parts of that relationship. The only person he could talk to about it without getting nothing but placation and pity. She listened. To the hard stuff.

And the spot up by the river was important to him. He didn't just take people there. Everyone had been up there for the memorial, but it was out of the way and it was secluded, and he had never gone up there with anyone since. But for some reason, he wanted her to see. Maybe just because it was another thing that felt not so lonely. He might not have been grieving strictly speaking for the last eight years, but he'd been isolated in a lot of ways. Shut down. And there was something about McKenna that made him feel like more.

McKenna didn't say anything when she got in the truck and saw the little potted poinsettia on the bench seat next to him. She didn't say anything the whole drive. Not even when they pulled off the paved road and went up a winding, mountain one that ended abruptly.

"You warm enough?" he asked as he put the truck in Park.

"I should be."

"Good."

They got out of the truck and he held on to the poinsettia as they walked into the forest toward the creek. He waited for her to make a joke. About him kidnapping her or something. But she must have known where they were going. Because she didn't make a joke. And that was the thing about McKenna. She knew when to joke. And she knew when not to.

"You know," she said. "Beatrix bought me this coat."

"She did?"

"I was really cold. My old coat wasn't good enough. She just…got this for me. Even though… She barely knows me. That's where I kind of understand how you feel about pity. But I've also been absolutely dependent on it. And when Bea gave me the coat it was about more than pity. I think she felt sorry for me, but she also just… Cared. Maybe it doesn't really matter. Maybe it all feels the same. But I think in some ways it does matter. I think pity without compassion looks down on you a little bit, like you said, like you're a sad puppy. And with compassion, a person might look at you, see who you are and want to make a difference. I've never been in the position to decline either one."

Grant's throat felt uncomfortably tight. "When you put it like that, I suppose I can see the difference."

"Maybe… Maybe that's just empathy, though," she said. "Maybe it's friendship."

He shook his head. "I wouldn't know. I'm not very good at having friends. Just the ones that I've always been around."

"I'm your friend."

He reached back and took hold of her hand, saying nothing as they continued to walk through the woods, stopping when they came to the edge of the creek. There was a small, wooden cross there that was beginning to show its age. Next to it was a potted poinsettia. He wondered if Cooper had left that.

"This was our spot," he said. "Well, it was my spot. Where I went to be alone, and be angry. I showed it to her after we had been studying together for a while. When I realized I was falling in love with her. We had our first kiss here."

McKenna squeezed his hand. "Can I ask you something really personal?"

"No one on earth has been as personal with me as you have. Go ahead."

"Why didn't… Why didn't you have sex with her when you were dating?"

"She was a nice girl. I was… I didn't feel worthy of her. I wanted to do things right. I don't think I would've waited for a long time. Not until we got married. But I wouldn't have married her so quickly if things had gone differently. She would have gone away to college. I would have waited for her. But things didn't go that way. They went to hell instead. And I never thought that the illness would mean… *Never*. Plenty of people who are sick have sex lives. It just so happens we got caught in a perfect storm that never stopped. And eventually… She would have done things for *me*, I know that. But… It was easier to just let that part go. And I did. I just… Did. She taught me a lot about how to be a man, McKenna, and we didn't have to have sex for her to do that."

McKenna pressed her head against his shoulder. "You're a good man, Grant Dodge. No one has ever loved me like that." The breeze wrapped itself around them, pushed them closer. At least it felt like it did. "I'm not sure many people have loved like that. Don't ever doubt that about yourself. That you're good. Not a saint. You wouldn't be half as much fun in bed if you were a saint."

"I want you to know," he said, turning toward her and grabbing her chin, tilting her face up toward his. "I didn't have sex with you because I thought… You weren't a good girl. Or because I thought you were something less than special. It's because I've changed. I don't want to wait on things anymore. Because if you wait… Sometimes you never get the chance."

She pressed her hand to his face. "You never made me feel less than special. No one has ever made me feel as special as you have."

He nodded, not quite sure what the hell was happening in his life, that he was standing next to the place where they had spread Lindsay's ashes, holding on to another woman. Except he knew… He knew it was what she had wanted for him. They'd talked about it. At length. In ways other couples rarely had to. Because the inevitability of it all was that Grant was going to have to face a life without her. She had known that.

But all those times, they had talked about him being with someone else. They had never talked about him loving anyone else.

It was something he still couldn't fathom. Couldn't fathom ever opening up his heart for.

He bent down and left the poinsettia next to the other one. Then he straightened. "It was her favorite flower."

"Can I ask… Did she die at Christmas? Your brother mentioned that it was a particularly hard time and—"

"No," Grant said. "She died in February. She took a turn for the worse around Christmas that year. And we knew it was coming after that. She'd stopped responding to everything." He swallowed hard. "I don't remember her that way. When I close my eyes that's not who I see. I see the girl who reached her hand out to me and saved my life. That's how I remember her. When everyone in town thinks of her, I know that isn't what they see. But it's what I remember. Her with all her blond hair, and blue eyes, that sweet smile and her whole life ahead of her."

His chest felt tight, and he couldn't speak anymore. McKenna said nothing, not for a long time. The only sound was the wind in the trees.

"I think anyone who's had a love like that is blessed," McKenna finally said. "To have someone love you who remembers your best, even when they've seen your worst, must be an amazing thing."

They stood there for a while, and he noticed McKenna dashing tears from her cheeks discreetly.

"You don't have to cry," he said.

"Well, you're not crying," she said, her voice breaking. "And someone has to."

"I cried mine out a long time ago," he said.

"These aren't for her. These are for you."

He squeezed her hand. "We can go."

They walked back in silence, and his hands were empty of everything except McKenna's. Leaving the poinsettia behind felt like something significant this year. Like he'd actually left something bigger there. And maybe it was because McKenna had come with him. He didn't know. He felt a little bit lighter. Not happy. The gravity of where they had been, of those memories, didn't allow for anything quite like that. But it was like his heart was buried beneath a pile of stones, and maybe he had just taken one off the top.

"All right," he said. "Let's go talk to your dad."

CHAPTER EIGHTEEN

McKenna's mouth felt like it was lined with chalk by the time they pulled up to the impressive ranch house. Gabe's text message hadn't indicated what her dad was thinking. What he thought about her, what decision he was going to make.

She had no idea how any of this was going to work, and the only thing that was keeping her upright now was the strong, steady hold that Grant had on her hand. And that was no less terrifying than anything else.

They got out of the truck and walked up to the house, and it was Gabe that met them at the door. Gabe looked down at their hands, and then back up at Grant. Grant lifted a brow, then a shoulder, and while McKenna might not have understood the exact tone of the masculine exchange, she had a feeling it had something to do with sisters.

Though that Gabe would think of her that way so quickly seemed...

She swallowed hard, and her tongue stuck to the roof of her mouth. She wanted this to work out. She wanted... She needed it. But this place was like a dream, and a handsome man standing there who was very likely her older brother only added to that.

That he could be hers. That this could be hers.

Though she had the feeling that if this were a hole

in the ground and Gabe were a troll she might feel the same way.

This was the first step toward roots.

And she could look at Grant and see what those roots cost sometimes, but she could look at the whole fabric of her own life and see what the lack of them produced.

Why couldn't she have this? Why *not* her?

She had spent her whole life feeling like... Of course. Of course no father had ever looked for her. Of course no boyfriend had ever really loved her. Because no one ever did. And that seemed okay to her, it seemed normal. But all of a sudden it didn't.

All of a sudden she thought maybe, just maybe, she could have everything.

"Dad is waiting for you in his office," Gabe said. "He wanted to talk to you alone."

Grant squared his shoulders, his expression stony. "That may not be possible," he said.

"Grant," she said. "It's fine. It's fine. I want to talk to my... To Hank by myself. I'll be okay."

"Can I get you a cup of tea?" Gabe asked Grant dryly.

Grant didn't say anything to that.

"Which way am I going?" she asked, feeling like she was standing in the middle of two dogs circling each other.

"Just up the stairs," Gabe said, "to the left."

McKenna moved through the entryway, and now that Gabe didn't loom so large in her vision, she could begin to appreciate the details of the house. The rough, repurposed barn wood floor, the pegs on the wall fashioned from horseshoes. Pictures of rodeo posters framed and hung everywhere, all featuring a Dalton as the headliner. There was a big set of polished longhorns hanging up on the wall, a cowhide rug on the floor. The stairs seemed to be made of branches that had been polished and varnished, but not cut in any way, the shape twisted and winding.

She took the first step slowly, then a little bit faster. Then suddenly, she couldn't wait. She ran the last few steps, and turned down the hall, her heart thundering. All of the doors were fashioned out of reclaimed wood, too, and there was one that was stained a darker color, the trim around the outside just a bit thicker.

The corner of her lips kicked up slightly. The Daltons were apparently rodeo royalty, and didn't pretend to be anything else. There was nothing understated about any of this, and somehow… Even though it was all impossibly expensive and fancy, that made her feel more at ease. This was all straight-up trailer-park fancy, and she felt right at home with that. None of that understated elegance that wealthy people often went in for. This was bedazzled.

She took a deep breath and knocked on the door.

"Come in," a voice said.

She paused for a moment, and then went inside.

She forced herself to take in her surroundings first. This office made the rest of the house look restrained. With memorabilia from the rodeo and knickknacks everywhere, it was like stepping into a Wild West museum. There were lariats, coiled up and hung on the wall, bronze statues of horses trying to buck off their riders, and McKenna's absolute favorite was the jackalope that was placed on the shelf behind the desk, seeming to survey everything.

"McKenna," he said.

And then she forced herself to look at him.

She blinked. He was like an older Gabe. His hair still dark, his skin like tanned leather, lined and rough from years of outdoor labor and probably a good dose of hard living.

And again, there was no denying that they all had each other's eyes.

"Hank," she said, taking a deep breath and squaring her shoulders.

"That's right," he said. "Gabe tells me..." The older man cleared his throat. "He tells me that you have reason to believe you're my daughter."

"I do. I have the..." She reached into her backpack and pulled out the birth certificate. "My mother is Annie Tate. And she put your name here."

She stepped up to the desk and handed the document over with shaking hands. Hank unfolded it and grasped it hard, looking down at the piece of paper.

He looked up at her. "I know Annie." He paused for a moment.

"You look a bit like her."

"I wouldn't know," McKenna said. "I don't know her."

"Did something happen to her?" His voice was full of concern, and McKenna didn't know why, really, but his concern surprised her.

"Not as far as I know," McKenna said. "She... She couldn't take care of me. When I was two she turned me over to child services."

Hank looked stricken. His dark eyes filling with tears. He wiped at them, then looked back down at the birth certificate. "Where did you grow up?"

"In foster care," she said. "I was never adopted or

anything like that. I was just… I've been moving around a lot," she said.

"What made you decide to come look for me?"

"I got a copy of my birth certificate when I aged out of the system. But the information was put in wrong. I finally got to see the original and it had your name on it."

"And it led you here," he said.

"Yes."

"I don't know how much you know about me, Mc-Kenna," he said. "But I was a foolish young man. I did a whole lot of things that I regret. One of the things I thought I did okay at was raising my kids. But now that I find out you were out there all that time… That you were by yourself… I didn't do a very good job, did I?"

"It doesn't matter now," McKenna said. "I'm here. I'm here and… I'm not angry. I'm really not."

"The other thing that I did that makes me ashamed," Hank continued, "is being unfaithful to my wife. She's a good woman. And she stuck by me professionally even when she couldn't personally. And I… I was young and I was stupid. A boy from nowhere and nothing who made it good. Who made a lot of money. Who met a beautiful rodeo queen and married her as quick as he could, but then could never give up all the attention he got from the buckle bunnies. I would go out on the road, and I would just forget. Forget that she was at home with the boys. That she was beautiful and I loved her, and more important than whatever I was feeling then. In the moment, only what I wanted was important. She left me. As she rightly should have. She left me many times. And it's just been in the last decade that she's forgiven me. And I've never strayed since then, not once. I'm not

a good man," he continued. "I thought that if I smiled
and tipped my hat and said, 'Howdy, ma'am,' that if I
held doors open for women and taught my boys everything I knew about being a cowboy, it would make me
a good man. If I went to church on Sunday, or just said
a prayer or two on days when I couldn't, I would count
as good. But that's not true."

He looked so sad, so genuine. "I've hurt people. I've
hurt you. Hurt your brothers, and my wife. I very likely
hurt your mother. She felt she couldn't come to me, and
that means I must have done something. The thing that
gets me now as I'm learning this lesson so late, I'm not
even sure I've been able to teach it to my kids. Charm
doesn't mean anything. Good looks don't mean much.
And they go away. What makes you a good person has
to come from somewhere deeper. Hell, I think I might
be a coward, McKenna."

A tear tracked down his cheek, and he opened his
desk drawer. He pulled out an envelope, and held it out
to her. "I wrote you a check. For a lot of money. I want
you to have it."

McKenna just looked at it like it was a snake; she
didn't know what to do, didn't know what to think or
say. "I don't… I don't understand."

"I just patched things up with Tammy. She's forgiven
me more than any woman should ever have to forgive
a man. And I just don't know if I can spring a daughter
on her now on top of everything else."

"You can't… Because I would remind her."

"That's the thing," Hank said. "And I feel like I'm
caught in the middle of a couple kinds of hell right now,
McKenna. But I have a family that I have to protect."

McKenna felt like all the air, all the words, had been

sucked right from her. "Well… I don't have a family. That's the thing. I don't have a family except for you. Except for Gabe and your other sons. That's it. I don't know my mom's family. Not any of their names—I don't how to find them. She doesn't want me and I—"

"This isn't something that I'm proud of, and it's not something I want to do. Believe me when I tell you, this is not a simple fix, darlin', it isn't. It tears me up inside, but I don't know what else to do. I can make sure you're safe. That you're taken care of. I can give you more than you came with. But I just can't… I've got so many sins to atone for, and this is one more. But I need to be able to… She's the best of me. My wife. I never deserved all that she gave me. I'm so sorry." Hank shook his head. "I'm so sorry."

McKenna felt like she had been stabbed clean through. Like her chest was caving in and she was going to die right there on the floor of the office of the man who was rejecting her like everyone else had.

He was handing her a check, which she supposed was more than anyone else had done, but somehow, it didn't matter.

She had come here for this. She had prepared for the eventuality that he would be like anyone else, that he wouldn't want her.

But it was that hope. That damn hope inside of her— it was stronger than any pragmatism that lived in her mind.

Damn *Anne of Green Gables*.

Because no matter what she said, no matter she'd hidden the book in a rage, part of her had believed. Had wanted to believe it so badly that reading it had made her eyeballs ache. She was torn right now. Between that voice in her head that said, *Take the money, because it's all you really wanted, anyway*, and that knot of pain inside her chest that said nothing mattered if she didn't have a family.

That said she was worth more than a check that could soothe an old man's conscience.

"I don't want your money," she said.

"What's that?"

"I don't want it. I can go out and I can earn money, Hank Dalton. And maybe it won't be that much. I don't know how much is in there. I don't want to know. But I can make my own money. I can't make family with... DNA. Believe me, I know that. But I don't need your permission to be happy. And I don't need your permission to have a family. And I damn well don't need your money."

Hank wiped a tear from his cheek. "I don't want to hurt you. It's killing me."

"Not enough. I'm not important enough. And you haven't learned your lesson. Not really. It was a real nice speech, Hank Dalton. But I don't actually think you've changed. You want to be comfortable. More than you want to do the right thing. Keep your money."

She turned and began to walk out the door, and then she paused. "I don't know what you taught your sons, but you have a daughter who had to learn everything all on her own. And I've learned that being comfortable and being happy are not the best things that you can be." She thought of Grant, the way that he had loved Lindsay. At such great cost to himself. The way that he endeavored to learn from that. From why she had loved him. From the way he tried to be that man every day.

"The important thing is how you love people. That's what makes you a man. It's what makes you matter."

And for her part, McKenna was going to love herself enough to walk away now.

She went out into the hall, and down the stairs, stopping at one of the rodeo posters with Hank Dalton emblazoned on it in big, red letters. She traced over it with her fingertips, and then put her hand back down at her side. She wasn't going to cry. Not after that.

She wandered into the living room, where she found Gabe and Grant sitting.

"I'm ready to go," she said.

"What happened?" Grant asked, almost leaping to his feet.

She felt like she was being pulled down through the floor. Not that her sadness was weighing her down, but that it was there beneath the earth tugging her through it.

"It's not going to work out."

Gabe looked frozen, his expression severe. "What'd he say?"

"He doesn't want to hurt your mother like this, Gabe. He offered me money. But I don't want it. I just want to go."

"It's not his choice," Gabe said. "You might be his daughter, but you're our sister. He can't decide whether or not we acknowledge you. Now that we have a chance to make some of his mistakes right, we have a say in it."

"I don't want to do that." She shook her head. "Can't you understand that? I don't want to be a bomb that blows your family apart because I want so badly to find a place in it. I wouldn't be able to stand coming here and having your dad angry, and your mother hurt.

I don't want to be halfway in. Maybe that makes me selfish. Maybe a sad little foster kid shouldn't have those kinds of standards. But… I already know what it's like to not be wanted. In excess. I'm not going to go through it again. I can't. Thank you, Gabe. For everything you did."

She turned and walked out to the truck, and that was when she dissolved. The first tear fell, and she couldn't stop it. Then another. Then another. By the time she got into the passenger side, she was crying like a little girl who'd lost her father.

Because she had.

Grant got in the truck a few minutes later, and started the engine. He didn't wait, or ask her if they should go. They just went.

"I wasn't going to cry," she said miserably. "I know better than to cry about things like this."

"Why didn't you take the money?"

She was stupid. She was an idiot.

She was changed.

"It's not what I want anymore." She let her head fall back against the seat. "Which is stupid, by the way. Because I still don't have a car, don't have an actual place that's mine and have, like, two outfits. Dumb. Straight-up dumbass."

"I can't blame you for not wanting to take the check off them."

"I blame *Anne of Green Gables*," she continued. "I *hated* that book, Grant. They never actually want the orphan. That's the thing. No one is ever secretly hoping that a scrawny little girl will come into their lives and change it for the better. No one."

"I can't claim to be expert on the topic of *Anne of*

Green Gables. But I know something about hope. And how it bites you in the ass."

"It does. It would be so much easier if I just didn't hope."

"I know what it's like to live without it. To know... to know that there's no light at the end of the tunnel. To know that you're walking in darkness for as long as you're on the path."

"What do you think? Is it easier to do that or...or to hope?"

Grant was silent for a moment. "I don't know. I lost my mother with no warning. On a normal day where everything seemed good. I lost my wife by inches. Certain, inevitable inches. At least then, I suppose, I knew how it would end." He cleared his throat. "Hope seems like a bitter, unfulfilled promise to me."

McKenna didn't say anything to that. It was true. And yet...

It was hope that was getting her through now, and she knew it. That even though she had turned down Hank Dalton's offer of money, even though she had lost that, she hoped there might be something more, something else, in the future. She had no real reason to believe that. And yet she did.

Hope had two sides to it, she supposed. It could be crushing, but it was also the thing that shone the light up ahead on the path, and gave you an idea of where you might go next. Everything hurt right now, but she had a place to go back to. She had Get Out of Dodge. She had Grant's bed. And there was a hell of a lot of hope in that.

"Take me home," she said.

The fact that he knew what she meant, and that he took her straight to his place, had to mean something.

Maybe if there was one lesson that she didn't learn, it should be not to hope.

CHAPTER NINETEEN

LINDY WAS IN full-scale planner mode. With Christmas only a week away, she had begun getting frantic with preparation. The shop in Copper Ridge for her winery was going to be manned by a few of her employees who would keep the place open for tastings, and she had decided she was going to have a big dinner at Grassroots Winery for the combined families of Get Out of Dodge and Grassroots.

Grant, for his part, wanted to stay home. But not because he wanted to drink by himself. Mostly, because he wanted to stay with McKenna. To keep her to himself. Anyway, it was safer than him being let out into town right now, because if he ran into Hank Dalton he was going to put his fist through the man's face.

The perk of that would be that when people saw him, they might not say, *There's Grant Dodge, widower.* They might say, *There's Grant Dodge, widower, who put his fist through Hank Dalton's face underneath the town Christmas tree.*

He could live with that.

He didn't think he had fully appreciated how... How soft McKenna was until that moment.

She played like she was all spiky edges and attitude, but she wasn't. There was more optimism in her soul than she would likely ever want to let on. Grant didn't envy it, but he admired the hell out of it.

And watching Hank shred it was infuriating.

"What do you think about Cornish game hens?"

"Why the eff would I want to eat a tiny bird?" Jamie asked.

"Because they are *fancy*," Lindy returned.

"I don't want fancy, I want tasty. Why can't we have steak?"

"Steak is not Christmas Eve dinner food," Lindy said.

"You don't have to go to this much trouble," Wyatt said. "We can just hang out at the house and have burgers."

"No," she said. "This is my first Christmas as your wife. My first Christmas not living at the winery. I want to… Bring everyone together. I want everyone to sit around a big table together and hold hands and sing songs."

"That isn't going to happen," Grant said.

"*I want Tiny Tim,*" Lindy insisted.

"No," Jamie said.

"God bless us," Lindy said. "Every one."

"Honey," Wyatt said, "I checked. It's way too late in the season to rent a small British child. They're all gone."

"You better get your knickers on, Dodge," Lindy said.

"Absolutely not," Wyatt said. "I don't do things like that. Anymore."

"Can't we just have turkey?" Jamie said. "That's at least a reasonably sized bird."

"I'll think about it," Lindy said. "Philistines." Lindy

abruptly stood from the table. "I have to go. Winery business. But we'll circle back to the menu. By which I mean you'll all cheerfully eat what I tell you to."

"I have a ride," Jamie said, standing, too. "See you later."

That left Wyatt and Grant at the table by themselves.

"You know I don't like a big party," Grant said. "I might come by for a while…"

"But what?"

"But I'm not sure I want to do this."

"It's just a dinner," Wyatt said. "And I know you're real attached to this brooding thing that you have going on, but it's really important to my wife, and that means it's really important to me."

"I'm not attached to the brooding thing," Grant said. "Gold Valley is attached to me brooding. Hell, half of Copper Ridge and the rest of Logan County is attached to me brooding, Wyatt. I'm going to go to this party and everyone is going to spend the entire time asking how I am."

"That's nice."

"It is. But I can't ever go out without being reminded. And hell, I remind myself." He shook his head. "I don't know the right balance. Between hanging on too tightly and letting go too much. I don't know what I want."

"You've seemed… Happier lately."

"Have I?"

"I thought maybe it had something to do with Mc-Kenna."

Grant gritted his teeth. For some reason he didn't want to talk about McKenna. It felt too deep, too personal. But maybe that was all part of those strangling roots, and trying to keep her out of them. Their time together was set aside from all the complications.

No one else owned that part of him.

That was the trouble with everyone knowing your pain. They all got a piece of it. They got to decide when they talked about it, when you thought about it. They had an opinion on when you should get over it, and when you shouldn't.

And there were good things. Support and prayers and dinners brought to your house, but all that sharing sometimes felt too heavy.

Still, he wasn't going to sit there and lie to his brother.

"We've gotten… Close."

"Are you sleeping with her?"

"Dammit, Wyatt, it's not really your business."

"So, you are."

A muscle Grant's jaw twitched. "Yes."

"That's good. I know you were in a relationship for a long time, but sex doesn't have to be that big of a deal."

"Says the guy that ended up marrying his last casual fling?"

"Well, then there's women who are different. Who change you. And make you into a guy who can't do that kind of stuff anymore, I guess. A guy who doesn't want to."

"The fucking problem, Wyatt, is that I met that woman when I was seventeen years old. I didn't want to play the field. Not even then. I wanted to marry her. And then she died, and I still don't want to do it. I'm living a life I don't want to live. So how do you help with that?"

Wyatt's eyes met his, serious and way too insightful for Grant's liking. "Make it a life you want to live, Grant. Because you aren't dead."

The words hung heavy between them. Filled the space, filled Grant with a kind of useless rage that had no function or form.

Because he was right. Dammit all, his brother was right.

But Wyatt being right didn't change anything. Didn't change the fact that everything in him wanted to tear his own heart out of his chest and demand it stop...

Feeling.

"I don't know what I want," he said. "I thought I wanted casual. Hell, Wyatt, I envied your casual. For years. I told you that. While I sat there in my house, with everything so heavy and real and tragic, I wanted a little bit of what you had. Or at least wanted to believe you were out there loving it. All the women you could handle, whose faces blurred together and names you couldn't remember. The applause and the glory and all of that."

Wyatt sighed. "Okay, you want to know the truth?"

"No. But I've had nothing but the hard truth about life for a long-ass time, so why stop now?"

"It's not fun. Casual sex like that. I mean, it feels good. For a little bit. But then you're left with you, and none of it changes you, except it makes you ask questions about yourself that you don't want to know the answer to. You don't do it because you're normal. You don't do it because you're emotionally stable. You do it because you're running. You do it because you're trying to fill the void inside of you with something. And yeah, you do it because it feels good. But again, that only lasts for a minute. And I... Look, having been with Lindy now, and knowing what more it can be... I couldn't go back. All the advice I gave you was from an idiot. You're more experienced than I am, Grant. Bottom line. Maybe it doesn't seem that way, but you are. And when I look back, as a man who had never been in love, telling a man who had, and lost it, how to behave... I'm just a jackass. I see things in a hell of a lot different way now. I used to say sex was no bigger a deal than a handshake. But I don't believe that now. And it's no surprise to me it's gotten you a little messed up."

"Everything's got me messed up." He wasn't going to go into the truth of his situation with his brother. There was sharing, and then there was...

McKenna was the only person that ever needed to know. What was between them, what they knew about each other, was no one else's business. For however long it lasted, it was no one else's business.

"On the subject of McKenna," Grant said. "Are you inviting the Daltons to the dinner?"

"No. It's just winery and Dodge people."

"Good."

"Are you in a pissing contest with Gabe over a woman?"

"No. He's McKenna's half brother."

Wyatt nearly choked on that. "Really?"

"It's why she's here. And Hank Dalton offered her a payoff to go away."

"I knew he was a hound dog, but I didn't know he was a dick."

"Yeah, well, apparently he is. I just don't want McKenna exposed to them right now."

"You care about her."

"I don't know how *not* to," Grant said. "I wanted to

try the casual-sex thing. But I'm tangled up in her, and I'm not sure I like it."

"I can relate to that."

"I don't know what I want."

"Come to the Christmas Eve thing. Think about that far ahead, and don't think any further. Maybe it's unreasonable to think you could stay completely emotionally unattached. Why can't you be her friend? And why can't it just...be what it is for now?"

"I like that better than just about any other scenario."

"Don't overthink," Wyatt said. "I know that's not easy for you."

"Surprisingly easier when I'm getting some."

He attempted a smile, and Wyatt laughed at him. "You have no idea how happy I am to hear that."

"You're overly invested."

"I just want you to be happy." He patted Grant on the back. "I mean it. Whatever this turns into, or doesn't turn into, be happy while you have it. Just to try something different."

"Screw you."

Wyatt laughed again. "I mean, it's nice to know you didn't have a whole personality transplant."

"I might like one."

"No." Wyatt shook his head. "We need you like you are. Bennett is the responsible one. I'm the irresponsible one. The only one that would have been stupid enough to convince everyone to go all in on this dude ranch business. And you care. You care deeper about things than I ever thought I could, before Lindy. It's not a weakness. It's something I've always admired in you. You saw what losing Mom did to Dad, and you... You married Lindsay knowing it would end that way. I know Bennett does medical procedures on big animals and puts his safety at risk there, and I rode bulls in an arena. You're the bravest one, Grant. The bravest of all of us. It's not a flaw to care."

Grant suddenly felt tired to his bones. "It's exhausting."

"I'm sure it is. But someday I hope you find someone who can give it back to you in the way you've given it out. And then maybe it won't be. Not quite so much."

MCKENNA STILL FELT bruised but hopeful by the time Christmas Eve rolled around. Lindy had loaned her a simple, long-sleeved red dress to wear to dinner. Though Jamie had insisted that a dress wasn't required, and that she wasn't going to wear one, McKenna had wanted to. Because she had wanted to do something special.

If anyone knew why, they weren't saying so.

But Grant had made it clear that she would be sitting with him at dinner, so she supposed it was a little bit like a date. Like a real date, in front of everyone, which felt very close to a declaration of some kind.

She shook out her hands, feeling slightly giddy and more than a little bit nervous.

Grant would be at her cabin any minute, and part of her wanted to tug him back to her room, take off both their clothes and just spend time in bed, where they were comfortable.

Because outside of that there were feelings and poinsettias and family who had rejected her, and it was all just a little bit much.

But another part of her wanted to do this. Wanted to be part of his story, part of his roots. Like he would be part of hers.

It was about making choices. She and Grant had talked about that when she had first come to live at the ranch. What were you going to do with your life now that you could control it? That was the question. There had been a whole lot of things that were out of her hands. A bad start that had been difficult to overcome. But when she had chosen to walk away from Hank Dalton's money, some things had become clear.

She didn't have to be that hard, desperate creature the world had tried to form her into. She didn't have to kill her hope.

She could choose happiness. She could choose joy. She could choose hope. She was only stuck if she didn't move forward. And she was done living in the past. Done laying blame for where she was. Because on the other side of blame she was free to move. And she needed that freedom.

She sure as hell didn't owe it to her mother. She didn't owe it to Hank Dalton. And she didn't even owe it to Grant.

She didn't know what he wanted. She knew that he had been through a lot. Knew that he didn't think he wanted a wife or a life of domesticity again. Didn't think that he could love.

But he had also shown her something different. His actions were deeper. The way that he held her, looked at her, made love to her. The fact that he had taken her to see Lindsay's spot.

That he had brought her into his pain, into his loss. Into his life.

They'd had more honesty with each other than either of them had had with anyone else, and that had to mean something.

She had been trying to keep it from being true, out of fear for what might happen, but she was tired of waiting on the whims of other people.

Something in life had to be her responsibility. Her choice.

She looked in the mirror and messed up her hair one last time, rubbing her lips together and admiring the dramatic effect of the red gloss she had put over the top of them. She didn't usually do makeup, but she had a little bit cobbled together from clearance end caps at drugstores and whatever samples she could get out of the salespeople in the nicer department stores.

And tonight it seemed like the kind of night to wear it. She had a date, after all.

A date with the most beautiful man she had ever known. She had a date with Grant Dodge; she had to look good for it.

There was a knock on her cabin door and she scampered away from the mirror, moving quickly to answer it.

She opened it, and her heart fluttered when she saw him.

She looked up at his face, at those glorious green eyes.

He felt familiar in a way no other person ever had.

He felt like home.

It hit her then, that that's what this feeling was. Not because of a place, but because of a person. A person she'd known for just over a month. She had lived so many places, met so many people, and none of them had ever made her feel like this.

It was a sense of right. A fitting. Belonging.

A feeling she had never imagined she might have.

"You ready?" he asked.

"Yes," she said.

He extended his arm, like a damned gentleman, and she looped hers through it, walking out to his truck with him.

She was getting inside of it when she realized. When she realized that she loved Grant.

And it was like a bright light went off in front of her eyes. It was hope, in its purest and most wonderful form.

McKenna had never loved another person in her entire life. That realization hit her, sharp and clear.

When she was a little girl, she might have loved the idea of her mother, before she had realized that the woman had left her. But she had never had her in her life. She had never loved any of the foster families she had lived with, never loved any of her boyfriends.

This feeling was new. And it wasn't... Easy. It was sharp and hard, it was too much. But it was certain. The most certain thing she had ever felt.

And she had nothing to assure her that everything would end up okay. There were so many things standing between them. So many roots that had him held down and held still.

But she hoped.

Because in that moment she thought... If she could love, after all this time, if she could want something other than the small, attempted cynicism she had tried to make for herself and call it a life, then why couldn't he change, too?

To know, so very suddenly, that something so beautiful existed in the world, and to not try to grab on to it with both hands... That was the real insanity.

To run away out of fear. No, she wouldn't do that.

She felt enervated now, not quite sure what to do with herself. What did you do when you realized that you loved a man?

She had no idea what to do.

Most of her life had been marked by grim determination. There had been very little in the way of desperation. Even when her situation was actually quite desperate. She hadn't allowed herself to care that much. If she didn't eat, she didn't eat. If the power was turned off, it was turned off. If this foster family didn't want her, the next one would work just as well, and either way, she would have a place to sleep.

But she felt desperate just now. To reach out to him, and have him reach back. Desperate to make him feel what she felt. To show him that something like this couldn't be…wrong. How could it be?

But she was hardly going to tell him right now. In the truck. Even though the silence was strange, and she knew it. But she also couldn't force herself to speak.

And he wasn't talking, either.

It made her wish she had stayed home. That she had dragged him back to bed, because at least then she might have shown him with her body. They were good like that. Good together that way. It was harder, the talking.

Especially when she barely knew what she was feeling, much less how to say it.

They drove through town, down the highway toward Grassroots Winery, which McKenna hadn't seen yet. When they turned onto the property, her jaw dropped slightly. The whole place was beautiful. Well-manicured with a large, gorgeous house overlooking the lawn, and barns that looked as if they'd been restored, lit up with

Christmas lights and decorated with wreaths. "It's beautiful," McKenna said, trying to do something to break the heaviness between them.

"Lindy loves this place," Grant said.

"It seems a lot more...her than the ranch."

"I guess Wyatt is more *her* than any place. He would have moved here for her, but Get Out of Dodge is our family property in a way that this isn't for her. She got it from her in-laws. Well, from her ex-husband. In her divorce. And it's definitely her pride and joy, but it's not the same—"

"It's not the same as roots," she said.

"Yeah," he said.

"What if some of your roots are poisoned?" she asked.

She knew she was pushing close to things she probably shouldn't be.

"I don't know," he said. "They're still yours, I guess."

"I guess," she returned.

They got out of the car, and Grant came around to her side, frowning slightly when he found her already outside the vehicle. "I would have opened the door for you."

"Oh, you don't have to do that."

"I wanted to."

She ducked her head. "Maybe you can just... Hold my hand instead?"

"I suppose I could do that."

He held his hand out, and she took hold of it, and the two of them walked toward the barn together. The structure was already full of people, seated at tables that were decorated with ornate centerpieces, great webs of twinkling Christmas lights strung from the rustic wooden chandelier at the center of the room, extending all the way to the far corners of the restored barn. Jamie was seated at a table in the center of the room, and Grant led her over that way. The family table, she assumed.

And he was including her.

Her heart gave a kick when she realized he hadn't dropped her hand when they had come inside. No. He was still holding on to her. He wasn't hiding that he was with her.

But to Jamie's credit, she didn't comment.

"I'm so glad you could make it," Jamie said, directing that at Grant.

"I couldn't disappoint Lindy."

"Well," Jamie said, her tone brooding. "She disappointed me."

"How so?"

"Cornish game hens," Jamie said, picking up a piece of paper set on the plate in front of her. "Cornish game hens. Stuffing with cranberries... I don't understand what any of this is."

"It's going to be good," Wyatt said, taking his seat next to Jamie. "Because Lindy made it."

Lindy snorted and sat down next to her husband. "I did not make it. But I delegated the making of it, and I have very good taste. Also, Pie in the Sky has provided little pies for everyone."

"I don't want *tiny* pies," Jamie said. "I want large pies."

"There will be extra pies," Lindy said, rolling her eyes. "I have one feral sister-in-law already. I didn't think I'd end up acquiring another one."

"Where *is* Bea?" McKenna asked, assuming that was who Lindy meant.

"I think she went to try and force Dane to come out for dinner."

"She cares a lot for him," McKenna said.

"He's basically a brother to her," Wyatt said, shrugging.

Lindy and Jamie exchanged glances. And McKenna knew exactly what they meant by them.

She was, yet again, so captivated by the connection between these people. To be here with them at the table was…amazing. She wanted to tell them that. Wanted to tell them all exactly how she felt. She wanted to start by thanking Bea so much for her kindness. Her friendship. And Jamie for the same. Wyatt and Lindy for bringing her into the ranch, for giving her a job.

And Grant… It wasn't a thank-you she wanted to give Grant. She just wanted to give him her heart. That was all.

She took a deep breath and tried to let herself get lost in the conversation around her.

"I better go check on the food," Lindy said.

"I'll go with you," McKenna said.

She scurried after Lindy, placing her hand on her arm. "Lindy… I just wanted to thank you."

Lindy stopped and frowned. "For what?"

"For giving me a job. For wanting to help me. Actually help me, not just do something out of pity, or to teach me a lesson. You and Wyatt are two of the most decent people I've ever known."

"I should be thanking you," she said.

"Why?"

"Grant."

"Oh… I…"

"He cares about you. And in all the time I've known

him I've never seen him with a woman. He's been completely consumed with the past."

"I don't know if that's it," McKenna said softly. "I think it's a little bit more complicated than that."

"I wouldn't know. Because he doesn't share. He never tells anyone anything. He's just always… Kind of isolated. I mean, he'll go out drinking with his brothers, and he'll come to the house for dinner, but there's always a distance. I hope with you there isn't."

"So do I," McKenna said softly. "But… I don't know."

"You're good for him," Lindy said. "You come from somewhere else completely, and you have had your own heart stuff. Your own life. I think it's good for him to care about someone else's pain. I think it's good for him to understand that there's a world out there that isn't this."

"I'm kind of amazed to find the world that's here," McKenna said. "I've never had a home or a… A family. Not really. I've never seen it. But the way you all are, with each other, with the town. You've shown me things that I didn't believe existed. And that's given me hope in ways I didn't know I could have it."

"I understand just what you mean, McKenna. Wyatt gave me hope I thought was gone. Love I thought I was too cynical to have. I like to think I did the same for him. It's amazing how two broken people can fix each other, and I wouldn't have believed they could, until him."

McKenna kept playing those words over and over in her head as she helped Lindy with some last-minute preparations. At that point, the rest of the family table was filled with the arrival of Bennett and his wife, and their son. Luke and Olivia joined not long after, followed by some winery employees and former winery employees that McKenna had never met before.

Including Clara and Alex Donnelly, who were apparently bison ranchers in the neighboring town, Sabrina Donnelly, Beatrix's sister and Lindy's former sister-in-law, along with her husband, Liam. And there were a few other Donnellys that arrived, as well.

"Is everyone in Copper Ridge related?" she asked.

"Not all of them," Lindy said. "Sheriff Garrett isn't a Donnelly. Nor is anyone in his family. Or Mayor West and her husband. Well, I guess they are kind of related to the Garretts by marriage because Kate Garrett is married to Jack Monaghan and he was the secret son of Nathan West. Who isn't really a secret anymore."

McKenna snorted. "More secret babies?"

"Every town has them, I suppose."

"Well, I guess I'm the lucky one for Gold Valley. Maybe I should meet Jack. We could start the Bastard Children's Coalition of Logan County."

In spite of her protests, Jamie seemed to enjoy dinner just fine. And much to McKenna's surprise, a band came out after dinner and began to play. There was a small dance floor area, and many of the couples—the sheriff and his wife, the mayor and her husband, the secret baby and his rodeo wife—all went out onto the floor.

McKenna watched them, her heart twisting. They were in love. And it was so blindingly obvious that it almost hurt to look at it. She looked over at Grant, twisting her napkin in her lap. "Grant," she said. "Will you dance with me?"

He looked shocked. "I don't... I don't know how."

"Neither do I."

"I've never danced with anyone before."

"I haven't, either," she said.

He had given her her first experience riding a horse. She had given him his first experience riding…well.

But here was something neither of them had done before, and she wanted so badly for him to say yes.

"Okay," he said, taking hold of her hand and leading her out onto the dance floor.

He pulled her out into the middle of all those couples, in the middle of all that love, and she thought her heart had possibly grown three sizes. She cupped his face and kissed him, right there, in front of everyone. She could feel eyes on them, but she didn't care.

Grant froze, as if he suddenly realized it, too. "I guess this is kind of a statement," he said.

That punctured her buoyancy slightly. She was sure he had realized that before now. But apparently not.

"Well, I guess this is… Not something you normally do."

"No," he said

"Do you regret it?"

"No," he said decisively.

"Good," she said, drifting closer to him and resting her head on his chest as they swayed to the music. She let her eyes drift closed, felt the beat of his heart, steady against her cheek. "Grant," she whispered. "I love you."

He went stiff, and then he released his hold on her.

He stood there, staring at her, still in the middle of the dance floor, and she knew she had made a mistake.

Oh, she had made a terrible mistake.

Whatever she had thought… Whatever she had been thinking…

She had been wrong. And she had been stupid. Because that wasn't what he wanted to hear. He was not happy at all.

And then he turned, walking away and leaving her on the dance floor. Her hero abandoning her in front of everyone.

Well, McKenna Tate was not the kind of woman who took things with grace, dignity or acceptance. No way. She was fire, brimstone and pointy elbows.

This would be no exception.

Ignoring the stares of the people in the room, McKenna went right out after him.

It was dark outside, freezing cold, the parking lot barely illuminated by the lights that covered the barn.

"Where are you going?"

"McKenna... Don't do this."

"Don't do what?"

"We had an agreement."

"This is the part where you lecture me about how just because I was a virgin doesn't mean it's... Oh, wait, that was you." She affected mock surprise and was gratified by how angry it made him look.

"Yes," he said, teeth gritted. "It was. And I wasn't a virgin by accident, McKenna. You know that I've been through some things. You know that my life hasn't been simple."

"Yeah, well, mine has been an absolute tea party. Waltzing through with my pinky out holding trays of tiny cakes."

"I'm not saying yours hasn't been hard."

"No, but yours is the hardest, and I can't ever know. Congratulations. You get your gold medal. Is that what you want?"

"I don't want a medal," he said. "I want to feel normal. For one second."

"I don't," she said, her voice scraping her throat raw. "I don't want to be normal." Oh, what a world it was that she realized this now. Right now when it was all falling apart. That she didn't want to just find a way to be like everyone else. She wanted to be special. She wanted to be Anne of Green Gables. That was why it ached like it did. She wanted it. So much. More than her next breath.

"I don't want to survive," she said. "I want to *live*, Grant. I want… I want everything. I want to be with a man who loves me and has great sex with me. I want to have a place that I can call my home. I want to have a family. I want it with you. I don't care if that's silly, or if I'm putting myself out there. I don't care. Why can't we have this? Why can't we have… Why can't we be happy? Why not, Grant?"

"McKenna, it's not that easy."

"Why the hell isn't it that easy? *Move forward, dammit.*"

"It's easy for you to say. You got nothing holding you down. I know you had it hard, but you've never had to let a damn thing go in your life."

"And you're bound up in roots. Poison roots. Things you won't let go."

"Things I *can't* let go."

"Why not?" she exploded.

He reached into his shirt and pulled the chain out, the chain with the rings. "I can't let this go. It's who I am and—"

"She's dead, Grant." The words spilled out on a cloud of frozen air. "And if you want to honor that, then you should live the life that her love enabled you to have."

"I don't understand what that means," he said.

"If she really changed you, then you wouldn't be standing here stubbornly clinging to your pain. That's the man you were in high school. The man who bullied people. The man who couldn't let go of his loss. At some point you have to move on. You have to release the anger. That doesn't mean forgetting the people you care about… But you have to… Grant, this isn't what your mother would have wanted for you. For God's sake, it's not what Lindsay wanted for you."

"You don't know what the hell Lindsay wanted for me."

"I know she loved you. I know she did. How could she not have? I'm sure she loved every single thing that I love about you. The way you care for people. The way you… Grant, the way you hold me." A sob blocked her throat, tried to stop her words from coming out, but she pushed on. "I'm sure she loved the way you held her. I'm sure she loved the way you looked at her—God knows I do. And if she loved you even the tiniest bit the way that I do, then this isn't the life she would have wanted for you."

He shook his head. "You can't know that. Married people say that all the time. *I would just want you to be happy*, but would they really? If you love someone, forsaking all others, do you really want them to move on after you're gone?"

"When you know from the beginning that moving on is what they'll have to do? Yes, I think so." She didn't know where her certainty came from, but it was there. Like the way she knew she loved Grant, it was there. And maybe she hadn't had a whole network of love and family all her life, so maybe she didn't have the experience to make those kinds of proclamations. But she knew it. In her heart. "Like you said, you knew that you weren't going to be like other married couples, and so did she. Just like you knew always that you would have to let her go, she knew she'd have to let you go, Grant, but this isn't the way she would have wanted you left."

"You can't…"

She closed her eyes. "Okay," she said. "Forget it. Forget what she would have wanted. What do you want? You keep saying you don't know. But you're not the kind of man who doesn't know his own mind. You make decisions. You're the kind of man that comes to my door late at night and takes me in his arms and kisses me till neither of us can breathe. That's who you are. So don't give me this BS about how you don't know what you want. I think you must. Forget what she wants. Forget what your mother would have wanted. Forget what the town expects of you. What do *you* want? Answer me that."

"I don't want to be hurt anymore," he said. "I'm tired of loving people. I'm tired of taking care of them. I wanted to get laid. That's it."

"Is that what you want now? Is that why you brought me here? Because you like sleeping with me? It has to be more than that."

"I don't want it to be," he said, his voice rough. "Just because I don't know how to not make it more doesn't mean that isn't what I want."

"So what, you feel something, but you don't want to?"

"I don't know what I feel. But I know I don't have the energy for it. You're another project, McKenna, and I don't want to take that on."

McKenna felt like she'd been slapped across the face. First Hank Dalton didn't want to take her on, because he couldn't possibly burden his wife... And now... Even to him, she was just another project.

"I see. Just another wounded bird for you take care of?"

"Hell," he said. "I don't know."

"Yes, you do. That's what you said."

"It's not really what I mean."

"Yes, it is."

"McKenna..."

She let out a sharp breath that cut her on the way out. "Do you love me?"

"What we have works," Grant said. "I don't want to get married again. I don't want to be in love. I don't want my whole future, my whole everything, tied up in another person. I don't want to do it again. But what we're doing right now works, and I don't see why we should rock the boat."

"Because I don't take half. Not now. Not anymore. I won't. I refuse. I'm not taking Hank Dalton's money, I'm not taking your pity sex. I deserve to be loved. I deserve it all. Everything you have to give. And you know what, if you don't have it in you to give everything, then you're right. We shouldn't be together."

"So you don't love me, then?"

"No, I do. But I deserve someone who loves me the same. Believe me when I tell you I would give you everything. But you need to give me everything, too. You wouldn't end up taking care of me, but God knows I might end up taking care of you. And I don't do trades. I'm not going to give you sex so you can give me a house, so we can pretend like we are a happy family. I want the real thing. I've never loved anyone before.

I've never told another person that I loved them. I love you. And if you're not willing to give me that back, then we're done."

"Just like that?"

She huffed out a laugh, a tear sliding down her cheek. "Yes, *just like that*. Weeks of sleeping together, talking with each other, sharing secrets. Confiding in each other. Holding each other, laughing, crying. Just like that. So fast and simple."

For a moment, she thought he'd run out of things to say.

"I can't," he said finally. "You knew. You knew in the beginning. I told you—"

"You told me not to talk. And yet then we did all that talking. So I guess I thought maybe somewhere along the line the rules might have changed, or that maybe there weren't rules anymore."

"I can't," he said.

McKenna stood there, her heart… She didn't think her heart could be broken any more than it already had been. She'd been rejected over and over again in her life. But never once by someone she loved. All the pain that she'd endured before had been a primer for this. This was what it meant to be shattered. To be broken. It was what it meant to be devastated.

"I'm leaving."

"How will you get a ride?"

"I'll call a cab."

"There are, like, two in Gold Valley."

"I'll figure it out," she snapped.

"McKenna, *I'll* go. Go back inside."

"No," she said, storming away from him. And she ran smack into Bea.

"McKenna?"

"Bea," she said. "Are you going inside?"

"No," she said, her voice sounding small and sad. "I'm leaving actually."

"So am I. Take me with you."

"What about Grant—"

"He's going to go back inside and join his family. I need to go home."

"I'll take you," Bea said, shooting Grant a wicked look, and wrapping her arm around McKenna's shoulders, guiding her to the truck.

When they were inside and on the road, McKenna spoke first. "Thank you," she said. "Not just for this. For everything. Everything... My coat. Being my friend. Thank you."

"You're welcome," Bea said. "What happened?"

"He doesn't love me."

Bea swallowed hard. "I know the feeling."

McKenna felt a pit growing in her stomach. She hated the idea of Bea being hurt. She was legitimately one of the sweetest people McKenna had ever known. Kind to small mammals and stray women who had been found sleeping in abandoned cabins. Dane should realize how lucky he was to have a woman like her love him.

But he was a man. So of course he didn't.

"Did he... Did Dane say something to you tonight?"

Bea's head whipped to the side. "I... No. I just... I'm not stupid. I know he doesn't see me that way. I'm like a sister to him. I hoped, for a long time. But... I can't even get him to come to a dinner that his sister is throwing. I don't have any kind of pull over him at all, and if he cared..."

"Well, sometimes men just can't see things clearly. On account of the fact that their heads are so far up their asses."

Bea laughed. "Yeah, I suppose that's true."

They lapsed into silence, and along with the quiet, a slow rolling thunderclap of pain went through her body. The road felt dark and closed in. There were no streetlights outside of town. Just a wall of dark, impenetrable trees that seemed to make it all that much more blank and hopeless.

She *had* hoped. For a brief moment, and now everything felt dark again. And she wondered if it had been wrong. If she had been wrong all this time. Maybe taking a chance had been wrong, because if she hadn't done that... Then she would at least still have him. As it was now, she was alone again. With no direction... No nothing.

Her phone buzzed, and she pulled it out of her purse, holding it up.

She had a message from Gabe.

She opened up her texts and began to read.

Can you come over tonight? Dad wants to see you again.

She set the phone down, just as Bea turned the corner, her headlights illuminating the road up ahead. And right then, she realized that her path hadn't ended. That hope was lighting the way.

It was always there. Even when it was dark.

"Bea... Can you take me to the Daltons'?"

"Sure," Bea said, sounding surprised.

"I have some business to take care of with them."

CHAPTER TWENTY

THAT WAS HOW she found herself in the Daltons' living room, surrounded by all of them—including Hank's wife, Tammy—and one of the largest Christmas trees she had ever seen inside of a house.

"You *are* Hank's daughter," Tammy said, her tone soft and even.

"I am mostly sure that I am, yes."

"I'm sure," one of the other Dalton brothers, Jacob, spoke. He looked a lot like Gabe, but was broader, more heavily muscled, with the same uncommonly handsome face. "She looks just like us."

Caleb, the other brother, nodded in agreement. "It's pretty clear to me."

"I never doubted it," Gabe added.

"I couldn't leave things like that," Hank said. "I kept thinking about what you said. About how I hadn't changed, after all. Because I was just looking out for myself. And you're right about that. Not only was I protecting myself, I was allowing my wife to keep on living with lies. And I told myself I wouldn't do that anymore. I promised her that was over. So that means airing it all. All my sins. Not that you're a sin."

"Sorry to crash your Christmas," McKenna mumbled, directing that at Hank's wife. She didn't know how she was supposed to respond to what he'd just said. And she was still so very raw from what had happened with Grant.

"No," Tammy said. "None of this is your fault. You existing isn't the hurtful thing, I hope you understand that. It's never fun to have to hear about Hank's past... misdeeds."

"In fairness," McKenna said. "As misdeeds go, I am a very old one."

Tammy nodded. "It's true. My reaction would be different if there was someone showing up with a baby on the doorstep. But I still wouldn't be angry at the baby. Believe me, McKenna, I can get redneck crazy with the best of them, but that's between me and my husband."

Everyone was looking at her expectantly. But expectant for what, she didn't know. "I don't... I don't understand."

"You're part of our family," Hank said. "You're my daughter. And... We can go forward and do DNA tests, or any of that, just to be certain, if you think that's important, though I did have a relationship with your mother, and you do look a hell of a lot like me. I already told you, if there's one thing I've ever been proud of, it's the kind of father I was. I know you're grown, and I know that you had the life you've had, and I'm not suggesting that I can just walk in and fix everything, or that this will be instant or easy. You deserve a place here. With us. Because you're mine just as much as these boys are. And that matters. You're my daughter, McKenna, and that matters."

"Are you... Is this real?"

"Yes," Hank said. "I'm very sorry for what I said to you when you came to see me the first time. I tried to do what I thought was the right thing, but it was wrong.

And now I'm trying again. Just to warn you, I'll probably do the wrong thing a few more times."

"We're about to have dinner," Tammy said.

McKenna was about to say she'd already eaten, but…

When in her life had she ever been offered the chance to eat two dinners? When in her life had she been accepted at one family table, and then at her own family table?

Never. Grant might have broken her heart, but right here, right now, she had found some roots.

She was trembling. Maybe because of this. Maybe she was just still shaking from what had happened with Grant. She wanted…

She was here in this living room, being brought into this family just like she'd barely ever allowed herself to dream she might be, and all she could think of was how much she wanted to run back to where Grant was.

Scream at him until he listened.

Until he understood.

But she'd spent so much of her life wanting what wasn't there. What she couldn't have.

The Daltons were offering her a space that Grant wasn't. And she was going to take it.

McKenna took a deep breath and tried to shift the weight in her chest. "I'd love to."

CHAPTER TWENTY-ONE

GRANT DODGE WAS ALONE, and theoretically, that was the way he liked it best. Alone, and about to be drunk. "And a bit of an asshole," he said into the silence of the cabin. He uncorked the bottle of whiskey, ready to pour himself some, when there was a knock on the door.

He opened it, and Wyatt greeted him, looking thunderous.

"Are you here to lecture me?"

"I sure as hell am."

Grant huffed out a breath. "Save it."

"Why did you do that?" Wyatt asked, his expression uncharacteristically fierce. Wyatt was usually a pretty easygoing guy. But apparently not tonight. "Why did you let the best thing that's happened to you in a long while walk away from you on that dance floor?"

"I think I walked away from her."

"Then you're an even bigger dumbass."

"Go ahead and lecture me," Grant said. "It won't make a difference. This isn't actually about what you think my life should look like. This is about what I feel like trying to survive."

"Love isn't about surviving. What you're doing... That's *just* surviving. Love is about living. I get it. I didn't want it, either—"

"I *had* it," Grant cut him off. "And I lost it."

"And you knew you would." Wyatt's words were hoarse and flat in the room. And true. "Dammit, Grant. What you did when you married Lindsay was a great thing. But you chose to do it. You knew you were going to lose her."

Grant swallowed hard. "I didn't know what it would feel like."

Wyatt shook his head. "I'm sure. But you watched our father contend with that same grief, and you walked into it. Because of love."

"I don't want to go through it again."

"Dad did. He found Freda, and they fell in love. It's as real as anything he had with Mom."

"Well, good for Dad. I lost Mom, and I lost Lindsay…"

"And you don't know if you'll lose McKenna. Is that it? Is that what you're looking for—certainty? You can handle grief, as long as you know it's coming?"

"No," he said, the knife twisting in his gut.

Because *maybe*. Maybe that was a little bit true. Losing his mother had blindsided him. And the anger that had come out of it was…hell.

Losing Lindsay by inches had been a nightmare, but Wyatt was right about one thing. The loss of her had been a certainty, and even if he had hoped… The surprise had been in every year she lived, and never when she had died.

"I don't want to go through anything like that again. I don't want to… Wyatt, it's like tearing my chest open and just letting the damn wolves feast on me."

"You don't want to be happy."

"I didn't say that."

"But it's true. You're determined to be miserable.

You don't want to be fixed. You don't want to move on, and for the life of me, I can't figure out why."

"Because there's... God knows what's up ahead. You don't know, I don't know. People die every day. That's the thing. Little boys lose their mothers, good women get cancer and they die. And there's just... I can move forward to *what*? Another love I might lose?"

Wyatt stared at him for a long time and Grant could see he was grappling with what to say next. With the fact he felt like, as an older brother, he had to say something. Grant was about to tell him to go when Wyatt spoke again.

"Maybe," Wyatt said slowly, "there aren't any guarantees in life. You can't have one. No one's going to give you one. But what you have, what you *know* you have, is a woman who cares a great deal for you. She might even love you. *That* you know. You might not have tomorrow, but you have today. You have yesterday, and no one can change it, no one can take that from you. I know that you're hurt by it. I expect you to have scars. But what will the legacy of those scars be, Grant? That you were still aboveground, breathing and walking around, but you let yourself die before you had to? Or that you got back up again."

Wyatt cleared his throat. "You know, that's how you become good at anything. When you ride bulls for a living, falling down is inevitable. You become a champion if you stand up enough times. That's the only way. Every damned asshole out in that arena will fall. And I didn't fall less, I just rode more often. And had to get up more often."

Grant huffed out a breath, his chest aching and

heavy. "And I appreciate that. But falling down in the arena is not losing people."

"I know that. But it's a pretty decent metaphor for life. The falling down isn't a separate part of the ride. It's all one thing. Just like life. There's bad, and there's good. But it's all your life. What are you going to choose to do with it? Because the choice is yours. No one is holding you back but you."

It was so very close to what McKenna had said to him earlier it was eerie. Made it ring true. Far truer than he would like.

What do you want?

And suddenly, it broke over him, clear as day. There wasn't a set, mystical lesson to be learned from the things he'd been through in his life. And pretending there was… It was holding him stuck in place. The poison roots had been planted by himself. And he'd stood there with them wrapped around his boots for all this time. Making excuses. Claiming he needed to hold on tight because he couldn't be a good man without Lindsay's influence.

It was fear. Fear to move. Fear he might just be headed into more pain.

But he could be free if he chose to be.

And the lesson was whatever he chose to carry with him.

Because it was his life, and no one could live it for him. He also couldn't live on solely as a memorial to someone else.

He couldn't live at all if he kept on trying to drink from a dry well.

The past was over. Tomorrow wasn't in his control.

But today could be whatever he made it as long as he was brave enough to try.

He knew he must have said goodbye to Wyatt, must have made the decision to get in his truck and drive up to Lindsay's spot. But until he was standing right at the edge of the river in the dark, he didn't fully realize he'd done it.

It was so dark he could barely see, but he knew he was in the right place. He could feel it. The way that it settled his soul, the way the breeze felt filtering through the trees. It had been his place before Lindsay, and it had become theirs together.

He sat down on the edge of the water until the sky started to turn from gray, darkness running from the rays of the sun slowly creeping over the edges of the mountain.

He was freezing. He was stiff.

But for the first time in a long while, he felt like things might just make sense.

He closed his eyes and thought of Lindsay, the way that he did. Blonde and smiling up at him, looking at him like he was someone who mattered. The way that it had inspired him to change. To become someone who was worthy of that kind of faith.

Maybe McKenna was right. Maybe a man had to have some good in him to respond to that in the first place. But it was because of Lindsay he'd found it. She had been exactly what he needed then. She had changed him. The experience of loving her, caring for her, losing her, had changed him. And on the other side of that...

McKenna was what he needed.

If he'd met her sixteen years ago, it wouldn't have worked. Not even close. But now...

She was exactly the right woman for the man he was now.

The man he had become because he had lost his mother. Because he'd loved Lindsay and lost her, too. Because he'd waited thirty-four years to sleep with a woman. Because he took things too seriously, and had been hurt too many times.

That was the man who loved McKenna Tate.

For the first time, he was happy to be that man. Because of McKenna.

He took a deep breath, and let it out. He knew he had to do this. It was something he had been avoiding for a long damned time. But now, he had a reason that meant he couldn't put it off any longer.

"I was so sorry when I lost you," he said softly, the sound of the running water nearly consuming the sound of his voice. "But I'm so damn glad that I had you."

He moved to his knees, leaning forward, touching the earth, taking a fallen a leaf between his fingers and turning it slowly. "You were the right woman for me when I needed you most. I hope I was the right man for you when you needed me."

He took a deep breath, his chest feeling like it might crack in two. "I know for a fact that you changed me for the better. I know for a fact that…if I can make a decision and move forward without fear, I'm going to do my damnedest to be the right man for McKenna. But you're part of that. You always will be. I'm the one that's kept me frozen for all this time. You saw an angry boy headed to nowhere and believed in him. All that I am now is because of who I was. And you were part of that. You gave me my future. I'm finally ready to have it."

He released his hold on the leaf, and let it fall into

the creek. Watched as the current carried it away. Took
it out of sight.

He lowered his head for a moment, then raised his
face to the sky. The sun moved up over a low point in
the mountain and spilled over the side, sending gold
piercing through the gray.

Light chasing the darkness away.

Hope.

Grant knew that his decision was made. He might not
be able to make sure there was no risk of loss, he might
not be able to protect himself forever, but it was a deep,
real love. A brave love that had changed him all those
years ago. And he needed deep, brave love now. But in
order to claim it, he was going to have to move forward.

Lindsay had made room in his heart to love. She'd
been the very thing he needed right then. Sweet and
kind, pulling him back from the edge. With her he'd
learned about the limits of love. That there were none.
That you could set physical need aside. That wedding
vows were real. That loving someone through sickness
was hard, but worth the pain.

On the other side of that, he needed different things.
He needed McKenna.

He didn't need that quiet, gentle love anymore. His
heart wasn't a quiet and gentle place. It was bruised and
battered from years of living. He wanted something
wild. Something sharp. Something that made him feel.
And damn but that was scary.

But with McKenna he felt it all. Not something bittersweet and quiet. But loud and all-consuming. Anger.
Passion. Laughter. All of him.

He could give her his worries. He didn't need to protect her from the world. She wanted his burdens, wanted to share them. He didn't have to hold back.

In the past, he'd been a shelter for his wife. Now, he and McKenna could shelter each other.

He didn't have to keep his thoughts, his fears, his passions, inside.

He wanted naked skin and deep kisses. He wanted to fight and make up. He wanted to *laugh*.

McKenna gave him all of that.

She woke up places inside of him he'd thought were dead. He'd felt empty. Like he'd poured out everything inside him he had to give.

Not now. He was full. Grief could drain, but love didn't. Love, loving McKenna, had restored everything the past had eaten away. He was so full of it now, he didn't think his body could contain it.

This was life. Real, full. Abundant.

And he was ready to live it.

With McKenna Tate.

WHEN MCKENNA WOKE UP bright and early on Christmas morning, the first thing she felt was a pain in her chest. That was because the bed she was in was empty. Grant wasn't with her, and it came flooding back to her with horrific clarity why, as soon as consciousness hit.

But then she realized she was in a completely unfamiliar bed, in an ornate and beautiful bedroom. And she heard the sounds of people moving around outside.

And she remembered.

She was at her father's house. Last night, in what was a true Christmas miracle, she had been welcomed into the Dalton family. She had sat around their dinner table and shared their food. Had traded stories, had laughed with them and had held back tears of her own when Hank had cried while giving her a hug good night.

And now it was Christmas morning.

She had gone to bed in the clothes she had come in, because she hadn't brought anything with her, so when she got up, she padded straight out into the main part of the house.

The family was sitting in the living room, holding mugs and looking at the tree.

"McKenna," Tammy said, smiling. "Sit down."

Even this early in the morning, Tammy looked like an homage to Dolly Parton. Big blond hair, and a button-up shirt with sequins and fringes. Enough makeup to outfit fifty states worth of beauty queens who had fallen on hard times.

"Thank you," McKenna said, edging into the room and taking a seat at the far end of the couch.

She couldn't believe that even Tammy was being so welcoming. She wouldn't blame the other woman for spitting in her face, or at least being a little bit chilly. But she wasn't. Tammy had an edge of hardness to her, a pragmatism that seemed to go deep. But there was something else there. Warmth. And...

Well, McKenna had to think it was hope. Because only hope could see you forgiving a cheating husband, after so many years of indiscretions. Hope that there was a better future. And it seemed like for the last decade it had been better.

Hope seemed to be the answer to everything. And in the future, it might even be the answer to her broken heart.

But right now, it was just broken. And there was no answer at all.

"Coffee or cider?" Tammy asked.

"You don't have to wait on me."

"I want to," she said. "Which will it be?"

"Cider," McKenna said. "Please."

She liked her coffee, but a little bit of cider seemed about right on Christmas morning.

Gabe, Caleb, Jacob and Hank were all there, as well as a woman McKenna had never met before, introduced to her as Ellie. Ellie had a little girl, who was bouncing in place, impatiently waiting for the time when presents would be opened.

She wondered at first if Ellie was Caleb or Jacob's girlfriend, but Tammy explained quietly that Ellie was the widow of a family friend who'd died in a helicopter crash years ago when the boys were out fighting fires.

McKenna looked at the pretty young woman, and the sweet little girl who no longer had a father, and decided life had a lot to answer for.

But then…they had the Daltons. And so did McKenna.

There was always light. No matter how dark it seemed sometimes, you could still turn on the light.

Soon, everyone was passing gifts around, and McKenna felt like she had stumbled into a strange, made-for-TV holiday movie. Because there was no way this was her life. No way this was reality. It didn't seem possible.

And then Hank handed her a tiny present, wrapped with brown paper and some twine. "It's not much," he said. "But I have something for you. And it's not an envelope full of money. Just so we're clear."

McKenna laughed, fighting tears. "Well, that's good. You know how I feel about that."

"Indeed I do. I pride myself on teaching my children life lessons. But you taught me one. I have a feeling it won't be the last one."

McKenna forced a smile, and untied the twine, pulling the top off the box. Inside was a key.

"That key is for the house, for every building on the property. You're a Dalton, McKenna. Even if you don't share our name. You're family. And this place is as much yours as it is mine, or Gabe, Jacob or Caleb's."

McKenna reached down into the box and held the key gently in the palm of her hand. "I don't know what to say."

"Say you'll use it. Say that you'll think of this as home. That you'll think of us as family."

Her throat tightened. "I do. I do… I just… Thank you."

She felt like she was in the middle of a Christmas miracle, but as they all went into the kitchen to eat cinnamon rolls, McKenna felt unsettled. Like she might want just one more miracle.

This was so much more than she'd ever imagined a girl like her could have. Just weeks ago she hadn't even let herself acknowledge that this was what she wanted. She'd put up defenses. Told herself all she needed was money.

No, she'd needed love. And now she was sitting here a whole different person. A person who'd been broken open, hurt and healed all in the same few hours.

It was a hell of a thing to have a dream come true and lose a different dream in the space of a night.

But the same thing remained that she'd always had. Hope.

But now she wasn't afraid of it.

The dangerous thing about hope was that now that she'd embraced it, she didn't see an end to it. Now that she'd gotten this, she wanted more.

Grant.

She needed Grant.

She loved Grant. And she wasn't going to go quietly. Wasn't going to sit and pretend she was happy right where she was when she wanted him.

She wasn't going to protect herself that way, not anymore.

"I have… I have someone I need to see," she said. "Would anyone be able to drive me…somewhere?"

"Personal business?" Gabe asked.

"Yes," she said. "Pretty personal."

"Dodge business, by any chance?"

She swallowed hard. "Yes."

"You can borrow my truck."

SHE HAD INTENDED to go straight to Get Out of Dodge. But something had compelled her to turn off that side road that went up the mountain, and led her to Lindsay's place.

She suddenly realized that the person she needed to talk to was different than the one she had originally set out to have some words with.

She parked Gabe's truck on the road, and started toward the river. She shoved her hands in her pockets and just stood there for a moment. It wasn't the exact spot they'd come to before. The cross and the poinsettias were a ways down. But she needed to just… Catch her breath. To just be here. Just for a minute.

She stood there and listened. To the leaves in the trees and the water rushing around her, and thought of all the times he'd stood there and listened to those same sounds.

She put her hand against her heart. Felt it pounding hard and steady beneath her palm.

"Thank you," she said. "For Grant. Grant the way that he is now, scars and all. I think things will work out. I have to believe that. But the man I love... He wouldn't be the man I love if he wasn't carrying that pain around inside of him. If he hadn't gone through what he had. He wouldn't be the man he is if you hadn't loved him. You changed him. Thank you. I'm going to love him for the rest of my life. I promise you that. I'm going to take care of him. And be there for him. I'm going to..."

Tears stopped her from speaking. Because she didn't know if she would be able to do all of that. She had no idea if Grant would ever be able to move forward. If he would ever be able to love her the way that she loved him.

"It doesn't matter," she said softly. "I'll love him, anyway."

She took a breath of the crystal-cold air and walked farther down along the creek, heading toward the site itself.

And when she got there, she froze. Because there were the little potted poinsettias, the ones that she and Grant had left, and ones that had been left by someone else. But draped over the cross was a chain with three rings on it.

Grant's rings.

McKenna's face crumpled, and she dropped to her knees, touching the rings where they hung.

Grant had been here. And he had placed the rings on the cross. And left them behind.

He had taken that burden he'd been carrying all this time and laid it down. Finally.

As tears rolled down her cheeks, hope burned in her chest, brighter than ever.

CHAPTER TWENTY-TWO

GRANT WAS ON the road, headed toward the Dalton place, when he saw her.

At first, he thought he was crazy. Seeing McKenna in what looked like a brand-new truck driving toward Get Out of Dodge. But there she was.

He slammed on his brakes and flipped a U-turn after he saw there were no cars coming, and went after her. She was exactly the woman he was after, and he wasn't going to let her get away from him.

He flashed his headlights, and revved up his engine, moving closer to her bumper. She tapped her brakes twice, then looked up into her rearview mirror. He saw the exact moment her eyes met his.

McKenna whipped to the side of the road, on the edge of the trees that surrounded the ranch. He parked right behind her, and got out, leaving the door open and the ignition on.

"What are you doing out here?" he asked.

"What are you doing?" she asked, her tone shrill. "Are you trying to run me off the road?"

"As a matter of fact, I was. So that I could talk to you."

"Pick up the phone like a normal person."

"I was on my way to the Dalton place." When he

couldn't find McKenna at her cabin, he'd called Bea and found out she'd dropped McKenna off there.

"Well, I was on my way to the Dodge place," she said.

"I can see that."

"Grant…" She looked up at him, her expression desperate, and he wanted to kiss away all the doubts that he saw there. "You left the rings."

She had gone to Lindsay's place.

The realization caused all of the remaining walls that surrounded his heart to crumble completely. If he'd had any doubts remaining that he could do this, she had just destroyed them all. Because she didn't approach his past with that distant pity, or fascination of the people who didn't know him. She saw it as part of him. And after he'd been up there reckoning with it, she must've been, too.

"I did," he said.

"I thought that had to mean something."

"You went up there," he said, his voice hoarse. "That has to mean something, too."

McKenna nodded slowly. "I was on my way to see you. But I felt like I needed to stop. And just… Grant, I'm so sorry about all the pain you went through. But I am so glad that you let her love you. Because I know that's part of why you're the man I love now. But I just wish—"

"I left them there," he said. "Because you're right. I'm grateful for the experience I had in my marriage. I will never regret the choice I made to marry her. It was hard. But I… She was worth it. But I didn't carry those rings because I felt married still. And I didn't carry them because I didn't think I could be a good person without them. I carried them because part of me wanted to use them as a shield. To keep from opening myself up. To keep from being hurt."

He hesitated. "Not even from opening myself up again. I genuinely loved Lindsay. And I don't want to say anything now that undermines that. Because I did. But… When I lost my mother I thought the whole world had fallen apart. It's why I walked around so angry. And with my marriage… I knew I would lose her. I did. Even though there was a small bit of hope inside of me, mostly I knew that losing her was the sure thing. I had to prepare myself for that from the beginning. And there's a kind of grim protection in that. A grim protection in the lack of hope."

A tear slid down McKenna's cheek, and he wiped it away. Not to protect her from the feeling. But to share it. He ached to share everything with her. "I understand that well," she said, the words a whisper.

"People think hope is weak," he said, his voice hoarse. "That dreaming of happy endings and better days is easy, but it's not. It's hard. So damned hard. So hard to let yourself want. I got very good at locking myself away and focusing only on what was right in front of me. But with you… I want everything. I want the whole future. It's wide open and bright and I want it so much it hurts. Growing old, having children. It scares the hell out of me. Because that's a whole lot of hope, McKenna. More than I've ever had in my whole life. I knew I couldn't have it in my first marriage. But we… we can have everything. It's love without limits, in a way I didn't know I could feel. In a way I never wanted to feel. It terrifies me. But I'm here. And I put all that self-protection away. I put my past where it belongs.

You're right. It will always be with me, but... It's time I chose what that meant."

She swallowed visibly, her face waxen. "What do you want it to mean?"

"I love you," he said. "And it's a whole different kind of love," he said. "Love like I've never had before. Love like I didn't know existed. It's not quiet, or sweet. It's not an organized little house on a quiet street. It's not me acting as a protector and a guardian, with all my anger and things I don't like about myself locked away where I don't have to deal with them. It's all of me, all of you. We're fire, sweetheart, and I think that scared me, because I knew it could burn me alive. But I'm ready for it now. To have what we can have. Laughing, yelling, screaming, making love. Everything."

She pulled a face. "Yelling and screaming? That's a lot of anger."

"What if I meant screaming because of sex?"

She laughed. "Okay, in all fairness, it's probably going to be a little bit of both."

"I know it will be, and believe me, knowing that I can be with someone who can take on all those parts of me is—"

"I don't need you to be perfect," she whispered. "Or always gentle. Or always protecting me. I need you to be you. So I can be me."

"I want that," he said. "So very much."

"You have it."

"McKenna," he said, his voice rough. "I want you to be the first woman and the last one."

She looked up at him, tears filling her brown eyes. "Grant, other men might have touched my body, but you're the only one who's ever touched my heart. I've never… You're the first person I ever said 'I love you' to. You're the first person I've ever loved."

He felt like his heart had been ripped in two. He hated that this beautiful, wonderful woman had been out in the world with no one to care for her for so long. But it had brought her to him. Much like the pain and loss in his life had brought him to her.

Without it, they wouldn't be here. Without it, they wouldn't be perfect for each other.

It was just like Wyatt had said. The fall wasn't different than the ride. It was all part of it.

The bad wasn't an interruption of life. It was just one of the threads woven into the fabric of it all.

It took the big picture to see it. Hindsight and distance. But now he knew if he pulled out those threads of pain, he'd be left with a completely different picture. This picture, the one with McKenna right in front of him, looking up at him like he was the most important thing in her world, was the picture he wanted.

"I love you. You're mine today, and if the sun rises tomorrow, I want you to be that, too. And every day after."

"I've never belonged to anyone before," she said. "I've never had any roots."

"Will you put some down with me?"

"Yes," she said. "I will."

When Grant Dodge went to bed that night, on Christmas, he wasn't alone. He was with McKenna Tate. And that was how he liked it.

EPILOGUE

CHRISTMAS HAD BECOME McKenna's favorite time of year. She had found her family on Christmas. She had found love on Christmas. And this year, she was getting married on Christmas.

She knew that everyone thought she was a little bit crazy for wanting to get married in the cabin. Not the cabin that she and Grant shared on the ranch property. But the one that he had found her in that first night.

Well, they weren't getting married in the cabin; they were getting married outside of it. She was currently in the cabin, which had some lace curtains put up over the windows, and quite a lot of white Christmas lights outside. Waiting. Waiting for the music to start.

The door opened just a crack, and Lindy rushed inside, wearing her red bridesmaid dress. McKenna smiled. She would have Jamie, Bea, Lindy and Kaylee standing with her. Her family.

Lindy was holding a small, wrapped present, and she handed it to McKenna quickly. "This is from Grant. He said to tell you to open it before you came out. And he would have delivered it, but he knows you would have killed him, because it's bad luck for him to see you before the wedding."

McKenna snorted. "Damn straight."

She loved that man.

She had loved him every day since the moment she had seen him, and she knew she would love him every day after.

Lindy scurried back out, leaving McKenna alone with the package. She frowned, tearing it open quickly, discovering that it was a book.

She turned it over and looked at the cover.

Anne of Green Gables.

She swallowed hard, tracing her fingers over the cover. She tried to laugh, a lump forming in her throat, a tear sliding down her cheek. She shifted it, and a piece of paper fluttered out from the inside of it, dropping to the cabin floor. She gingerly bent to collect it—careful not to get her wedding dress dirty—standing again and holding it up to the light.

Grant had written her a note.

Just remember, that even though you weren't what I ordered, you were exactly what I needed. And I want to keep you forever. So I guess this book isn't a lie, after all.

McKenna held the book to her chest, her eyes closing.

She was going to read this book to their children. Whenever they had them.

They were going to have them. She and Grant. The whole family. A whole life. Together.

The door opened again, and this time it was Hank.

"Don't you look pretty," her father said, smiling.

"Thank you."

"I never thought I'd get to do this," he said, clearing his throat. "Of course, now I'm doing it a hell of a lot sooner than it seems like I should be. Just a year after getting my daughter, I have to give her away."

McKenna grabbed hold of her dad's arm, and squeezed it. "I never thought I'd ever get married. Much less have my dad at my wedding. And you know... I'm not going anywhere."

"That's good to know," he said.

"I've got some pretty strong roots holding me here," she said.

Roots that were grown out of love. And she knew that they would never, ever be broken.

* * * * *

Return to Gold Valley, Oregon,
where the cowboys are tough to tame, until they
meet the women who can lasso their hearts.
Look for Dane Parker's book,
Unbroken Cowboy,
from Maisey Yates and HQN Books!
Read on for an exclusive sneak peek...

CHAPTER ONE

BEATRIX LEIGHTON WAS a friend to all living things.

She cared for creatures large and small, domestic and wild, both in her job at Gold Valley Veterinary Clinic and in her everyday life.

Whenever she found a wounded critter on the side of the road she always stopped and tried to help it. If ever she found a sickly mouse or a sad, stranded kitten, she nursed it back to health.

She never lost her cool or brought harm to any being.

But she was close, very close, to administering grievous bodily injury to one *extremely* irritating cowboy who was—no doubt about it—the worst patient she had ever tended to in her life.

Not that Dane had asked for her to tend to him, as he was the first to point out, often.

But if she didn't, what was going to happen to him? Who else could care for him?

She had a special place in her heart for Dane. She always had. From the first moment she'd met him. She'd known him for so many years now it had settled into being part of who she was. She loved him. And it was as much a part of her as her love of nature, animals and pie.

Something so ingrained in her fabric didn't require her to be conscious of it at all times, or to live with expectation about it. It simply was.

As simple and plain as the fact that Dane saw her as a sister, and yet she loved him still.

Well, most days she loved him. Today he was being an ass.

But the care and keeping of Dane was currently a responsibility she couldn't turn away from.

She lived in a cabin on the property of Grassroots Winery, happily tucked away in the woods, and currently Dane was the only person occupying the main house.

His sister, Lindy, had moved to Get Out of Dodge—the dude ranch owned by the Dodge family, which sat on the outskirts of Gold Valley—when she and Wyatt Dodge had gotten married, and when Dane had been horrifically injured a few months ago during a championship rodeo competition, it had made the most sense to move him into that house.

And there he had stayed ever since. With Bea on the property basically taking the place of his sister, when the last thing she felt for this man at all was *sisterly*.

It, along with his grumpiness, was getting old.

The grump she'd been able to cope with. After all, he was incapacitated and stuck indoors. Bea had made sure that she checked in with him now and again just to make sure that he was doing okay, but his unwillingness to follow doctor's orders and his inability to be even remotely civil was amplifying, and Bea was a hair's breadth away from clubbing him fiercely with his own crutch.

She supposed she should be grateful that he was on crutches at all. But he was overdoing it. He had just begun transitioning from his wheelchair and doing physical therapy to get walking again a week ago. But from the moment he had stood up he had refused to get back into his chair and he never admitted when he was tired.

Today he'd been God even knew where the whole day. Then she'd heard he'd been out in the field making sure the grapes weren't going to die in an upcoming frost and then she'd heard through the workers that he'd *fallen down* because his leg had given out, and the bastard hadn't even come in then.

He wasn't doing the prescribed exercises from the physical therapist. He was *literally* trying to walk it off.

It drove her absolutely insane.

The fact that she didn't need to be there—the fact that no one had actually asked her to take him on occasionally did occur to her.

But then, she had not asked her heart to fall resolutely and ridiculously in love with her former sister-in-law's brother all those years ago, and yet it had.

So here she was. And here he was.

Being a total jerk.

"Bea, I'm fine."

"You're not fine," she snapped, looking at where he was sprawled out on the couch, appearing as if he had just run a marathon.

A stupid marathon of idiocy through a vineyard *on crutches.*

As soon he had been able to get a bit more mobile, he had been on his feet. And he had been trying to get back into what he called fighting shape.

Bea was actually shocked at just how close he was to at least looking like he was back in fighting shape. His muscles weren't nearly as diminished as she would have expected—his thighs still thick and muscular, his stomach flat, his chest broad and his arms...

If anything could entice a person to write poetry about forearms, it would be Dane Parker's very loaded-looking guns.

"Take a pain pill," she said, standing there holding a glass of water out, with a pill flat in her other out-stretched palm.

"I don't need a pain pill," he growled.

She wanted to punch his sculpted, handsome face. Right in the scar that he'd gotten in this accident. That still hadn't marred his beauty. No, it made him more roguish, if anything. With his blue eyes and blond hair, he could easily trick someone into believing he was angelic.

The scar made it much clearer that he was more of a fallen angel.

"I'm going to put it in a piece of cheese and trick you into eating it," she said.

"I'm not a schnauzer," he said.

"Then stop acting like one." She didn't know if he was particularly acting like a schnauzer. Actually, in her experience schnauzers were much better patients. In her experience, basically everything was a better patient.

"Bea..."

"Dane," she said, perilously close to stamping her foot. "Lindy asked me to check in on you."

"Lindy needs to realize that just because she's my older sister doesn't mean that I'm not a grown-ass man."

"A grown-ass man who got trampled near to pieces because he insists on earning money by engaging in...a measuring contest for private parts."

Her cheeks heated intensely and she tried to keep her expression steady.

"For private parts?" he repeated.

"You heard me," she said, the glass of water and the pill still held determinedly out in front of her.

"I did hear you," he said. "I just didn't realize that you were in the third grade." He shook his head. "Private parts."

"Stop it," she said.

"I don't want to take a damn pain pill," he responded.

"Then drink some damn water." She slammed the glass down on the coffee table in front of him and stood there expectantly.

"I want a beer."

"Yeah, great," she said. "Drink a beer, don't hydrate."

"I'm fine," he said again. But he did sit up and lean forward, picking up the glass of water.

"You need to be careful with yourself," she said. "If you overdo it then it's entirely possible you'll set back some of your progress. You don't want to cause any internal bleeding or anything like that."

"I have been stuck in here, sitting on my ass, going on eight months. I'm over it."

Bea sighed and took a seat in the chair across the room from him. She really did feel for him. She did. A man like Dane was…almost impossible to contain.

Snowed in
with the Cowboy

CHAPTER ONE

"WHAT DO YOU want for Christmas, Chloe?"

Chloe Nolan looked over at her stepbrother's wife, who was busily loading food into the back of their SUV, and mentally scrolled through any number of possible—yet impossible—responses.

She was not going to say: *for Tanner to realize that I am a woman and not a child, and for him to realize that I am his stepsister, and not his biological sister, and it actually wouldn't be weird at all if the two of us were to maybe get together even if only for some physical action*

Also off the table was: *to lose my virginity.*

Probably equally as inappropriate as: *a night of hot sex.*

Something. Anything to deal with her Tanner feelings once and for all.

"I like candles," she said finally.

Candles were innocuous. They were a great thing to ask for when you had everything you wanted in the whole world—a place to live on a beautiful ranch, a thriving business as a riding instructor—except the stepbrother you found unreasonably hot.

A scented candle could never a bad thing, she supposed.

"That's impersonal," Savannah said, closing the

back of the SUV and looking down at her phone, obviously checking items off of a to-do list. "I don't want to get you something impersonal. If I wanted to do that I would've gotten you shower gel and a loofah."

"That's a very practical gift," Chloe pointed out.

"I don't want practical!" Savannah said. "Practical is what you get yourself when you go into town. Gifts are not meant to be practical."

Chloe didn't tell her step-sister-in-law that gifts were also not meant to be mental chores for the people who were supposed to be receiving them. Savannah was far too nice for Chloe to say that. "Well, I don't really know what I want."

And what she wanted was off-limits anyway.

"All right, then I'll have to surprise you. We are going to do a little shopping before we head up to the cabin. Are you going to ride with us?"

Chloe knew that *us* meant Jackson, Savannah and their toddler, Lily.

And as much as Chloe loved her niece, she was going to have to pass on sharing a car with the noisy creature.

"I'm going to head up later. Plus, I want to have my own car."

"That's probably a good idea. But I did hear that the weather is going to take a little bit of a turn."

"They always say that," Chloe said, waving a hand. "Endless forecasts of snowpocalypse this and that and the other, and you know it never happens. Much to the chagrin of people who would like to be skiing right about now. At best we'll get some anemic frost. Maybe some hail."

Savanna laughed. "True. In Colorado, when they promise snow, we listen. But I can see why you're a little more lackadaisical about it here. Having spent a whole winter here last year I was disappointed bitterly in what you considered a white Christmas."

"The grass *was* white," Chloe pointed out.

"The song does not go, 'Please have *frost* and mistletoe.'"

"Fair enough. But I bet there will be some snow up at the cabin we're staying at. It's at a higher elevation."

"Here's hoping. I'm sure Ava and Grace will be hoping for snow," Savannah said, talking about their brand-new nieces. The youngest Reid brother, Calder, had recently married a single mom, and her two daughters—both teenagers—and their mom were the center of his world. "Though I so hope it stays contained to the mountain and not the roads."

"It will be fine," Chloe said.

Their part of Oregon was so rarely buried underneath snow that Chloe wasn't worried about it at all. It was a little bit of a drive from Gold Valley up to Granite Pass, but she figured that it would be fine. She might have to chain up when she got to the mountain road that she knew would carry them to the cabin that they'd rented for their big family Christmas, but that was no big deal.

The cabin rental was a plan thrown together by Jackson, Calder and their wives to do something *special*. Particularly for Calder, his new wife and stepchildren. It was their first Christmas as a family, and he really wanted to do something extra for the girls. Chloe wasn't opposed. Especially since her mother was coming in from out of state for a visit. It would all be very nice.

A very nice Christmas of watching her stepbrothers happy and paired off. And watching the one that she'd had inappropriate feelings for since she was a child be resolutely single, and resolutely off-limits.

Which, in fairness, was nothing new. It honestly shouldn't upset her. She should be used to it. She literally lived in the house with Tanner. They were in each other's pockets all the time. Changing a venue shouldn't bother her. And she shouldn't be ruminating like she was.

She and Tanner didn't spend all their time together or anything. They didn't act like a family living together. They only ate dinners at the dining room table when the rest of the Reids came over. Otherwise, Chloe usually ate in her room before Tanner came in from working the ranch. He would microwave something for himself and eat in front of the TV.

Then she would often come out to graze for a while, and they'd exchange some words about the day, standing with the kitchen island between them.

They watched one TV show together, because they both liked it. Chloe always sat on the chair. Tanner always took the couch.

There were unspoken barriers between them, and both of them seemed to easily keep those in place. There wasn't any tension between them. Not really.

But there were fences.

It was Christmas. That was the problem. It made everything feel just a little bit bittersweet.

The sparkle of magic felt just out of her reach.

Like it was always for someone else, and never for her.

Christmas had always felt like that to her growing up. At least, until they had come to live on the ranch, when her mother had married Tanner's father. Here, she had actually found a sense of magic. Something that went beyond the vague disappointments her meager childhood had provided.

But then, that was part of the problem.

Her crush on Tanner was all about security, at the end of the day. Security and wanting what you couldn't have.

They had moved on to the ranch, she had met him—the oldest, tallest and most handsome of all of her stepfather's sons—and it had been love at first sight.

He had also been utterly and completely out of bounds when she had been twelve. Just like he was now.

She had never pined after anyone else. Not ever.

She imagined that much like making outlandish Christmas gifts when she was a little girl, before her mother had married Jim Reid, knowing she wouldn't even receive one small thing, it was a way of protecting herself.

If you went bold, and you went crazy, and laughable, then you knew that you were never going to get your way at all.

She'd heard it said that you should shoot for the moon, so that even if you missed you landed among the stars.

As far as Chloe was concerned, it was better to fantasize about the moon, knowing there was no way in the world you could jump that high, than try to jump over a small fence and land on your face. Or something. It was maybe a clumsy metaphor. But it made enough sense to her.

"I just need to make sure the horses are squared away. I know that Jacob Dalton is going to do a decent job taking care of them, but I want everything in order."

"They're horses," Savannah said, laughing. "Not children."

"Well, they're all I have," she pointed out.

Savannah cringed. "I didn't mean to say it like that or make it seem like I thought they didn't matter."

"I didn't think you were," Chloe said, gently.

Savannah was so sweet, and such a wonderful addition to Jackson's life. When he had unexpectedly found out he was a father, and had ended up raising his infant daughter on his own, he'd hired Savannah as a live-in nanny, and the two of them had fallen in love. As far as Chloe was concerned it was something out of a fairy tale. The kind she would have said didn't exist if she hadn't seen it with her own eyes.

"Well, we'll see you up there then. Calder, Lauren and the girls are already on the road. He didn't have any confidence in their ability to get there quickly. Apparently there will be a lot of stopping. Shopping, views and bathrooms."

Chloe laughed. "I'll see you there."

Jackson came out of the house then, cradling his daughter, Lily, in his arms. He shifted the little girl and waved. Lily copied him, waving a chubby hand until he set her in the car and began to buckle her into her car seat.

Chloe stood and watched as they drove off of the ranch property and headed down the highway.

She took a deep breath, trying to do something to ease the strange heaviness that she felt in her chest. She didn't know why her more melancholy Christmas feelings were surfacing. Well, she wasn't sure why particularly this year more than any other year. Unless she was really so small and petty that it was about everyone being paired off in a way that she wasn't.

She hoped she wasn't that small and petty. She really did.

She took a fortifying breath and turned, heading toward the barn, where the horses were. The horses were her pride and joy, the ultimate gift that her stepfather had given to her. A love of horses, and a knowledge of how to handle them. Something she never would have had if Jim Reid had never come into her life.

He had been imperfect, and she knew that. He was gruff, and it was difficult for him to show emotion. But she had always felt like he showed it with what he had. By giving out responsibility on the ranch that he loved, and entrusting his children, his sons and his stepdaughter, with the care of it.

She'd found her purpose on this ranch. Her calling.

Sure, it wasn't the most lucrative career, giving riding lessons—mostly to children—but it was rewarding, and the ranch was set up in such a way that it was possible for all of the siblings to live there if they wanted to.

Of course, Calder had moved into his wife's house, their brood of children too large for the cabin he once lived in.

And really, Chloe was supposed to be moving into his old place on the property so that she didn't have to be in the main house with Tanner, who had that place simply because he was the oldest. But she just… Hadn't. She had stayed, because while coexisting with Tanner wasn't comfortable per se it was also…

She just liked to be near him. And as pathetic as that was, it was also undeniable.

She went over the detailed list of instructions that she

was leaving behind for Jacob. She had already walked him around the place and given him a good look at the facility, but she had also made sure to leave as much direction behind as possible.

He would be taking care of the horses, but also the cattle that lived on the ranch. It was a rare and strange thing for the entire family to leave the property. In fact, they had never done it. Not in all the time that Chloe had lived there. It was a big thing. A marker of the changes that had occurred recently. And she wondered if perhaps that was partly why she was feeling a little bit strange.

Like things were moving faster than usual. Like it was all getting away from her, with everyone moving forward, and her standing still.

Tanner hasn't changed...

Maybe not.

She sighed heavily. She needed some time to clear her head. She ignored the gathering clouds in the sky and decided to get her horse out of her stall. All of these strange emotions were nothing that a ride through the countryside wouldn't fix.

She would do that and then she would head up and be as festive as anyone could possibly ask her to be.

And hopefully no one would realize that she was grappling with any kind of weird emotion.

Least of all the stepbrother who was causing them.

WHEN TANNER SAW that Chloe's car was still parked in front of the ranch house he swore. He was hoping that Chloe would have already taken off. Hours ago, preferably, because if his much younger stepsister had, then none of this would be his problem. But he had just gotten a call from his brother Calder, who was already at the cabin a couple of hours away, and he'd informed him that the roads were ice covered. There was no way that Chloe was going to get up there in her little car.

And that meant that she had to ride with Tanner.

Of course, he lived with her, it wasn't like he wasn't exposed to her all the time. But that didn't seem to help with the inappropriate attraction to her he'd been dealing with since she was about eighteen, and way too young for him to be looking at her that way.

He didn't know when it had started, not exactly. It wasn't as if he'd been struck with lightning one moment, but somehow she had gone from being something not quite a sister, but certainly not eligible, to being…a woman.

No. A lightning strike would have been easier.

He'd have been able to go back to the scene of that crime and do something about it. He'd have been able to get to the damn root of it all and tear it out, if it had been that simple.

It hadn't been a moment. It had been a subtle build. Something about the way the light would catch her short, curly dark hair sometimes. Or a mischievous grin she would give him.

The way that her laugh rolled through his body and landed with that kind of exhilarating feel that he got when he rode horses and a strong breeze came through and took his breath away.

He'd done his best to ignore it. He really had. And then, one day she had bent over and he had looked. He had seen the way that her jeans cupped her perfectly rounded ass, and he hadn't ever been able to lie to himself again about what those breathless moments between them were.

For years it had been like this, and over the past few months it had been even worse. A damned torturous slog. Like the buildup of a dam about full to bursting.

Being in an enclosed truck cab with her for the next couple of hours did not sound good. It sounded like it might put a crack in the dam, and that was something he couldn't afford.

The last thing he needed to do was breathe the same air that Chloe was breathing, before he had gotten his libido under control. That was the real issue with why it had been getting so bad lately, he was sure.

He had *not* had any sex recently. It was tough. He was busy running the ranch, and he wasn't particularly open to the idea of a long-term relationship. Hookups were what he thrived on, but with his brothers happily settled into marriage, arranging times when he could go out and fool around and they would hold down the fort for him had gotten fewer and farther between. That was the issue. Not so much Chloe herself, but the fact that he hadn't been near enough to a willing woman in longer than he could remember.

Well, he could remember. It was just that it didn't do anything for him. He had tried. He had tried in the dead of night to imagine his last partner, a woman named Alex who worked at the tattoo parlor down in Tolowa.

She had a lot of ink, and piercings in interesting places.

She was so different from Chloe. And as much as it pained him to admit it, that had been the primary attraction to most women he'd been with over the past few years.

Not Chloe.

Alex fit that bill, and nicely. And he'd had a good time with her when they'd been together. But now?

The memory did absolutely nothing for him. For some reason, imagining her thick eyeliner and pouty lips didn't fire his blood at all. No, it was fresh-faced Chloe that kept imprinting herself on his mind. And he didn't like it at all.

A man's life had cornerstones. And his had a few. This ranch. His brothers.

Chloe.

Chloe had been the key to him deciding that the ranch mattered. Seeing it through her eyes had been a revelation, and it had stirred something in him he hadn't imagined was there. Teaching her to ride, and how to perform chores around the property, had breathed new life into all of it.

Chloe wasn't a sister to him, but she was something. Something definitive.

Something essential.

He'd never wanted to risk that. Ever. An attraction to her had seemed like the worst thing possible, though he'd figure out how to tamp it down.

He could never risk disrupting a cornerstone. Not just in his life, but in his family's. All it would take was a crack, and all that he was, all they were, could come tumbling down.

Because Tanner couldn't keep it in his pants.

And no, that wasn't going to happen.

As if she had been conjured up from his imagination, Chloe came riding toward the barn, her hair flying behind her in the wind, her lithe, strong body guiding her horse exactly where she wanted her to go.

She pulled to a stop when she saw him, a slight frown on her lips.

"You're still here," she said.

"So are you."

She frowned. "Yeah, I wanted to get in one last ride and make sure that all the instructions for Jacob Dalton were in place."

"Well, now it's too late for you to drive yourself. Calder called. The road is not going to be passable in your little two-wheel drive, so if you have anything packed up in that Civic of yours you better throw it in the back of my pickup truck."

Oʜ I ᴊᴜsᴛ... I thought it would be more convenient if I had a car..."

"Hey, no argument from me on convenience," he said. "But it's not going to be very convenient if you get stuck in a ditch."

"I have chains," she said.

"Calder said that wouldn't cut it."

"Right," she said.

"It'll be fine. It'll be fun. We'll sing," he said, because if he couldn't feel normal he'd try to trick himself into thinking it was normal.

She shot him a look. "We will not sing."

He followed her into the barn while she untacked her horse.

"Why not?"

"Because you don't sing. Actually, you're pretty terrible at it."

"You're no Miranda Lambert."

"Lucky for you," she said. "I might get a little crazy and light something of yours on fire."

He chuckled, ignoring the way that her hair moved when she brushed it back off her face. Ignoring the tightening low in his gut that accompanied it.

"I guess I'll get ready then."

She moved, and he caught her scent, and then she stopped dead, her luminous brown eyes connecting with his. It was like a band of tension had stretched tight between them, drawing them together.

"You better do that," he said, taking a step back, breaking the tension. Because, oh, hell no. He did not need this. Not now. Not ever.

Most of all, Chloe didn't need him lusting after her.

He couldn't offer her anything. He had watched his own father go through marriage after marriage, making a hash of it.

The only real reason his marriage to Chloe's mother had lasted was her sheer grit and stubbornness.

And...

Chloe's mother was about the best thing that had ever happened to his family. He couldn't imagine taking a risk like that. Detonating a bomb in the middle of what they had.

No.

Just about every way of getting laid was a hell of a lot cheaper. He was not going to go there.

No matter how beautiful his stepsister was, he was never going to touch her. No matter that he'd spent seven years wanting her.

If he had to spend the next seven wanting her, he'd do just that. But he wasn't going to have her.

And that was his final word on that to himself.

CHAPTER TWO

BY THE TIME they were on the road, Chloe was feeling antsy. And by the time the stretch of road in front of them began to grow thick with snow, she was feeling even more antsy. And it wasn't even the proximity to Tanner.

"This is looking ugly," she commented as they went around the corner and the tires on Tanner's four-wheel-drive clung fast to the ground. Much to her relief.

"Yeah, but we should be fine," Tanner said. Normally she found his confidence...well, pretty sexy, sadly for her. Right about now she was dubious about it.

"I'm glad that you have so much confidence," she said. "I'm not sure that I do."

"I know how to drive in all weather," he said. "Need I remind you, I'm a very experienced driver."

"Is that a euphemism for *old*?"

He looked over at her. "Maybe."

"Well, you are certainly old."

She didn't know why she was jabbing him like that. Maybe to put a bigger gap between the two of them. Maybe for her own benefit, because she was being maudlin and a little bit silly about him.

But then, she often was. No matter how hard she tried not to be.

The drive had been fine so far. Punctuated by such

in-depth observations as *Oh, an elk crossing sign*. And *The trees are so tall*.

They'd stopped for gas and Fritos. The Fritos had been a mere excuse for Chloe to get out of the car for a while.

Tanner seemed tense, too, and Chloe couldn't figure out why. Maybe he wasn't as confident about driving on these roads as he said he was.

Up ahead, there was a tunnel carved deep into the mountain, the snow building up steadily around it, making Chloe feel vaguely nauseous as they went through it.

"That's sketchy," she said, gripping the door handle as they drove through, the car passing underneath the earth for one second.

Two. Three.

She held her breath going through the tunnel, it was a habit of hers from childhood, and now a sort of superstition she wasn't about to break when the snow looked like it might tumble down avalanche style at any moment.

"It'll be fine," he said.

They came out the other side, and when they did, a massive bank of packed snow dropped down over the exit to the tunnel.

"Well, fuck," he said, pressing down on the brakes and looking back behind them. More snow tumbled down off the mountain, covering the tunnel completely.

"We could have been stuck in there," she said.

"No," he said, he shook his head. "I would've dug us out."

"Right," she scoffed. "With your bare hands?"

He lifted a shoulder. "I have a shovel in the back."

"Well, it doesn't seem very safe."

As soon as the words exited her mouth, a tree came unrooted from its spot on the hill, pushed down by the wet snow, and it tumbled down the mountain, falling down over the tunnel exit, on all the packed snow.

"Shit!"

"No kidding," she said. "You wouldn't have been digging that out of the way with your shovel."

The look he gave her was searing enough to melt the snow, and she ignored the little flip in her stomach. "Let's just hope we make it the rest of the way without incident. I bet you're really glad that you're not driving your Civic."

"Pretty glad," she said.

They drove on, yellow caution lights flashing over the top of a `ign that warned of slick road conditions, and then farther ahead was a temporary road sign with orange lights on it. It proclaimed the mountain pass closed.

"Well, hell," he said. "We're supposed to go up the mountain pass."

"Now what are we going to do? The path back is blocked, and apparently the way forward is closed."

"We'd better stop," he said, looking up ahead, squinting through the falling snow. A sign that was mostly covered in thick white powder came into view, and Chloe could see part of the lettering and filled it in for herself.

Granite Ridge.

The town was tiny, more wooded than brick, unlike Golden Valley, with small cabin-like structures. A diner, an ice cream shop, and the larger general store.

"I wonder if we should stop at the general store," she said. If nothing else there would be warmth, food and a bathroom. So basically all the essentials should the world continue turning into an icy hell.

Tanner whipped his truck into the parking lot and the two of them got out. Chloe stepped gingerly into the snow, the powder covering her boots up to the top of her laces.

"This is just insane," she said. "I had no idea that it was going to come down like this."

"Because it never does," he said. "They always say this, and then we get a few wet flakes."

"No kidding." The snow was pelting her face like frozen crystals being dumped from a sugar shaker, leaving little pinpricks of ice on her cheeks.

She followed Tanner into the store, banging her shoe against the side of the door frame to knock off the snow before the two of them walked inside.

The interior of the place was a patchwork of merchandise. From a swivel rack of dog-eared novels being offered up for trade or inexpensive purchase, to power bait, fishing line and live night crawlers in a cooler not far away.

There was a mounted bobcat on top of a shelf holding picnic essentials like mayonnaise, pickles and breadcrumbs for fried trout. On the rough-hewn walls were several sets of antlers from different sorts of animals, and there was a small jackal open mount sitting on the counter by the register.

There was a woman standing behind that register, dressed in a plaid shirt, her long black hair tied back away from her face.

"Hi, there," Tanner said. "I'm just wondering if you have any idea what the situation is with the pass."

The woman, whose name tag said *Elena*, regarded

them with dark eyes. "The pass is not going to open," she said. "At least, not for a couple of days. I haven't seen snow like this in…fifteen years?"

Judging from the woman's youthful face, she would have been maybe twelve at the time of the last snow. At least, that was Chloe's estimate.

"Anyway, any snow tends to make the pass a complete mess. But with the rest of the roads getting all of this, and I hear the tunnel is closed back out of town… They're going to be working overtime to clear up the main roads."

"Well, dammit," Tanner said. "What are we supposed to do? Because we can't turn around and get back at this point."

"You should go up behind the store here. There's a lodge. But you better hurry. The rooms are going to fill up fast. If people are stuck on this side, this is going to be the best place for them to get a bed. Otherwise, they have to drive all the way to Maverick River. That's the next place with lodging, and it's going to be harrowing getting over there."

"I have four-wheel-drive," he said.

Elena chuckled. "I don't know that four-wheel-drive is going to help you in this, cowboy."

"Great. Thanks."

The two of them walked back out of the store and Tanner cursed. "Just great."

"It's not that big of a deal," Chloe said, a knot of strange dread tightening in her stomach as soon as she said it.

"It's not bad," Tanner said. "It's just… Let's go. The last thing we need is to be out of a room at this point."

"True."

They followed Elena's directions and drove down a winding road that pushed back off of the highway, toward a large building with a sign over the top proclaiming it to be the Granite Ridge Lodge.

"Here's hoping there's room," Chloe said drily.

The parking lot was surprisingly full, especially given the barren-looking state of the town.

The lodge had a wide wooden porch with rocking chairs on it, and there was a stack of wood right next to a red door that had a cheerful wreath wishing the world a Merry Christmas.

The two of them walked in and saw a harried-looking older woman with gray-streaked dark hair. She bore a striking resemblance to Elena, with a few more years lining her face. "Can I help you?" the woman asked.

She didn't have a name tag.

"We were just at the general store, and were told we might come see you about a room."

"Oh, yes," the woman said. "My daughter must have sent you. She's sent through fifteen people in the last hour. And now I hear that the tunnel is closed."

"Definitely," Tanner responded.

"You're lucky," she said. "I have one room left."

Chloe's stomach twisted tight. "One room?"

"Yes," the woman said slowly. "Is that okay?"

Tanner looked at her sideways. "We were hoping for two. She's my sister," he said, by way of explanation.

And that made Chloe's stomach get even tighter. Because she was not his sister. And *step* was a one-syllable word. *Stepsister* was *not* much harder to say.

It was so strange and twisted and utterly messed up, because if the circumstances were any different she would probably like that he didn't take pains to make it clear the two of them weren't related. That he seemed to accept her with such ease.

Except she didn't think of him as a brother, and she never had. And so it made her feel distant, because it didn't allow her the kind of closeness that she wanted.

"Sorry," the woman said. "It's all I have. We are slammed, and this place isn't that big."

"Yeah," Tanner said, looking around. "I get that."

It was rustic, with a big living area, a massive fireplace that was currently roaring, and rocking chairs placed all around. There was a station for coffee and hot chocolate, and for all that it was rustic, it was also incredibly homey.

"We'll take the room," Chloe said.

Tanner looked over at her. "It's not like you're going to go out and sleep in your truck," she said.

"Fair enough."

He reached into his pocket and took out his wallet, offering the woman his credit card.

"You don't have to pay," Chloe said.

"I'll tell you what," Tanner said. "You can buy me a coffee."

She rolled her eyes. "A coffee is not going to cover the cost of the hotel room."

"Don't worry about it, Chloe," he said. "I know where you live. I'm going to go grab our bags." He left his credit card on the counter and walked back outside. Chloe watched him go, her body jangling with nerves.

"He's your *brother*?" the woman questioned.

"Stepbrother," she said absently.

"Oh," she said, as if that made much more sense. Chloe truly didn't want to inquire as to why.

Tanner returned a few moments later, and at that

point they were checked in and ready to go. The woman handed them a metal key with a big round piece of wood attached to it. It had etching on it, identifying it as a key for room 15 at Granite Ridge Lodge.

Chloe swallowed hard, and determined that she wasn't going to allow the weirdness in her to be spread around.

"Which way do we go?" Chloe asked.

"Up the stairs," the woman said. "First door on the left."

Chloe nodded affirmatively, and she and Tanner walked toward the sweeping wooden staircase that would take them to their room.

When they reached the top of the stairs, they headed down the hall, pausing at the door, and Chloe stopped, her eyes lingering on the view of the lodge over the top of the railing, and the coyote hide that was draped over the log posts.

She heard the lock click, and something in her body went tight. She didn't know why she was reacting like this. Like it was anything other than normal.

They shared the same house all the time. There would be nothing significantly different about sharing a room for a couple of hours.

Tanner pushed the door open and the two of them walked in and then Chloe stopped cold.

The furniture was made from natural wood, large pieces of trees that seemed to be twisted into shapes. But the largest, heaviest-looking piece of furniture was the massive bed that dominated the room.

The only bed.

Chloe looked over at Tanner, and for just one moment she was certain that she saw heat blazing in his eyes.

CHAPTER THREE

TANNER WAS ABOUT to throw his bag through the window down to the snow below, and follow it with his body. This was getting out of control. He was going to be snowed in, in this tiny room that had one bed, with Chloe. Overnight. With all that inappropriate attraction that lived inside him, deep and dark and shameful.

At least, it should be shameful.

Rather than giving him any pleasure. Rather than making him feel...

He should've gotten laid before they left Gold Valley. He should've gotten laid a long time ago.

He looked over at Chloe, who seemed serene.

That was the other damned ridiculous part of all this. It wasn't like Chloe had any idea her older stepbrother was lusting after her like a pervert.

None of this probably seemed weird to her. They shared the same house. This probably seemed completely normal to her.

To him it was all about the space surrounding them. Or the lack of it.

There wasn't enough space here. There weren't enough walls.

"I'll take the floor," he said, walking in past her.

"You don't have to do that," she said. "You don't

have to pay for the hotel room and then gallantly take the floor."

"I'm not being gallant." She had no idea. "I'm being practical. Anyway. When I go hunting I'm more than happy to sleep in my truck, or in the bed of it if I want to stretch out. I don't have any issue with a hard surface."

She looked at him, her expression bordering on being so bland it had to be intentional. "What makes you think I do?"

"You're a woman," he said, through gritted teeth. "I'm being chivalrous."

Much to his surprise, Chloe rolled her eyes. If there had been a foot stomp involved he wouldn't have been surprised. "Oh, because I'm a *woman*?"

"Yes," he returned. He slammed the room door shut behind them, trying not to be too conscious of the fact that it seemed to make the air a hell of a lot thicker.

"It's just that you introduced me as your *sister* downstairs. I wasn't sure that me being a woman factored into anything."

He frowned. "That bothers you?"

"It doesn't bother me," she said, so huffily that it was clear that she was intensely bothered. "It's just that I'm not your sister."

"I'm aware of that."

"You called me your sister."

"You're my stepsister. It's close enough."

"Except your father died. He died and our parents aren't married because he died."

He gritted his teeth. "I'm well aware that my father died, Chloe, you don't have to repeat it four times."

"Well, me, too," she said, looking ferocious. "I loved your father. I did. He was the only father that I ever knew. And it's not… I'm not minimizing that. But I'm just saying."

"I don't know what the hell you're saying," he said, choosing to ignore her now that she was in such an unreasonable mood.

He was the one that should be in a mood. He was the man stuck sleeping on the floor for the night. He was the man who had increasingly inappropriate thoughts about the woman he was trapped in a room with overnight.

"I'd better call Jackson," he said, pulling his phone out of his pocket and dialing his brother angrily.

Chloe was staring at him, her eyes luminous. And he didn't want to analyze what they might be illuminated with.

"Hello?" His brother answered on the first ring. "What's up?"

"Chloe and I are stuck in town," he said. "Not Gold Valley. Granite Ridge. The tunnel is blocked behind us and the mountain pass is closed, so we can't get up to the cabin tonight."

"Hell. What are you going to do?"

"We got a place at some lodge," he said. "We'll be fine."

"Well, I hope you can make it up," Jackson said. "We're going to have burgers tonight."

"We are *not* making it up tonight. The snow was falling heavy down here."

"Damn," Jackson said. "I was hoping that maybe it was just that thick up here."

"Apparently not. Apparently, the forecast snowstorm finally came through, and it's making up for all the years it didn't."

"Well, that's damned inconvenient."

"You're telling me. But it looks like there's food around here, so it isn't like we're going to starve."

"As long as you're not stranded by the side of the road," Jackson said. "When you didn't turn up yet I was getting kind of worried."

"We should have left earlier. Who knew."

"Well, hopefully we'll see you tomorrow morning."

"Yeah," Tanner agreed as he ended the call.

He and Chloe didn't speak at all for a while. She was practically snarling around the room, placing her bag in various locations around the space, each and every movement trailing a spark of irritation behind it that he could almost taste.

"What's up?" he asked.

"Nothing," she said. "I'm just agitated."

For some reason, the cranky look on her face reminded him of the first time he'd seen her. She'd been about twelve years old and suspicious as hell of the new situation she seemed to find herself in. At that point in time Tanner had been around home as little as possible, life being much more interesting when he was fishing with friends, drinking beer and hooking up whenever he could.

But Chloe had seem to find a connection with his father that he never had, and she seemed to relish her position on the ranch in a way that Tanner had been vaguely envious of.

And ultimately, there had been something about the way she'd responded to the ranch, the horses, that had given him a kind of new appreciation for a place he had always taken for granted.

Seeing it all through new eyes.

Something about the way that her interacting with

horses had transformed her, from a wary, angry creature into one that smiled and laughed.

He had *always* been around horses, and he hadn't understood the different kinds of healing they could bring.
He had taken it all for granted. The sky, the mountains
and the security of having a house to grow up in.

His life had always had a thread of insecurity, since
his mother had left the family. Since his father had ro-
tated stepmothers through his life, unable to connect
with them, unable to connect with his kids.

But the ranch had been home. It had been stable and
sturdy and real.

He had learned something from watching Chloe
flourish. The importance of the place. The importance
of *a* place. Of home and belonging. And what it could
do when you found a place that fit you.

Watching her on the ranch had made him understand
just how much it was that place for him.

And then later, watching her had been about something else entirely. Whether he could put a pin in that
place on his life's map or not, it existed. That moment
when he'd looked at her and realized...

And realized they might fit together.

She was right. She wasn't his sister.

And he was so much more painfully aware of that
than she had any idea.

"Let's get something to eat," he said, needing to get
out of the enclosed space, needing air that wasn't tangled up with Chloe's scent. "I noticed a diner across
the street from the general store. We might as well get
some sustenance."

"Good point," she said.

She looked at him, as if she was daring him to make

some kind of comment about the situation, and he had no idea what in hell comment she wanted.

So he ignored it. Ignored the challenge on her face and walked over to the door, stuffing the hotel key as far into his pocket as it would go, the wood keychain draping over the edge. "Let's go," he said, holding the door open.

"Okay," she said.

They marched out the door, back down the stairs and passed the front desk, which now had a line of people who were looking more than a little bit upset, and who sounded like they were making arrangements to pay reduced fees to sleep in the lobby.

"I guess it could be worse," she said.

He was seriously considering bunking down in the lobby, now that those people had had the idea.

"I guess so," he said instead of voicing his thought.

When they went outside, things had changed even just in the twenty minutes or so they had been up in the room. The snow was falling more heavily, and the parking lot was now cluttered with cars. The road was so covered with snow that Tanner figured they were probably better off walking.

Chloe echoed his thoughts a moment later. "We might as well just walk."

"Yeah," he said. "Might as well."

They trudged down the snowy road, the only two people that seemed to be out and about right then. The road was lined with tall pine trees that were shrouded in a thick layer of snow that had fallen on top of the branches. The wood all around them groaned with the weight of it, the smell in the air fresh and snappy, mingling with the cold air that bit against his skin.

"I loved snow when I was a kid," he said. "And now, it usually just bugs me."

"I guess that's being an adult," Chloe pointed out.

"I guess. I don't necessarily like having to get out and work in it, that's for sure."

"I don't mind so much," Chloe said. "But then, I didn't necessarily like the snow when I was a kid. Growing up, we never lived in one place very long, but a lot of times there wasn't really anywhere to play. And bad weather just meant being cooped up indoors. It didn't snow much in Portland, but even when it did it wasn't fun. Because the parking lot would get grimy almost immediately. Tires would just pack the snow down and make it icy, and everything was muddy."

"It must've been a big change for you. Moving from Portland out to Gold Valley."

"It was. But I loved it. I was afraid to love it at first. Because I didn't trust that it wouldn't just be taken away from me. Everything in my life up to that point... My mom is wonderful. You know that. And she did her best, but she had bad taste in men for the longest time. Until she met your dad."

"It could definitely be argued that my dad is not the best example of good taste in men."

"They seemed happy, didn't they?"

"Yes," he said slowly. "I suppose it's all complicated."

"Relationships always are." Chloe shrugged, and he looked over at her, trying to read her expression. "I mean, so I hear."

That was the problem with being as close in proximity as the two of them were. He knew full well that Chloe had never had a relationship.

The very idea of it bothered him. Sent a streak of possessiveness through him. He didn't know what the hell to do with that.

"You know what else we used to do when we were kids in the snow?" he asked.

He was looking for a subject change. One for himself. A way to shift the direction of his thoughts and get everything back in order.

"What's that?"

He bent down, closing his hand around the heavy, wet snow, the cold making him regret the decision as soon as he did it.

"Snowball fights."

Luckily, he didn't hold onto the lump of snow for all that long. He let it fly, sending it in Chloe's direction. She shrieked when the ball of snow hit her shoulder, broke apart and sprayed down beneath the collar of her jacket.

"You're a menace!"

"I'm not so bad," he said, keeping his tone and expression innocent.

"You'll pay," she responded, bending down and picking up her own handful of snow.

Tanner took off running down the fully empty street, and Chloe was giggling and shouting after him.

When the snowball hit him, it was hard in between the shoulder blades, with a taste of vengeance buried in it. She had packed that tight before sending it his way.

"Brat," he said, turning around and starting to make another snowball. But Chloe had already packed together more, and he found himself assaulted as he attempted to replenish his ammunition. So he did the only sensible thing. He stood up and went straight for her, grabbing her around the waist and listening to her shriek as he flung them both down into a snowbank.

"That was pointless!" she shouted. "Now we're both wet."

"Worth it," he said.

The cold from the snow was sinking through his jeans, chewing on his knees, and suddenly he was very aware of Chloe's warmth.

Of the way her body fit snugly against his. He could feel how soft she was, even through the layers of her jacket and when she wiggled underneath him he let go of her like she was a live snake he'd pulled up out of the ground by mistake. He jumped up to his feet, gritting his teeth against the rising tide of desire in his system.

He'd been trying to get back onto a different footing. Talking about simpler times. Simpler memories. When they'd both been young, and she sure as hell had been too young for him to find attractive.

But his walk down memory lane had ended up in one hell of a problematic snowbank.

And he had no one but himself to blame.

He had underestimated this thing that was growing inside of him. Taking root in his gut. It had existed in him for so long he'd thought it was handled in many ways. But this only proved to him that it was a hell of a lot closer to getting out of control than he'd imagined.

"Let's go," he said, knowing that his tone was overly brisk, and not quite sure what he was supposed to do about it.

"Okay," Chloe said, sounding muted and a bit uncertain. He should say something to reassure her, but he didn't have anything to say.

He didn't know how to fix this thing. Not even remotely. Didn't know how to repair the damage that was settling between them. Mostly because he was afraid that if he tried to make amends he would only make it worse.

Chloe hauled herself up out of the snowbank on her own steam, brushing herself off, and the two of them continued on silently down the snowy road.

Every so often the new falling snow would disturb some of the snow that had settled on the branches and a large chunk of it would slide off, crashing down to the ground and breaking branches along the way. A testament to how wet and thick and horrendous the stuff was. Not a friendly powder, but a sodden blanket.

The highway was completely covered now, the road totally empty. But the parking lot in front of the diner was bursting to overflowing, there were so many people out in front of the place. Tanner groaned.

"Great."

"It looks busy," she said.

"It seems like we're not the only people stuck in Granite Ridge."

"I bet not."

They made their way to the diner, and Tanner greeted a couple of people who freely offered up the information that landslides up ahead had made it difficult to get to Maverick River, and many of them had turned back on the way.

"This is a shitshow," he muttered as they wove through the people and inside.

There was a hostess standing there, looking very harassed. "I don't have any tables," she said. "And no, I can't ask people to share with you. Because we're already doing that. Every single chair and every single bit of space is occupied by a body already."

"Well, damn," he said. "Do you at least have food?"

"We're making burger patties in bulk. So if you want something quick, I suggest you go with a cheeseburger with the fixings, and we can have that out to you pretty quick."

"We'll take it," he said. "And beer."

"I can send a bottle out with you. Because where you eat it isn't my problem."

"Cheeseburger fine?" Tanner asked.

"Fine by me," Chloe responded.

True to their word, the diner had the cheeseburgers out to them within fifteen minutes, along with an overflowing bag of French fries that he had a feeling was an apology.

He took the burgers, and Chloe held the fries, nibbling on them as they waded back through the snow, heading toward the lodge.

"This is insane," she remarked, pulling a crunchy French fry off the very top of the bag and chewing it as they walked, each footstep of hers raising her up half a foot before she sank down into the white.

Tanner just pressed through, his thighs aching with the effort, the snow seeping into his jeans.

"Pretty insane," he agreed.

And he didn't just mean the snowstorm and the ensuing crowd. But the way that everything had fallen into place just so, and his own idiocy in putting his arms around her.

"It's kind of…"

She trailed off, and she didn't continue. He waited, and she still didn't go on.

"It's kind of what?"

"Nothing," she said.

"Chloe, it's something." He really didn't have the patience for her to be vague. He was on edge, and apparently not even freezing his balls off was enough to take the heat out of his veins right now.

"I trailed off for a reason," she said. "Because it was stupid. And not what I meant."

"Well, tell me what it was."

"I don't want to."

He saw another opportunity to tease her, to make it light, and he took it. "It's almost… Like the beginning of a horror movie and I'm going to get ax murdered and then you're going to spend the rest of the day running around in the snow trying to escape a madman?"

"No," she said angrily.

"It's almost like Jack Frost is plotting against us specifically?"

"Romantic," Chloe said. "It's almost romantic."

The word slugged him in the gut, the breath in his lungs rushing into the frigid air on a cloud.

"I didn't mean with *you*," she said. "I just meant that if it were with anyone else, being snowed in at a nice little lodge and forced to share a room and carting around cheeseburgers that we had to go eat back at the hotel would be romantic."

"Huh," he said.

"I imagine being trapped indoors is nice when you actually want to get cozy with someone."

"Probably," he said stiffly.

"But that doesn't apply to us."

"Nope."

Silence lapsed between them and they tromped up

the front steps and back into the inn, which was now loud and overfull of people, sitting on every available surface in the lobby, talking on their cell phones and clearly explaining to family members why they wouldn't be arriving at their intended destination.

"Want to eat upstairs?" she asked.

"Why not?" Because for fuck's sake it was just past the point of lunacy right now. Down at the diner, in the lobby. In his body.

"It'll be quiet, at least," she pointed out.

Yeah, but he wasn't sure that quiet or privacy was his aim. Not at this point.

He was feeling more than aggrieved by the time they got back up the stairs and into the room.

The bed loomed large, and he gritted his teeth. And he definitely didn't allow himself to think what it might be like to spend some time with Chloe in that bed.

Just the very idea was laughable. Because whatever their relationship was, and it was definitely a complex one, it wasn't complicated to the rest of the family.

Jackson and Calder had made it clear that they had always only ever thought of Chloe as a sister. And he knew that Chloe's mother thought of him as one of her children. That right there made everything impossible.

Anyway, for all he knew Chloe saw him totally and completely as a brother.

Chloe flung herself onto the bed, taking the bag of French fries with her and sitting cross-legged on the quilt, holding the bag with one hand as she peeled off her coat, first slowly tugging her arm out of one side, then transferring the bag and peeling herself out of the other side.

"Don't eat all the French fries," he said, passing her one of the hamburgers.

"I can't help it," she said. "This weather is making me want carbs." But she took the hamburger and passed the French fries over to him as she unwrapped it slowly.

He put the fries on the nightstand, sitting his own ass on the ground and turning his full attention to his food, so that he didn't have to pay any more to Chloe.

"It's going to be nice to have the whole family together," Chloe said.

"Yep," he said, taking a big bite of hamburger and giving all his focus to that.

"I mean, my mom. We see Jackson and Savannah and Calder and Lauren all the time."

"Yes, we do."

"But it's kind of nice to be here with the two of us."

He paused and looked up in spite of himself. "Yeah," he said.

He didn't agree, but saying no wouldn't have gone over very well. He'd have had to explain himself, and he didn't want to. Not even a little.

"I… I have something to tell you." She set her hamburger down, scrambling to the edge of the bed and looking at him. "And I would never have said anything, but we are stuck here. We're stuck here overnight, and… Savannah asked me what I wanted for Christmas. And I made myself a little Christmas wish, which I haven't done since I was a kid. I used to wish for things that I knew I could never have."

"I'm not sure I follow you."

"You know when I was a kid we didn't have any money. I thought it was easier to wish for things I knew I couldn't get. A pony. A trip to Paris. Well, if there is no hope in hell of even getting a doll, you might as well dream big, right?"

"I...guess so." He'd never thought of it that way. In truth, Christmas in his house had been a pretty sparse affair. Chores had to get done on a ranch whether it was a holiday or not. But they'd always had a tree, and their father, for his sins, had always gotten them something. Even if it was a new pocketknife or a new pair of work boots.

"So this year Savannah asked me what I wanted," Chloe continued, "and I played that game in my mind. The one that I used to play. Where I wish for something outrageous, something I knew I could never have. But now we're here, and I swear, Tanner, it's like my crazy Christmas wish is trying to force itself to come true."

Her eyes were luminous as she stared at him. Large and full of meaning he couldn't quite divine. "What was your wish?"

He regretted asking. He regretted asking and he didn't even know why. Except that on some level, he knew. He knew, and he also knew that if she said the words he wasn't going to have the strength to turn her away.

"I've always had a fantasy," she said slowly. "About the two of us together. And it doesn't have to be romance, Tanner. It really doesn't. But maybe what happens in a snowy lodge can just stay in the lodge."

CHAPTER FOUR

CHLOE DIDN'T KNOW what was inspiring her to be so brave. Except maybe it wasn't bravery. It was just that maybe something had broken inside of her that moment Tanner had swept her into his arms and down into the snowbank. It had been almost a perfect representation of their relationship in general.

They'd spent so much time together over the years. Racing horses through a field. Tanner deciding to spray her with the hose on a hot day and laughing his ass off when she screamed. Tanner getting angry and railing about one of her teachers when she got a bad report card.

She and Tanner sitting on separate pieces of furniture in the living room when they watched TV. As if they were being careful to never touch.

Playful. Protective.

Tense.

The act had been playful, but it had been completely overtaken by tension toward the end. And then he had been cool and remote once he let her go. The more she thought about that, the more she realized it couldn't simply be because he was irritated at her.

There was no reason for him to be. He had instigated the snowball fight, and he was the one that had tackled her. And the only thing that made sense in all the world for why he was annoyed was that he had felt the same thing she had. That he was feeling that tension that had overtaken her, too.

And if he was feeling it, then why couldn't they have it?

She didn't expect Tanner to randomly fall in love with her, to upend their entire family dynamic just because she had a crush on him. But she also knew that her feelings weren't going away anytime soon. And maybe at the end of the day in order to move on from him she needed to have experienced him.

He had taught her a lot of things.

He had taught her how to ride a horse.

Maybe he could teach her this? And why not?

"Chloe…"

"If you're horrified by that then of course… I'm obviously not asking you to do something that disgusts you."

"What exactly are you asking me to do?" His face looked carved from stone, each line etched deep and hard into his skin.

"I want you to… I…"

She couldn't get the words out. It was too difficult. Too humiliating.

Particularly if he didn't feel the same way that she did.

So she launched herself off the edge of the mattress and down to the floor in front of him, where he eyed her like she might be a poisonous snake.

She reached out slowly, pressing her hand to his thigh, the heat of his body burning her through the thick denim. She was so very, very aware of him. She didn't know how it could be possible that he didn't feel this, too. Not because she was so confident in herself and her appeal, but because this thing felt too big to be contained in one person. It simply seemed impossible.

She licked her lips, and watched, glimpsing that same fire that she had seen in his eyes right when they had opened the hotel room door and seen that there was one bed.

No, she wasn't imagining this. She wasn't.

She leaned in slowly, and he didn't pull away.

And when their lips touched, she caught fire.

As if the heat from his eyes were burning right through her, like they were sharing it. And hell, they were sharing breath, so it didn't seem quite so crazy. His lips were firm and glorious, and she felt like she had thrown herself into the deep end for sure, but she didn't feel like she was drowning.

No. Instead, she felt like she was *breathing* for the first time. She had wanted this, fantasized about it, ever since she knew what the tightening in her stomach when he was around meant. What the racing in her heart signified. She had seen too much to believe in happily-ever-afters. Even her mother's marriage to Tanner's father had been far from perfect. It had been a lot of fighting, a lot of work and a lot of stubborn grit on the part of her mother, who mostly had differentiated herself from his past wives by her refusal to leave.

Chloe didn't fancy herself above any of that. She didn't think that she was destined for something greater than her mother in terms of romance. But that didn't mean she couldn't want this. Couldn't want pleasure and fantasy, and a moment to get a little taste of everything that she had always wanted.

She had wished and wished for a pony. It had seemed out of this world, and ultimately, she had become a girl who had learned to ride, who made her living riding horses. So maybe things weren't so far-fetched after all.

He pulled away, his dark eyes grim. "Do you know what you're doing?"

She laughed. "No," she said. "Not at all. But I don't understand why this can't stay here. Why you and I can't... Can't just be this. This whole thing has been surreal. And look at it. The snow falling outside, the entire inn is full. The town is full. And we're stuck. You and me, and that bed. And I just think... You could go downstairs and sleep in that crowd. You could sleep here angrily on the floor. Or you could... You could sleep with me, Tanner. You could sleep with me."

"Chloe... What will this do to us? To the family?"

"Nothing," she said quickly. "It doesn't have to do anything. Tanner, if you don't want me then I'll go sleep downstairs myself. Or sleep on the floor. Or in the bathtub. Whatever you want. But if there's even the smallest chance that you do..."

He growled suddenly, his arm wrapped around her waist, and he propelled them backward, pinning her down onto the floor, his eyes intense as he stared down at her. "I've wanted you for so long. It's been driving me crazy. Chloe, if I'd had any idea that you wanted me..."

"What?"

He shook his head. "Nothing. Absolutely nothing. Because how can I do anything? You're my stepsister, Chloe. But that's not the most important thing. The most important thing is our family. And how they feel."

"They don't have to know."

"And that's why even if I had known that you wanted this we couldn't have done anything then. But here..."

"Blame it on the blizzard," she said softly. "On this

bed. On the fact that no one is around. But there's a boundary."

"Yes there is," he said roughly. "Maybe it's that boundary that will make crossing the others not quite so bad."

"Tell me," she whispered, feeling a growing hardness between them, satisfaction roaring through her. "Tell me when you first started to want me."

"It's the damn way you ride those horses," he said. "The way that you move with them. It's like nothing I've ever seen. Once I noticed how good you look doing it…"

"So it's not just that you think I'm pretty."

"Does that matter?"

"Yes," she said softly. "It does. Because I know that you've slept with a lot of women. And I want to know if I'm different than that. If I'm more than just pretty."

"If it's for a night, does it matter?"

"Yes. It matters to me."

"It's not just that you're pretty. Though you are. It's that you glow. I've never seen anything like it."

After that, he kissed her, his mouth rough over hers, his hold intense and masculine, and everything she had ever fantasized that it might be.

When they parted, she was breathless, her heart threatening to thunder right out of her chest. She had to tell him. She wasn't scared, not really. But if he hadn't guessed already, she really, really needed him to know.

"I'm a virgin," she said softly.

He stopped, his head rolling back, his eyes closing. "You don't want to do this." The words sounded like pain. Like they'd been scraped raw on their way out, and it was how she knew he *did* want to do this.

It made her even more sure of her decisions.

"I do," she said.

"You want to have a one-night stand for your first time?"

Tanner had been an essential part of her life for so long. A sounding board, a protector. Something never quite like a brother. But someone she trusted.

Had trusted from the moment she'd met him.

There was no other way she would have ever gotten up on a horse if she hadn't. He was strong. Dependable. Capable.

Sexy.

The only man she'd ever wanted.

The only man she could ever see having this conversation with.

"Yes. I want to be with somebody that I trust. I want to... Tanner, there are not very many people in the world that know me better than you do. There might not be any. But I want you. I want this to be my first time. And it's okay if it can never happen again. I mean... It's been hard for me. To go out and find a relationship. Especially after my mom's experience. The last thing I ever wanted was to be left with a child to raise on my own. To be betrayed the way that she was over and over again. But it's not enough to be alone anymore. I don't like an empty bed. But now I'm twenty-five and I'm desperately inexperienced. And... It's going to have to be with you. I'm afraid it'll never be with anyone."

"Do you want me?" The words were low and surprisingly intense.

"Yes," she said. "I do. What made you think I didn't?"

"If all you want to do is lose your virginity, then that's not the same thing."

"That's not all. I've wanted you forever. And don't… Don't make that weird. Or anything like that. But it's like… You know when you dream of something. When you have fantasies of it for a long time, and you kind of need to know… If it's going to live up to the hype, if it's going to be what you want, or if it's just going to disappoint you. Well, I need to know. If you're going to live up to the hype."

"I have to live up to the hype," he said.

"Yes," she said.

"What hype, exactly? Do I have a reputation?"

"No. It's hype that I've built up in my mind. Based on very little. I've never actually done this before, so…"

"What have you done?"

"Nothing," she said.

He swore, and slid his hands down her back, holding her hips. "Sweetheart," he said. "Nothing?"

"Nothing."

He shook his head, then leaned in, pressing a slow, lingering kiss to her neck. "That should scare the hell out of me."

"It should?"

"Instead it turns me on," he said, the words rough. Sending an illicit thrill through her.

"Well," she said, "if this is a fantasy, if we are just living things out, why can't it turn you on?"

"It works for me, too."

"Just tonight," she whispered.

He kissed her again, and they quit talking. And she quit thinking. About what might happen next. About the fact that this moment couldn't last any longer than the snow outside. Less even.

She had one night to extinguish the flame that had been burning for years. One night. That was it.

She grabbed hold of him, rocking against him, relishing the feeling of his hard length against her. He did want her. He did. Tanner. Her Tanner, who had been the object of her desire for so long. She had been convinced that she was being silly, wanting him like that. That there was no way it wasn't anything more than all in her head. But he wanted her. He did. He wanted this.

She reached down and pushed her hands beneath his T-shirt, the breath hissing through her teeth when her skin came into contact with his. So hot and hard and beautifully muscled. Then she ran out of patience, and she didn't care if she was being too bold or if she was revealing the fact that her feelings went deeper than lust. She just didn't care. Not right now. She ran her hands over his body, his muscular back, down his chest, covered with dark hair and so outrageously sexy in ways she couldn't begin to describe.

It was those contrasts between them. The differences. The ways in which he was rough, and so very much a man. Something different and fascinating and glorious in her eyes. But then, it was his turn. His movements were rough and uncontrolled as he stripped her shirt up over her head. "I've been waiting a long time to do this," he said. "So long."

"You have?"

He pulled his shirt off, and Chloe basked in the glory of all those muscles. "I've wanted you since you were eighteen years old," he said. "And I knew that I was sick to want it then. I knew it. I'm even sicker to want it now. To have it. Just once." He chuckled, lowering his head and brushing his lips against the soft, curved part of her breast. And then he tasted her. The flat of his tongue was hot and wet and it made her tremble inside and out to have him touch her like that.

He reached up then, cupping her breast, his thumb tracing a line over the lacy cup of her bra, torturing the tightened bud that strained beneath the fabric.

Wanting him had been a strange kind of torture for the last decade or so. But this was the sweetest and keenest of all. Knowing that she was actually going to have him. Wanting to rush it, so that she could finally know what it was like. And wanting it to go on forever, because once it happened, it wasn't going to happen again.

She was made of contradiction and desire, and she wouldn't have it any other way.

He grabbed hold of her pants, a thick, insulated, stretchy black fabric that kept her warm in the snow, but had her far too hot now, and pulled them down her hips, leaving her in nothing but her underwear, which did not match her bra, and had she known that she was going to be losing her virginity, she definitely would have put some thought into color coordination.

"Fuck," he breathed, pushing himself up onto his knees, his muscle shifting with the motion.

He looked like a wild and feral thing, and it was so strange to see him like this. This man that she knew so well. Whom she lived with, day in and day out. She was familiar with almost every aspect of Tanner's routine. Of who he was. But she didn't know this part of him. This secret part that made him so much more a man than anything else.

Sexual, raw. Animal.

There was nothing civilized about the expression

on his face, nothing restrained there. It was like being struck with a match to realize that. That this man whom she had known for so long, that she had wanted for even longer, had been carrying all this around with him the entire time. Did those other women that he slept with get to see this? Did they know this Tanner? It made her feel unspeakably jealous.

She'd always been a little bit jealous.

Knowing that he touched other women. But now she realized it was more than that. It was the intimacy of it. It wasn't just having his naked body beneath their hands, it was getting to see this. This part of him that only a lover could ever see.

But she'd also seen so much more than just this. She'd seen how he was with his brothers. How he was to her mother. The way that he treated his nieces.

The way that he trained horses, and the way that he worked the land.

She knew him in all those ways that his various lovers never would.

And now she knew this, too.

As if she had finally found the last piece of Tanner Reid and claimed it for her own. All the pieces locking into place. Perfect and hers.

Emotion swelled in her chest and she tried to shove it aside. Tried to embrace her arousal. Because that at least was safe. She wasn't scared. Plenty of people had sex and survived it. She knew that it hurt the first time, but she also knew that so many people kept doing it, so that meant that it was worth it. No, she wasn't nervous physically. Because Tanner's reputation really did precede him. And there was no small amount of hype when it came to conversation surrounding his prowess.

More than that, she knew that Tanner would never hurt her. At least, she knew he would never let pain be the last word on their experience together.

She was confident in that.

No, there were no nerves. But there were feelings. And she didn't especially want them.

"Let me just look at you for a second," he said, the lust in his eyes taking her by surprise. The desire there so much deeper, so much more intense than she had ever imagined it could be.

She wondered how the two of them had managed to carry all this around inside of them for so long and never act on it. She really, really did.

"Okay," she said. "But I think I like it better when you touch me."

"I will," he replied. "I promise you I will. I'm going to touch you until neither of us can breathe. But... You're my darkest fantasy, Chloe. Nobody knows. I could never afford for anyone to know. Can you imagine? My dad would have taken me out behind the barn and shot me."

"That would have been a waste. Since I wanted you, too. And nothing about this feels dark or forbidden to me. It just feels like a Christmas wish."

"That's real nice. But I aim to make it feel a little bit dark and forbidden, too."

"I'm okay with that."

Those words came out trembling as he leaned forward, but he didn't kiss her mouth. No, he kissed her stomach, his lips lingering there for a moment before taking a path down below her belly button. Her breath hitched. She didn't think that this was the order of things. The way that he was moving down, the way that his fingers hooked in the lace of her panties and began to drag them down her thighs. She was still wearing her bra. Very clearly, in her mind, bras were supposed to come off first. But that wasn't what he was doing. No, it wasn't. Not at all.

She wondered if Tanner had any idea that he was supposed to be following the rules.

She felt like he should. All things considered.

But he was doing it, whether it was against the rules or not, and before she could protest, he had grabbed hold of her hips and dragged her down an inch or so, forcing her legs apart, fear fluttering in her chest as she realized exactly what he was about to do, exactly how close to her he was.

He kissed her inner thigh, and this time, she did reach out and try to push him away. This time, she did try to scoot back. But he held her firm, chuckling as he moved his mouth to her center, the groan on his lips like a man who was tasting an ice cream cone for the first time, as he slowly pulled the tip of his tongue through her folds.

She arched her back, screaming as he did, humiliation rolling over her when she realized how strong her reaction had been. But… Nothing had prepared her for that. She had gone from kissing, to him licking her there in a matter of only a few moments, and it was all just too much. It was all just… He moved forward, deepening the strokes of his tongue, bold and luscious, and suddenly not too much at all. Suddenly not quite enough. Because something had changed inside of her. Like a switch being flipped.

And suddenly, all of her common sense and any feelings that she had about propriety or the order of operations when it came to the removal of underwear had been wiped clean from her mind.

His mouth was wicked, and he was bringing her closer and closer to the edge, making her feel wild and uncontrolled. And she loved it.

Because this was Tanner, and with him she knew she was safe, even as wild and reckless feelings rioted through her. Knew she was safe even though she felt like she was falling. He moved his hand around, gripping her bottom hard as he shifted his other hand and pushed a finger inside of her, slowly. Very slowly.

She wiggled against the unfamiliar invasion, focusing on the magic that he was creating with his mouth. He was drawing her closer to release, closer still. And when he added a second finger, she was so wickedly aroused that it was welcome, rather than uncomfortable. He stroked her, teased her, made her feel like the world might come to an end with the appropriate flick of his wrist, and yet, he refused to give it.

He pumped his fingers in and out of her, and shifted, sucking on that sensitized bundle of nerves there. And the light burst behind her eyes. She outright exploded, her whole being utterly and completely captivated by what was happening. Wave after wave of pleasure rolling over her, leaving her spent and breathless.

She was limp, when he made his way back to her lips and kissed her there, leaving behind ample evidence of her downfall.

But she was too exhausted to care. He reached behind her, unhooking her bra and leaving her completely naked.

Another thing she was far too boneless and exhausted and satisfied to care about.

"You still have your clothes on," she said.

That she cared about. Seeing Tanner naked. She wanted that. More than just about anything, right in that moment.

Her satisfaction was already starting to ebb, a hollow feeling inside of her. She had the sense that it wasn't finished. She knew it wasn't. That there was so much more for her to have. All of him.

He undid his belt buckle slowly, then the snap on his jeans, followed by the zipper, and she caught and held her breath.

She had never seen a naked man before. She licked her lips.

It was like her own personal strip show, and she had never really imagined that she would like one of those. She really liked this one. If she had a couple of singles, she might have given him one to show her appreciation. But in lieu of that, she simply watched.

He pushed his jeans down, exposing himself, leaving her slightly breathless with the knowledge of what was about to happen next. All of it. Displayed before her.

He was so large. Fully erect and very male, and actually very beautiful.

She imagined he wouldn't appreciate her characterizing his body that way. But it was true.

"You okay?" he asked.

"Yes," she said. "I'm… I'm good."

"Good," he said.

He kissed her, flattening her out on the floor, his big body covering hers entirely.

"The bed started this," he said, his lips pressed against hers as he spoke. "I think we should give the bed its due."

"Okay," she said, the word ending on a breathless note as he swept her up off the ground and brought them both down onto the bed. Naked. Skin to skin. Breast to chest. Their legs tangling, their bodies arching against each other in time as their kissing became more fevered. More desperate.

"I want you," she whispered. "Please."

"Just a second."

He left her for a moment, and she felt cold. Bereft. He grabbed hold of his jeans and pulled his wallet out of his pocket, retrieving a condom before returning to the bed. He tore it open quickly, rolling it on his length with no small amount of experience and then returned to her, nestling himself between her thighs and guiding himself to the entrance of her body. He pressed in slowly. Very slowly, but it did nothing to diminish the stretching, fierce pain that she felt as he breached her, as her body began to expand to accommodate him.

She bit her lip, not wanting him to know, because if he knew that it hurt, he might stop. And she wouldn't be able to stand it if he stopped.

She did her best to hide her discomfort as he began to move. As she arched her hips upward, trying to take more of him. Trying to take all of him. This was what she wanted, and she would not be thwarted by virginal logistics. He kissed her, and she relaxed slightly as his tongue swept against hers, and then he thrust all the way home. She gasped, unable to keep back the cry of pain that resulted from his action.

"Do you need me to stop?"

"No." They had one night. One night, and she wasn't going to waste a moment of it on letting pain have a foothold. She wasn't going to waste anything. She was going to take it all in. And she did.

The feel of him, hot, hard and strong inside of her. The way he smelled, the way his body felt beneath her fingertips. All of it. The way he tasted. She buried her face in his neck and swept her tongue over his skin, the salty, masculine tang of him like balm for wounds she hadn't even known she had.

He was everything, and this was like healing.

She didn't even know what. Except that she felt…

Whole. Complete in ways she never had.

The only thing that had ever made her feel like this was the first time he'd put her up on a horse.

She supposed that was fitting.

Both times he had taught her to ride.

As pleasure rose inside of her, motion did, too. A great, swelling need that surrounded her heart, threatening to overtake the desire that made her internal muscles pulse low and hot in her body.

The pain began to fade, giving way to pure pleasure. To a deep, endless ache that he filled with each and every thrust of his body into hers.

"Tanner," she whispered his name, and he shuddered.

So she did it again. And again, and again. It didn't matter that she was a virgin, she knew how to make this man shake. And that made anything feel possible.

When he flexed his hips forward, pleasure broke over her for a second time, and when she cried out her release, he gave up his own, freezing above her, his length pulsing inside of her as he came.

And when it was over, she really couldn't handle the fact that it might be over. Because she needed more of this.

Tonight. They had tonight.

He was breathing hard, jagged when he rolled to his side. And she looked at him, gazed at the lines on his handsome face.

"I need to know two things," she said.

He looked stricken. "What?"

"Do they have hot chocolate downstairs. And do they have more condoms."

CHAPTER FIVE

TANNER GOT DRESSED and went down to the lobby, and discovered that the answer to both of her questions was yes.

There was hot chocolate, and he could bring it up to the room, and they did indeed sell condoms at the front desk. He felt the need to make sure that the woman knew that Chloe wasn't actually his sister. He had been met with a strange, enigmatic expression that he hadn't been able to decode, but it didn't matter, because she had sold him the condoms, and then he had gone back upstairs with two cups, a small paper bag and a decently sized amount of guilt.

No, he wasn't going to feel guilt. Not tonight. Because tonight was all about that fantasy. Tonight was all about the thing he'd denied himself for so long because it was wrong on every fucking level.

But he had wanted this woman for seven years. And it was the sweetest thing on earth to finally have her.

He had lost his control. He had known that tasting her like he had was going to push her past her comfort zone, maybe even a little bit too early. When he returned to the room, he found her there, sitting cross-legged on the bed, wearing a pair of the most ridiculous, fuzzy-looking pajama pants he had ever seen. They were red, with white reindeer on them. She was wearing a matching long-sleeved top, with no bra underneath.

"You're dressed," he said, feeling vaguely disappointed.

"Yes," she said, reaching down into the French fry bag and fishing out what had to be a cold, soggy fry by now.

"*You're* dressed," she pointed out.

"Well, I didn't want to excite anyone downstairs too much. In this circumstance, it might have caused a riot."

"Hmm. Yes, I would say you have a riot-worthy body."

That shouldn't turn him on. Dammit.

"Anyway," Chloe continued. "I didn't want to sit here freezing the entire time I was waiting for you."

"Here you go," he replied. "Hot chocolate with no small amount of whipped cream. And I put sprinkles on it. This is most definitely a Chloe hot chocolate."

She glowed, and it just about killed him. "Thank you," she said.

"And condoms," he said.

"Very important," she said.

They were silent for a moment. "This should be weirder than it is," she pointed out.

"You don't find it weird?" In point of fact, he didn't, either, but he was relieved that Chloe didn't seem to feel any differently. Or maybe, relieved was the wrong word. Maybe it wasn't so much about relief as it was about not wanting anything to invade this evening they had set out before them.

There was a reason that he was baiting her with hot chocolate and whipped cream, after all.

It was a funny thing. To know a woman that he was sleeping with like this.

He didn't, typically. Not because he didn't respect women, or didn't enjoy their company, in theory. It was just that his father had made relationships look a whole lot like hell, and he'd never been particularly driven to pursue them as a result.

"Thank you," she said, taking a sip of the hot chocolate. "For this."

"Well, I had forgotten to get you a present."

She narrowed her eyes. "This is perilously close to you claiming you gave me a particular part of your anatomy."

He shrugged, a smile tugging at the corners of his lips. That was weird, too. The conversation after the sex. The fact that he felt in genuine good humor.

He shouldn't. He should probably feel guilty. But hell, this was the thing he had been avoiding for a long-ass time. Something that he had been trying to deny inside of himself.

And maybe this was confirmation that he was more like his old man than he had ever wanted to believe.

His father, who had never seemed to put much thought into anything, but had just jumped from relationship to relationship, cruising through that part of his life without giving deep thought to how it impacted other people.

He had tried to consider Chloe. He had tried to be better than that. Ultimately, this was the end result. But Chloe certainly didn't seem upset. She had said she wanted it.

He was her Christmas present.

And that did things to his ego.

He sat down on the bed with her, holding his own hot chocolate, which did not have whipped cream and sprinkles, thank you very much.

"I think," she said, "you should take your clothes off again."

"Do you?"

"I do."

"But baby, it's cold outside," he responded, taking a sip of his drink.

"I'll keep you warm," she said, treating him to a suggestive expression that should have been over the top, but left him hard and aching and ready to take her there and now.

"What about you?" he asked, looking her over slowly. There was something enticing about her in the pajamas. They weren't sexy, not in the traditional sense. No lace or cut-outs or anything to offer a suggestive peek at her body. But it made her look cozy and warm, and made it seem like the best idea in the world would be to wrap his arms around her and hold her against his body.

He took her cocoa out of her hands and set it on the nightstand, placing his own beside it, and then he stripped down as quickly as possible. She said nothing, watching his every movement.

"Come over here and keep me warm," he said, pulling her up against him.

She giggled. And he couldn't remember if he'd ever made a woman giggle like that before. Like that silly, breathless excitement they showed in movies. He shouldn't like that, either. That should worry him. Concern him. But it didn't. Instead, he wanted to cling to it. Claim it for himself.

"Do you wear these pajamas at home?" he asked.

"Only around Christmas time," she said solemnly. "They have reindeer on them, Tanner. Anytime would be ridiculous."

"Sure," he said, letting his hands slide down her back, moving to cup her butt.

He groaned as he took a handful of her, squeezing, before going back to stroking. Working his hands beneath the waistband of those reindeer pants and relishing the soft, silky feel of her skin.

She wiggled against him, draping her leg over his, her hand resting on his chest, stroking him, moving down to his stomach, and lower still. Her eyes met his, her lips parted slightly as she curled her hand around his length.

He closed his eyes, and then forced them to snap open again. He wanted to look at Chloe while she touched him. He wanted to be fully present, fully aware of the woman who had her hands on his body. Because this was everything, and so was she. This woman who was made of every fantasy he'd never wanted to have.

He had thought the snow was an inconvenience. But now, right about now, it was looking like it was his Christmas present, too.

Those soft hands, that beautiful body, yes, all that was for him.

And when she stripped those pajamas off and revealed the full beauty of herself to him again, when she pleasured him, with her lips, her tongue, her whole body, and when he sank into her again, just as the clouds cleared and a shaft of moonlight slid into the window, illuminating her all in silver, he was sure that this was going to be the best Christmas of his life.

CHAPTER SIX

TANNER WOKE UP with Chloe tangled around him in the early hours of the morning. He looked outside, angling his head, keeping one arm firmly wrapped around her as he did. The sky looked clear. It was a pale blue, but there were no clouds, and the sun was shining. It had that cold look to it, like the rays were far too peaked to cast any warmth down below. Like they might freeze into golden shards and break off before they were able to hit the earth.

But it wasn't snowing.

The warm weight of her soft body against his was like every fantasy he'd tried so hard to never let himself have. It wasn't just physical satisfaction, lying here with her like this. It was more. It was deeper.

It was terrifying.

"Chloe," he said roughly. "Wake up."

She stirred slightly, and he got out of bed, leaving her there. Then he started to collect his clothes.

He made his way downstairs, where there were people still sound asleep all over the lobby. There was a sign hanging on the desk.

All Roads Are Plowed.

Well, good. That was what he was here to find out.

He ignored the kick of disappointment in his stomach. He shouldn't be disappointed about the fact they needed to leave. What had happened last night was good, but it needed to be contained there. It was his one chance. His one chance to explore that fantasy, before putting it to rest again. And it was done. Now they were going to get on with this trip. Get on with the holiday.

He went back upstairs and found Chloe partially dressed and with a strange look on her face. It was so different than the way she had looked last night. She seemed guarded now. Diminished.

And he should be glad about that, too. Not resentful that his beautiful, generous lover was gone.

"Are the roads open?"

He nodded wordlessly.

"Good," she said, her tone overbright. "Now we can get on with the trip. And see…everyone. I'm excited to see my mom."

"Yeah," he agreed.

There wasn't really anything else to say.

They packed up the rest of their things in silence, and by the time they were back in the truck, Chloe had descended into total silence. Tanner figured that was a good thing, and he could go ahead and put his focus on driving.

The road was cleared, but the banks on the side of the road were built up high, and he didn't want to hit any patches of ice and slide into them. The way up to the mountain cabin was still a bit slick, and he gritted his teeth, trying to keep his focus on that, rather than recurring memories of what had happened the night before. Of how her body had felt. How it had tasted. How much he wanted her then. And how much he wanted her still.

When the cabin came into view, they both let out relieved breaths. He would have laughed, but he didn't want to acknowledge it. Didn't want to acknowledge the fact it was so obvious the two of them were tense.

"We're going to have to do better than this," Chloe said softly.

"What do you mean?" he asked, digging into the denial, as he pulled his truck around to the front of the two-story home with large windows overlooking the mountains around them.

"You know. You can't even look at me. We can't talk to each other. And we can't be behaving like this when everyone sees us."

"I think everyone will be distracted by themselves," Tanner said. "The kids will do a pretty good job of filling in all the spaces."

"Why isn't it easy?" she asked.

She sounded genuinely confused.

She'd been a virgin, and he'd love to blame that for why she was confused now. But the fact of the matter was, he'd had sex with plenty of women and had no trouble talking to them the next day like all they'd done was shake hands.

But he'd never thought this would be easy. Not Chloe.

"Chloe, I've been inside you," he said. "It's not going to be easy to pretend that didn't happen. You don't go back to normal from there. You just fake it."

"But I… I wanted you. All that time. I don't see why I was able to act a certain way around you then, and I can't seem to do it now. All I can do is picture you naked."

"We had a deal," he said.

"Well, I was a virgin. And I didn't know better. *You* should have known better."

"You're right. And I did know better. But I'm just

a man. And men are stupid when their penises get involved."

Her cheeks turned pink. "Don't say that word."

"Sorry. Any other words I shouldn't say?"

"Yes. And I think you can guess most of them. Don't say any words you wouldn't say to a sister."

His chest felt like a rock had fallen on it. "Well, that's the trouble. You really aren't my sister."

"I know," she said.

"But I guess I can pretend."

Silence fell between them, the only sound the ticking of the engine as the truck cooled down.

"Ready?" she asked.

"You just said you *weren't* ready."

"I'm not," she said. "But we have to be, don't we? We have to go in right now and greet everyone. And pretend that none of that happened."

"Just pretend it was a dream," he said.

A dream he was wishing that he hadn't woken up from.

But it didn't matter what he wanted. No, what should matter was that everything needed to go back to normal.

It was the only thing to do.

WHEN THE FRONT door to the cabin opened, Chloe had to fight to paste a smile on her face, and not put an unnatural amount of distance between herself and Tanner. Acting natural was something much easier said than done, when she could still feel her stepbrother's hands all over her body. Thankfully, it was Savannah that opened the door and ushered them inside.

She needed a second before she could face down her mother. Her mother, who had always been just a little bit too good at reading her. Her mother, who would be shocked, appalled and angry if she ever knew what had happened between Chloe and Tanner.

The cabin was beautiful, Christmas decorations festooning every available surface. Pine boughs twisted around wooden beams, lights twinkling from beneath the dark green branches. Pops of red, cranberries on strings along with large velvet bows, were everywhere. It was clear that whoever owned this rental considered it their sacred duty to make the place as festive as possible. And for a moment, Chloe welcomed the explosion of cheer as a distraction from the decidedly uncheerful feelings in her chest.

Lauren and Calder were sitting on a couch in the living room, wrapped around each other, and Jackson was sitting in a chair opposite them, holding Lily in his lap. She was wiggling, clearly unamused at being restrained by her father. Jackson looked over at Chloe.

"Hi," he said. "I am tired of chasing this one around and making sure she doesn't trip and fall into the rock fireplace."

"Yikes. I guess we needed some foam buffers for the hard edges," Chloe said.

Jackson shook his head. "Everything is dangerous."

It amused her still to see her stepbrother acting like a mother hen. Fatherhood had definitely changed him, in about a thousand amazing ways. But this was her favorite. He was so bold and brash before, and he still was when it came to himself. But when it came to Lily... He fretted, worried and protected. She could definitely see why Savannah had fallen head over heels for him.

Who could resist a man who was such a great father?

The thought gave Chloe a strange, hollow pang in her stomach.

Tanner would be a good father. She knew that he would be. He was a great uncle, and he had such a deep, serious sense of responsibility when it came to caring for what was his.

I wish I could be his.

She banished that thought and shoved it to the side. She wasn't, and she wouldn't be. And she needed to remember that.

"Where's Mom? And where are the girls?" Chloe asked.

"The girls have been outside basically since yesterday," Lauren said. "Frostbite is not a deterrent to this much snow. It's kind of nice because usually all I get is sullen teenage behavior. So it's refreshing to watch them enjoy something."

"Your mom has been watching them," Calder said. "I think she's enjoying her instant grandma status."

That created another pang in Chloe's stomach, and it wasn't fair. But the fact that her mother was not a grandma because of Chloe, and wouldn't be anytime soon, if ever, stuck just a little bit right now. Because she'd had a taste of the ultimate fantasy, and now she was brooding about the potential of what life could be if things were different.

But they couldn't be. And pondering it was all pointless.

It just didn't stop her.

"Why don't you put your things away?" Lauren asked. "I'm making sandwiches for lunch, and then I figured we could play some board games or something."

Chloe felt like she hadn't thought through just how

domestic this whole situation was. The weather didn't make it the most conducive to spending time in open spaces, and that meant a lot of inside time in close proximity with Tanner, but also with people all around them, watching their behavior.

"Sounds good," Chloe said.

They gathered up their bags and walked up the stairs. "The two bedrooms down at the end of the hall are still free," Lauren called out.

Tanner looked over at her, and Chloe swallowed. Then they made their way down the hall, and Chloe pushed her bedroom door open, so very aware of the fact that they were right next door. That Tanner was going to be sleeping right on the other side of the wall.

They might live together at home, but her room was downstairs, in a back corner, while his was up the stairs, with a whole lot of square footage and space between them.

Also, they hadn't been back home since they'd slept together.

She had no idea how any of this was going to work. It all seemed so stupid now.

The feverish wishes of a woman who wanted, far too badly, to touch the man she'd always fantasized about, justifying and making up stories about how it would be okay if she did.

Hindsight was twenty-twenty, or so they said.

In this case, hindsight had very clear memories of Tanner *naked*, and she didn't know how in the world she was ever going to forget that.

She wasn't even sure she wanted to.

She was left with a host of uncomfortable feelings

and questions, and no real desire to sit down and sort them out.

She went into the bedroom and closed the door firmly behind her, not looking at Tanner. She was going to rally, go downstairs and have lunch. She was going to be normal, and act normal, and she was not going to let what had happened between the two of them ruin anything. She was resolute and determined on that if nothing else.

Lunch went well enough, with Chloe making sure to position herself at the end of the table opposite of Tanner, so that she wouldn't have to engage him in conversation. She focused on catching up with her mother, whom she hadn't seen in a couple of months. They talked on the phone all the time, but it was different. They'd always been very close, because for most of Chloe's childhood, it had just been the two of them.

They managed to get through board games without any sorts of issues, and at a certain point, the men wandered off and left the women to roll dice with the teenage girls. For dinner, Calder declared that he was going to fire up the barbecue underneath the awning outside, even though it was insane, but he cooked salmon for everyone, so no one complained.

Then, he lit a bonfire in a hollowed-out brick pit in the center of the patio area.

They all bundled up and went outside, setting up for roasting s'mores in the snow.

Again, Chloe was careful to position herself far away from Tanner. She was pretty sure they had actually managed to figure out a way in which they didn't have to speak even two words to each other in anyone else's presence today.

But she knew that wouldn't last. "Anything new?"

Chloe's head whipped around while she was putting a marshmallow on her skewer. Her mother was standing there, eyeing her far too intently.

"I... No. Not really."

"No new students at the barn?"

"Oh," Chloe said. "A couple. Yes, actually there are a couple."

"Are you still living in the house? Or have you moved out to the cabin yet?"

Chloe blinked. Her mother should know that if she'd made any big changes, she would have talked to her about it by now.

"I'm still in the house."

"Chloe," her mom said, grabbing her own skewer and sticking a marshmallow on the end. "You need to be careful."

Chloe felt like she was being pinned to the spot, and she was thankful that it was dim outside so her mother couldn't see her face clearly.

"I need to be... Of what?"

"I'm just afraid that you're letting yourself get into a very stagnant place. And I know that we had some difficult times when you were growing up. I know that we moved around a lot, and I'm sure that it felt haphazard to you. But I just want you to make sure that you don't get so terrified of change that you keep yourself from experiencing life."

"I'm not," Chloe said, so relieved that this conversation had nothing to do with something that her mother had witnessed between herself and Tanner.

"That house is safety to you. And I understand that. When we moved to the ranch our lives changed for the better. And I loved it. But there's a reason that even I moved away after your stepfather died."

"I know," Chloe said, swallowing hard.

"Do you? Because Tanner and Calder and Jackson made it absolutely clear that I was welcome to stay. But I needed to keep on in my journey. My husband was a huge part of that. I loved him dearly. Our marriage wasn't perfect, no marriage is. Ours might've had more struggles than some, but I loved him, and that's what matters. I grew on that ranch. I know you did, too. But I'm in a different part of my life now, and I mean to keep on changing. Not sit and never grow. Like plants, when your roots start to get too big for the pot you're in, you need to transplant yourself. I needed to. I've got a whole group of friends in Arizona, and I love it. The weather is warm, I've picked up new hobbies. I go out dancing. He would have hated that. And I didn't know I would love it. But now I've learned that I do. You have to... You have to go out and experience things sometimes. You really do."

"I love horses," Chloe said. "I love working with kids. I love what I do on the ranch. I truly do. I'm not afraid of anything. I just... Can't you just grow where you're planted?"

"I think it would have to be a pretty special circumstance."

"Did you feel stifled there?"

"Not stifled, not really. But there was a definite way to life there. A definite way things work. I spent so many years as a young adult struggling. And then I found safety and security in that place, in that marriage. A consistency that truly allowed me to find out more about myself. When you're not living just to survive, you grow so much stronger. But now I'm in a phase in my life that feels more about freedom."

Chloe thought about last night. About the way it had felt to be in Tanner's arms. That had felt a whole lot like freedom.

She imagined a life with him, a life where she was allowed to touch him the way that she wanted, kiss him the way that she wanted.

Love him the way that she really wanted.

That sounded like the ultimate freedom, and anything else felt a whole lot like hiding.

She gritted her teeth, because she didn't want to admit any of that to herself. She didn't want to acknowledge the fact that her feelings for Tanner went somewhere far beyond simple fantasy and lust, like she had told him last night when she had said she wanted his body for Christmas.

"I think that freedom looks different for everyone," she said. "I think that for me it looks a lot like riding horses around the fields on the ranch."

She didn't say anything about Tanner. She didn't want to think about Tanner, not right now.

All those thoughts she just had made her feel fragile and small, and very concerned.

"You know you don't have to have the kind of life that I like to have," her mom said softly. "But I just want to make sure that you don't miss out on having a life."

"I know," she said. "And I appreciate that."

She retrieved her marshmallow and went back to the fire pit, feeling melancholy. But everyone around her was smiling and talking, the girls dancing around excitedly, and Lily getting her first taste of s'mores and waving her chubby hands happily.

This was her family. This was her life. And she could understand why her mother—who had always been somewhat feral—would have found freedom in a little bit of distance. In a bit of time spent finding out who she was apart from anyone else. Because she had been linked to Chloe's birth father—the one Chloe had never known, since he'd been off being an asshole, with not a care for the child he'd had—and then she had spent all her time and energy worrying about Chloe.

After that she had gotten married. And then some of the burdens had been shared, but there had been another person to consider yet again.

Chloe, for her part, had spent her life void of those kinds of responsibilities. And it had given her a lot of time to think about who she was and what she loved.

She loved to ride. She loved her horses.

She loved the ranch.

And very unfortunately she loved Tanner. She wasn't quite sure what she was supposed to do about that. She put her skewer out and touched it to the flame, lifting her marshmallow up when it began to smoke.

"You're going to light it on fire."

She looked over just as Tanner took a seat next to her.

She wanted to snap at him for violating their unspoken agreement. The one that clearly stated they were not supposed to be anywhere near each other, nor were they supposed to be speaking to each other.

But nobody was paying attention to them, her mother having moved on to talk to Savannah and watch Lily delight in the sticky marshmallow, chocolate and graham cracker concoction.

"Thank you," she said. "I will submit that to the

marshmallow roasting review board and let you know if we decide to alter the technique."

"That's a lot of bureaucracy for a marshmallow."

"We live in a civilized society, Tanner, and bureaucracy, while inconvenient, definitely ensures that proper protocols are followed."

"Well, we wouldn't want improper marshmallow protocol."

"Indeed. I myself am highly concerned with propriety."

"That is true," he said.

She moved the marshmallow down toward an ember, daring him to comment again.

"Today went well," he said.

"Why are you over here?"

"Because it's where I would be no matter what."

Those words settled funny in her chest. Would he be over here talking to her no matter what had happened last night? And what would it have meant then, versus what it meant now? Did it mean the same thing?

Them being together had only further exposed feelings for him she already had. He had always been attracted to her, but did he have any other feelings?

What did he feel for her? Because it was obvious that she wasn't a sister to him. Last night had made that abundantly clear. But he had never said exactly what he did see in her. What he did feel.

"I've admired you since the moment I met you," she said, turning the marshmallow slowly. "You were so tall and strong and serious. I wanted to capture that sense of solidness that you had and hold it close. Make it mine. I had spent my whole life feeling like everything could spin out of control at any moment. One missed payment and my mom and I would be out on the streets, or we wouldn't have heat or water or food. Everything had felt precarious, and then I met you, and you were like this mountain. A rock. You taught me how to ride, and you taught me by extension what I wanted to do with the rest of my life. I don't think I can possibly overstate the influence you've had on me, Tanner. I never saw you as a brother, not really. But you started out as an idol, and then you became something else. I have a lot of twisted, tangled-up feelings where you're concerned. But one thing that I'm really not sure of... Especially after last night... What am I to you? You said I was more than pretty, but what does that mean?"

"I'm not sure this is a good discussion for us to have," he said flatly.

Her marshmallow began to smoke again and she drew it back. Then she stuck it closer to the flame again. "I'm curious," she insisted. "I want to know. I know it doesn't change anything, but I just want to know."

"When I met you, you were a little scrap of a thing. Like a stray cat. You didn't want to be talked to, you didn't want attention, and yet it was all you wanted. And the horses were like a breakthrough. I was a pretty insensitive young guy at the time, and even I could tell that the horses did something to you. Change something in you. And there was something about that that made it different for me, too. I took the ranch for granted, I took that life for granted. I only focused on what I felt like I didn't have. My mother, a father who wasn't able to let his sons know he was proud of them. He treated us like ranch hands, but suddenly when I saw the ranch through your eyes I could see the value in that. I could understand how a plot of land could be more than rocks and dirt. You gave me a heart for the ranch in a way I didn't have before. If there is such a thing as a muse for a cowboy I guess you would be it."

Her throat felt dry, her heart racing erratically in her chest. "Oh," she said. "Tell me more. About how you wanted me."

"I wanted you well before I should have. And I wanted nothing to do with it. Because I wanted for everything to stay the same. And for you to say exactly as you were to me. Because that was simple. Because it was right."

They looked around the campfire. Everyone was making their own conversation and no one was particularly looking at them. Still, Chloe felt like she had been pulled apart and exposed. His words revealing all kinds of hidden things inside of her. Making her ache. Making her long. Because this was about more than lust, and that was a lot more than she had expected. From him. From this.

"And everyone thinks we're like brother and sister," she said quietly.

It was so much bigger than that. So much more. They had given each other things, taught each other things that no one else ever could have.

"And that's for the best," Tanner said. "Because these kinds of things are important. This vacation. The connections."

"Yes," she said, her heart squeezing tight.

She wanted to ask him why they couldn't just be together. Why they couldn't make a family. Why it couldn't be forever. Because the only reason it was a problem was the fear that it would end. But what if it didn't end. Ever.

But she couldn't ask that. Because there was no way his answer would be yes. And she was too afraid to take that chance. Oh, she remembered her mother crying after men. Men who didn't want to have a wife and daughter. Men who had taken all of the good and all of the beauty in her mother's heart and taken advantage of it. Twisted it. No, she didn't want that kind of pain. She wouldn't be able to endure it.

Her marshmallow suddenly burst into flame and she drew it back quickly, blowing on it.

"I told you it was going to catch fire," he said, his tone maddeningly calm.

And suddenly it seemed like the world's most unfortunate metaphor.

"Yes," she said solemnly. "You did."

She left him then, angrily making herself a s'more and taking a position at the opposite end of the fire.

This was going to be her life with Tanner from now on. Wanting, knowing and not having. Because.

Because. Because. Because.

The word repeated itself on a refrain inside of her until the fire died down and everyone slowly trickled back inside. Everyone except for Tanner. Everyone except for her.

"Are you ready for bed?"

"It's no business of yours," she said. "Especially since I'm going to bed without you."

She licked the remainder of the sticky marshmallow off of her fingers and walked defiantly back into the house.

Her heart felt like it was shattering with each beat, but she managed to head straight to her room and not pause. And not beg. And not tell him that she wished things could be different.

The fact of the matter was they couldn't be. He had said that.

One more time with him would only make things impossible. Would only make it so that she absolutely couldn't let go.

And she needed to be able to let go.

It was essential.

So she ensconced herself in her bedroom, and got back into her reindeer pajamas, which would now always have sexual significance, and she got beneath the covers, convincing herself that her bed wasn't cold, and that she wasn't lonely.

She was a liar.

But she preferred a lie, to crying herself to sleep.

CHAPTER SEVEN

TANNER WAS MISERABLE, and he couldn't sleep. The cold shower that he took hadn't helped. He kept replaying the conversation that he'd had with Chloe by the fire over and over again.

He had been an asshole. Lecturing her like he had. Especially on the heels of telling her that she was his muse. His muse, dammit. Who talked like that? He certainly didn't.

He didn't entertain thoughts like that. And yet, the moment they had left his mouth, he had known the words were true. She was something so much more to him than a sister ever could be. Something so much more than a simple object of desire.

And yet, she was all of that and more.

He couldn't reduce the attraction between them by saying it was only sex. Because sex between them had never been a simple, solitary thing.

For some reason, he had taken a chance with her and potentially compromised the foundation of his entire life.

How could you call it only sex when it was not much of a risk? When it rocked you down to your core.

No, there was no *only* about it.

Something was pounding through his veins, and it was more than just arousal. He couldn't put a name to it, couldn't organize his thoughts. If it was desire, then it would fade. Desire always did. Desire was present, but it was more than that. It was so much more.

He wasn't going to be able to sleep tonight.

Not for wanting her.

And he was the one that had put such a hard limit on their night together.

And he should know, more than her, that it wasn't essential. He was the one with experience. He wasn't the one who should be obsessing.

She had been a virgin. *Her*.

She was the one that should be confusing sex with emotions. If one of them was going to.

But for some reason, something was shifted inside of him, and for the life of him he couldn't seem to push it back into place.

He let out a long, slow breath, hoping that he could settle the pounding of his heart. That he could somehow cool down, slow down, the way the blood was moving through his veins. He couldn't seem to. He kept thinking of her. Remembering what it had been like to have handfuls of her hair, her ass, her breasts. To be deep inside of her. Chloe. Finally.

He'd taken that bag of condoms from the inn and packed it in his bag.

Because he was a liar. Because he had been lying to himself from the moment they had left that inn.

He had just thought he might need them later. That it would be a waste of money to leave the box behind. But now it seemed so glaringly obvious that he would never use a box of condoms he had bought for *Chloe* with any other woman. Never.

Those condoms were for Chloe.

His body felt like it might be for Chloe, from now until forever.

The very idea of touching another woman after he'd been with her felt like a blasphemy in a church. A stain on pure white sheets.

No. He couldn't do it. He wouldn't.

But that left him grappling with the implications of that. What it meant to want her. What it would mean to have her.

And before he knew what he was doing he was getting out of bed. He opened the bedroom door and stood in front of hers. For a long time.

The house was quiet, everyone long gone to bed. But he didn't want to chance someone hearing him knock on her door. He tried the knob, and it didn't budge. A smile curved his lips.

He sort of hoped that she had locked him out. Not that he was going to let it deter him now. But he liked the fact that she had either tried to lock herself in to keep herself from coming to him, or that part of her had known that he would do this. That he was going to be weak. That he wasn't going to be able to leave this alone.

That whatever they'd agreed about what happened in a snowed-in lodge staying there, he wasn't going to be able to honor it. Not now. Not ever.

He licked his lips, adrenaline coursing through him, his stomach tightening, his cock getting hard. He tapped on the door with one knuckle.

He heard nothing. He looked down the hall and knocked slightly louder. Then waited. He thought he heard the rustling of sheets and blankets, but it could also be wishful thinking, for how subtle the sound was.

But then he heard the sound of the lock turning. And nothing else. No voice. No open door. He tested the knob, and it gave. By the time he pushed the door open, Chloe was back in bed, the blankets pulled up to her chin. He shut the door behind him quickly, locking it.

"What are you doing here?" she asked.

"You know," he said, the box of condoms in his hand a glaringly obvious statement.

"You said one night. You said one night was all it could be."

"And I meant it, when I said it. At least, I convinced myself that I did."

"You lied," she said simply.

"To myself."

"What if we get caught?"

"I don't know," he said, his voice rough. He stripped his shirt off, and made his way to the bed, setting the box of condoms down on the pillow and climbing under the sheets, not touching her yet.

"But I can't stay away from you either way. And I'd rather deal with the consequences of all of that than I would sleep alone."

"You were so adamant about the way things could work between us, by the fire earlier. So much instruction. From marshmallows to the attraction between us."

"Because I'm an asshole. And apparently I only get more sanctimonious when I know that I'm going to fail a test. But you locked the door. So my question is… Were you locking me out or locking yourself in?"

She lifted a shoulder. "Probably both."

"But you unlocked it," he pointed out.

"You came," she said simply.

"I meant what I said by the fire."

"I'm going to burn my marshmallow?"

"No. That you mean something more to me than anyone else. Something different than a sister. Something not quite like anyone that's ever been in my life. You changed me."

"How nice for me," she said loftily. "To be a muse set up high on an unreachable shelf."

"You're not unreachable now," he said, putting his hand on her hip and smoothing it up and down over her curves.

His body let out an enthusiastic hallelujah. Because he had been committed, knuckling down and telling himself that he wasn't going to touch her again, and the fact that he was...an illicit shot of arousal fired through his veins. Yes, this was exactly what he wanted. Exactly what he needed.

They still weren't home. Surely that had to count for something. Surely that had to count as some kind of specious boundary that they could call okay. "What if I wanted to be unreachable?"

"Do you?"

"No," she said, her voice muted. "And I judge myself for that."

He gripped her hips and rolled her over to the top of him, positioning her so that her core was directly over his hardening body. "Good."

"Tanner," she breathed, bending down and fusing her lips to his. Her kiss was wild, deep and unrestrained, and completely at odds with the cool, arched tone she had taken with him only moments earlier. She kissed him like her life depended on it. Kissed him like they might both drown if they didn't get a taste. Kissed him like she was dying. Like he might be able to heal her.

He wanted to. Whatever she needed, he wanted to be. He felt an ache grow, expand in his chest.

As he realized fully what he had admitted to her, what he had admitted to himself. That she was somehow the agent of change in his life. Somehow everything. The root of him finding who he was meant to be. And she had been. But she had to be old enough for that to become this. He had to wait, and now suddenly it was like all the pieces of his life had locked into place. This woman, who had made him the man he was, was finally in his bed. Finally over top of him, arching her body against him, beautiful and wild in his arms.

It was love, he realized, as she pulled her shirt up over her head, exposing her breasts to him.

He had never given any credibility to romantic love. Not really. And yet, suddenly it all made sense. Not only this feeling that he had for her, but the ways in which it had changed his father's life. No, it hadn't made him perfect. And Tanner's relationship with him had never become what he might have hoped. But his stepmother had changed him. And by turn, his father had changed her. Their marriage, their love, had actually changed the lives of all the children involved for the better.

And had enabled him to find this.

It was suddenly like he could see every stage of his life at once, from a high vantage point, watch it all coming together in a single, glorious motion.

As if every pitfall, and every step, suddenly made perfect sense.

He had never been a man who believed in fate, but he felt like he was staring at his right now. Luminous, glowing and perfect in the pale moonlight that filtered through the window. He moved his hands to her breasts, cupped her, gloried in her. And then he slid his hands around her back, moving them down, all the way to her ass. He maneuvered her from one side to the other, removing her pajama bottoms and then putting her back just as she was. She leaned forward, pressing a kiss to his chest, down to his abs, her hands working diligently on his belt and tugging his jeans down just enough.

His breath hissed when her slick, wet body made contact with his cock.

She arched her hips forward and back, rolling herself along the ridge of his arousal. Stoking the fire in his stomach that he didn't think would ever be extinguished.

This was different. This was more than sex. It was Chloe. And it was love. And it reached every part of who he was. From his body down deeper. All the way to his heart.

She was the one who reached for the box of condoms, and she took a packet out slowly, her expression veiled as she clumsily placed the latex over the head of his arousal and squeezed him as she rolled it on slowly, protecting them both. Though it didn't seem so bad, the thought of having unprotected sex with her. The idea that she might get pregnant. Have his baby.

Those thoughts came fast, hitting him hard, and leaving behind a certainty that overwhelmed him.

He would be fine with that future. More than fine.

With Chloe in his house forever. In his life forever.

And as she positioned herself over him, taking him slowly into her tight, wet body, his desire so great he thought his chest might burst, he held her hips tightly and pushed her down onto him fully, growling with approval as she took him all the way.

She gasped, experimenting with little movements at first, rolling her hips back and forth, establishing a rhythm that pleased them both. Everything she did was magic. Everything she did was bound to please him.

Being in her was like being home. All those feelings of rightness that she'd given him about the ranch, about his future, it was all in her.

It was all Chloe.

Chloe.

He wanted to make it last, but desire was like a hot fist, clamped around his throat, and he couldn't fight it. It grabbed him, shook him, and threw him over the edge, his release bursting like a bomb in his gut, making him growl as he slammed up inside of her. He felt her own release hit at that moment, a sweet cry of pleasure on her lips as her internal muscles pulsed around him, and then she collapsed against him, her breath hot over his chest, her hair spreading out over his body. And he held her. He was in no hurry to move, but he was going to have to get up and deal with practicality soon.

He didn't want to. He just wanted to hold her.

He wanted to hold her forever. And he was going to have to figure out exactly what that meant. Exactly what that looked like. Because one night was never going to be enough.

Forever was barely going to be enough.

Tanner Reid had spent most of his life giving no thought to love, and now it was the only thing that mattered.

Because it was Chloe.

Love all on its own was one thing, was for other people.

Loving Chloe was for him. He had never been more certain of anything in all of his life.

"Chloe," he said, his voice rough.

"What?" she asked, her tone sleepy.

"I was wrong."

"Well, that's the first time I've ever heard you say that," she said, moving away from him and rolling to her side of the bed.

"I was wrong about boundaries," he said.

"Which boundaries?"

"About the ones that mean we can't be together. About drawing lines around things, and pretending like this never happened."

"But…" She blinked. "But our family…"

"Can learn to adjust."

"And what happens if the two of us break up?"

"Well, then everyone would have to deal with that, too. But I'm not planning on breaking up with you."

"How can you not be? You've broken up with every woman you've ever been with."

"But I've never loved any of them."

Those words brought about a crashing silence.

"You've never… What?"

"I've never loved any of them. I love you."

CHAPTER EIGHT

CHLOE THOUGHT SHE was going to have a panic attack. She had been fantasizing about this very thing earlier. That he would tell her that he cared for her. That he would offer her forever.

But suddenly, he was presenting it in front of her like an enticement, and all she wanted to do was run away from it. More than run, she wanted to roll off the bed and hide under it, do something to cover herself, protect herself. Because this was so exposing, so terrifying. This offer of something that sounded a lot like forever.

This answer to the biggest Christmas wish she'd ever had.

She knew how to wish for the unrealistic. The unreasonable.

She knew how to long for things that she could never have. But she really didn't know how to have them presented to her. Not long-term. One night...a little taste of what she wished for, a chance to build up more fantasies, to store up more dreams—that she could fathom. But this? She had no idea what to do with it. And it terrified her.

"You don't want that," she said.

"I don't?"

"Tanner, you have never shown the slightest bit of interest in me."

"And you've never shown the slightest bit of interest in me, but I know that you were. What we showed each other was not the truth. And what I told myself wasn't the truth, either. But I had...a revelation, Chloe."

"During sex?"

"You're damn right during sex. When I was inside you. It was like I had a sense of myself, really and truly for the first time in my entire life. And I am not the kind of man who says shit like that. Who feels shit like this? I'm not the kind of man that believes in fate, or the one, or this kind of spiritual connection that comes with physical pleasure, but dammit, it's all there with you. And I believe it. For the first time. I get it. I understand why people go to war for it. I understand why people die for it. I understand why people are willing to change their whole life for it. Because I'm willing to. Whatever the consequence. Whatever happens. I'm willing to do this for you. For me."

"Why?" she asked, choking. "Why for me?"

"Why not? You are the single greatest force of good in my life, Chloe. You made me the man that I am. I have no doubt about that. I was aimless and drifting until you showed me why ranch work mattered. Until you made me see everything around me with fresh eyes. And you keep doing it. Again, and again. You've done it with sex. You've done it with this feeling that has taken over my body. It's like I'm seeing everything for the first time. All because of you."

"Well I... I'm very honored to have provided you with the revelation, but that's not any kind of guarantee. Of anything."

"I'm not asking for a guarantee. But I am asking that we take a chance."

"I don't… I don't want to." Suddenly she saw it. Her life as she knew it slipping away. Oh, she had imagined for a few heady moments that building a life with him would look like freedom, that it could be everything, but now she could see two sides of it. She could see losing him. Losing her place on the ranch. Her job. Everything that had ever mattered to her.

Because she would never be enough for him. She never could be.

Her own father had wanted nothing to do with her, why would he?

It would never work. Ever. She might be broken and bruised for a while if she left now, but if she wanted everything and lost it, then she would be so much more than bruised. She would be shattered. And she didn't think she could handle that.

"We can't," she said, her voice hoarse and husky and colored with all the jagged edges that seemed to be rising up inside of her, all her secret fears, all her broken parts. All of the things that she had conveniently been able to ignore for years while her life was set in a comfortable pattern.

Just how terrified she was of losing her security.

How much she feared all the ways in which she might find herself inadequate if she ever really got the opportunity to try. To try for what she really wanted.

"Why not?" he asked.

"For all the many valid reasons we came up with at the inn. For all the reasons that it was valid beforehand. All the reasons that we never acted on these feelings. There were reasons. There were always reasons."

"And I've decided that none of them are as important as what I feel for you. My father spent his entire life trying to learn how to love somebody, and I'm not sure that he ever did it right, but he did try. He spent his life looking for that person. He found it in your mom. We have it now. We don't have to wait that long. I'm going to try. That's all I can do. All I can do is try to be the best that I can be. But I will put everything on the line to do it. Everything."

"No," she said. "And that's where you are acting more like your father. He was selfish. And he didn't consider you. You or Calder or Jackson. The way that he lived his life… It wasn't for you. I know that he was better later. I do. But that… What if this is actually just that. For you. You justifying what you would be putting our family through because you think it's going to make you happy. I'm not convinced it will. Not me. Not you. Not anyone else."

"Why don't you think it would make you happy?"

"It probably would. For a while. For a while, and then what? Then what? I just…"

"You're afraid," he said.

"I'm not afraid," she said. "I'm being practical. You've never had a relationship in your life. Not a real one. And you know that I haven't. So we aren't going to take the chance and blow up everything that matters. Everything that made us good, and do that for… For what?"

"On the chance that this could be forever," he said. "On the chance that it's love."

"No," she said. "It's… It's not right…"

"I understand," he said, his voice rough. "You're scared. You're scared because you don't know what to do when things are going your way. You're independent, Chloe, and I admire that about you, but I also think it's because you don't like to depend on other people. Because you don't know how. You told me that you like to make wishes you know can't come true, and I believe it. I believe full well that you don't want to go after something that you can have. Because if you were to get it, then you have to be able to give back. You have to be able to open yourself up, and admit how much something means to you. And then you might be afraid of losing it. And I think... I think that's what scares you."

"It's easy for you to say. It's easy. You didn't live a life like I did. You didn't live with things being promised to you and then taken away. With not being sure how long a nice apartment might last, before you get thrown out. You can enjoy a nice meal one day and go right back to starving the next, because nothing in this life is certain. And you're not guaranteed a damn thing. I know that. When your whole life is waiting for the other shoe to drop because it always does, then you're just always waiting for the inevitable. I'm not going back to that."

"You think I'm going to drop the other shoe?"

"Yes. And I don't think you would do it on purpose. But it's just... There's too much at stake here. There's too much to risk. For sex. We can't."

"But it's not too much to risk for love, is it?"

He knew at that point he'd pushed her too far. He knew that she couldn't follow him there right now, whatever the reason.

Fear. That was the reason. And he understood that.

Because in the end, that was the real reason he had held back from her. Fear.

Fear that he was just his old man. That he was going to disappoint her. That he was going to hurt her. And it wasn't until he had realized that he loved her, really, that he'd been able to get over that fear. She'd trusted him with so much so far. But this was too much for her, apparently. The end of her trust. It stabbed at him like a knife, but he couldn't blame her, either. Not really.

He got up and began to get dressed, slowly, methodically. And then he turned toward the door, but he paused before he opened it.

"Be sure of this," he said. "I'm the Christmas present you can have. Whatever you want, that's all for you. I swear it. You're going to have to be brave enough to come to me and ask, though. You're going to have to trust me. You're going to have to trust yourself. That we are not our parents. Even the good parts, we are going to handle differently."

"How are you so confident in that?"

"Because I don't like the alternative," he said.

"Well I don't see any possibility but that."

"Get back to me when you change your mind," he said.

He walked out of her room, and the next beat of his heart seemed to break fragments off of it, shocking him with the pain. With the intensity of it. He had never felt like this before. Not even when his mother had left. This intense hopelessness that seemed to drain the strength right out of his body.

He was used to a life he could control. But for so many years, the one thing he couldn't change were his feelings for Chloe. As it turned out, the most important thing he couldn't change was her feelings for him.

"Merry Christmas to me," he muttered, as he went back to his bedroom. Alone.

Facing a future that would be just as lonely.

CHAPTER NINE

CHLOE DIDN'T SLEEP for the whole rest of the night, tears eventually drying and sealing her eyes shut. But still, she was restless. By the time she dragged herself down to breakfast the next morning, she had a feeling that she looked severely compromised. Probably as much as she felt. Thankfully, the boys had all gone out to go shooting somewhere in the snow, and she didn't have to face Tanner just yet.

She needed the reprieve.

And it made her wonder if what she was doing was insanely stupid.

Because she had rejected everything he offered her to avoid pain, and she wasn't sure the pain in her chest could ever be matched. Except, that was the problem. It could be. If she decided to start a life with him, and he then decided that it wasn't working out, then she would be blindsided and devastated. If she trusted it… If she trusted him… Then what would happen when it all crumbled?

You're so certain that it's going to crumble?

Yes, she was. Because that was life as she knew it.

That's not fair. Your mother's always been there for you.

She ignored the argumentative voice inside of her that seemed bound and determined to encourage her to go forward with Tanner and get herself shattered completely.

"You don't look like you slept very well," her mother said, coming into the kitchen and giving her a critical eye.

"Thank you," Chloe muttered, moving over to the coffeepot and filling up her mug.

"It wasn't an insult," her mom said. "I was just commenting."

"Well, you certainly weren't saying that I looked pretty," Chloe pointed out.

"You look unhappy."

"I just didn't sleep well. New bed. And all of that."

"Is that it?" The telling pause before her mother spoke told Chloe that she didn't believe her at all.

"Yes." Chloe was committed to her narrative, dammit. "What else could it be?"

"I don't know," her mother said. "Maybe what you and Tanner were talking about so intensely last night by the fire."

"Why would you think we were…talking intensely? We were just talking."

"If that's the story that you want to tell, Chloe, I can't make you tell me anything but that. I was watching the two of you last night. I've been watching the two of you for a long time. And I'm not an expert on everything by any means, nor am I a psychic. But I am your mother. And I can certainly tell certain things by watching people's body language. Anyone can. There's a way that you are with Jackson and Calder that you've never been with Tanner."

"He's the oldest," Chloe said, feeling itchy and uncomfortable. Defensive. "And we've spent a lot of time together. It's just…with me staying at the ranch and how it worked out so that I was in the house even after you left and Jim died." She was simply staring at Chloe. "I'm not sure what you're saying."

"You have feelings for him," her mother said. "I've been aware of that for quite some time, but I've never known how to approach it. I tried last night to check in on you and see how things were going. I was hoping that you might confide in me a little bit, but I can see now that you're not going to. Not about this. I don't want you stuck there pining after him forever."

"I'm not… That's ridiculous," Chloe said. "It's ridiculous."

"Is it?" her mother asked. "He's a handsome man, and you were older when I married his father. Why wouldn't you see him for what he is?"

"Because it's dangerous. And it doesn't make any sense. And it has the potential to destroy this," she said, waving her hand around the kitchen. "Our family. Which was so hard won. For years it was just you and me, Mom. It was good, don't get me wrong. I know you did your absolute best, and in spite of the fact that we went through hard times we were happy. We were."

"But they were very hard times," her mother said. "I know that things were better when we moved to the ranch. And I don't think for one moment that I was the best mother to you that I could have been. Not when I was under so much stress all the time. Not when I worried about basic things like keeping a roof over your head. I know that our lives were better for having them in it. For having that family."

"Yes," Chloe said. "Exactly. That was when it got better. And I do love Jackson and Calder like brothers.

I do. And Savannah and Lauren are like sisters to me already, and my nieces are so precious. Visiting you and having us all together like this is so precious. And me having stupid, inappropriate feelings for Tanner can't ever disrupt that."

Her mother looked out the window, and then back at Chloe. "Does he have feelings for you?"

"It doesn't matter."

"It does," her mother said. "Let me tell you something, Chloe. Trust is the hardest thing to give when it's been abused. And you had your trust abused again and again as a child. I appreciate that you feel like I did the best that I could. Your forgiveness for the mistakes I made means more to me than you can ever know. But the fact of the matter is, even though I tried to shoulder all the burdens, I know you took them on, too."

Her dark eyes, so like Chloe's, were full of hurt. Full of regret. "I know you did. You had to worry about where we would live. You couldn't trust that you would have a room to come home to when school ended on any given day. You couldn't trust that one of the men that I tried to make things work with would be kind, or that he would stay. You were thrown into any number of situations where most children could have just trusted that their basic needs would be met, and yours weren't. I'm sorry. It took me a long time to figure out how to get things together, and in order to do that I had to trust Jim. It wasn't easy. And our marriage was never the easiest, and I'm sorry for that. I'm sorry that it was the example that you did have. But I loved him. I loved him, and I didn't stay with him just for security. Because that wouldn't have been a better lesson to teach you. I stayed because what we had was worth fighting through the hard stuff. It was worth fighting through his issues, his own difficulty opening himself up. After the boys' mother left things were hard for him. It was difficult for him to fully open himself up to anyone. From his sons to his wives. And the fact of the matter is, he did try to push me away when things got too real. But I wouldn't go. I wouldn't be pushed away, because I finally recognized all of that for what it was. The exact same thing I was doing. Trying to keep someone from knowing me. From lulling me into a false sense of security."

"I had no idea," Chloe said.

"Of course not. You were a child, and I don't know why you would have ever been able to sort through any of that. But I know that it sticks with you. I know it's there under the surface. It's the foundation of what built you."

"But, Mom," Chloe said, "you can't seriously be advocating for me being in a relationship with my stepbrother."

"I want you to be happy. That's what I'm advocating for. I meant what I said to you last night. I wouldn't mind if you went and moved across the country for a while and found yourself some freedom. But if freedom for you is him, then you should go after that. It doesn't matter what anyone thinks."

Chloe felt miserable. Miserable and like a timid little mouse hiding underneath the furniture. "I'm not worried about what anyone thinks, I'm worried about it ruining our entire family structure."

"I believe that you're worried about that a little bit, but I think you're much more worried about being hurt.

I think you're much more worried about trusting and having that trust abused."

"He said he loved me," Chloe said. "But I don't understand how he could. He's...he's so beautiful and strong and wonderful, and he's everything I've ever wanted, and I don't understand how I'm not for him. And he told me that I was. But I don't understand. I don't understand how I could be so special to him."

"Oh, Chloe," her mother said, pulling her into her arms. "I did more damage than I realized."

"You didn't," Chloe said.

"You should know what you're worth, baby girl, and if you don't, I don't know who else to blame."

"I don't know, maybe my father who wouldn't stick around?"

"I tried to be enough."

Regret lanced Chloe. "You were. You were, and I don't want to hurt you."

"This isn't about me. It's about you. Don't worry about hurting my feelings. I'm just sorry. But I also can't lie to you and say that loving him means it will solve all your problems. Because you know it won't. Love solved a lot of my problems, Chloe, but then I had some new ones. Loving somebody does mean opening yourself up to being hurt. Loving someone means having to try, having to put in an effort. Loving someone means you can't protect yourself. And I think in the end, that's what you're really afraid of."

Chloe stared down into her coffee. She couldn't really deny her mother's words.

They went so nicely with all things Tanner had accused her of before. Because if she tried to make things work with Tanner, then she would have to trust him.

She would have to open herself up, all of herself, and not have any self-protection left at all.

Tanner had been a form of self-protection, and then he had suddenly become available. And it had terrified her.

Because the reality of Tanner had the power to devastate her in the way that the fantasy of him couldn't have.

"I just can't," she said.

"Then I think it's time you went and found your freedom. Because if you stay here with him, and don't let yourself have him, you're clipping your wings for sure."

CHAPTER TEN

"WHAT CRAWLED UP your ass and died?" Jackson asked as Tanner swore when he missed the target yet again.

"Nothing," he insisted. He *lied*.

"Right. Okay. But you're a terrible shot today, and you're being grumpy about it."

"It's nothing," he said.

"Right. Well, it seems like it's a pretty serious nothing if you ask me."

"I agree," Calder said.

"Shut up."

"Make me," Calder said.

Tanner was about to bang both of his brothers' heads together. None of this was any of their business, and if they had a clue what was bothering him they would be scarred onto their souls.

And that made him want to tell them. It made him want to take control of it that way. Because why the hell not? Really, why should Chloe get to control the whole thing? Why should she be able to tell him no, and use the family as an excuse? When, really, she was scared. She didn't trust him. Or she didn't know how.

"It's Chloe," he said finally.

Jackson and Calder's heads whipped around. "What?" Jackson asked.

"Chloe. She is my problem."

Jackson and Calder exchanged knowing looks that made Tanner want to punch them both. If they had any idea...

"Did you finally figure out she has a crush on you?" Jackson asked.

He blinked. They had known that *Chloe* had a crush on him? And they had thought that was all it was? They hadn't realized that Tanner wanted her?

"No," Tanner said. "She rejected me. After I had sex with her."

"What the *fuck*?" Calder asked.

Jackson might have said something similar, but he slammed his forearm over his mouth. It was mildly satisfying to see that he'd succeeded in shocking his brothers to that degree.

"Yep. So now you know. You were so curious. And now you know."

"I want to go back to not knowing," Jackson said, his face contorted with disgust.

"Too late," he said. "You were nosy, so you got the story."

"What do you mean she rejected you?" Calder asked.

"I said I was in love with her," Tanner said.

"No shit," Calder said. "You're in love with her?"

"Yeah," Tanner said. "I have no idea what in hell to do about that."

Jackson's expression took on a solemn shade. "Nothing you can do about it," he said. "Once that happens, and once you're ready to admit it... There's just nothing for you."

"Great," Tanner said.

"But you already knew that," Calder added. "Because if you didn't, you sure as hell wouldn't have said anything to us."

It was a good point.

"What am I supposed to do?"

"I mean, I suggest not being a dick. Because when you reject their offer of love they leave in the dead of night and you end up heartbroken, and you have to crawl back to them on metaphorical broken glass. My experience," Jackson said, and Tanner knew that he was speaking of his relationship with Savannah, and the rough patch they'd hit before they'd ultimately decided to spend forever together.

"Coming on strong doesn't hurt," Calder said. "You've got to basically offer the whole world. Hold nothing back. That's what I would do. That's what I did."

"Yeah, yeah. I get it. The two of you have functional love lives." He shook his head. "But none of you fell in love with your stepsister. Anyway, she said we couldn't because of what it would do to the family."

"She's hilarious," Jackson said. "Because we all know that she likes you. I'm much more surprised about you liking her. That I never got a whiff of."

"Me, either," Calder confirmed.

"Nice to know I hid my inappropriate feelings for so long. They were definitely there."

"Did you tell us so that… What? So you can tell her that everything's fine?"

"No, because I don't think that's a real problem. I think it's an excuse. She doesn't trust it will last. I just want to take away all her excuses."

"I'm not college-educated or anything," Jackson said. "But I think that might be your first problem."

"What?"

"I think you shouldn't focus on taking anything. I think you have to figure out just how much you can give. And you're going to have to keep doing it until she can find the trust. It doesn't matter what you think she should know or see or feel. She's been hurt. And if we were completely unaware of your feelings for her, I imagine she didn't know about them, either. She's going to need those reinforced."

"I don't know what to give."

Calder shrugged. "Everything."

"What does that mean?"

"I don't know," Jackson said. "It's kind of open-ended and vague. It's something you're going to have to figure out for yourself."

"You guys are my younger brothers, and this is really annoying. Getting advice from you."

"I imagine it's even more annoying to be dependent on that advice," Calder said smugly.

"Yeah," Tanner agreed.

"*Everything* is going to be the thing she needs," Calder said, overly sage in tone.

"That is a mouthful of nonsense," Tanner said.

"Is it?"

And immediately everything clicked into place for him. There was no woman on earth who would ever entice him to make such a rash or impromptu decision. But she did. Because he suddenly realized what she needed.

She needed someone who would go all the way and hold nothing back. Someone who gave all their trust so that she could begin to give hers.

And he was more than ready to do that. For her? He would do it.

"Okay, I might be getting frostbite. Because this is starting to make sense."

CHAPTER ELEVEN

CHLOE WAS STANDING on the deck looking out at the snowy view when she heard muted footsteps coming from behind her. She looked over her shoulder and froze. It was Tanner.

"What are you doing?" she asked.

"I came to talk to you."

"Why?"

"Because we need to talk. Actually, I need to say some things."

"Tanner…"

"No. You took a step out in faith with me when you asked for a night together. That was a lot. I know it was. And what did you get back from me? You got the promise of a single night. And then, because I was good and ready I told you that I loved you. But that wasn't enough for you, either, and I actually understand why. You deserved more. You deserved better. From me. You absolutely did. But I didn't understand that. I was waiting for you to give me something. I was waiting for give-and-take. You need a reason to trust me. And I haven't given it. That's not your fault, that's mine. I love you. I love you, Chloe. I'm ready to give you anything. Any damn thing you want. I swear it. You can have it. I want to offer you this. Me. Forever. Marry me, Chloe. Make us a family. The most important family. It'll be you and me. And it will be forever. I've never made a vow I haven't kept, not to my father or the land, and I sure as hell won't make one that I'll break to you. You wanted to know how this was different. And why I had confidence that we could do this. It's because we are not like anything. And I want to show you that. Be my wife. Be my everything."

Chloe was stunned. The last thing she had expected when he came walking toward her with his eyes blazing was that he was going to propose. She'd thought he might yell at her, and she could understand why. But she hadn't thought he was going to do that.

"But why… Why?"

"Because this is about trust. I am putting all of mine in your hands. All of it. I don't have any more protection left, Chloe. I want you. Nothing else. No one else. And it's been like that for a long time. For every reason that you're special, for everything that you taught me. For the way that I feel when I'm with you, and the shady way I feel when I'm not. I want to be with you. I swear that I will give you everything that's in my power to give. You have nothing to fear from me."

And just like that, she felt her resistance crumble. Felt the walls inside of her start to give way. He was taking all her concerns and dealing with them. He was giving to her with no guarantee in return.

"I told Calder and Jackson about us," he said. "At first because I was angry at you and I wanted to take away your excuses, but then because I was just desperate for some advice, and somehow, those idiots managed to get themselves wives."

"They know?"

"They do. And they're not shocked or upset or angry.

But they did tell me that I was being a little bit of an idiot. Trying to strong-arm you into something, trying to take away your defenses. When I needed to set down my own."

"I love you," she said softly, her heart pounding like a butterfly trying to dry its wings. Tentative, hopeful. So very, very fragile. "I love you, and I'm so scared of what might happen if you don't love me. I'm so scared to hope."

"Let's hope together," he said. "Because if we do it together, then neither of us are sitting around waiting for something to happen. This isn't a passive thing. Love is active. I love you. You love me. And we want it. If we want it, we'll work at it. I see that with you and your horses, with your business. You've seen that with me on the ranch. It's who we are. When we love something, we don't let it die. And we're certainly not going to let this die."

She swallowed hard. "I know," she said. "I know you're right. I was just... I hoped for it for so long, and I think I don't really know how to have nice things."

"I want to give you a whole lifetime of them. I do."

"I want that," she whispered. "With you. Only you."

"What do you want for Christmas, Chloe?" he asked, his voice rough, the kiss that followed even rougher, leaving her dizzy.

"What I've wanted for as long as I can remember. It's you, Tanner. It's always been you."

"You have it. You have me. Forever."

EPILOGUE

"WHAT DO YOU little rascals want for Christmas?" Tanner asked, looking down at his niece, who was nearly three and had a comment for everything, and her little brother, who was one and had nothing but spit bubbles and very loud sounds.

They were all gathered at the family ranch house for a Christmas Eve celebration. They'd decided not to go up to a cabin this year, and Tanner felt like that was somehow more special. That this place, this home, was the most special place on earth to all the Reid brothers, their wives and their children.

"A pony," Lily said, with utter confidence.

And he smiled, because he already knew Jackson's plans for his daughter. "Do you think Santa could fit that in his sleigh?"

Lily looked worried at that.

Chloe slapped him on the shoulder, her wedding band glistening on her finger. It was such a nice distraction he didn't even mind being slapped. But then, he didn't much mind anything Chloe did to him.

"Of course it could," Chloe scolded. "Santa is magic."

"He brought me a pony," Ava said, grinning at her little cousin. "I'm sure he could bring one for Lily. Hers would be tiny!"

"And this year he's bringing you a brother," Tanner said, looking over at Lauren, who was nearly at the end of her pregnancy.

Calder was never far from her side, his hand perpetually rested in a protective fashion over her baby bump. "Or sister," Calder said. "We don't know what it is yet."

Lauren smirked. "I do."

"Don't tell me," Calder said. "I want to be surprised. And I love having daughters. I won't be disappointed if it's not a boy. I have the best women around."

When Calder went to the fridge for a beer, Lauren turned to Tanner and Chloe and mouthed, "It's a boy."

Only a few years ago he wouldn't have been able to imagine his brother in this life. Hell, a few years ago he wouldn't have been able to imagine himself married.

Looking forward to children.

To the whole life he and Chloe had ahead.

"Dinner is served!" Savannah announced, coming out of the kitchen, with Jackson in an apron trailing behind her. "Come on and get it while it's hot!"

Chloe grabbed hold of his hand and held him back. "Just a minute," she said softly.

"What?"

"I have a present for you."

"You do? I don't think we have time for the kind of present I like best," he said, raising his eyebrows suggestively at her.

She slapped his shoulder. "No. We don't. It's something else."

"What is it? You don't have a box big enough in the house for a motorcycle."

"It isn't a motorcycle. And you aren't allowed to have

one anyway. Because they aren't safe and you have to worry about safety now."

"Oh, do I?"

"Yes. Because you, Tanner Reid, are going to be a father in about seven months."

The words stopped the whole world turning. "I am?"

"Yes," she said, looking up at him, her eyes shining with tears, her face glowing with love. "Merry Christmas, Tanner."

He looked around, at the house, at his wife. His rock. His cornerstone.

His very foundation.

Years ago, Chloe had changed the course of his life. And she just kept on doing it. Kept on bringing him into his purpose. Making him the man he was always meant to be.

He bent down and kissed her, slow and deep.

"Merry Christmas, Chloe. Merry Christmas."

* * * * *

Read on for a sneak peek of
Want Me, Cowboy
the latest in New York Times *bestselling author*
Maisey Yates's Copper Ridge series.

⬡HARLEQUIN®DESIRE

When Isaiah Grayson places an ad for a convenient
wife, no one compares to his assistant, Poppy
Sinclair. Clearly the ideal candidate was there all
along—and after only one kiss he wants her without
question. Can he convince her to say yes without
love?

November 1st, 2018
Location: Copper Ridge, Oregon

WIFE WANTED—

Rich rancher, not given to socializing. Wants a
wife who will not try to change me. Must be tolerant of moods, reported lack of sensitivity, and
the tendency to take off for a few days' time in
the mountains. Will expect meals cooked. Also,
probably a kid or two. Exact number to be negotiated. Beard is nonnegotiable.

November 5th, 2018
Revised draft for approval by 11/6

WIFE WANTED—

~~Rich rancher, not given to socializing.~~ Successful
rancher searching for a wife who enjoys rural living. ~~Wants a wife who will not try to change me.~~
~~Must be tolerant of moods, reported lack of sensi-~~
~~tivity, and the tendency to take off for a few days'~~
~~time in the mountains.~~ Though happy with my

life, it has begun to feel lonely, and I would like someone to enhance my satisfaction with what I have already. I enjoy extended camping trips and prefer the mountains to a night on the town. ~~Will expect meals cooked. Also, probably a kid or two. Exact number to be negotiated. Beard is nonnegotiable. I~~ I'm looking for a traditional family life, and a wife and children to share it with.

"This is awful."

Poppy Sinclair looked up from her desk, her eyes colliding with her boss's angry gray stare. He was holding a printout of the personal ad she'd revised for him and shaking it at her like she was a dog and it was a newspaper.

"The *original* was awful," she responded curtly, turning her focus back to her computer.

"But it was all true."

"Lead with being less of an asshole."

"I *am* an asshole," Isaiah said, clearly unconcerned with that fact.

He was at peace with himself. Which she admired on some level. Isaiah was Isaiah and he made no apologies for that fact. But his attitude would be a problem if the man wanted to find a wife. Because very few other people were at peace with him just as he was.

"I would never say I want to—" he frowned— "'enhance my enjoyment.' What the hell, Poppy?"

Poppy had known Isaiah since she was eighteen years old. She was used to his moods. His complete lack of subtlety. His gruffness.

But somehow, she'd never managed to get used to *him*. As a man.

This grumpy, rough, bearded man who was like a brick wall. Or, like one of those mountains he'd disappear into for days at a time.

Every time she saw him it felt as if he'd stolen the air right from her lungs. It was more than just being handsome —though he was. A lot of men were handsome. His brother Joshua was handsome, and a whole lot easier to get along with.

Isaiah was...well he was her very particular brand of catnip. He made everything in her sit up, purr...and want to be stroked.

Even when he was in full hermit mode.

People—and interacting with them—were decidedly not his thing. It was one reason Poppy had always been an asset to him in his work life. It was her job to sit and take notes during meetings...and report her read on the room to him after. He was a brilliant businessman, and fantastic with numbers. But people...not so much.

As evidenced by the ad. Of course, the very fact that he was placing an ad to find a wife was both contradicting to that point—suddenly, he wanted a wife!—and also, somehow, firmly an affirmation of it—he was placing an ad to find her.

The whole situation was Joshua's fault. Well, probably Devlin and Joshua combined, in fairness.

Isaiah's brothers had been happy bachelors until a couple of years ago when Devlin had married their sister Faith's best friend, Mia.

Then, Joshua had been the next to succumb to matrimony. A victim of their father's harebrained scheme to marry him off, the patriarch of the Grayson family had put an ad in a national newspaper looking for a wife for his son. In retaliation, Joshua had placed an ad of his own, looking for an unsuitable wife that would teach his father not to meddle.

It all backfired. Or… front fired. Either way, Joshua had ended up married to Danielle, and was now happily settled with her and her infant half-brother whom both of them were raising as their son.

It was after their wedding that Isaiah had formed his plan.

The wedding had—he had explained to Poppy at work one morning—clarified a few things for him. He believed in marriage as a valuable institution, one that he wanted to be part of. He wanted stability. He wanted children. But he didn't have any inclination toward love.

He didn't have to tell her why.

She *knew* why.

Rosalind.

But she wouldn't speak her foster sister's name out loud, and neither would he. But she remembered. The awful, awful fallout of Rosalind's betrayal.

His pain. Poppy's own conflicted feelings.

It was easy to remember her conflicted feelings, since she still had them.

He was staring at her now, those dark eyes hard and glinting with an energy she couldn't quite pin down. And with coldness, a coldness that hadn't been there before Rosalind. A coldness that told her and any other woman—loud and clear—that his heart was unavailable.

That didn't mean her own heart didn't twist every time he walked into the room. Every time he leaned closer to her—like he was doing now—and she got a hint of the scent of him. Rugged and pine-laden and basically lumberjack porn for her senses.

He was a contradiction, from his cowboy hat down to his boots. A numbers guy who loved the outdoors and was built like he belonged outside doing hard labor.

Dear God, he was problematic.

He made her dizzy. Those broad shoulders, shoulders she wanted to grab on to. Lean waist and hips—hips she wanted to wrap her legs around. And his forearms…all hard muscle. She wanted to lick them.

He turned her into a being made of sensual frustration, and no one else did that. Ever. Sadly, she seemed to have no effect on him at all.

"I'm not trying to mislead anyone," he said.

"Right. But you *are* trying to entice someone." The very thought made her stomach twist into a knot. But jealousy was pointless. If Isaiah wanted her…well, he would have wanted her by now.

He straightened, moving away from her and walking across the office. She nearly sagged with relief. "My money should do that." As if that solved every potential issue.

She bit back a weary sigh. "Would you like someone who was maybe…interested in who you are as a person?"

She knew that was a stupid question to ask of Isaiah Grayson. But she was his friend, as well as his employee. So it was kind of…her duty to work through this with him. Even if she didn't want him to do this at all.

And she didn't want him to find anyone.

Wow. Some friend she was.

But then, having…complex feelings for one's friend made emotional altruism tricky.

"As you pointed out," he said, his tone dry, "I'm an asshole."

"You were actually the one that said that. I said you *sounded* like one."

He waved his hand. "Either way, I'm not going to win Miss Congeniality in the pageant, and we both know that. Fine with me if somebody wants to get hitched and spend my money."

She sighed heavily, ignoring the fact that her heart felt an awful lot like paper that had been crumpled up into a tight, mutilated ball. "Why do you even *want* a wife, Isaiah?"

"I explained that to you already. Joshua is settled. Devlin is settled."

"Yes, they are. So why now?"

"I always imagined I would get married," he said simply. "I never intended to spend my whole life single."

"Is your biological clock ticking?" she asked dryly.

"In a way," he said. "Again, it all comes back to logic. I'm close to my family, to my brothers. They'll have children sooner rather than later. Joshua and Danielle already have a son. Cousins should be close in age. It just makes sense."

She bit the inside of her cheek. "So, you...just think you can decide it's time and then make it happen?"

"Yes. And I think Joshua's experience proves you can make anything work as long as you have a common goal. It *can* be like math."

She graduated from biting her cheek to her tongue. Isaiah was a numbers guy unto his soul. "Uh-huh."

She refused to offer even a pat agreement because she just thought he was wrong. Not that she knew much of anything about relationships of...any kind really.

She'd been shuffled around so many foster homes as a child, and it wasn't until she was in high school that she'd had a couple years of stability with one family. Which was where she'd met Rosalind, the one foster sibling Poppy was still in touch with. They'd shared a room and talked about a future where they were more than wards of the state.

In the years since, Poppy felt like she'd carved out a decent life for herself. But still, it wasn't like she'd ever had any romantic relationships to speak of.

Pining after your boss didn't count.

"The only aspect of going out and hooking up I like is the hooking up," he said.

She wanted to punch him for that unnecessary addition to the conversation. She sucked her cheek in and bit the inside of it too. "Great."

"When you think about it, making a relationship a transaction is smart. Marriage is a legal agreement. But, you don't just get sex. You get the benefit of having your household kept, children…"

"Right. Children." She'd ignored his first mention of them, but…she pressed her hands to her stomach unconsciously. Then, she dropped them quickly.

She should not be thinking about Isaiah and children or the fact that he intended to have them with another woman.

Confused feelings was a cop-out. And it was hard to deny the truth when she was steeped in this kind of reaction to him, to his presence, to his plan, to his talk about children.

The fact of the matter was, she was tragically in love with him. And he'd never once seen her the way she saw him.

She'd met him through Rosalind. When Poppy had turned eighteen she'd found herself released from her foster home with nowhere to go. Everything she owned was in an old canvas tote that a foster mom had given her years ago.

Rosalind had been the only person Poppy could think to call. The foster sister she'd bonded with in her last few years in care. She'd always kept in touch with Rosalind, even when she moved to Seattle and got work.

Even when she'd started dating a wonderful man she couldn't say enough good things about.

She was the only lifeline Poppy had, and she'd reached for her. And Rosalind had come through. She'd had Poppy come to Rosalind's apartment, and then she'd arranged for a job interview with her boyfriend who needed an assistant for a construction firm he was with.

In one afternoon, Poppy had found a place to live, gotten a job and lost her heart.

Of course, she had lost it, immediately and—in the fullness of time it had become clear—irrevocably, to the one man who was off limits.

Her boss. Her foster sister's boyfriend. Isaiah Grayson.

Though, his status as her boss had lasted longer than his status as Rosalind's boyfriend. He'd become her fiancé. And then after, her ex.

She'd lived with a divided heart for so long. Even after Isaiah and Rosalind's split, Poppy was able to care for them both. Though she never, ever spoke to Rosalind in Isaiah's presence, or even mentioned her.

Rosalind didn't have the same embargo on mentions of Isaiah. But in fairness, Poppy was the one who had cheated on him, cost him a major business deal and nearly ruined his startup company and—by extension—

nearly ruined his relationship with his business partner who was also his brother.

So.

Poppy had loved him while he'd dated another woman. Loved him while he nursed a broken heart because of said other woman. Loved him when he disavowed love completely. And now she would have to love him while she interviewed potential candidates to be his wife.

She was wretched.

He had said the word *sex* in front of her like it wouldn't do anything to her body. Had talked about children like it wouldn't make her... yearn.

Men were idiots. But this one might well be their king.

"Put the unrevised ad in the paper."

She shook her head. "I'm not doing that."

"I could fire you." He leaned in closer and her breath caught. "For insubordination."

Her heart tumbled around erratically and she wished she could blame it on anger. Annoyance. But she knew that wasn't it.

She forced herself to rally. "If you haven't fired me yet you're never going to. And anyway," she said, narrowing her tone so that the words would hit him with a point. "I'm the one who has to interview your prospective brides. Which makes this my endeavor in many ways. I'm the one who's going to have to weed through your choices. So, I would like the ad to go out that I think has the best chance of giving me less crap to sort through."

He looked up at her, and much to her surprise seemed

to be considering what she said. "That is true. You will be doing the interviews."

She felt like she'd been stabbed. She was going to be interviewing Isaiah's potential wives. The man she had been in love with since she was a teenage idiot, and was still in love with now that she was an idiot in her late twenties.

There were a whole host of reasons she'd never, ever let on about her feelings for him, Rosalind and his feelings on love aside.

She loved her job. She loved Isaiah's family, who she'd gotten to know well over the past decade, and who were the closest thing she had to a family of her own.

Plus, loving him was just…easy to dismiss. She wasn't the type of girl who could have something like that. Not Poppy Sinclair whose mother had disappeared when she was two years old and left her with a father who forgot to feed her.

Her life was changing though, slowly.

She was living well beyond what she had ever imagined would be possible for her. Gray Bear Construction was thriving, the merger between Jonathan Bear and the Graysons' company a couple of years ago was more successful than they'd imagined it could be.

And every employee on every level had reaped the benefits.

She was also living in the small town of Copper Ridge, Oregon, which was a bit strange for a girl from Seattle, but she did like it. It had a different pace. But, that meant there was less opportunity for a social life. There were less people to interact with. By default she, and the other folks in town, ended up spending a lot of their free time with the people they worked with every day. There was nothing wrong with that. She loved Faith, and she had begun getting close to Joshua's wife recently. But it was just… Mostly there wasn't enough of a break from Isaiah on any given day.

But then, she also didn't enforce one. Didn't take one. She supposed she couldn't really blame the small town location when the likely culprit of the entire situation was *her*.

"Place whatever ad you need to," he said, his tone abrupt. "When you meet the right woman you'll know."

"I'll know," she echoed lamely.

"Yes. Nobody knows me better than you do, Poppy. I have faith that you'll pick the right wife for me."

With those awful words still ringing in the room, Isaiah left her there, sitting at her desk, feeling numb and ill used.

The fact of the matter was, she probably *could* pick him a perfect wife. Someone who would facilitate his life, and give him space when he needed it. Someone who was beautiful and fabulous in bed.

Yes, she knew exactly what Isaiah Grayson would think made a woman the perfect wife for him.

The sad thing was, Poppy didn't possess very many of those qualities herself.

And what she so desperately wanted was for Isaiah's perfect wife to be *her*.

But dreams were for other women. They always had been. Which meant some other woman was going to end up with Poppy's dream.

While she played matchmaker to the whole affair.

*Will Poppy find Isaiah the perfect wife?
Or will he realize Poppy may be just the woman he's
been looking for?*

Don't miss what happens next in New York Times
bestselling author Maisey Yates's

Want Me, Cowboy

*available November 2018 wherever
Harlequin® Desire books and ebooks are sold.
www.Harlequin.com*

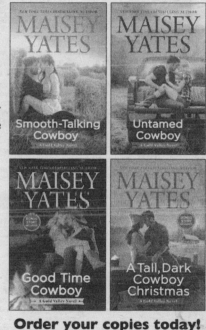

Get 4 FREE REWARDS!

We'll send you 2 FREE Books plus 2 FREE Mystery Gifts.

FREE
Value Over
$20

Both the **Romance** and **Suspense** collections feature compelling novels written by many of today's best-selling authors.